DECIMUS
and the
Wary Widow

EMILY LARKIN

Decimus and the Wary Widow / Emily Larkin. ~ 1st edition

ISBN 978-0-9951436-9-2

Cover Design: Jane Smith (JD Smith Design)

Larkin Font Design: Georgina Kerby (Georgie Graphic Design)

Series Logo Design: Kim Killion (Killion Group)

Author Photo: Tim Cuff (Nelson Creative)

Silhouette Effect: Melissa Evans (SunRoom Web Design)

Regency Audiobook Listener:
Emily Gee in combination with Midjourney

A Baleful Godmother

Novel

It is a truth universally acknowledged,
that Faerie godmothers do not exist.

CHAPTER 1

*D*ecimus Pryor—Dex to his family and friends—enjoyed being the center of attention. He'd never minded being gossiped about. What wasn't to like about being pointed out as a notable rake? The man who'd seduced the ravishing Lady Winslow from under the nose of a rival, the dashing buck who'd been the first to snare Lady Brereton when she entered the ranks of available young widows, the Lothario with the legendary stamina who'd entertained the Cleweston sisters in their hunting box for one blissfully strenuous week.

A wit had once labeled him *le jouet des jeunes veuves*. As sobriquets went, it hit the mark; Dex was only interested in young widows, and he was extremely happy to be their plaything. Assignations with the lovely young relicts of deceased noblemen were his *raison d'être*. Flirtations and stolen kisses and amorous liaisons with ladies who knew exactly what they wanted—and with no need to worry about outraged husbands, because the husbands in question were dead. So, yes, Dex was very happy to be called *le jouet des jeunes veuves*.

But no one had called him that for several months. The name that followed him around these days was Vigor, and while that nickname could be taken as a compliment, it was not.

Vigor, but no finesse.

An observation that Lady Twyckham—beautiful and viperish—had made about him.

Dex liked making people laugh. Jokester, jester, wag—those were all labels he was happy to own—but while he liked making people laugh, liked being laughed *with,* he didn't particularly like being laughed *at,* and he especially didn't like being mocked.

That's what was happening at Wimbledon House this evening. The ball was in full swing, couples whirling around the dance floor while matrons and dowagers gossiped on the sidelines, ostrich feathers nodding in their headdresses. A promising number of young widows were present, but instead of sending him come-hither glances and roguish smiles, they were whispering behind their fans. "Look, it's Vigor," he heard one of them say to another. Her companion shushed her, and they both tittered and turned away.

Dex gritted his teeth behind a smile and made a note never to pursue either lady. It was their loss. His stamina—his *vigor*—was legendary.

Too legendary, alas.

It was four months since acid-tongued Lady Twyckham had made her unfortunate comment about his prowess, but whispers and laughter still followed him. Some of it was friendly laughter, like at his club, where he was openly ribbed, but some of it wasn't. Those two young widows and their barbs of laughter weren't friendly.

Both ladies turned back to him, lowering their fans and giving him the sorts of smiles he was used to receiving from young widows, playful and provocative, flirtatious, but Dex mistrusted them. If either—or both—of them invited him into their beds, he rather thought it would be to laugh about it afterwards with their friends.

He aimed an indifferent nod at them, an indifferent smile, and moved on, heading for the far side of the ballroom, where a footman presided over a tureen of punch that was as potent as it was fragrant. Every time the laughter and mockery became too much, his feet led him back to the tureen. The punch was the only good thing about tonight's ball. It took the edge off his anger. Dex wasn't used to being angry. He was used to flirting and joking, to making ladies blush and laugh and invite him into their boudoirs. But not tonight. Tonight he was stewing in wounded pride.

His punch procured, Dex leaned his shoulders against a silk-covered wall, trying to look nonchalant, as if he didn't care that half the ballroom was covertly—or not so covertly—laughing at him.

Hyperbole, he scolded himself, sipping the punch, tasting rum on his tongue, champagne and orange zest, sugar and spices. It wasn't half the ballroom. It wasn't even a quarter. It was mostly just the young widows. His sole purpose for attending this ball.

Damn Lady Twyckham to perdition.

He ought to have stayed in the country. The Little Season had seemed tempting when he was buried in Gloucestershire, but now that he was in London he'd far rather be back at his grandfather's estate, where there were no enticing young widows, but equally there was none of the mocking laughter that so stung his pride.

His gaze drifted over the assembled guests. It wasn't a crush, but it was full for a ballroom in early September. But then, balls at Wimbledon House were few and far between, invitations highly sought.

A sprightly *contredanse* was underway, the musicians plying their bows with fervor, young ladies and sprigs of fashion dancing vigorously. Vigorously. *Pah.* Dex's upper lip curled involuntarily, angrily. He hid it behind the rim of his glass.

He would probably be able to laugh about this one day, but that day was very far off.

He sipped the punch, his gaze drifting over the dancers. Débutantes held no attraction for him, be they the shy, shrinking ones who dared not meet his eyes or their more confident peers who boldly flirted with him, hoping to snare a duke's grandson as a husband. He had no interest in virgins and no interest in marriage, just as he had no interest in other men's wives. Young widows on the other hand, experienced and enticing, unfettered by husbands . . .

Dex sighed into his fifth glass of punch. Or was it his sixth?

If he couldn't remember how many glasses he'd had, it was probably time to leave.

He scanned the ballroom, unerringly finding the young widows—a cluster of them in the farthest corner, several on the dance floor, the pair who'd given him those coquettish smiles he mistrusted. There, near the door to the cardroom, was the delectable Viscountess Fortrose—or more properly, the Dowager Viscountess Fortrose, given that the current viscount, her late husband's cousin, had a wife who was also Viscountess Fortrose.

One needed that qualifier "dowager" when both ladies were in town, but now that autumn had taken hold and the viscount and his wife had retreated to their country estate, it was unnecessary. Such a disconcerting term, dowager. It brought to mind elderly matriarchs, stately and gray-haired and with formidable bosoms, but Eloïse Fortrose was slender, not stately, and her hair was a striking white-blonde. She wasn't someone you could easily overlook. She was pretty, yes, and the white-blonde hair was unusual, but it was her clothing that really captured the eye. The dowager viscountess favored bold, vivid colors. Rich yellows and deep crimsons, emerald greens and azure blues. Gaudy, the most disapproving of the matrons called her, but they were wrong; there was nothing flashy or garish about Lady Fortrose's wardrobe. Not that she cared what people said about her. She possessed a cool, aloof confidence that was almost, but not quite, hauteur. She was frosty with rakes, coolly friendly with everyone else, and notoriously picky when it came to lovers. As one Casanova had so aptly observed, "Every time she sees a rake coming, she

4

raises the drawbridge, lowers the portcullis, and sends archers to man the ramparts."

That comment had led to her being dubbed Lady Fortress.

Dex found the juxtaposition of vivid color and cool reserve intriguing. Eloïse Fortrose was an enigma, a puzzle, a challenge. He wanted to joke, cajole, and wheedle his way into her boudoir and melt her frosty heart.

Unfortunately, the viscountess had rebuffed every approach he'd made—and he'd made a number over the years. Dex hadn't given up hope yet. He would continue to lay siege to the Fortress, but not right now, when his pride was so dented.

At that moment, Dex discovered that his evening was looking up, for there, having newly entered the ballroom and not two steps from the viscountess, was Lady Swansea.

Lady Swansea's proximity to Viscountess Fortrose was unfortunate. The viscountess was resplendent in eye-catching pomegranate red; Lady Swansea wore fawn trimmed with blonde lace. Alongside the viscountess she looked mousy, dowdy even. But, unfortunate choice of gown aside, she was an undeniable beauty, a voluptuous treasure, ripe for the plucking. Or at least, she'd been ripe for the plucking four months ago.

He and Lady Swansea had been getting along very well indeed when Dex was last in town, their flirtation rapidly heading towards an affair. They'd been on the brink of a liaison, and if his cousin hadn't dragged him off to Hampshire in pursuit of a red-haired governess, Dex had no doubt that he and Lady Swansea would have been intimately acquainted by now.

He set aside his empty glass and sauntered across to her. His smile was jaunty, the familiar swagger back in his step.

"Lady Swansea, how delightful. I had no notion you were in town." Dex bowed over her hand with a flamboyant flourish, kissed her gloved fingertips, then offered an extravagant compliment: "Your beauty is dazzling tonight. You outshine the sun, the moon, and all the stars in the sky."

Lady Swansea used to blush and giggle when he paid her such fulsome compliments; now, she tittered and said, "You look very well, Mr. Pryor. Very . . . vigorous."

Dex's smile congealed on his lips. Was she poking fun at him?

He looked into those blue eyes, discovered a glint there, and realized that she was.

But perhaps it was a friendly glint? They'd laughed together often enough, he and Lady Swansea, before he'd left for Hampshire. Perhaps this was her idea of a joke, some friendly teasing between the two of them?

"Would you care to dance, Lady Swansea?"

"Oh, no," she said, removing her fingers from his clasp. "Too *vigorous* for my taste tonight."

Dex decided that it wasn't a friendly glint in her eyes. He kept his smile with effort. "Another time, then." He inclined his head politely, stepped away, and willed his face not to become a humiliated red. His feet wanted to march from the ballroom, but he refused to give Lady Swansea the satisfaction of seeing him leave so soon after her little witticism. So he had a sixth glass of punch, or perhaps it was a seventh, and then strolled out to the vestibule and requested that his carriage be brought round—he was *ambling*, not running away—and had to wait an interminable fifteen minutes before it drew up at the door. That was the problem with balls at Wimbledon House. One couldn't just walk home. One had to drive the five wretched miles back to London before one could bury oneself in one's club with a bottle of good claret and get comfortably drunk.

Unfortunately, Viscountess Fortrose had also decided to leave the ball early, along with her two companions, the diminutive and aging French comtesse with whom she resided, and a stout, gray-bearded Russian baron. Dex kept his distance. He didn't need a rebuff from the oh-so-ravishing viscountess tonight.

Coaches came, coaches went, and finally it was his turn.

He stepped outside to the accompaniment of the lilting strains of a quadrille. The carriage sweep was lit by torchlight and moonlight, dark inkblots of cloud smudging a starry sky.

The coach had a crest on the door and came with a coachman and a footman. Neither the crest nor the servants were his. Dex owned a curricle and a phaeton, but he had no reason to own a town carriage, not when his uncle, the Marquis of Stanaway, and his grandfather, the Duke of Linwood, had carriages and servants to spare.

He climbed aboard and flung himself into one corner, head tipped back, eyes closed, then sat up abruptly and rifled through the roomy pockets beneath either window. Was there a hip flask of whiskey tucked into one of them . . . ? Yes, there was. Excellent.

Dex cracked open the hip flask, slouched back in the corner he'd chosen, and settled in for a good sulk lubricated by strong spirits.

His good sulk lasted all of five minutes before the coach drew to an unexpected halt.

Dex opened the window and peered out. They were on Wimbledon Heath. He saw the dark shapes of trees, the silver disk of the moon, the shadowy figures of the coachman and footman perched high on the box.

"Something wrong?" he called out.

"Highwaymen," the coachman replied in a low voice. "They've stopped a coach up ahead."

Stopped a coach?

The viscountess's coach?

Dex flung open the door and jumped down. "How many of them?"

"Looks like three, sir."

"You have a blunderbuss?"

"Yes, sir." The footman flourished it, the barrel glinting dully in the moonlight.

"Loaded?"

"Yes, sir."

"Good. Stay at the ready, both of you. I'll shout if I need assistance."

"But sir—" the coachman protested, at the same time that the footman said, bewildered, "Don't you want the blunderbuss?"

Dex ignored them both and set off in the direction of the beleaguered coach. Highwaymen generally didn't harm their victims—but that didn't mean that people weren't sometimes hurt, or even killed. If Lady Fortrose was too uncooperative or if the highwaymen noticed her striking good looks and decided to ravish her . . .

He ran towards the dark shape of the coach sixty yards ahead, his dancing shoes almost silent on the hardpacked dirt. The moon was full and currently unconcealed by clouds, its light illuminating the road and himself, but no one noticed his approach. One masked and mounted man held the coachman and footman at gunpoint; the other two ruffians had dismounted, the better to assist their victims in the removal of their valuables. No removal of valuables appeared to be taking place, however. The French comtesse was in the throes of rather loud hysterics, collapsed on the ground with Lady Fortrose attending her, her shrieks shrill and incoherent. The baron was berating the villains in overwrought Russian, arms flailing, voice booming, as stentorian as a watchman, quite drowning out the rogues' attempts to impose order. One scoundrel was futilely commanding everyone to shut up, while the other was repeating, in rather harassed tones, the standard demand of highwaymen everywhere: "Your money or your lives!"

The French shrieks and Russian oration perfectly concealed the ever-so-faint crunch of Dex's footsteps. He slowed from headlong run to stealthy tiptoe, slipping silently into the shadows on the far side of the coach, directing his attention to the mounted highwayman first. He appeared to be the least distracted of the three villains, and it wouldn't do for anyone to be shot.

Dex didn't have a blunderbuss, but that didn't mean that he was helpless. Far from it. He was one of only ten people in England who possessed magic—the other nine being his father, grandfather, three uncles, and four cousins—and he could rout a trio of highwaymen with both hands tied behind his back.

He needed to rout them without anyone noticing the magic, though.

Rather obligingly, a cloud drifted over the moon, plunging the road into gloom.

Levitation was the magic that Dex possessed, and he used it now, lifting the mounted highwayman from his saddle, hoisting the man high, flinging him into the clutch of one of the hulking, shadowy trees that lined the road. He floated the blunderbuss from the villain's grip while he was at it and lobbed it into the dark embrace of the night.

The man yelped, but the sound was swallowed by the comtesse's shrieks and the baron's bellows.

One ruffian down.

The coachman and footman were dim shapes on the box, staring stiffly ahead, fearful of the blunderbuss. Dex hurried to them and gripped the coachman's ankle. The man yelped, much as the highwayman had yelped.

"Quiet!" Dex whispered fiercely. "Hold the horses steady and leave everything to me."

The highwayman's mount stood riderless. Dex released the coachman's ankle, scooped up a stone, and flung it at the horse's hindquarters, his aim aided by more judicious application of his magic.

The horse bolted down the road at a gallop.

Dex slipped around to the other side of the carriage.

The moon began to reappear, shedding ghostly silver light upon the scene. The comtesse's shrieks petered out and the baron fell silent. Everyone—robbers and victims alike—was staring in the direction of the rapidly departing and riderless horse.

"Joe? You all right?" one of the two remaining highwaymen called out.

"Help!" Joe wailed from the tree Dex had flung him into.

The two villains exchanged a glance. Both had mufflers concealing their lower faces. One man leveled a pistol at Lady Fortrose and her companions; the other holstered his weapon, strode to his horse, grabbed the reins, and swung up into the saddle. Dex assisted him, his magic boosting the man up and over his horse. He fell in the dirt on the other side with a thump and a squawk.

There was an astonished silence.

Dex chortled soundlessly, and used his magic to relieve the fallen highwayman of his pistol, levitating it from the man's holster, disposing of it stealthily in the shrubs on the far side of the road. The moon was fully out now, but no one would notice such sleight of hand.

"Harry?" the last highwayman standing said. "What you doin'?"

Harry scrambled to his feet and ran around his horse, belligerent and bewildered in the moonlight. Dex stepped forward to meet him. He punched the man solidly on the chin. A touch of levitation and the highwayman soared backwards across the full width of the road before tumbling into the ditch.

It looked rather impressive.

"Heh," Dex said, rather pleased with himself. He shook out his fist and turned to find everyone was staring at him—comtesse, baron, viscountess, highwayman.

The sole pistol was pointing at him now, too.

He realized his danger an instant before the highwayman fired. There was a crack of sound, but his magic levitated the bullet, up into the dark sky, where it expended its lethal energy harmlessly.

Dex strode to the highwayman, took hold of the barrel of the pistol, wrenched it from his grip, and tossed it away.

The highwayman uttered a sound that was neither yelp nor

squawk but more a bark of astonishment. He put up his fists.

Dex punched him. The blow didn't connect well, his knuckles barely grazing the man's cheek, but only he and the highwayman knew that. His magic did the rest: lifting the man off his feet, hurling him back into the carriage with a resounding thud.

The highwayman slid down the side of the carriage as if his legs were boneless and collapsed in a heap on the road.

"Heh," Dex said again, very pleased with himself. It was rather fun playing the hero. He shook out his fist for verisimilitude and turned to his rescuees. Was that a word? Rescuee? He decided it was.

They were all staring at him, the comtesse lying on the road, propped up on one elbow, Lady Fortrose kneeling alongside her, the baron standing, with his mouth open and his arms frozen in mid-oratory flail.

"Everyone all right?" Dex inquired.

His rescuees gaped at him.

While they were gaping, the second highwayman, Harry, scrambled out of the ditch and attempted to mount his horse. Dex assisted him magically again, up and over and into the dirt on the other side. He couldn't repress a cackle. This was rather amusing. He grinned at his audience and repeated his question: "Everyone all right?"

There was a moment's pause, and then Lady Fortrose said, "Yes. Thank you."

"My pleasure, ma'am." He gave a sweeping bow.

Harry made another attempt to climb onto his horse. Up and over he went, landing in the dirt again. Dex decided that three times was enough for that particular trick. He crossed to the confused horse and gave its haunch a hearty slap. The beast took off into the night.

Harry looked up at him from the dirt. His muffler had slipped down below his nose. Above it, his eyes were very round, the whites showing.

"I'd run, if I were you," Dex informed him.

Harry hauled himself to his feet and did just that.

Dex listened until the man's footfalls had faded to nothing, then turned back to the carriage. Lady Fortrose and the baron were fussing over the comtesse, helping her to her feet, brushing the dirt from her gown. The footman had climbed down from the box and was gingerly brandishing a blunderbuss at the third highwayman. The coachman sat high above them all, reins in hand, horses firmly under control, commanding the footman to "Hold the fiend there! Don't let him get away!"

The footman looked as if he wanted to climb back up on the box. He retreated a step as the third highwayman staggered to his feet. The ruffian steadied himself against the coach for a moment, then lurched towards his horse.

"I think not," Dex said. A flick of his fingers and a stone levitated up from the ground and pinged the horse on its rump. The animal set off down the road with a thunder of hooves.

The highwayman stared after it in dismay.

The footman gingerly brandished the blunderbuss again.

Dex removed the weapon from the servant's grip. He was likely to shoot someone's foot off, holding it like that. "Off you go," he told the highwayman. "Unless you wish to decorate the gallows?"

The highwayman tottered hurriedly into the darkness.

Dex chortled under his breath, very pleased with himself. He turned back to the coach. The viscountess, the comtesse, and the baron were all staring at him.

Dex stopped feeling quite so pleased with himself. Why were they looking at him like that? It wasn't as if anyone could have seen him use his magic. It was nighttime, after all. They'd think he'd thrown that stone at the horse, not flicked it with his magic.

"Well, that was an adventure!" he declared, rather inanely.

The comtesse and the baron exchanged a glance. Lady Fortrose regarded him with narrow-eyed thoughtfulness.

The footman scurried over to the comtesse and busied

himself brushing the most obvious dirt from her gown, the coachman was intent on his horses, but the viscountess, comtesse, and baron were all looking at Dex as if they might possibly have noticed the magic. Which they couldn't have, because it was the middle of the night and the moon, while bright, wasn't *that* bright.

Dex cleared his throat with a disconcerted "Er-hem," and turned away from those unsettling stares. He gave a piercing whistle and shouted, "You can come along now!"

His grandfather's carriage came along.

"The rogues are long gone," Dex assured Lady Fortrose and her companions. "You're safe now, I promise."

His rescuees didn't look completely convinced. In fact, they looked rather dubious. And they were all still staring at him.

Dex decided that those stares were because they doubted their safety. It had been a rather alarming incident, after all. They'd probably been in fear of their lives.

"I tell you what, I'll ride up on your box with the coachman. I'll carry this blunderbuss. No one will dare stop us."

This pronouncement didn't appear to overwhelm his rescuees with relief. They still showed an alarming tendency to stare at him. They did, however, climb back into their carriage. Dex closed the door and scrambled up onto the box seat, alongside the coachman and footman.

The coach lurched into motion with a *clip-clop* of hooves. His grandfather's coach fell in behind.

Dex cradled the blunderbuss on his lap. Wimbledon Heath trundled past on either side—shrubs, bushes, trees. The moon shone down, a bright silver disk, beautiful and indifferent.

All was well in the world—viscountess rescued, highwaymen routed—but he couldn't quite shake the feeling that something was wrong.

CHAPTER 2

"Did you see that, *mes amies*?" Minette asked, in the dark, swaying closeness of the carriage.

"I saw a number of things," Ella replied. "Which one are you referring to?"

"That *is* rather the question," Arthur rumbled, from his corner of the carriage.

Ella nodded, although it was too dark for either of her companions to see that gesture.

Minette and Arthur had been their usual marvelous unflappable selves, setting up such a fuss that the highwaymen had been on the verge of abandoning them to seek easier prey . . . and then *that* had happened. Although Ella wasn't quite certain what *that* had been.

"His punch sent the fellow clear across the road," Arthur said. "Five or six yards. Not sure if that's possible, not without a rope and pulley."

Ella agreed: she didn't think it was possible. The highwayman had pitched across the road as if a giant invisible hand had grabbed the back of his coat and yanked.

She'd also seen the same highwayman fling himself over his horse and land in the dirt on the other side, which could conceivably happen if a man were panicked enough, but . . . three times?

14

Again, it made one think of giant invisible hands.

And then there'd been that stone. She could have sworn that Mr. Pryor hadn't thrown anything, but she'd definitely seen a stone strike the final horse's rump.

Which brought one back to invisible hands.

"What happened to *le troisième brigand*?" Minette asked.

"Who knows," Ella said, but something obviously *had* happened to the third highwayman, because there'd been that plaintive "Help," from back in the trees. What had Pryor done to the man, and how?

She frowned. Decimus Pryor had singlehandedly defeated three highwaymen. Without a weapon. It did seem rather unlikely. Pryor was a dilettante, not a soldier. He was skilled at flirting, not fighting.

But the alternative, that he'd had help from an invisible person—a giant?—a ghost?—seemed even more unlikely.

"I think . . . I shall invite him to take tea with us tomorrow afternoon."

"An interrogation?" Arthur inquired.

"An interrogation," Ella agreed.

Minette gave a delighted clap of her hands. "We shall pluck out his secrets like a worm from its shell!"

There was a beat of silence; then Arthur said, "Snail."

15

CHAPTER 3

$\mathscr{A}$s a fifteen-year-old, Ella had stepped out of the schoolroom and into marriage with a man forty years her senior. A man who'd ruled every aspect of her life.

Her husband had chosen the clothes she had worn, her gowns and her bonnets, her shoes, even her underclothes: stockings, petticoats, chemises. He'd decided how her hair was styled and what perfumes she wore, what jewels she adorned herself with—diamonds and pearls only—just as he'd decided when she left the house and when she didn't, which shops she patronized, which invitations she accepted, which books she read, even what food she ate.

It had almost been a continuance of her childhood— obedience to a stern parent's authority—except that Francis had been assiduous in asserting his conjugal rights. Not that his assiduousness had been fruitful; Ella had proven barren, her monthly flow so intermittent that it barely qualified as a yearly flow.

Francis had favored cool shades of gray and white, with the occasional foray into pale, icy blues and delicate celadons. After his death, when she'd begun to think for herself, Ella decided that he'd chosen her as his bride because of her coloring: the white-blonde hair and wintry blue eyes.

In the six years of her marriage, Ella hadn't been allowed to make a single decision. At first, it hadn't occurred to her that she could. Later, she hadn't dared. Widowhood had been a liberation, an escape from a cramped and cloistered prison. With Minette and Arthur's help she'd avoided a return to her father's house and his power over her, just as she'd avoided being subsumed into the new viscount's household and the rôle he'd intended for her, that of grateful, mouselike widow.

Ella had been the most meek and obedient of wives, but as a widow she had learned to be colorful, bold, free. No one told her what she could and couldn't do, what she couldn't eat or wear or think or say. No one said, "You can't have marigold *and* amber *and* gold all in one room," or "You can't wear crimson." Instead, Minette and Arthur encouraged her to live as loudly and brightly as possible. Her wardrobe brimmed with color and so did her house. There were no diamonds and pearls in her jewelry box, not a scrap of pastel in her wardrobe, just as there were no rooms decorated in cool, pale colors, no whites, no smoke grays or dove grays, no frosty blues, no celadon. Everything was a feast for the eye: clothes that made her feel happy, rooms that were vibrant and welcoming, furniture that was exuberantly comfortable.

Francis would have hated the house and her clothes; Ella loved them. "*My* life, *my* choice," she sometimes whispered to herself when there was no one to overhear, touching fingertips to a sumptuous brocade curtain, a saffron-colored cushion, a flamboyant ormolu clock.

One such clock, with frolicking nymphs and satyrs, was currently gazing down upon Ella, Arthur, Minette, and Decimus Pryor from the mantelpiece in Ella's second-best parlor. The nymphs and satyrs were all beaming sunnily; Ella was not, because a man she'd sworn never to encourage was sipping her tea and attempting to flirt with her.

It wasn't that Pryor was repugnant. He was as good-looking as he was personable, which was to say, very—the midnight black hair, the dark eyes, the strong jaw—but he had no substance. He was a bandbox creature, a man with nothing better to do than to look handsome, crack jokes, and talk his way into ladies' beds.

Ella had held few opinions about men before her marriage. She'd dreamed of being swept off her feet by a dashing hero or a handsome prince, as most schoolgirls did. She had spared little thought as to what the character of that hero or prince might be, other than that he'd be noble and virtuous and, in some nebulous way, perfect for her. By the end of her marriage, she'd wanted nothing to do with men—not to be controlled by them, not to be told what to do by them, not even to be touched by them.

But then Minette and Arthur had swept into her life, bringing with them color, warmth, laughter, *joie de vivre*. To her astonishment, she'd discovered that life could be enjoyable. Eventually, she'd wondered whether sexual congress could be enjoyable, too. She hadn't wanted a husband—she never wanted one of those again—but lovers? Why not?

Rakes had never tempted her—who wanted to be a notch among many on a bedpost?—but dandies, with their dazzling appearance, briefly had. She'd quickly learned that color didn't equate to character. Her preference was for men with more depth than shallow, frivolous popinjays like the specimen currently sitting in her second-best parlor. Men who didn't look for the mirror whenever they walked into a room and who didn't surreptitiously preen when they thought no one was looking. Not that Pryor had done either of those two things yet. He was too busy responding to Arthur's effusive compliments and Minette's rather less effusive words of praise, while simultaneously drinking his tea and attempting to flirt with Ella.

Ella eyed him over the rim of her cup. Decimus Pryor. Possessor of a handsome face, a glib tongue, and no substance whatsoever. A rake and a dandy, a libertine, a man whose sole purpose in life was to inveigle his way into young widows' beds.

A man who had put three highwaymen to rout.

Or possibly, one whose invisible companion had put three highwaymen to rout.

Arthur was still in his Russian manifestation, jovial and big-bellied and bewhiskered, taking up most of the three-seater sofa. Minette, petite and elegant, was perched on a sumptuous Louis XV *bergère*. Pryor had chosen what was Ella's favorite armchair, a Chippendale with a winged back, red upholstery, and lion's paw feet. It irritated her, somewhat irrationally, that out of all the chairs and sofas in the room, he'd chosen her favorite.

Arthur was currently extolling Pryor's bravery in thickly accented English speckled with the occasional Russian word, a pastiche that rolled off his tongue as easily as if he had been born in Saint Petersburg, not Bristol.

Pryor appeared rather disconcerted by the deluge of praise but, disconcerted or not, he was also throwing out lures to Ella: laughing glances and playful little smiles, compliments turned deftly away from himself and presented to her instead—forays into flirtation that Ella was ruthlessly ignoring. She had no intention of inviting Pryor into a dalliance, however good-looking he might be and regardless of whether they had the same taste in armchairs. He met none of her criteria in a paramour. He had no substance, no seriousness. Ella had so far had four lovers—an earl's son who wrote poignant sonnets, an aristocratic sculptor who was fascinated by the female form, a quiet baronet who painted watercolors, and a gentleman scholar who wrote essays on emancipation and civil society—all earnest, erudite men, men who held women in high regard and didn't reduce them to playthings and conquests.

Unlike Decimus Pryor.

"But you were not alone, no?" Minette said. "Who was your companion?"

Pryor stopped looking at Ella and returned his attention to Minette. "My companions? You mean the coachman and footman? They were behind—"

19

"No, no. I mean the person who helped you to fight *les brigands*."

Mr. Pryor's smile began to look wary rather than playful. "I assure you, ma'am, I was alone."

"But you were not. There was someone to help you."

"It was a frightening experience, ma'am," Pryor said, his manner becoming slightly condescending. "You were overwrought—"

"Bah! I was not overwrought. *Moi*, I see everything, and I see a man fly across a road as if he has been seized by an invisible giant."

An expression that could almost be alarm flitted across Pryor's face, and was immediately replaced by a charming smile. "Ma'am," he said, his tone light and amused and still with that hint of condescension. "I can assure you that there were no invisible—"

"I saw it, too," Arthur put in. "Thought perhaps it was a ghost. Was it?"

Pryor chuckled, a sound that was probably meant to be merry rather than uneasy. "I assure you, sir, there were no invisible men or ghosts with me."

"Then who threw that stone?" Ella asked.

His gaze flicked to her.

Ella gave him a steely smile. "The stone that hit that last horse on the rump . . . who threw it, Mr. Pryor?"

Pryor put down his teacup and uttered another uneasy laugh. "I did, of course."

Ella shook her head. "No, you didn't."

"Someone else threw it." Arthur leaned forward on the sofa, ponderous and dignified, pinning Pryor with an imperious stare. He was channeling one of the many kings he'd played on stage. "Just as someone flung that highwayman across the road."

"An invisible person!" Minette declared.

"Or a ghost," Ella put in, although she wasn't certain she believed in ghosts.

"There was no ghost," Pryor said emphatically. "And no invisible person."

"Then it was . . . how do you call it? . . . *la magie?*"

"No, of course it wasn't magic."

Pryor's voice was just as emphatic, but his pitch was a little higher, a little sharper, his cadence slightly staccato.

Arthur had spent years treading the boards, pretending to be people he wasn't, surrounded by other actors who were also pretending. He was good at hearing when something didn't quite ring true. Ella didn't have that skill, so she glanced at him to see what he thought of the change in Pryor's voice.

Arthur looked dumbstruck. Which meant . . .

That Pryor had just lied?

That what they'd witnessed last night *had* been magic?

Ella glanced at Minette, so that they could share a moment of shocked incredulity, but Minette was looking at Pryor, her eyes narrow with speculation.

Arthur recovered his voice. "Aha!" he cried. "It *was* magic!" He forgot his Russian accent in his excitement, but Pryor didn't notice.

"Nonsense! Magic doesn't exist." He slipped his watch from its pocket in his waistcoat and glanced at it. "Oh, is that the time? I really must—"

"All three of us saw it, *monsieur*," Minette said.

Mr. Pryor shoved his watch back into his pocket and stood. "It was dark and you were overwrought and—"

"I was playing *la dame hystérique* and Arthur was playing *l'homme frénétique*, but we were not overwrought and we were not blind," Minette told him rather tartly.

"It's not magic!" Pryor said. He'd lost his duke's-grandson cockiness and the rakishness. Gone was the suaveness, the playfulness, the swagger.

"Does your grandfather know?" Ella asked.

Minette seized upon that idea. "But of course! We must visit *le duc* and ask him."

"Excellent notion," Arthur said, his Russian accent firmly back in place. "Where does the duke live? Here in London?"

"Gloucestershire," Ella informed him. "Linwood Castle. If we leave at first light tomorrow, we'll be there by—"

"Don't!" Mr. Pryor said, putting up both hands in a gesture that shouted *Stop!* "Please, don't."

"Does he not know about *la magie*?" Minette enquired.

Pryor parted his lips, and then closed them again without speaking. He looked worried, hunted, harassed.

Ella was conscious of a prick of conscience, a prick of guilt. Pressing him like this wasn't kind; it was, in fact, akin to bullying.

If Pryor did indeed possess magic, it was a sizable secret to have. A potentially dangerous secret. A secret that he would naturally be afraid to share with anyone.

"We're very good at keeping confidences," she assured him.

Pryor's glance was sardonic and mistrustful and more than a little bitter. A corner of Ella's brain noted that he was surprisingly attractive when he looked at her like that. Here was the substance that she liked in her men, the authenticity, the absence of affectation and calculated charm.

She ignored that observation, just as she was ignoring the fact that they had the same taste in armchairs. "How about a bargain, Mr. Pryor? We give you one of our secrets in exchange for your secret."

Everyone in the room frowned at her—Arthur, Minette, Pryor.

"We're asking him to trust us," Ella told her companions. "Therefore, we should show him that *we* can be trusted."

Minette and Arthur exchanged a dubious glance. Ella understood their concern. The secrets the three of them shared were mostly Arthur's and Minette's, not hers.

Arthur stirred uneasily on the sofa. Minette plucked at the rings encrusting her thin fingers. Pryor's gaze flicked between them. His eyes were narrow and he was clearly wondering what secrets a French comtesse and Russian baron could possibly be hiding. Then his attention shifted to her. There was nothing flirtatious in that gaze, just pure suspicion.

Ella noted again that he was very attractive when he wasn't playing the rake.

Arthur inhaled a deep, bracing breath and reluctantly opened his mouth.

"I'm not a comtesse," Minette declared.

Pryor blinked, and looked away from Ella. He frowned at Minette. "You're not?"

Ella understood his doubtfulness. Minette occupied the Louis XV *bergère* as regally as if it were a throne. Her silvering black hair was immaculately coiffed, her posture was proud, the thin arch of her eyebrows supercilious, her nose patrician. She was elegant and aristocratic from the crown of her head to the very expensive tips of her shoes.

"*Non.* Me, I am an opera dancer."

Pryor's frown deepened, eyebrows drawing together until they almost touched. He had the expression of a man who believed his leg was being pulled.

Minette smiled at him, aloof and haughty, every inch a comtesse, and then she tilted her head slightly and the smile became saucy and more than a little wicked. The comtesse was gone; seated in Ella's second-best parlor was a retired opera dancer.

Pryor uttered a startled, uncertain laugh. "Good Lord. You mean . . . it's true?" He glanced at Ella, as if for confirmation.

She nodded.

Pryor's bemused gaze returned to Minette.

Minette's smile become roguish, almost vulgar. She winked at him.

Pryor rocked back on his heels and gave another of those uncertain laughs. He looked quite nonplussed.

Ella waited for his bemusement to reshape itself into outrage. He was a duke's grandson, after all. He wouldn't approve of a French opera dancer infiltrating the *ton*.

Pryor let out a guffaw, so loud and unexpected that Ella jumped in her chair. "Bravo, madam," he exclaimed, clapping his hands. "You must have set the stage on fire."

"I was *très magnifique*," Minette said, with no modesty whatsoever.

"I don't doubt it. I'm sorry I never saw you perform." And he did indeed look sorry to have missed that spectacle.

Ella eyed him. Decimus Pryor clearly had more depth than she'd thought, but that didn't mean that she *liked* him. "A secret for a secret, Mr. Pryor?" she reminded him.

Pryor lost his grin.

"You can see for yourself that we know how to keep secrets."

Pryor glanced at Arthur, as if wondering whether the Russian baron wasn't who he claimed to be either.

Arthur gave him an inscrutable smile.

"*La magie,*" Minette prompted.

Pryor shifted his weight from one foot to the other. He clearly didn't want to reveal his secret to them. He looked at Ella, nothing flirtatious in his gaze, just . . . worry.

Botheration, there was the substance again, making her almost like him, making her want to reassure him that whatever he told them wouldn't leave this room, that he was safe from exposure.

"I won't reveal your secret to anyone," Ella told him. "I give you my word of honor." If she'd heard the lie in Pryor's voice earlier, she hoped he heard the truth in hers now.

Pryor stared at her for several seconds, then pressed his lips together and sat. He picked up his teacup, frowned at it, and drank what was left.

No one prompted him to divulge his secret. They all knew surrender when they saw it.

Pryor put the cup back in its saucer with a clatter. He lifted his head and looked from Arthur to Minette, his expression close to scowling. "I must have your words of honor, too."

"*Je te donne ma parole d'honneur,*" Minette said, laying a hand over her heart.

Arthur made the same gesture. "You have my word," he said, his Russian accent firmly back in place.

Pryor's almost-scowl didn't abate. Ella preferred it to the many times he'd tried to flirt with her. This was the real man, harassed and uncertain. Not flippant, not cocky, and definitely not swaggering.

Pryor blew out a breath and rubbed above one eyebrow, as if a headache gathered there. "You weren't supposed to notice, any of you," he said accusingly. "*You* were having hysterics and *you* were pounding your chest and shouting and *you* were being a ministering angel—"

"Appearances can be deceptive," Arthur reminded him.

Pryor harrumphed and rubbed his forehead again.

"Were you alone last night?" Ella asked.

He glanced at her and nodded.

"So . . . it was magic?"

He grimaced, then nodded again.

"How?" Ella asked.

"Yes, how?" Minette leaned forward, alert and expectant.

Pryor pulled a face. "You won't believe me."

"Don't make assumptions, young man," Arthur told him.

Pryor huffed out another breath, rubbed his forehead again, and said, "I have a Faerie godmother."

Ella barked a laugh of disbelief, clapping a hand over her mouth too late to muffle the sound.

Pryor tipped his eyebrows up, a sardonic *I knew you wouldn't believe me* on his face.

Ella liked him even more. She lowered her hand. "How is that possible? A Faerie godmother!"

Pryor shrugged. "No one knows. Lost in the mists of time."

"What does she look like?" Arthur asked, at the same time that Minette said, "Did she give you three wishes?"

Pryor glanced from one to the other. "She looks rather like you, ma'am, except that her eyes are pure black and her teeth are as sharp as a fox's. She gives us one wish each, on our twenty-fifth birthdays. I chose levitation." He looked at Ella as he said those last words, as if challenging her to scoff at his choice.

"You can fly?" Arthur asked.

"After a fashion. And I can make things fly. Any person or object."

"*Les brigands!*" Minette cried, clapping her hands.

"That stone," Arthur said.

Pryor nodded.

"So, when that highwayman leaped right over his horse three times . . . ?" Ella asked.

Pryor grinned, a startlingly attractive flash of amusement. "That was me." A hint of cockiness returned in the tilt of his chin.

"Who else in your family can do magic?" Arthur asked.

Pryor lost his grin and that cocky chin-tilt. "A few of us. Not everyone."

"The duke?" Ella asked.

Pryor hesitated, and that hesitation was as good as a *Yes.*

"What can *le duc* do?" Minette asked eagerly.

Pryor hesitated again. "It's not that I don't trust you, ma'am, but it isn't my secret to tell."

Minette accepted this with a nod. "But of course. You must protect your family." She leaned across to pat his hand. "You are a good boy."

Pryor went faintly pink at this praise.

"So you were alone when you vanquished *les brigands* last night? Bravo! You are *un héro.* Tell us it all, from the very beginning."

Pryor became even pinker, ducking his head a little and glancing at Ella again. He looked bashful and boyish and not at all rakish. Ella had to remind herself that she didn't like him. Decimus Pryor was a dandy and a flirt, and as soon as he recovered from his uncharacteristic and momentary bout of modesty he'd resume his attempts to cajole his way into her bed. That, or look for a mirror to preen in.

He told a good tale, though. Ella found herself leaning forward like Minette and hanging on his every word. She listened raptly to Pryor's account of the previous night's events, from the moment his own carriage had halted to the stone that had encouraged the final horse to gallop away.

In the middle of the recital, Pryor mentioned the bullet he'd turned aside.

Ella had forgotten about the bullet. Pryor's magic wouldn't have protected him if that bullet had struck him in the heart. Or the face. Or anywhere else, for that matter.

He could have been maimed, or worse, killed.

It was a horrifying thought. Decimus Pryor might be a peacock and a libertine, but he'd come to their aid last night, had confronted three armed highwaymen, had saved them.

Ella was uncomfortably aware that she might have misjudged him. Pryor wasn't the lightweight she'd thought him. Not if he'd hidden a secret of this magnitude for years. Not if he was prepared to risk his life for people he barely knew. The cockiness had fooled her, the swagger, his incessant need to flirt. Beneath the frivolous veneer was someone who possessed discretion, ingenuity, and courage.

She poured fresh cups of tea all around, listened to Minette and Arthur's eager interrogation, and tried to ignore how attractive Pryor was—that mobile mouth, the laughter in his eyes, his hands.

Hands were one of the things Ella always noticed in a man, and Pryor's hands were just about perfect: broad palms and long fingers and blunt, clean nails. Masculine hands, strong and capable. His calves and his shoulders were good, too, no padding there. The nape of his neck was fortunately hidden beneath shirt and neckcloth, waistcoat and tailcoat.

Napes were her Achilles heel.

There was something about the bare nape of a man's neck that plucked at her heartstrings, something vulnerable. Ella had only discovered this weakness in herself recently and she was determined not to indulge it. Men were anything but vulnerable, bare napes or not, and imagining that they *were* vulnerable was the sort of thinking that made women fall into the trap of marriage.

Her motto regarding matrimony was simple: Never again.

"Could you lift me up to the ceiling?" Arthur asked.

Pryor shrugged. "If you wish."

Arthur stood with alacrity.

"Ah . . . the servants?" Pryor glanced at the door. It had no lock. Few of the doors in the house did.

"The servants won't enter unless we ring for them," Ella said. "I told them we weren't to be disturbed."

Pryor nodded, and turned to Arthur. "Are you ready, sir?"

"*Da!*" Arthur said, grinning and bouncing on his toes. He looked as excited as a boy.

Pryor made a gesture, a turning up of his palm.

Arthur rose from the floor. He ascended gently, slowly, until his grizzled gray hair almost brushed the ceiling. The polished toes of his shoes dangled above the sofa he'd been sitting on.

Ella gazed up at him, open-mouthed and amazed.

"Make him fly!" Minette requested excitedly.

Pryor waited for Arthur's nod, then obeyed this decree. Arthur canted in the air, his legs rising until he lay almost flat, his not-insubstantial belly bulging downward, gravity warring with his corset. After a moment, he put his arms out like wings.

"Ready, sir?" Pryor asked.

Arthur grinned down at them. "Ready!"

He began a slow circumnavigation of the room.

Ella discovered that she was holding her breath and clutching her hands to her breast.

"Faster!" Arthur cried.

Pryor obeyed that decree, too. Ella watched, open-mouthed, hands still clutched to her breast, as Arthur began to glide more swiftly—to *fly*—swooping around her second-best parlor like a great gray-haired, big-bellied bird.

She hoped he'd glued his wig on well. Otherwise he might become a big-bellied *bald* bird.

Arthur was hooting with laughter. Ella discovered that

she was laughing, too. This was absurd and impossible and breathtaking and *it was happening in her parlor.*

Magic. Flying.

She wanted to fly, too.

"A figure eight!" Arthur cried, so excited that he'd forgotten his Russian accent again.

Pryor obliged, steering Arthur into a figure eight, once, and then twice, and then he brought Arthur low, his belly barely skimming above the tea table, a swift swoop that made them all shriek with alarm—including Arthur—then shriek equally loudly with laughter.

Ella heard the noise they were making—more noise than she'd ever made in her life—and couldn't quite believe it. Was this her? This hysterically laughing creature? It didn't seem possible.

The servants must think they'd gone mad.

Pryor took Arthur on another lap of the parlor—more sedately this time—then tipped him upright and set him on his feet on the floor.

Arthur was red-faced with mirth, his whiskers and his wig still miraculously glued in place. He seized Pryor's hand and wrung it vigorously. "*Blagodaryu vas!*" he said, which Ella guessed meant thank you. She pressed a hand to her chest. She was breathless, her ribs ached, and her face was damp with tears of laughter that she had no memory of shedding.

Arthur relinquished Pryor's hand and collapsed into the embrace of the sofa. "Never in my life," he said, groping for his handkerchief. "Never in my life did I think . . ." He waved the handkerchief, clearly lost for words, and dabbed at his sweaty forehead.

Pryor was smirking, his natural cockiness back in full force. For once, Ella didn't find that cockiness irksome. He had every right to be pleased with himself. He'd made her laugh more than she'd thought humanly possible.

She reached for the red-and-gold *chinoiserie* teapot—and decided that the moment called for something stronger than tea. "No magic," she warned, crossing to the bellpull and summoning one of the footmen.

Five minutes later, they each held a goblet of her best champagne, a beverage that was much more suited to magic and merriment than tea.

"To you, Mr. Pryor," Ella said, lifting her glass. "Vanquisher of highwaymen."

Unexpectedly, Pryor flushed faintly pink.

"To our savior!" Arthur declared, with a flourish of his goblet.

"Our hero!" Minette agreed.

Pryor went beyond pink, to a deep rosy red. "To Faerie godmothers," he said, turning the toast away from himself, raising his own glass.

The four goblets clinked together. Arthur tipped his back and drained it in one long gulp. Minette, a twinkle of devilry in her eyes, did the same. Pryor laughed and followed suit.

Ella attempted to copy this feat. She didn't quite make it. She coughed, and laughed, and set about refilling their goblets. She felt as lighthearted and effervescent as the bubbles sparkling in the champagne.

Arthur didn't gulp the champagne this time, but settled in for a comfortable coze with Mr. Pryor, leaning towards him, gesturing expansively with his glass.

Instead of flirting with Ella over the rim of his goblet, Mr. Pryor gave Arthur his full attention. They looked well on the way to becoming bosom beaux. They also looked oddly alike for two men who didn't resemble each other at all, an intangible similarity that Ella's eyes told her existed but that her brain couldn't identify.

"*Ma chère,*" Minette murmured. "Will you step out with me for a moment?"

Ella's effervescence was instantly quenched. "Of course." She set down her glass and followed Minette into the corridor and across to the dining room. "Is something wrong?" she asked, closing the door behind her.

"*Non,* not at all, it is merely . . ." Minette folded her lips and appeared to debate her next words.

"Merely what?"

Minette gave a very French shrug. "Me, I think you ought to give Monsieur Pryor a reward."

CHAPTER 4

"*A* reward?" It took a moment for Ella to fathom Minette's meaning. "You mean . . . give him *me*?" She took a step back, affronted. "I'm not a prostitute."

Minette sniffed. "You say that like it's a bad thing."

"I beg your pardon," Ella said hastily. She hadn't meant to offend Minette, who'd been a *fille de joie* as well as an opera dancer and who was unashamed of either profession. "What I meant was . . . I don't wish to intrigue with Mr. Pryor."

"No? You like his looks, *c'est* évident. And why not? He's a very pretty boy."

Ella ignored the first part of that statement. "He's not a boy. He's at least as old as I am."

Minette waved this quibble away. "Boy, man, who cares? He did us a favor; now you may do him one. Teach him finesse."

Ella opened her mouth to tell Minette that if anyone taught Mr. Pryor finesse, it wouldn't be her . . . and then closed it again.

It *would* please her to thumb her nose at Venetia Twyckham. The woman delighted in belittling people, in uttering comments that appeared artless but which were deliberately hurtful.

Decimus Pryor possibly did have more vigor than finesse, but that was no reason not to invite him into her bed. Not liking him was sufficient reason, but Ella could no longer claim not to like him. It was impossible to dislike a man who'd made her laugh so loudly, a man who'd risked his own life to save hers.

But . . .

"He has a swagger."

Minette lifted elegantly plucked eyebrows. "So?"

"I dislike men who swagger."

Those eyebrows stayed raised, so Ella clarified: "A swagger denotes arrogance and conceit."

"Most often, yes. That dreadful Baron Rumpole. Bah!" She gave an extravagant shudder. "But your Monsieur Pryor? No. He's like Arthur, that one. Likes to be the center of attention, likes to make people laugh. Should have been *un acteur*, not a nobleman."

Ella frowned at this assessment. Pryor was nothing like Arthur . . . was he? "He's too cocky."

Minette grinned, looking very like an opera dancer and not at all like a comtesse. "Me, I like *un gros pénis* on a man."

"That's not what I meant."

"Bah!" Minette said again, with another dismissive wave of her hand. "There are different types of cocky, just as there are different types of swagger. Your Monsieur Pryor, he is *un comédien*. That is why he has the swagger: because he should be on stage making people laugh."

"He's not my Mr. Pryor."

"He could be. He would be, if you gave him *un peu d'encouragement*."

Ella didn't want to encourage him. Pryor was too conscious of his charm as it was.

She was rather too conscious of his charm, too. And not entirely impervious to it. Nor was she impervious to the laughter in his eyes.

"I think you should tumble with him," Minette declared.

"It would be *très agréable* for you. Enjoy a frolic, teach him finesse, and then *adieu.*"

Put like that . . . it wasn't unappealing.

"Me, if I were thirty years younger, I would do it myself."

"I shall think about it," Ella said noncommittally.

"*Bon.*" Minette gave a short nod and swept out of the dining room, diminutive and regal.

Ella followed. As they entered the parlor, both men looked up. The similarity between them jumped out at her, so blindingly obvious that she couldn't believe she hadn't been able to identify it earlier. They looked nothing alike—the shapes of eye sockets and noses, foreheads and jaws were vastly different—and yet they could almost have been father and son. The resemblance was in the way that they sat, the way that they held themselves, confident and relaxed, each man owning his seat. Their heads were cocked at precisely the same angle, as were their eyebrows. Laughter brimmed in their eyes, as if they'd been telling jokes to one another—which was probably exactly what they'd been doing. Arthur adored making people laugh, and if Minette was correct, Decimus Pryor did, too.

Ella sat and picked up her goblet, feeling rather disconcerted.

Arthur was loud and exuberant and irreverent, but he was also the best man she knew, goodhearted and kind and steadfast, one of only two people in the world whom she trusted implicitly. He undeniably had a swagger, but it was a showman's swagger. It had never annoyed her. It was part of him, just as his outrageous sense of humor was part of him.

Ella sipped her champagne, letting the bubbles fizz and pop on her tongue while she listened to Arthur and Pryor bounce witticisms and jokes between them. By the time she reached the bottom of the glass, she decided that Minette was correct about Pryor: beneath the layers of rake and dandy was a man who delighted in making people laugh. Which meant that she'd been overly harsh in her estimation of him and that he deserved a chance. Possibly.

Ella didn't refill her goblet; she felt off-kilter and confused enough as it was. She poured herself a cup of tea instead. The tea was barely lukewarm, over-steeped and astringent, but it was also steadying. Conversation flowed around her while she sipped. Minette had discarded the cool, reserved comtesse's hauteur she wore in public and was showing some of her real self, vivacious and a little earthy, dark eyes snapping, hands punctuating her remarks. Arthur was still playing the rôle of Russian baron, but Ella thought he'd probably let Pryor in on that secret soon, and as for Pryor . . . he was still a popinjay and a peacock, but he was also . . . annoyingly attractive.

He was flirting with her again, trying to draw her into the conversation, but Ella ignored the playful looks, just as she ignored the conversational gambits. She was happy to observe. It gave her time to think, time to come to a decision.

During her marriage, she'd kept a mental diary. She'd not dared to keep a real one; Francis had read every letter she received, every letter she wrote. Nothing had been private—except her own thoughts. Now, for the first time in years, Ella reached for that mental diary and opened it. She turned to a fresh page, picked up her imaginary quill, and began to list the things that she liked about Pryor.

His hands.

His physique.

His grin.

The ready laughter.

The irrepressible cheerfulness.

Ella set down the imaginary quill and closed the diary. A list was no way to decide whether or not to invite someone into her bed. Lists were impersonal and dispassionate, the opposite of sex. Sex was intimacy and carnality, sensation and passion.

There was only one reason to embark on an affair with Decimus Pryor: because she wanted to kiss him, to touch him, to feel his mouth and his hands on her skin, to ride his *gros pénis*, as Minette had phrased it.

Ella looked across at Pryor, confident and cocky in her favorite armchair, laughing at something Arthur had just said. Would he be that cocky and confident in her bed? That willing to laugh?

She rather thought that he would be.

Pryor noticed her glance and raised his glass with a flourish, offering her a silent toast, one eyebrow and one corner of his mouth ticking up in blatant invitation. It would have been irritating an hour ago—but now Ella saw the man behind the rake, the laughter brimming beneath the flirtatiousness.

Ella had never laughed while in bed with a lover. Lovemaking had always been serious—a duty when she was a wife, a new skill to master once she was a widow. With Pryor, she rather thought that laughter would be inevitable.

On the heels of that thought came a pull of curiosity and interest, of attraction.

Ella looked down at Pryor's hands. They weren't the plump, soft hands that so many men of the *ton* possessed. She liked the assertive shape of his thumbs and the robustness of his knuckles, the long, masterful fingers, the strong sinews across the backs of his hands, the neatly trimmed nails.

If the nape of a man's neck was her Achilles heel, then hands were her second greatest weakness. Hands exactly like Mr. Pryor's, large and strong and masculine.

What would it be like to be touched by him? To be kissed by that annoying, playful mouth? To hear Pryor laugh low and teasingly in her ear? To have those hands roam her body?

The pull of attraction intensified. Ella was aware of a shiver across her skin and a bloom of warmth in her blood. The muscles one used for lovemaking contracted slightly, readying themselves for pleasure in a visceral stir of arousal that was as unexpected as it was unmistakable.

Which meant that the decision had made itself without the need for any lists.

Ella put aside her cold, tannic tea and shared the last of the champagne between the four goblets. There wasn't much left, barely a mouthful each, but it would suffice.

"To us!" she declared.

"To us!" Minette and Arthur echoed.

"To us," Pryor said, placing emphasis on the *us* and sending her another of those suggestive little glances.

His unquenchable confidence didn't annoy Ella; it made her laugh. She tipped her glass up, drank that mouthful of bubbles and joy, then set the glass down decisively. When she looked at Minette she found the older woman watching her, a question on her face.

Ella answered with a nod.

Minette beamed at her. She put down her own goblet and stood. "*Mon cher baron,* if I might have a word?"

Arthur looked startled but he complied, heaving himself out of the sofa's embrace and following Minette to the door. They stepped out into the corridor. The door closed with a quiet little *snick*.

Ella found herself alone in her second-best parlor with the rake she'd sworn never to encourage. The rake she was about to invite into a dalliance.

Pryor's gaze went from the closed door to her. His grin became jaunty.

Ella jumped in before he could embark on unnecessary flirtation. "Yes."

Pryor's grin acquired a slightly puzzled edge. "Yes?"

"Yes, I'll have a liaison with you."

He was momentarily lost for words, something Ella hadn't thought possible, but then his confidence reasserted itself. Even though he was seated, his posture acquired more than a hint of swagger. A smirk claimed his mouth. "I confess I had thought you immune to my charm."

Ella had become familiar enough with him in the past hour to spot the humor lurking beneath the smirk and that hint of swagger. "I am immune to it," she told him dryly and not quite truthfully. "What do you say to a month? Until the end of September."

The smirk faded. His eyebrows ticked up. "Do you ordinarily set an end date to your liaisons?"

"Yes."

His eyebrows stayed up a moment longer; then he said, "Very well. Until the end of September." The smirk returned. "You won't regret it."

Ella laughed at that blatant piece of conceit. "Neither will you. I shall spread it about town that you have both vigor *and* finesse."

The smirk vanished. Pryor surveyed her through slightly narrowed eyes. "This isn't because of last night, is it? It's not . . . *payment* for helping you?"

"No, Mr. Pryor, I assure you it's not. I have the strongest dislike of Venetia Twyckham's cattiness; it will give me great pleasure to tell everyone that she's wrong."

He didn't look wholly convinced.

"We shall enjoy ourselves," Ella told him. "You'll show off your skills and perhaps I'll learn to laugh more, and once it's over I shall proclaim far and wide that you are a virtuoso among rakes, *not* because you saved us last night, but because it's true!"

"It *is* true," Pryor said, and then, "Is that what you'd like? To laugh more?"

"Possibly." Ella lifted one shoulder in a shrug she'd learned from Minette. "But perhaps it isn't in my nature to laugh very much." Just as it wasn't in her nature to fall in love. Her heart was too stunted for romance, too cold and too colorless. She had learned to feel sexual pleasure, but she doubted any man could teach her how to fall in love—and if such a man existed, he definitely wasn't Mr. Pryor.

"I can teach you to laugh more," Pryor declared, his cockiness returning. "Among other things." The smirk made a reappearance. The look he gave her was bolder than any he'd yet bestowed on her. It held heat and intent, the promise of pleasure.

Ella's pulse responded with an eager little leap and then settled into a fast, nervous trot. Her skin tingled in antici-pation of his touch and her innermost muscles contracted again. She felt shy and excited and flustered, all at the same time, which was ridiculous in someone who'd lost her virginity twelve years ago. She sprang to her feet. "Then it's settled. One month."

Pryor stood, too. "One month," he agreed.

They shook hands over the tea table, with its litter of cups and empty glasses. Pryor's hand was warm, his clasp firm and strong. Heat came to Ella's cheeks. The amatory muscles in her loins gave another of those fluttering and disconcerting contractions. She reclaimed her hand, not quite certain what to do next. She'd never started an affair so quickly and so un-ceremoniously. She'd also never been so blunt about the end date before, despite what she'd told him, but Pryor was quite unlike the other men she'd invited into her bed and she didn't want him to get the wrong idea.

Did he expect to start now?

Ella decided that while she wanted to kiss Decimus Pryor in theory, she wasn't ready to kiss him in practice. Not quite yet, and not in a room that had no lock on its door.

Pryor's natural confidence had reasserted itself, but she thought that perhaps he felt a little awkward, too. He was used to lengthy flirtations and seductions, not sudden, businesslike plunges into intimacy. Was he wondering what she wanted from him, what she expected?

Ella smoothed her skirts. "I hope that you can join us for dinner tomorrow," she said, crossing to the door.

"Thank you. That would be delightful."

Pryor followed her to the door. Everything felt a little off-kilter, the moment needing something more than a polite leave-taking. Perhaps she ought to kiss him?

Ella glanced up at him—and found herself unable to look away. His eyes were a warm brown. Smiling eyes. Laughing eyes. And, at this moment, eyes that held heat and promise. She could tell that he wasn't thinking about tomorrow's dinner while he gazed down at her. He was thinking about more carnal things.

Foolish heat rose in her cheeks. The awkwardness between them blossomed into something else. Something that felt rather like anticipation. Ella's heartbeat sped up.

Pryor noticed the blush. His smile acquired a hint of smirk. "Good day, my lady." He took her left hand and, with a rakish flourish, bent his head to lay a kiss upon its back.

He didn't release her hand afterwards, nor did he straighten. Instead, he glanced up at her through his lashes, a look that was arch and mischievous and somehow absurdly attractive.

Ella's pulse gave a little flutter. Her amatory muscles did, too.

Pryor turned her hand over and kissed her palm. His lips were soft. Warm breath tickled her skin.

Ella's pulse fluttered more strongly. She had to suppress a tiny shiver of arousal.

Pryor glanced at her again, laughing brown eyes seen through a fringe of black lashes. He kissed her palm a second time. She felt soft lips—and then his tongue, a playful flicker, unexpected and ticklish.

It was impossible not to shiver, not to give a shocked, breathy little giggle. Arousal bloomed inside her from one instant to the next. Her amatory muscles contracted eagerly. She was aware of strong, masterful fingers holding her hand, aware of warm breath feathering across her palm, aware of the tingling patch of skin where his tongue had licked. Her heart beat rapidly with anticipation, but she didn't know exactly what she was hoping for.

Pryor smirked, his eyes laughing at her through that veil of lashes; then he dipped his head and tasted her skin again, his tongue warm and bold, thorough, tickling, blatantly erotic.

Ella shivered again, giggled again, and felt like a foolish young débutante encountering her first rake. Except that this rake had no interest in débutantes. The polite world knew that he only chased widows.

Ella was suddenly very glad that she'd caught his eye.

Pryor straightened, but didn't release her hand. They stared

40

at one another for a strangely breathless and heated moment; then his eyebrows tipped up and so did one corner of his mouth.

She'd ignored his previous invitations, but this time the answer was an unequivocal *yes*. She wanted more than a kiss on her hand, more than the flicker of his tongue over her palm.

Her lips parted, but she found herself unexpectedly mute. Her heart felt as if it had taken up residence in her throat, where it beat strongly and rapidly.

Pryor correctly interpreted her parted lips as acquiescence. His slanting smile grew into a smirk that was more than a little cocky—and how could something so annoying be so attractive? Ella had no time to unravel that puzzle, because he was dipping his head again, still smirking at her, and then his lips were on hers.

It wasn't a forceful kiss, a seizing of possession, a claiming; rather, it was a question, an invitation, warm and soft and light—and far too brief.

Pryor made as if to draw back, but Ella stopped him. He was still holding her left hand, but her right hand was free. She used it to clutch at his lapel and tug him closer. She gripped the material, stood on tiptoe, and kissed him.

This kiss was forceful, possessive, claiming. Pryor released her hand. His arms came around her and he kissed her back. His mouth was hot, his tongue clever. Ella sank into the kiss, losing herself in it until a desperate need for air obliged her to release his lapel and step back.

They both gasped for breath. Ella felt lightheaded and a little delirious, almost feverish. There was a hectic flush in Pryor's cheeks and his pupils were dilated—but even as she watched, they dwindled to their normal size. He inhaled a deep breath, refilling his lungs, then grinned at her, triumphant and cocky.

How could she find that cockiness attractive?

It was a great mystery.

If she and Decimus Pryor had been awkward and off-kilter

before, they weren't now. The only thing Ella wanted to do was kiss him again, but Arthur and Minette might reenter the parlor at any moment. She forced herself to turn away and open the door, to step out into the corridor.

In the vestibule, Pryor accepted his hat and gloves from the butler. "Until tomorrow, Lady Fortrose."

"Until tomorrow, Mr. Pryor."

He bowed with another of those ridiculous flourishes—a showman's flourish—and departed into the gathering dusk. He was definitely swaggering as he strolled down the steps to the street, and most likely smirking, too, which should have been annoying—which *was* annoying—and yet Ella found herself looking forward to their assignation tomorrow with all the eagerness of a giddy young girl.

CHAPTER 5

T here were things Dex was good at and things he wasn't. He was a bruising rider, but an indifferent boxer. He was a competent swordsman, but his marksmanship was nothing to boast about. He'd never been one for book learning, but he did enjoy drawing—not painstaking sketches where everything was picturesque and precise, but quickly dashed-off caricatures where noses were too big and legs too skinny. The sorts of drawings that made people laugh.

His letters to his sister Phoebe had always been more pictures than words and his latest epistle was no exception. *Dearest Fleabee,* he'd written at the top of a sheet of hot-pressed paper, *herewith an account of my EPIC BATTLE on Wimbledon Heath.* The rest of the letter was a pictorial rendition of his encounter with the highwaymen, each scene inside its own little box. He'd drawn himself with a barrel-like chest and great ham-like fists. *Take that!* his figure cried, punching a highwayman. In the next box, the man flew across the road.

It hadn't been clever, that dramatic punch. He should have just let the highwayman drop where he fell. Now three people knew about his family's rather malevolent Faerie godmother.

Even his cousin Ned, who was the idiot of the family, had never made such a cursed botch of things.

Dex sighed gustily. He'd have to tell his father, and more importantly, his grandfather. His father wouldn't be angry. Scoldings weren't Secundus Pryor's métier; as he cheerfully admitted, he'd made every mistake Dex had ever made and more. Grandfather wouldn't scold either, but he would be disappointed, and he'd look grave and worried, and, damn it, Dex liked making the old man laugh, not giving him cause to worry.

He could write to them both now, father and grandfather, but it felt cowardly to confess on paper when it was really something he ought to do face to face, so that he could shoulder his grandfather's disappointment and assure him that there was nothing to worry about, that Lady Fortrose and the baron and the comtesse-who-wasn't-a-comtesse were good at keeping secrets.

He gave a little grunt of laughter, remembering Comtesse de Villiers' admission that she'd been an opera dancer in her youth. *That* was audacity.

It was almost impossible to believe such a wild imposture. Her carriage was so regal, her countenance so patrician, everything about her so aristocratic, so blue-blooded. He might know the truth, but it would be impossible to treat her as anything other than a comtesse.

His amusement, his admiration, ebbed away. Dex heaved another gusty sigh. The letter fluttered on the desk. *Take that!* his caricature cried, his error in judgment immortalized in ink.

Dex was tempted to screw up the letter and toss it into the fire, but the drawings would make Phoebe laugh, and he liked making her laugh, so he scrawled *Love from your prodigiously valorous brother, Dex,* at the bottom. He folded the letter, sealed it, and set it to one side, then called for his manservant: "Hicks!"

His lodgings were in Clarges Street, three rooms on the second floor, so he didn't have to yell loudly for Hicks to hear him. The manservant stepped out of the bedchamber, boot in one hand, polishing cloth in the other. "Sir?"

Hicks had pock marks all over his face, and thick fingers, and a gruff manner. He looked as if he ought to be hauling bricks, not dressing gentlemen, but he was a genius with clothes. His eye for color was far superior to Dex's and he could put together an ensemble and match it with just the right accessories in a way that Dex had never been able to equal. "I'm having dinner with a lady," Dex told him. "I want to look less frippery than I usually do, more sober." Eloïse Fortrose seemed to prefer men who were intelligent rather than waggish, men who had serious thoughts and who could have conversations about weighty matters. But she had also said that she wanted to laugh more. "But a dash of *joie de vivre*, you know?"

Hicks nodded as if he did indeed know—which was a feat, considering that Dex didn't—but an hour later, when Dex was bathed and dressed and standing in front of his mirror, it was clear that Hicks had understood perfectly.

The manservant had chosen brown, accented with plum red and hints of gold. The brown was dark and masculine, stern almost, but the red was rich and warm and the gold thread gleamed subtly. It was the sort of outfit Dex wore at Linwood Castle, when he wasn't trying to impress any ladies.

His cuffs were less frothily abundant than usual, his neck-cloth less effusive, and his jewelry was limited to a mere tiepin, signet ring, and the buckles of his shoes.

The buckles were set with rubies, though, as was the tiepin, little glints of bright, laughing red. The *joie de vivre* he'd asked for.

Dex missed the frivolous froth of fabric at his wrists and throat, the peacock colors of his brightest waistcoats, but there was no denying that he looked less frippery than he usually did, less rakish. Dressed like this, he was dependable rather than dashing, a man capable of thinking serious thoughts if he wanted to—which he didn't particularly.

"You are worth every guinea of your exorbitant wages," Dex declared, smoothing his hand over the brown, plum red, and gold waistcoat and thinking that he almost looked like an intellectual, which was an achievement indeed.

Hicks merely grunted. He had an unmatched ability to dress a gentleman, but few social graces. He was blunt in his criticism, stinting in his praise, and he never flattered Dex's vanity—which had taken some getting used to, because Dex rather liked having his vanity flattered. He'd been considering letting the man go, until the day Hicks had said, "You look ridiculous in that, sir," and Dex had looked at himself in the mirror and realized that he did indeed look ridiculous.

He'd doubled Hicks's wages then and there. That had been five years ago, and Dex intended to employ the man until they both died of old age.

An honest valet was infinitely more valuable than an ingratiating one.

Dex admired himself in the mirror one last time, donned his hat and gloves, and departed for his club. He'd flick through the newspapers and catch up with the latest *on-dits* before his engagement with Lady Fortrose this evening.

His rooms were just around the corner from Piccadilly and only five minutes' walk to his club on St. James's Street. "Evening, Vigor," someone said, leaving that establishment as Dex entered.

Dex managed to smirk rather than snarl. He added more swagger to his step, sauntered into the front parlor, and looked around. The room was less than half occupied. Several men read newspapers by the fire, others lounged in the armchairs by the bay window.

One of the men by the window raised a hand. "Vigor!"

Dex pinned his smirk firmly in place and strolled across to join him.

"Didn't know you were in town," the man, a chap he'd been to school with, said. "Haven't seen you for an age. What have you been up to?"

Now was the time to boast about vanquishing three highwaymen, but Dex found himself reluctant to mention that incident. It was also the time to let drop that he was engaged to dine with a certain lovely young widow, but he was strangely reluctant to mention that, too. "Not a lot," he said. "You?"

They gossiped over a decanter of the club's best claret for the next hour. Dex tried not to notice how often he was called Vigor, but it was difficult not to when every person who entered the room felt obliged to use that wretched appellation.

"I say, look, it's Vigor!"

"Fancy a hand of piquet, Vigor?"

"Try this, Vigor. It's a new blend. Tell me what you think."

"Want to join us at billiards, Vigor?"

He tried the snuff, declined the offers to play cards and billiards, smiled and laughed and didn't gnash his teeth until he was outside again and heading for Lady Fortrose's house on Old Burlington Street. He did *not* need finesse, damn it. He'd brought Venetia Twyckham to climax every time they'd danced the feather bed jig.

He stomped down St. James's Street, turned right into Piccadilly and then left into Old Bond. It wasn't in his nature to be angry, though, so he was whistling by the time he reached the lane that ran behind Burlington House's expansive gardens.

Old Burlington Street was a short, elegant avenue. Each house possessed a garden of its own, although those gardens were nowhere near as vast as the gardens of Burlington House, with their lawns and tree-lined walks. Dex halted in front of the viscountess's residence and gazed up at the tall windows and elaborate brickwork. Finally! The most tempting of all London's widows, the one he'd hankered after for years, the one who'd ignored every approach he'd made.

Eloïse Fortrose's mouth was sweeter and hotter than he'd imagined it would be. Yesterday's kiss had been scorching, exhilarating—and a mere taste, a mere tease. Tonight, he'd do far more than kiss her.

He couldn't regret revealing his family's secret, not if it had brought him to this moment.

Dex smoothed his lapels, tweaked his cuffs, and tilted the brim of his hat to a dashing angle. His pulse gave an excited little skip. If he hadn't been a rake with a reputation to maintain, his feet might have given a little skip, too. As it was, he climbed the steps with an appropriately rakish swagger.

He plied the door knocker with confidence—*rat-tat-tat*—and recalled that he was attempting to be sober rather than dashing. He adjusted his hat brim to a more dignified angle.

Lady Fortrose's entrance hall was a cozy oasis of color and lamplight. The walls were yellow, the carpet a bold strip of red. Pink, purple, and blue Michaelmas daisies rioted exuberantly in a vase on the pier table, and cupids and songbirds danced overhead in a sunlit *trompe l'oeil* sky.

Dex surrendered his hat and gloves to a footman.

"Her ladyship is in the drawing room, sir," the butler said. "If you will be so good as to follow me?"

Dex followed, a jaunty spring in his step and more than a hint of braggadocio in his stride—and then he remembered that braggadocio was probably something the viscountess didn't like. He tried to walk more sedately, to match the butler's solemn dignity, but his legs weren't made for solemn dignity. Before he had mastered the knack of walking sedately, they arrived at their destination.

The drawing room was no less colorful than the foyer, although it didn't have a *trompe l'oeil* ceiling. What it did have was a French opera dancer turned comtesse and a Russian baron. Dinner would be no *tête-à-tête*.

Dex tried not to let his disappointment show. Comtesse de Villiers resided in this house to protect Lady Fortrose's reputation. If not for her presence, the viscountess wouldn't be able to have gray-bearded Russian barons stay under her roof or rakes dine at her table.

Eloïse Fortrose was resplendent in cerulean satin. Sapphires gleamed in her white-blond hair and against the creamy skin of her throat. She looked like one of Poseidon's daughters newly risen from the sea, lissom and sylphlike, the sort of woman kings fought battles over.

Dex planned to place kisses where those sapphires lay, to peel off that spectacular gown and plunder her most intimate secrets. He'd take his time, learn the places that made her body sing. It would be a delightful game, the most diverting of treasure hunts.

He stepped into the room with his jauntiest swagger, kissed Lady Fortrose's fingertips with a flourish and then Comtesse de Villiers's, offered both ladies extravagant compliments, bowed to Baron Zhivot and offered him a fulsome compliment, too.

The baron gave a great guffaw, the comtesse twinkled at him, and Eloïse Fortrose looked as if she didn't know whether to laugh or roll her eyes, pursing her lips in a way that almost brought dimples to her cheeks, making her look less like a sea nymph and more like a mortal.

As he sat, Dex remembered that he was trying to be sober rather than flirtatious. But the viscountess had almost laughed, so . . . perhaps it hadn't been a blunder? In his experience, getting a lady to laugh was the first step to charming her into bed.

Dinner was announced shortly, and while it wasn't the intimate occasion he'd been hoping for, it was surprisingly enjoyable. The comtesse and the baron were excellent companions, *bon vivants* both of them, and there was considerable merriment around the table. Dex was almost sorry when the comtesse folded her napkin and declared that she and her *très cher baron* must depart if they were to catch the first act of the new play at Drury Lane.

He *was* sorry when Baron Zhivot bade him farewell and announced that he was leaving London tomorrow.

"It's been a pleasure meeting you, sir," Dex said sincerely, making his bow, but bows were too formal for the old gentleman. He shook Dex's hand vigorously and kissed him on both cheeks with unrestrained Russian enthusiasm.

The departure of the viscountess's two companions meant that at last he and Eloïse Fortrose were alone.

"Shall we remove to the drawing room?" she suggested. "Unless you'd like some brandy or port? I can have them set out the decanters for you."

Dex declined this offer. One couldn't show off one's finesse if one were half-cut.

The fire had been stoked in the drawing room and a tea tray laid out. Finally, Dex was having the *tête-à-tête* he'd hoped for. He and the viscountess together, alone.

Lady Fortrose hesitated, then crossed to a three-seater sofa near the fire.

Dex decided that her choice of seat was an invitation and crossed to the sofa, too. He settled himself not too close, but not too far away either. Less than two feet of cushion separated his thigh from hers. Beneath the glorious cerulean satin and the frothy layers of petticoat and chemise would be warm, creamy skin.

Dex's pulse began to beat a little faster, excitement and anticipation tempered with an uncharacteristic dash of nervousness.

He thought Eloïse Fortrose might be feeling a little nervous, too. She didn't look completely at ease as she poured them both tea from a pretty *chinoiserie* teapot.

Dex fell back on his customary method of putting ladies at ease: a joke, something silly to make her laugh and bring almost-dimples springing to her cheeks.

One joke led to another, and by the time they'd drunk their tea the dimples in Eloïse Fortrose's cheeks were no longer hiding.

She set aside her teacup.

So did Dex.

Their eyes met. A *frisson* zigzagged down the nape of his neck, as if static electricity lifted the hairs from his skin. Dex found himself holding his breath. Anticipation thrummed in his blood. He watched as faint color rose in the viscountess's cheeks, a delicate wash of pink. Was that blush shyness? Desire? Both?

Her hand rested on the sofa within easy reach.

Dex reached out and traced a fingertip over the back of her hand, light, tickling, teasing.

She shivered and inhaled a short breath, her gaze caught in his.

The drawing room was hushed and breathless. Nothing moved except the flames in the grate and Dex's finger roaming lightly across Eloïse Fortrose's hand. She shivered again. Her cheeks became pinker. The sapphires glinted, their facets catching the candlelight as her bosom rose and fell.

Dex smirked, and lifted his hand to one rosy cheek. Four fingertips, resting lightly on warm, silky-soft skin.

He watched her pupils dilate, felt the heat of her blush beneath his fingers. She didn't pull away, didn't shiver or gasp, just watched him, waiting for whatever he'd do next. Expectancy hovered in the air, silent and alert, holding its breath.

Dex traced a path down her cheek with the tips of his fingers, whisper-light, making her shiver again. He followed the curve of her jaw, tipped her chin up and waited a moment, giving her time to draw back, to tell him he was moving too fast.

Her cheeks grew a little pinker. Her eyelashes swept down, swept up. Her lips parted, a silent invitation.

Dex leaned closer and kissed her.

Eloïse Fortrose's mouth was as soft and sweet and eager as he remembered. She kissed him back without hesitation, a dance of lips and tongues. Several minutes passed. Heated, delightful, intoxicating minutes, but also minutes while Dex kept an ear cocked for approaching footsteps and opening doors—because although they were alone, they were sitting in a drawing room in a house filled with servants.

He didn't pluck the pins from the viscountess's elegant chignon, although he longed to feel her silky hair tumble over his hands. He didn't bend his head and place kisses where the sapphires rested so temptingly above her neckline, because kisses there would glow like brands upon her pale skin. And he most definitely didn't get down on his knees, push her lush cerulean skirts up, and show her what he could do with his tongue.

Those were all things he planned to do, but not while a butler could walk in on them.

At last, they drew apart. Eloïse Fortrose was panting and flushed, lips rosy and kiss-swollen, eyes hot and dark. Dex knew that he was just as flushed, just as dark-eyed, just as breathless.

"Shall we go upstairs?" she said.

CHAPTER 6

$\mathcal{E}$lla had two bedrooms: the one she slept in and the one she allowed her lovers to enter. A large dressing room separated the two bedchambers. The pleasures of the flesh through one door; the comfort of a serene night's sleep through the other.

Her bedchamber, the one her lovers never saw, was a sanctuary, a place of privacy and repose. Its palette was very different from the rich, sensual crimson and gold of her boudoir. It was a warm blush pink with notes of amber and peach and ripe apricot, the colors of soft sunrises and peaceful summer mornings.

This morning wasn't a summer morning, though; it was an autumn morning, and a cold one at that. A fire burned in the grate in the dressing room, pressing back the chill the room had acquired overnight. The candles in the *girandole* mirror above the mantelpiece were lit, the light reflecting to illuminate the room. The bathtub she'd washed in after her romp with Mr. Pryor no longer sat in front of the hearth. It was back in the corner, where it lived when it wasn't in use.

Ella allowed herself a small, secret smile at the memory of that romp—although romp was perhaps not quite the right word. Their lovemaking had been playful rather than strenuously athletic, a lingering, candlelit interlude of murmurs and laughter and teasing caresses. Pryor had acquainted himself with her body without haste, making discoveries no one else had ever made, learning things that Ella hadn't even known about herself—that soft kisses behind her knees made her shiver and sigh, that she squirmed and giggled when someone licked between her fingers, and—most surprising of all—that gentle bites to the side of her waist were ridiculously arousing, making her buck helplessly and demand to be mounted *right now,* something that Ella had never demanded of anyone before, something she'd never imagined she could ever *want* to demand.

Ella gazed at herself in the mirror. She'd chosen raspberry red kerseymere this morning, rich and warm and cheerful. She touched her waist lightly where Pryor had bitten. The skin was unmarked, hidden beneath gown and petticoat, stays and chemise.

Last night had far exceeded her expectations. Pryor had eased them into intimacy with levity and laughter, banishing awkwardness with a few easy jokes, everything playful and lighthearted. It had been impossible to be embarrassed while they were disrobing, impossible to be embarrassed when she grabbed his arm and demanded that he mount her immediately.

"Will that be all, ma'am?" her maid, Hedgepeth, asked.

Ella removed her hand from her waist. "Yes, thank you."

Hedgepeth bustled over to the dresser and began setting everything to rights, aligning the brushes, tidying away the hairpins. She hummed as she did so, soft and melodious.

Ella stayed where she was, standing in front of the tall cheval mirror. Ormolu figures frolicked along the frame, mermaids and dolphins to match the blue-green décor of the dressing room. It *was* the room where she bathed. What better theme than the ocean?

The dressing room was blues and sea greens, she herself was wearing raspberry red, but . . .

What color is my heart today? Ella asked herself silently.

Last night had been so enjoyable, so beyond her previous experience of sex, that she almost thought that the answer might have changed, but no, it was the same as it always was: *No color.*

The vividness and vibrancy that surrounded her was all on the outside. Inside, she was as colorless as glass. Not even two hours of laughter and pleasure with Decimus Pryor could change that.

Ella sighed.

She wanted a heart that matched her private bedroom, those rich apricots and pinks, but perhaps some people never had color in their hearts? Just as some people never fell in love.

Ella turned away from the mirror and made her way down to the breakfast parlor.

If her private bedroom was a peaceful summer's dawn, then the breakfast parlor was a golden summer's afternoon. It was daffodil yellow and buttercup yellow and sunflower yellow, joyful and cheerful and uplifting. Displayed over the sideboard was an array of bright, childish drawings, courtesy of Arthur's young great-nephew, Phillip, an orphan who resided with his spinster aunt in Bristol.

Minette was already ensconced in the parlor, nibbling a warm brioche and sipping bittersweet chocolate. She set her cup down, eyes sharp with curiosity, thin black eyebrows arched inquiringly. "Well, *ma chère*?"

"Good morning," Ella said, crossing to the dishes lined up on the sideboard.

Minette batted that greeting away with her hand. "How did *le beau monsieur* acquit himself? Is it true? He has no finesse?"

It was very *un*true. Pryor had shown off his finesse unequivocally, and then he'd demonstrated his vigor just as thoroughly—but the events of the boudoir were private and not for gossip over the breakfast table.

"Who believes a word Venetia Twyckham says? I certainly

don't." Ella picked up a plate and perused the offerings on the sideboard. She piled her plate with kedgeree, hesitated, then added a poached egg. When she turned back to the table, Minette was still staring at her with those eagle-sharp eyes.

"I'm not going to give you the details!" Ella protested.

"Not the details, no, but surely you can give me a . . . how do you call it? A tittle bit."

"Tidbit," Ella said, setting the plate down and taking her seat at the table. "Very well: He has a great deal of finesse."

"And?"

Ella reached for the teapot, debated what else she could tell Minette. Not that Pryor did indeed have *un gros pénis,* nor that, despite being informed that she was barren, he'd withdrawn at the last moment, gentlemanly even in the throes of passion. Finally, she said, "He has a great deal of stamina as well."

Minette cackled with laughter. "He is a stallion?"

Ella poured herself a cup of tea with dignity and didn't reply, choosing to eat her egg instead.

"Will we be seeing more of Monsieur Pryor, *ma chère?*" Minette asked, when Ella had finished the egg.

"I invited him to dine with us tomorrow." A tryst that she was looking forward to more than she'd ever looked forward to a tryst before.

"*Bon.*"

Ella plied herself to her kedgeree. Minette resumed nibbling her pastry. They ate in silence for several minutes, then Minette said, "Did you learn anything last night?"

"I'm not giving you any more details." Ella selected a fragrant brioche from the basket in the middle of the table and broke it open. Warm apple nestled inside, seasoned with sugar and cinnamon.

"I mean other things than that."

Ella felt her brow wrinkle. "Such as?"

Minette gave a very French shrug. "Did you laugh with him?"

"Yes."

"*Bon.*" Minette gave a satisfied nod. "That is a good thing to learn. Bedsport, it is not meant to be a serious thing."

Ella glanced down at her brioche, and then back at Minette. "But it usually *is* serious. It's a duty or it's . . . how one earns one's living."

Minette regarded her across the table with wise, dark eyes. "We barter our bodies in exchange for many things, *ma chère*—money, food, security—but sometimes we are lucky enough to find joy as well." She smiled a tender, reminiscent smile and her eyes were momentarily luminous with grief.

Ella looked down at the brioche split open on her plate. "Not everyone has a great love." Or even a heart capable of love. "And even if I *do* have a great love, it's not Mr. Pryor. He's a rake and a dandy and a . . . a clown!"

"Your aunt was a clown."

Ella glanced up to see that Minette's smile had become even softer, her eyes more luminous with grief and memory; then Minette blinked the sheen of moisture away and reached for the chocolate pot. "Do not disregard clowns, *ma chère*. The best lovers are those who make you laugh."

Ella opened her mouth to argue this statement—and decided to eat her brioche instead. She bit into it, tasting buttery sweetness, apples, and cinnamon. "How was the theater?" she asked, when she'd swallowed the delicious mouthful. "Has Arthur decided who he'll be next?"

CHAPTER 7

A different butler admitted Dex to the house on Old Burlington Street. The fellow he'd seen previously had been middle-aged; this chap looked to be in his early sixties. He was spindle-shanked and stoop-shouldered and rather doddery, with a fringe of graying ginger hair around a bald pate.

He was also oddly familiar, even though Dex was certain he'd never seen the man before.

The butler set a tottering pace to the drawing room, where he announced Dex's arrival. There was no Russian baron tonight, just one delectable dowager viscountess and one French comtesse. Lady Fortrose was wearing spring green shot with threads of gold, like sunshine filtering through leaves. Peridots glittered at her ears and throat and nestled in her hair.

She looked bright and vivid, cool and confident, and a tiny bit shy.

She'd kissed him open-mouthed the night before last, when they'd frolicked in that cloud-soft feather bed, but with Comtesse de Villiers and the butler as audience, Dex bowed and kissed only her fingertips. She'd invited him to call her Eloïse then, too, but first names were another intimacy that was appropriate only in privacy. "Your beauty dazzles the eye, Lady Fortrose. You shine more brightly than your jewels."

She laughed at that, blushed at that. Dex wished they could pick up where they'd left off, but first there was dinner to be undergone. He turned to Comtesse de Villiers, kissed her fingertips, and offered her a compliment, too. "*Vous* êtes *magnifique, madame.*"

Her dark eyes twinkled at him. "*Merci. Vous* êtes *magnifique vous-même, monsieur.*"

"Thank you, ma'am." Dex managed not to preen, although he knew he did look rather handsome. Hicks had excelled himself again, pairing a midnight blue tailcoat with a waistcoat in cream, gold, and fuchsia. The blue was sober, steady, unimaginative, the sort of color worn by statesmen and intellectuals; the waistcoat was *joie de vivre* stitched in silk thread.

They sat down to dine shortly after. Without Baron Zhivot, conversation around the table was less animated. Dex was sorry that the old gentleman wasn't still with them. They were cut from the same cloth, he and the baron.

Perhaps it was the baron's absence, perhaps not, but Dex found himself more aware of the butler than he usually was. Everything the man did was unobtrusive—he removed the dish covers without dropping them, poured the wine without spilling anything, directed the footmen with a mere flick of a finger and twitch of a faded ginger eyebrow—but Dex couldn't help thinking that the fellow ought to be sitting in front of the kitchen fire, with slippers on his feet and a nightcap on his head.

The butler stood to attention at the sideboard while they ate the first course, ready to leap—or totter—into action if anything were needed. Dex ate soup à la Reine and a stuffed quail and a portion of artichokes in Italian sauce . . . and watched as the butler's eyelids drooped and his head began to nod. Lower and lower sank those eyelids. Each nod of the man's head was longer and deeper, until finally his chin came to rest on his neckcloth.

Dex paused with his fork halfway to his mouth. Had the butler gone to sleep, standing by the sideboard?

He ought to do something to wake the man before the others noticed, make a loud noise, clatter some dishes.

Before Dex could do so, the comtesse noticed him sitting with his fork poised between his plate and his mouth. She glanced behind herself—and uttered an unladylike snort of laughter. "Monsieur Pettislaw," she said loudly. "Have you fallen asleep again?"

The butler jerked awake. "I beg your pardon, sir?"

There was a beat of silence, and then the comtesse gave vent to a cackle of laughter. Dex was hard put not to cackle, too. He bit the inside of his cheek to hold the sound back.

The butler drew himself up with dignity. "Do you require something, ma'am?" he inquired loftily of the comtesse.

"*Non, non.* Go back to sleep, my old friend."

Pettislaw gave the haughty sniff of a man who had been falsely impugned, picked up one of the wine decanters, and doddered around the table, refilling their glasses. Then he returned to his post by the sideboard . . . and promptly fell asleep again.

Dex didn't dare resume eating. A laugh was building in his chest. If he tried to swallow anything, he'd surely choke. He glanced at Lady Fortrose. Her cheeks were pink and her lips tightly pressed together. Mirth sparkled in her eyes like sunlight on water.

In that green dress shot with gold thread, laughter shining in her eyes, she looked radiant and beautiful, a woodland nymph, a spring goddess. If Dex had paid more attention at school he'd know which nymph or which goddess; as it was, all he could do was stare at her and think that she was one of the loveliest women he'd ever seen in his life.

As if she felt his regard, Lady Fortrose glanced at him. Dimples danced in her cheeks. They stared at one another, both brimming with mirth, both struggling not to laugh. Something intangible passed between them, a connection that had nothing to do with sex, an intimacy that felt like . . . the beginnings of friendship?

The butler uttered a faint, whistling snore.

Lady Fortrose's gaze jerked to the man. Her cheeks became pinker with suppressed laughter. The dimples danced more deeply. She bit her soft, rosy lower lip, giving Dex a glimpse of white teeth.

Dex's attention became divided. Most of his focus was on the butler standing sleeping like a spindle-shanked, stoop-shouldered, balding stork, but some of it was on the viscountess, marveling at how extraordinarily beautiful she looked right now, how *alive*.

"He has done it again, has he not?" the comtesse said, not bothering to look behind herself, her attention on the lobster she was elegantly picking away at.

As if to answer her, the butler gave vent to another snore. It went on for rather a long time, high-pitched and nasal, before ending with a comical squeak.

It was the squeak that undid Dex. He couldn't hold back a hoot of laughter. Lady Fortrose exploded into giggles and the comtesse joined in, all three of them laughing over their plates.

Pettislaw didn't wake up.

Dex knew he ought to feel ashamed of himself, laughing because an elderly man had fallen asleep. He *was* ashamed of himself—but at least the laughter wasn't cruel. The comtesse had called Pettislaw "old friend." The butler wasn't going to be berated or turned out onto the street.

Even so, he ought not to laugh.

Dex mastered his amusement, caught his breath, and cleared his throat loudly. "I say, Pettislaw!"

The butler jerked awake again. "Yes, ma'am?"

Don't laugh, Dex told himself, jamming his molars together. *Don't laugh.* It was touch and go for a moment, though. He unclenched his jaw, swallowed twice, and managed to say, in an almost-steady voice, "You have any champagne over there?"

"Of course, sir."

Pettislaw brought the champagne over and poured. Dex

expected the butler's eyes to be rheumy and groggy, bleary with age, but they were a surprisingly bright hazel, clear and alert.

The man didn't fall asleep again. Dex drank his wine and sampled a little lobster, a smidgen of Venetian cream, and some very tasty trifle. He didn't want to fill his belly with food, not given his plans for the evening.

Lady Fortrose ate sparingly, too, and it wasn't long before the covers were removed. When the ladies withdrew to the drawing room, Dex accompanied them. He had no desire to sit in lonely splendor in the dining room, sipping brandy or port.

They played loo with mother-of-pearl counters instead of guineas. Comtesse de Villiers won the first two tricks, until Dex realized she was shamelessly cheating. He started shamelessly cheating, too, which led to several rapid and rowdy games, the three of them competing to outdo each other in underhandedness.

As the clock struck ten, the comtesse set aside her cards and rose to her feet, diminutive and regal. "Good night, *mes poulets*. Don't do anything I wouldn't do." She patted Lady Fortrose's cheek, winked at Dex, and swept from the room.

Dex watched her depart, then transferred his gaze to Eloïse Fortrose. "If you don't mind me asking . . . how is it that you have Comtesse de Villiers as your companion?"

The viscountess picked up the discarded cards and began to shuffle them, her lips pursed thoughtfully. Dex thought she was sorting through answers, much as she was sorting through the cards. "You don't have to tell me," he hastened to say.

Lady Fortrose gave a shrug that was very like one of the comtesse's, elegant and graceful. "I have one of your secrets; there's no reason why you shouldn't have one of mine." She set the cards aside and sat back in her chair, lacing her fingers together. "You know that Minette was an opera dancer . . . well, my uncle was one of her patrons. Lord Cameron. He wasn't a very kind man, he liked to flaunt his infidelities in front of my aunt, but from the moment she and Minette met they became the very best of friends. When my uncle passed away, they decided to set up house together, and the Comtesse de Villiers was born."

Dex felt his eyebrows climb halfway up his forehead. "Audacious."

"Yes, very. Minette claimed to be my aunt's long-lost cousin and everyone believed her, even my father, and he was a stickler of the highest order. I grew up calling them Tante Minette and Aunt Clara. They lived together until Clara died."

Dex almost said "audacious" again, but it was more than that. It was impressive, a magnificent deceit, the stuff of stories and legends. "When did you learn the truth?"

"After my husband's death. Father was insistent that I return to live with him and the new viscount wanted me to occupy the Dower House." Her expression changed, an infinitesimal tightening of the skin around her eyes, a faint pinching of her mouth.

"Is it a very . . . *dour* dower house?"

"Very dour, yes, and my father's house was little better. Fortunately, Minette offered herself as an alternative—a respectable companion. Or at least, respectable insofar as everyone knew." She laughed. "I chose Minette, of course. I wanted to be free."

Lady Fortrose was certainly free now. Free of husbands and fathers and dour dower houses, free to do as she wished, free to conduct discreet liaisons under her own roof.

Dex tilted his head slightly, let his eyes become hooded, looked at her through his lashes. He curled up one corner of his mouth in what he thought of as his bedroom smile.

Eloïse Fortrose's cheeks became faintly pink. She glanced away, glanced back, flushed a little more vividly.

Dex put more bedroom into his smile.

The viscountess laughed and shook her head. "You're doing that on purpose, aren't you?"

"Is it working?" He gave in to impulse and fluttered his

lashes coquettishly at her, even though gentlemen wearing sober blue tailcoats oughtn't be so silly.

Eloïse Fortrose shook her head again, laughed again, and said, "You, sir, are a clown."

"I'm wounded," Dex said, pressing one hand to his chest.

"No, you're not." Dimples quivered in her cheeks, and then she dipped her head and looked at him through her lashes, giving him her own bedroom smile. "Shall we go upstairs, Mr. Pryor?"

CHAPTER 8

What color is my heart today? Ella asked herself the next morning while surveying herself in the mirror. Outwardly, she was a cheerful jonquil yellow—a color chosen to combat the closed-in grayness of the day and the steady drip-drip-drip of rain. Inwardly, the answer was the same as it always was: *No color.*

Ella headed downstairs. Today, she was the first one to the breakfast parlor. She had only taken a few mouthfuls when Minette joined her.

"Someone had an energetic night, *non?*" Minette said, when she saw the amount of food on Ella's plate.

Ella tried not to blush, and failed. She busied herself with slicing her sausages into bite-sized pieces.

"So?" Minette said, pouring herself a cup of hot chocolate.

Ella didn't look up from her task. "I'm not giving you any details."

"*Non,* you misunderstand."

Ella glanced across at her.

Minette sipped the fragrant chocolate, her eyes bright with curiosity. "Did you learn anything more?"

Ella frowned at her. "More?"

"About him. About yourself."

Ella looked down at her dismembered sausages, then back at Minette. Decimus Pryor was good in bed, he was amusing, what else was there to know about him?

Minette's cup steamed gently. The scent of chocolate drifted across the table, dark and rich. Minette sat with her head cocked and her eyebrows raised, waiting for Ella's reply.

Ella thought back over her two trysts with Pryor. "I think . . . he believes he must play the more active part, that it is his rôle to lead and mine to follow."

"A common misconception among men," Minette put down her cup and selected a brioche from the basket on the table. "A shame. I had thought him more égalitariste. And what did you learn about yourself?"

"Nothing. What do I have to learn?"

Minette became engrossed in pulling the brioche apart. Today, the treasure hidden inside the soft pastry was berries.

"What?" Ella said. "What do you think I need to learn?"

Minette glanced at her. "To laugh more."

"I do laugh." In fact, she'd laughed rather a lot last night in the privacy of her boudoir.

"And to open your heart."

"To *him*?" Ella said, appalled. She put down her cutlery with a loud clatter.

"In general. You have a wary heart, *ma chère,* and I understand why, but instead of holding it so tightly closed, let it bloom."

"I love you and Arthur," Ella said, a defensive note in her voice.

"And we love you. But I'm talking about a different kind of love. One you've never experienced. And if you keep your heart closed, you never will."

"I don't want to love Decimus Pryor." Ella wrinkled her nose. "He's an amusing flirt, but that's all. He's not someone I want to have feelings for. He's too . . . lightweight."

"Do you know what I most loved about your aunt? Her sense of humor. Her silliness. She made me laugh every day. If you can find both laughter and love, you will be most happy."

"I am happy," Ella said, the defensive note returning to her voice.

"Yes. But if someone who could make you happier should, how do you say . . . present himself, don't close your heart to him."

"I won't. But it's not Decimus Pryor."

"If you say so, *ma chère.*"

"I do." Minette was possibly right about Ella's heart, but she was definitely wrong about Pryor.

Ella ate her eggs and sausages. When she'd finished, she plucked a brioche from the basket and broke it open. The berries had stained the dough a red so rich that it was almost purple.

Hearts that loved deeply must be that rich a red.

Minette's heart would be that red. And Arthur's heart.

Was her heart colorless because it held some deep, integral flaw? Had she inherited that flaw from her father, who'd been incapable of loving anyone? Was she incapable of romantic love, too?

Not for the first time, Ella found herself wondering what the mother who'd died giving birth to her had been like. Had her heart been as stunted and colorless as Ella's? Or had it been like Aunt Clara's, capable of deep love?

"Good morning, ladies!" Arthur beamed at them as he entered the breakfast parlor.

"*Mon ami,* you were dreadful last night, simply dreadful! I thought I should die with the laughing!"

Arthur swaggered across to the table. "Good, wasn't I?"

"You were superb," Ella told him. "That snore!" She laid the brioche on her side plate and clapped.

Minette clapped, too.

Arthur puffed out his chest and preened, basking in the applause. "Thank you," he said, bowing with a showman's flourish to the left and to the right. "Thank you, thank you."

Ella laughed and shook her head. He was even more of a comedian than Decimus Pryor.

Arthur gave a theatrical start and raised a hand to his brow, like a mariner peering out to sea. "What's that I spy? A letter for me?"

A letter did indeed lie alongside his place setting. The postmark said Bristol, which meant that it was probably from his niece.

Arthur rounded the table and picked it up. "It's from Sarah," he declared, eagerly breaking the seal and unfolding the paper. In the blink of an eye he went from swaggering showman to doting great-uncle. "Another of Phillip's drawings. Look!"

Ella and Minette *ooh*ed and *ah*ed over the drawing—a bird striped like a bumblebee, or perhaps it was a bumblebee that looked like a bird?

Arthur proudly added the drawing to the collection displayed over the sideboard; then he filled a plate and took his place at the table. "When's Pryor next dining with us?"

"Tomorrow."

"Who shall I be?" Arthur mused, cutting into his sirloin. He had his plotting face on.

"Colonel Withers," Minette declared. "You can dine with us and then escort me to the theater, give the young ones some time alone."

"The colonel it is." The way Arthur inhabited his chair changed, spine straightening, shoulders squaring. His eyebrows beetled and his jaw acquired a bulldog jut.

"He'll guess eventually," Ella felt compelled to point out.

Arthur became himself again. "I'm counting on it," he said cheerfully. "The look on his face will be priceless!"

Pryor didn't guess when he dined with them, and Minette's departure for the theater with her elderly military admirer was most welcome. Ella and Pryor retired early and spent quite a few hours rumpling the sheets and laughing.

Her mood was light the next morning. Hedgepeth wasn't the only person humming as she moved about the dressing room. Ella crossed to the cheval mirror and examined herself. She was wearing cornflower blue today, a color that made her eyes look brighter and less wintry.

What color is my heart? she asked herself, and to her surprise the answer was . . . not completely colorless?

Her heart held the faintest hint of color, a pinch of rose gold, like the sky before the sun peeked up above the horizon, a color that was possibly . . . contentment?

Ella stared at herself, disconcerted. After all these years— twenty-seven of them!—her heart was finally gaining some color?

The phenomenon was as unexpected as it was unprecedented, but there was no mystery as to its cause.

Decimus Pryor.

She had laughed before, she'd experienced physical pleasure before, but never at the same time and never so fulsomely and unrestrainedly.

Ella turned away from the mirror. She didn't skip down the stairs, but her feet almost wanted to. She was still humming when she entered the breakfast parlor.

"Someone is *joyeux* this morning." Minette's expression was wicked and knowing, opera dancer, not comtesse.

Ella didn't blush. She smiled and crossed to the sideboard like the bold, confident widow that she was and piled a plate high with food.

Minette waited until she was seated to ask, "You learned something last night, no?"

"I learned that laughter is more important than I thought," Ella said, pouring a cup of fragrant tea. "You were right." When she next took a lover, it would be someone like Pryor, someone who liked to laugh.

Minette sat back in her chair, looking smug.

"He's not my Clara, though, so don't think that he is," Ella told her, before Minette could start building castles in the air. But perhaps there *was* a man out there who could fully awaken her heart. Someone who liked to laugh, but who wasn't a rake.

Ella busied herself with her eggs. When she'd taken the edge off her hunger, she looked up from her plate. "Minette?"

"*Oui?*"

"Is there a name for when a woman is, ah, astride a man?" She'd done it with two of her lovers, but neither had given it a name.

"Riding St. George, they call it here, but in France we call it *Diligence de Lyon.* The Lyon stagecoach."

Ella filed away that piece of information, then said, "Do some men not enjoy it?"

Minette paused in sipping her hot chocolate. "I have never met a man who didn't. Why?"

"I don't think Mr. Pryor likes it. He didn't want to do it." Now she did blush a little, warmth rising in her cheeks.

Minette looked even more surprised. "But why not?"

"I don't know."

"How peculiar. Perhaps you ought to ask him why."

"Ask him? I couldn't do that!"

Minette gave one of her elegant shrugs. "However else will you find out, *ma chère?*"

Arthur chose that moment to stroll into the breakfast parlor. "Good morning, ladies! What are our plans for today? When will your swain next be joining us, my dear?"

"Tomorrow evening. I've invited him to escort me to the theater. *The Merry Wives of Windsor.*"

"Oh ho!" he exclaimed. "A public outing!"

"Yes." The blush threatened to rise in her cheeks again. Ella lifted her chin. "We shall show each other off to the *ton.* That is, if you'll accompany us, Minette?" Bold, confident widow or not, she still needed a companion if she wished to appear in public with Decimus Pryor without ruining her social standing.

"But of course. I would not miss it for the world."

"I'll join you," Arthur declared. "What fun!"

*C*HAPTER 9

*D*ex wrote to his sister every week, filling one or more sheets of paper with drawings and anecdotes. His activities with the delectable Eloïse Fortrose weren't something he could tell her, so instead he wrote: *Dearest Fleabee, this week it rained a lot.*

Beneath that he sketched a dandy strolling along Piccadilly. He gave the man an absurdly pinched waist, padded shoulders, and a very tall hat. Behind him, he drew the bay windows of Hatchard's bookshop.

In front of the dandy, Dex drew an innocent seeming puddle.

That filled one page.

On the other side, he left space to write Phoebe's direction. Below that, he drew Piccadilly and Hatchard's again. All that could be seen of the dandy was his head emerging from the puddle. Dex sketched in dripping hair, boggling eyes, a wide-open, horrified mouth. The hat bobbed jauntily off to one side. What else? Ah, yes, a tiny fish leaping from the dandy's mouth.

There was just enough room at the bottom to pen: *I'm off to the theater this evening. I'll tell you all about it the next time I write. Your spectacular and inordinately handsome brother, Dex.*

He folded the sheet of paper carefully, wrote the direction in the space he'd left blank, and sealed it; then he wandered through to his bedchamber. What sober-with-a-dash-of-*joie-de-vivre* ensemble had Hicks put together tonight? Dark green was the answer, with a cream, gold, and bright leaf-green waistcoat.

Dex whistled while he dressed. He tied a sober mathematical neckcloth. The tie pin Hicks handed him wasn't emerald to match the tailcoat, but a twinkling yellow citrine that brought out the gold in his waistcoat. More *joie de vivre*. His buckles were set with citrine, too, little flashes of sunshine on his feet.

Hicks possessed magic, even if the man had no Faerie godmother.

"Excellent, Hicks. You have surpassed yourself yet again. I don't know what I'd do without you."

Hicks accepted this praise with a grunt and handed him his hat. Dex placed it on his head, tilted the brim jauntily, and set off for St. James's Street. Rain pattered steadily down, but he'd long since mastered the trick of levitating raindrops away from himself—not all of them; one needed to get a little damp for verisimilitude, but he only needed to brush off a scattering of drops when he reached his club.

"Vigor!" someone greeted him when he strolled into the main salon. "What's this we hear about highwaymen? Is it true you fought off five of them?"

Conversations stopped, heads turned, and a great many pairs of eyes skewered him.

Dex felt unaccountably self-conscious. It wasn't an emotion he was used to experiencing. "Only three, actually."

This was where he should swagger and strut and spin a great tale, making himself more heroic than he'd actually been, but the incident on Wimbledon Heath felt like something private, a secret known only to a few people. He was strangely reluctant to share it.

Everyone was agog, though, so he did his best. The tale soon caught him up. "I threw him into the bushes," Dex said, and, "I punched him clean across the road," and, "The bullet only just missed me," all of it true, but not the whole truth. "And then I escorted them home," he finished.

There was applause and more than one "Bravo!" It was impossible not to swagger a little, not to strut a little. Someone pressed a glass of brandy into his hand. Men crowded close, asking questions, and for half an hour he was all the rage. Dex basked in the adulation, but much as he enjoyed being the hero of the moment, he had somewhere else he needed to be.

"If you'll excuse me, gentlemen, I have a dinner engagement." He couldn't repress a smirk as he uttered those words.

"Oh?" someone enquired. "Who's the lucky lady?"

"That would be telling," Dex said loftily, although there was no reason to keep it a secret any longer. As soon as he and Eloïse Fortrose set foot in the theater, London's rumor mill would run riot. By tomorrow everyone would know that he, Decimus Pryor, rake extraordinaire, had conquered the impregnable Fortress. What a triumph *that* was! But it didn't feel like a conquest, nor was it something he wanted to boast about. It felt like something to be held close to his chest, not broadcast to all and sundry.

Usually Dex loved being the subject of salacious gossip, but as he walked the half mile to Old Burlington Street he found himself wishing that he was a nobody and that Eloïse Fortrose was, too, and that the polite world wouldn't notice when he accompanied her to the theater that evening.

Another of the comtesse's elderly admirers joined them for dinner. His name was Entwhistle and he was as different from the last fellow, Colonel Withers, as chalk was from cheese. The colonel's iron-gray hair had retreated to the back of his head; Entwhistle had a thick mop of fluffy white curls that fell over his brow. The colonel possessed luxuriant mutton-chop whiskers; Entwhistle had a short, feathery beard along the very edge of his jawline that made him look as round-faced as an owl. The colonel was lean and stood ramrod straight, barking out his remarks as if he were giving orders on a parade ground; Entwhistle was round-shouldered and had a bit of a paunch. He was also rather deaf. So far, his conversation had consisted mostly of, "Eh? What's that you say? Eh?" He peered at the world through a chased gold quizzing glass, a genial smile on his face, looking like a rumpled white barn owl that had just woken from a nap. Or perhaps a barn owl that was about to take a nap. Dex wouldn't be at all surprised if the old fellow fell asleep during the play.

There was no chance of Dex falling asleep. Their arrival caused quite a stir in the boxes. Heads turned, people nudged one another, and a hum of gossip had arisen, audible in snatches beneath the clamor rising from the pit. Fortunately, they'd entered Lady Fortrose's box mere moments before the play started. Once the players came onstage, it became much easier to ignore the attention.

The Merry Wives of Windsor was an amusing piece of nonsense. As always, Falstaff's antics made Dex chuckle. And, as always, they reinforced his decision to never pursue married women. Lord, that was a game for fools! Creeping and sneaking and risking a husband's wrath.

That wasn't the only message in this play. Falstaff was a warning to all rakes. Dex had no intention of becoming an elderly *roué*, a ludicrous figure to be sneered at and ridiculed, the butt of jokes. He would quit his raking long before that fate had a chance to befall him. One had one's pride, especially if one was a Pryor.

On stage, the two wives convinced Falstaff to hide in a basket of filthy laundry. Dex laughed at the actors' silliness and glanced at Lady Fortrose—only to encounter her glancing at him. She looked amused, but also . . . a tad thoughtful.

Dex looked back at the stage, unease mingling with his enjoyment of the play.

Was Eloïse Fortrose comparing the rake alongside her to the rake climbing into the laundry basket onstage? She *had* called him a clown several nights ago, and she hadn't been wrong.

Was he as foolish as Falstaff in her eyes?

An uncomfortable suspicion took root that perhaps this wasn't the best play for them to be attending. He should have countered her invitation by suggesting something more weighty, a play about virtuous people performing heroic deeds. Or something depressing, where everyone died, the sort of play that made one long for levity and foolishness.

The fourth act came to its end. There was a brief burst of conversation in the box. "Vastly amusing," Lady Fortrose said, and "*Très drôle!*" agreed Comtesse de Villiers, and "Eh? What's that you said?" from Mr. Entwhistle.

Despite that "Vastly amusing," Eloïse Fortrose still had a disconcertingly introspective expression, as if she was thinking deep thoughts.

Dex waited until the comtesse and her elderly admirer were engaged in a rather one-sided conversation before leaning close to the viscountess and murmuring, "You're looking rather thoughtful. Are you not enjoying the performance?"

"Oh, yes, I am! It's quite absurd!"

"But . . . ?"

She bit her lip briefly, which confirmed his suspicions: there was more on her mind than the antics of a fat old *roué* and two quick-witted wives.

Did she think he was like Falstaff?

Dex didn't want to know . . . but he also did.

He gave her his most winsome smile. "You can tell me," he said coaxingly. "I promise I won't bite . . . unless you wish me to?" He waggled his eyebrows at her.

Eloïse laughed and shook her head. She glanced at the stage, then at him, hesitated, and took a breath.

Dex braced himself for whatever she was about to say. If it was *Falstaff reminds me of you,* he would abandon his career as a rake and take up one as a hermit instead.

76

"Your attire."

Dex glanced down at himself, and then back at her, mystified by that utterance. "My attire?"

"You used to dress a great deal more flamboyantly."

So that was what had caught her eye: Falstaff's gaudy clothes.

"Yes," Dex admitted. "I did. But I thought that you'd prefer something a little more sober."

Now it was her turn to look baffled. "I like color." She gestured to her gown, which was a lush color that reminded Dex of ripe apricots.

"On yourself, yes, but your gentleman friends have always been more, ah, sedate in their clothing choices."

"Yes, you are a departure from my norm." She smiled briefly, as if at some private joke, then said more seriously, "Don't alter yourself for my sake, Mr. Pryor. Wear whatever pleases you most."

"But . . . you don't like dandies or rakes."

"I don't like men who are vain and conceited and look no further than their reflections in the mirror," she told him bluntly. "Most rakes and dandies fall into that category."

Dex wanted to protest that he didn't, but it would be untrue. "I am a bit vain," he admitted, and then, preening slightly, tossing his head, making a joke of it, "It's hard not to be when you're as good-looking as I am."

Eloïse laughed. A dimple danced in her cheek. She shook her head and glanced at the stage, where the fifth act had started. Falstaff was strutting, vain and silly and foolish, his clothes as bright as a peacock's feathers.

Was that how she saw him?

"Does Falstaff remind you of me?" Dex blurted out.

"What? No, of course not."

Her startled expression, her unhesitating reply, set his mind at rest. He might be a rake and a dandy, but he wasn't a Falstaff. Dex reminded himself that he *had* saved her from three highwaymen. According to some people, that even made him a hero.

On the subject of highwaymen . . .

"The tale is out," he said in a low voice, beneath Falstaff's exchange with Master Brook. "About our adventure on Wimbledon Heath. Did you mention it to anyone?"

Eloïse shook her head. "No, and I'm certain Minette didn't either."

Baron Zhivot was no longer in London, so the gossip probably hadn't originated with him. Which meant it must have come from the servants. His grandfather's footman and coachman. Lady Fortrose's footman and coachman. And why not? It was a tale worth recounting. He *had* been rather valiant.

Onstage, actors disguised as Faeries pestered poor Falstaff, darting madly about the stage. One fellow stepped too close to the musicians' pit, teetering on the brink of that drop. Dex nudged with his magic, the merest smidgen of assistance.

The actor caught his balance and pranced on. *The Merry Wives of Windsor* hastened towards its conclusion, the final scene wrapping up with everyone laughing and gay, virtue rewarded, love prevailing. The actors took their bows. When the applause had died down, Eloïse said, "Does anyone wish to stay for the farce?"

"For me, no, that was *comédie* enough." The comtesse turned to her elderly admirer. "Do you wish to stay for the farce, Monsieur Entwhistle?"

"Eh?" the old gentleman said, peering through the lens of his quizzing glass with a bright, hazel eye. "What's that you said? Eh?"

Half an hour later, Dex accompanied Eloïse Fortrose up the stairs to her boudoir, a sumptuous chamber decorated in crimson and gold. Candlelight cast an intimate glow and a fire danced in the grate. The room was cozy and welcoming, voluptuous and sybaritic.

It was Dex's fourth tryst in this den of pleasure, the fourth time he and the viscountess had undressed one another. She was luscious in that delectable gown, practically eatable. Dex peeled her clothing off, exposing the mouth-watering treasures beneath.

Formality fell away with their garments. They called each other "Eloïse" and "Decimus." Dex unpinned her hair. It cascaded across her shoulders, as bright as moonlight, as soft as silk.

Together they tumbled onto the wide, soft bed, kissing and touching one another. After three nights in her boudoir, Dex knew what made her gasp and what made her giggle, knew how to make her sigh and melt, how to bring her to climax. She was learning him, too, but that was by the by. In this bedroom it was his rôle to give pleasure and hers to receive it. He was the virtuoso, playing her body, plucking at strings of pleasure and desire, bringing her to crescendos with his hands, his mouth, his cock.

But tonight, before he could perform that final delightful deed, she drew back in his embrace and said, "I should like to ride you."

Dex felt his shoulders tense. "Ride me?"

"Like St. George."

Like a dead dragon, in other words.

He was a master in the bedroom. He wasn't about to lie flat on his back like a toothless old man and let his lover do all the work. Might as well be a capon that had been castrated for the cooking pot!

Eloïse was stunning in the soft candlelight, a vision of rosy lips and sultry eyes, her skin flushed pink with arousal. Gold thread glinted in the crimson bedhangings overhead and her hair gleamed silver-bright. Dex might not have paid much attention at school, but he knew which goddess she was right now: Venus.

He told her so, which made her blush and laugh, but didn't distract her sufficiently, for she said, "May I? Ride you?"

Only the laziest of sluggards would let a woman ride

him, but telling her that might quench her ardor, so instead Dex said, "Have you ever made love in mid-air?" Slowly, he levitated them both from the warm tangle of sheets.

Eloïse gasped and clutched him and laughed breathlessly.

Dex held her close, drifting upward until they hovered just beneath the crimson-and-gold canopy. "I won't drop you. I promise."

He kissed her deeply, plundering her mouth, and when they drifted down to the bed several minutes later he plundered her body, too, making her arch and cry out and dig her nails into his back. The levitation had done its trick; she'd forgotten all about St. George and dead dragons.

*C*HAPTER 10

*E*lla examined her reflection carefully, but she looked the same as she always did. Shouldn't there be *some* difference? Something in her eyes perhaps? Some sign that she was changing on the inside.

But no, the Ella gazing at her from the mirror looked identical to the Ella of last month and the month before that.

She wasn't, though.

What color is my heart? Ella asked for the second time that morning, and the answer was still the same: sunshiny.

She stared at her reflection, trying to see some indication of her sunshiny heart, but she looked exactly as she always had. There was no extra bloom in her cheeks, no new warmth in her eyes. The glow in her heart was indiscernible.

Ella knew it was there, though. She could *feel* it, warm and golden inside her.

Her heart was smiling. It was happy, joyful.

She knew why: laughter. Laughter and sex. She'd enjoyed last night tremendously—the exuberant ridiculousness of the play, Arthur's masterly performance as Mr. Entwhistle—but most of all, she'd enjoyed the hours with Decimus Pryor. He was irreverent and silly, diverting and amusing. Quite simply, he was *fun* to be with.

Not to mention, he was extremely skillful in bed.

Laughter and sex. They were the ingredients for a sunshiny heart.

Ella hummed as she descended the stairs. If Pryor's levity was the catalyst she'd needed for her heart to finally start thawing, perhaps she ought to extend their liaison long enough for her heart to become like Arthur's and Minette's: capable of romantic love. Another month or two, and then she could release him back into the pool of rakes. He'd prowl off after another young widow and she could look about for a *cher ami* she could have warm feelings for.

Marriage was a trap she had no intention of falling into again, but she wouldn't mind a long-term liaison, something similar to what Minette and Aunt Clara had had, friendship and love combined, a relationship capable of enduring the vicissitudes of time.

As she entered the breakfast parlor, Ella came to two realizations. The first was that she had no idea what kind of man she could fall in love with.

The second was that she and Pryor hadn't ridden St. George last night. Not that it mattered. They were trysting again tomorrow; they'd have the opportunity to do it then.

Ten days later, Ella still hadn't ridden St. George, although they'd had half a dozen more assignations. Pryor was skilled at distracting her, exceptionally skilled, but tonight she wouldn't let him divert her from her goal. Minette and Count von Klöppel—Arthur in his Teutonic manifestation—were bound for Vauxhall to watch the fireworks, and she and Pryor were going to stay behind and ride St. George. He wouldn't sidetrack her with jokes and skillful nips of his teeth, or even with magic.

She crossed the dressing room with purpose in her stride. "St. George or die!" she vowed as she opened the door that gave on to the corridor.

"I beg your pardon, ma'am?" Hedgepeth said.

Heat flamed in Ella's cheeks. "Nothing!" she said, catching up her skirts and hurrying downstairs in a swirl of fox-glove-pink silk.

Arthur was already in the parlor, his girth alarmingly enlarged thanks to a corset. Minette followed shortly after. Together they waited for Mr. Pryor to join them. *St. George or die,* Ella vowed again, silently this time. She would not be diverted from her mission. She would not allow him to sidetrack her.

The butler announced Pryor's arrival.

Ella forgot about dragons and knights. Pryor entered the room with a swagger and a smirk, a gleam of laughter in his eyes. He was wearing peacock colors tonight, indigo and azure, purple, emerald green, gold. He looked like a rake and a dandy, a seducer of young widows, a cockerel, a popinjay, but also an actor strutting onto a stage, ready to entertain and amuse, to enchant, to delight.

Ella's heart, which had been sunshiny and smiling all week, seemed to grow a little more sunshiny. "Mr. Pryor," she said, rising to her feet and crossing to him. "Good evening."

He kissed her fingertips. His eyes laughed at her and his smirk became more pronounced, promising wicked things.

Ella's heart grew even more sunshiny. "May I introduce you to Count von Klöppel?"

Arthur played his rôle with aplomb. He was fussy, pedantic, precise, and verbose. The salt cellar set him off on a long-winded and painfully boring anecdote about salt. His fork prompted an equally long-winded monologue about forks. When he began to reminisce on the subject of carrots, Minette leaped in to divert him.

Pryor caught on to this trick immediately. For the rest of the meal, whenever Arthur drew breath and declared, "This reminds me off the time ven . . ." the pair of them vied to divert him—and it *was* diverting. Ella ate with a smile plucking at her lips. It was difficult not to burst into laughter when Arthur speared a mushroom on his fork and said, "This mushroom reminds me off ven I voss a boy," and Minette said, "We have mushrooms in Paris—they grow *souterrain,* in the cellars," and Arthur persevered with, "Ve picked mushrooms in der voods. They grow underneath the leafs."

"There are *beaucoup* tunnels under Paris. Did you know that, Monsieur Pryor? And catacombs!"

Pryor opened his mouth to reply.

"Now, catacombs, they are *sehr* interesting. Ven I voss a young man, I visit a catacomb . . ."

And so it went on until Minette and von Klöppel made their goodbyes and departed for Vauxhall. The last thing Ella heard was the count's voice drifting back: "You say there vill be firevorks tonight? That reminds me off ven . . ."

"Whew," Pryor said, once the door had closed behind them. "That fellow has enough tongue for two sets of teeth. How long is he staying?"

"He's leaving tomorrow." None of them, Arthur included, had the stamina for more than one performance of Count von Klöppel.

Pryor leaned back in his chair. His smile was slow and suggestive, his gaze heavy-lidded and wicked. "So . . . ?"

"So," Ella agreed. She stood and held out her hand.

Pryor took it. Together they climbed the stairs to her crimson-and-gold bedchamber. *St. George or die,* Ella reminded herself, but it was difficult to remember her mission when Pryor was peeling off her clothes and she was peeling off his. He was very much the dandy in that glorious ensemble, but as she divested him of the garments, he became someone simpler, no longer Mr. Pryor, duke's grandson and plaything of young widows, but merely Decimus.

He was beautiful, if a man could be said to be beautiful. Ella liked the angles and planes of his body, the lean flanks, the taut buttocks, and she most especially liked his hands, the shape of fingers and thumbs, their strength and dexterity. She was rather fond of his mouth, too, for his smirk and his grin as much as for his skill in using it as a lover, the kisses and nips that he gave her, the marvelously wicked things he could do with his teeth and his tongue. And as for his virile member, well . . . it *was* rather magnificent.

So far, she'd avoided looking at the nape of his neck. She knew it would be just as beautiful as the rest of him and she dared not catch a glimpse of it, because she'd see the vulnerability as well as the strength and her heart might be tricked into thinking that he was someone worth falling in love with, when he most definitely wasn't.

Decimus Pryor was a rake, not a man with whom one embarked on a long-term liaison.

Ella divested him of his drawers; he divested her of her silk stockings, her chemise, her hairpins. This was the eleventh time they'd lain together, and with familiarity came a lack of ceremony, a lack of reserve. Decimus plucked out the last hairpin. Her hair spilled about her shoulders. He scooped her up in his arms—part manly strength, part magic—and swung her around before tumbling them both onto the bed. They bounced lightly and laughed, kissing one another, limbs tangling playfully, skin sliding deliciously. Ella had never frolicked like this in her crimson-and-gold four-poster bed. No one had ever teased her as Decimus was teasing her, biting and tickling, pressing his mouth to her stomach and noisily blowing air until she laughed at the ridiculousness of it.

Their play slowed, becoming tender and intense, and Decimus proved, yet again, that he had a great deal of finesse. His mouth was magical, his fingers were magical, and Ella nearly forgot her mission.

She remembered it when they were almost at the point of no return. Decimus was poised above her, eyes dark and hot, skin dewy with exertion, no longer laughing but intent on his goal, on *their* goal.

"Wait," she gasped, dazed by the pleasure his clever tongue had just given her.

Decimus paused and drew in a ragged breath. His black hair tumbled wildly over his brow, damp with sweat.

Ella clutched his arm and tried to capture her wits, but they were still spinning giddily.

"Wait what?" he asked, his voice gravelly with desire. The muscles in his arm were taut, trembling with eagerness, and his virile member was a hot brand, burning against her inner thigh.

"I'd like to ride you."

Something changed in his arm, a tensing that seemed almost like a flinch; then he bent his head and nipped her shoulder. "You do, do you?"

Right at that moment, Ella didn't really care how they did it, just as long as they did, but this mission had seemed important earlier, so . . . "Yes. I do."

He nipped her shoulder again. Ella found herself floating several inches above the bed. Decimus gathered her close. "If I'm to be your dragon," he whispered in her ear. "Then you must fly with me first."

They floated upwards. The magic thrilled her to her bones, as it always did. It was dark and shadowy under the crimson-and-gold canopy, mysterious, the candlelight barely penetrating the gloom, and she was *floating in midair,* as light as a petal. Their kisses grew heated, scorching, until Ella drifted in a haze of pleasure and arousal, feeling as if she might combust.

"I need you inside me," she panted in his ear—words she'd never uttered to any man before, words she'd never dreamed she would ever utter. "Now."

Decimus laughed and lowered them to the wildly disordered sheets. He positioned himself between her thighs again, fitting perfectly there. Ella groaned and pressed herself urgently against him, gripping his arm—exactly as she had five minutes earlier.

He'd distracted her again. Consummately.

Did it matter? She didn't care how he was inside her, just that he *was* inside her, but . . .

St. George or die.

"I'd like to ride you," Ella managed to gasp out.

Decimus froze. His arm tensed in a way that was almost a flinch.

Or . . . *was* it a flinch?

The candlelight was soft and shadowy, golden and intimate, lacking the bright clarity of day. Ella tipped her head back on the pillow, wishing she could see his face more clearly, because her intuition was telling her that . . . "You don't want to, do you? You don't like it."

Decimus exhaled and closed his eyes, head dipping, shoulders sagging. His breath feathered across her skin.

Ella gentled her grip on his arm, turning it into something soothing. "Why not?"

He sighed again and rolled off her. Which wasn't at all what she wanted.

Ella sat up. "Decimus? What is it?"

CHAPTER 11

*E*lla hurried down to breakfast the next morning, eager to speak with Minette. To her relief, Minette was already in the cheerful yellow parlor, sipping hot chocolate and nibbling on a brioche. Ella crossed to the sideboard and chose her food hastily. She set the plate on the table and took her seat, impatient to ask the question that had consumed her all night . . . and was unable to find the right words. How did one broach such a subject?

She spread her napkin on her lap.

She poured herself a cup of tea.

She picked up her fork and put it down again.

"Minette . . . ?"

"*Oui, ma chère?*"

Ella met that alert, questioning gaze and looked down at her plate. She rotated it until the egg was at twelve o'clock, then glanced back at Minette, petite and elegant, head tilted at an inquiring angle, eyes as dark and bright as a starling's.

"Do men . . ." No, that wasn't how she wanted to ask this question.

Ella rotated her plate another quarter turn clockwise and started again, directing her words to the kedgeree and eggs. "Do you think that . . ."

No, she'd had it right the first time. She took a deep breath and blurted, "Do men think that riding St. George is emasculating?"

She peeked at Minette, trying to read her expression. What she saw was a blink of astonishment and a little pleating of creases between those thin black eyebrows. "Émasc*uler*? Of course not. Why?"

Ella picked up her fork, stirred the kedgeree, and put the fork down again. "He thinks so. Mr. Pryor, I mean. He said only toothless old men would ever do it that way."

Minette cackled with laughter. "He is very wrong, *ma chère.* Why, one of my most youthful patrons, it was his favorite way. Always, he wanted to ride St. George. *Là,* but it was hard work!" Her expression became roguish. "But most enjoyable."

Ella looked down at her plate, trying not to envisage the scene Minette had just painted. "I think that's why he thinks it's emasculating," she said to the kedgeree. "Because the lady is uppermost and she does all the work. He sees it as . . . an affront to his virility?"

"Then you must teach him otherwise."

Judging by Pryor's reaction last night, it wouldn't be an easy lesson to impart.

Ella picked up her fork again and stirred the kedgeree. "Maybe it's an English thing, to not like it?"

Minette snorted, an inelegant sound that was quite at odds with her appearance. "*Quelle absurdité.* I did it in England as much as I did it in France."

Ella looked up with a frown. "But he said that when he was at school, everyone mocked men who did it that way."

"Ah," Minette said, setting down her cup. "Now, we get to the heart of it. What else did he say?"

"That they used to pass around drawings. Lewd drawings."

Minette nodded. "I have seen such drawings."

"He said . . . the drawings made it very clear that riding St. George was only for old men and sluggards. They all vowed they would never be so . . ." What was the word he'd used? "Pusillanimous."

Minette snorted even more loudly. "You must help him get the bee out of his hat, *ma chère.*"

"Bonnet."

Minette's brow pleated in confusion again. "Men do not wear bonnets."

Arthur chose that moment to enter the parlor. "Good morning, ladies!"

"Good morning," and "*Bonjour,*" they replied.

Arthur filled a plate from the dishes on the sideboard and joined them at the table. "These sausages remind me off ven I voss a boy."

"*Non,*" Minette said firmly. "One meal with Count von Klöppel was enough."

Arthur chuckled, and dug into his breakfast.

Ella dug into her breakfast, too. She ate slowly, letting Arthur and Minette's conversation flow around her. Last night had been . . . interesting. Unusual. She remembered the way Pryor had sighed, the halting way he'd spoken.

There had been nothing flirtatious in his voice, nothing playful in his manner. For a few minutes, he'd been quite serious. He'd told her one of his secrets. One could almost say that he'd bared part of his soul to her.

They'd made love after that, but it had been unlike all the other times. There'd been no lighthearted teasing, no conspicuous display of skill. Their lovemaking had been quiet and simple and . . .

The word that came closest was beautiful.

There'd been a strange sense of connection, something that had almost felt emotional.

Ella chewed her kedgeree without tasting it. She didn't want to feel an emotional connection to Decimus Pryor.

"*Ma chère,*" Minette said loudly, in the tone of someone who had repeated herself several times.

Ella looked up. "Yes?"

"When will Monsieur Pryor next be visiting us?"

"Tomorrow evening."

"Is that enough time to find them?" Minette asked Arthur.

"It should be."

"Find what?"

"The drawings Monsieur Pryor mentioned."

"You told Arthur?" Ella's voice squeaked with dismay.

"But of course. Why not?"

Ella felt heat rise in her cheeks. Discussing her liaisons wasn't something she was comfortable doing with Arthur.

"You want to see them, no? I know I do." Minette reached over to pat Arthur's hand. "*Mon cher* Arthur will find them for us, and then we will know how to change Monsieur Pryor's mind."

"When did he see them?" Arthur asked. "Ten, fifteen years ago?"

"Thereabouts," Ella agreed faintly.

"*Bon*! It is agreed then. Arthur will go to Holywell Street and find them for us." Minette set her napkin aside and stood briskly. "Now me? I am going to play on *le pianoforte*."

CHAPTER 12

Arthur didn't return from his mission until dinnertime. Once the covers had been removed and the servants had retreated downstairs, he laid seven sheets of paper on the table. "Here you go, ladies. My haul!"

"These are what he saw?" Ella rose from her chair and went around the table for a closer look.

"Most likely. Some of 'em at any rate."

The illustrations were similar to those one found in magazines, caricatures drawn in ink and then tinted with color. Three of them featured Catherine, Empress of Russia. She was depicted as an obese giantess riding the puny figure of her husband, the man she'd overthrown to seize Russia's throne.

Ella picked up one of those illustrations for a closer look. "Goodness."

There was nothing titillating about the scene. On the contrary, it was quite distasteful. Catherine had huge pendulous breasts and a vast belly like a sack of grain about to burst at its seams. Her husband was all but squashed beneath her bulk. The artist had depicted him as weedy and pale, unresisting.

If Pryor had seen this when he was in his teens, no wonder he'd decided that being ridden was emasculating.

Ella wrinkled her nose and placed the illustration back on

the table. Beside her, Minette clicked her tongue disparagingly and muttered something under her breath.

"Ladies, would you like something to drink?"

Ella nodded absently, perusing the other images. Two featured men in their dotage, wizened and wrinkled, toothless. That was a word Pryor had used last night—toothless—which suggested that he might have seen these very images.

The elderly men lay passive and all but impotent while their much younger companions labored over them.

Arthur handed her a glass of port.

Ella sipped it and examined the last two images. One showed a corpulent gourmand. He sprawled on a bed, a haunch of ham in one hand and an enormous drumstick in the other, more interested in his food than the beauty attempting to ride him.

The subject of the final drawing also sprawled on a bed. No pot-bellied glutton this time, but a country bumpkin with straw in his hair and a rather impressive member rising from the thatch of hair at his loins. He lay back, grinning like a simpleton, while two whores squabbled over who would ride him first.

Tom Gapeseed discovers the delights of the metropolis, read the caption.

Ella wrinkled her nose again. She stepped back and sipped from the glass Arthur had given her. The port was rich, mellow, raisin-sweet. Her gaze skipped from one illustration to the next.

"Well?" Arthur said. "What do you think?"

"I think that they're unpleasant. Every last one of them." Any of these drawings would convince an impressionable youth that being ridden was shameful, something fit only for doddery old men, gluttons and sluggards, ignorant yokels, or browbeaten husbands.

"Unpleasant, yes," Minette said. "But he was a boy when he saw these. He is a man now. He is old enough to know better."

Ella wasn't certain she agreed. Was there an age at which one ought to know better about everything? Sometimes the opinions one formed when one was young became unquestioned convictions.

She thought back to herself at fifteen, on the eve of her marriage. How unformed she'd been. How malleable. How ignorant. If she'd seen these drawings then, she would have leaped to an opinion that was as strong as it was erroneous. An opinion she would probably still hold.

Francis had taught her about sex—and everything she'd learned from him had been wrong. In their marriage, *she* had been the toothless old man, lying unresisting on her back. If not for Minette, she'd still believe that sex was nothing more than a tedious duty, that there was no pleasure in the act, that she could have no rôle beyond that of passive receptacle of a man's seed.

She sipped the port, tasting the sweetness of exotic lands, and said, "I don't know that age has anything to do with it."

Adulthood hadn't taught her that everything she believed about sex was wrong. It wasn't a realization that had miraculously occurred when she'd turned twenty-one. On the contrary, it had taken many hours of conversation with Minette and even more hours of experimentation with a succession of lovers to unlearn the lessons that Francis had taught her.

"He needs a Minette," she said.

There was a brief, stunned silence, during which Ella tipped up her glass for the last of the port.

"*Moi? Non, non, non!* Absolutely not!"

Ella choked on that final mouthful of port. She coughed and spluttered and wheezed. When she finally regained her breath, she croaked, "I meant that *I* will be his mentor." If she could. Only a week remained of the agreed term of their liaison—unless she extended it, which she wasn't yet certain she wanted to do.

Minette's face cleared. "*Bon.* I think that will be very good for you both." She gave a decisive nod and gathered up the illustrations. "These, they are for the fireplace. Thank you for finding them, *mon cher*, but I do not like them at all! They are *très désagréable*."

*C*HAPTER 13

*D*earest Fleabee, Ned is a knucklehead and a jobbernoll—
*and you may tell him that from me! If he tries such a trick again,
my advice is to upend a vase over him.* Dex drew a picture of his
cousin, Ned, dripping with water, a bedraggled flower sticking
out of one ear. A victorious Phoebe stood to one side, empty
vase in hand.

Truth be told, he rather missed his sister and his cousins,
even Ned, who was the loudest and most annoying gollumpus
to have ever been born.

Dex dipped his quill in ink and launched into the description of *The Merry Wives of Windsor* that he'd promised
Phoebe. *Of course,* he concluded, *the final act would have been
<u>much</u> better if I could have made the Faeries fly.*

He drew a cowering Falstaff, with Faeries darting and
diving overhead. It really was a damned shame he couldn't
use his magic overtly, that he was limited to surreptitious little
saves and unobtrusive acts of assistance.

Turning the page over, he wrote: *You'll be proud of me. I
stopped an actor falling off the stage.*

He sketched a man cartwheeling into the pit where the
orchestra played, his arms windmilling. Musicians cringed in
their seats, eyes starting from their sockets, mouths aghast.

Alas, you and I are the only ones who know the shining extent of my heroism. A silly little sketch accompanied that statement: himself with a saintly expression and a halo.

Dex snorted. Saintly was not a look that suited him.

There was just enough space at the bottom to scrawl: *Remember to tell Ned he's a jobbernoll! Your incomparably magnificent brother, Dex.*

He folded the paper carefully, hiding the words and sketches, turning the quarto page into a small rectangle that needed merely a wax seal and Phoebe's direction.

Dex put it aside. He might miss his family, but wild horses couldn't drag him away from London right now. Not while he was trysting with Eloïse Fortrose. Their last encounter hadn't been the most successful he'd ever had—in fact, it would rank among the most awkward, alongside the time he'd overbalanced and fallen out of bed, knocking over a bedside cabinet, a chair, and all the trinkets on the dressing table, and the time when he'd brought the bedhangings down on himself and his inamorata in a smothering flood of heavy brocade. He'd managed to recover from both those mishaps, turning them into acts of comedy that made his partners laugh, but he hadn't managed that feat with Eloïse Fortrose. The playful mood had been punctured and their lovemaking had concluded on a note that had been subdued rather than spectacular. But tonight was a clean slate, a chance to erase the awkwardness of their previous encounter from her memory, an opportunity to dazzle her with his prowess. He wouldn't just bring her to climax three times tonight, he'd aim for *five.*

An hour and a half later, Dex strolled into his club. "I say, Vigor, over here!" one of the chaps seated by the window called out.

Dex put a little more swagger in his stride as he crossed the room, because he *was* intriguing with the most delectable of all London's widows, a feat no other rake had managed.

"Glass of brandy, Vigor?"

He settled into an armchair, accepted a glass of brandy, and caught up on the latest news, the latest gossip, the latest wagers. "You're in the betting book, you know," someone informed him.

Dex did know. The bet had been laid the night that he and Eloïse Fortrose had attended the theater.

Decimus Pryor to wed the Fortress by the end of the year, 100 guineas.

It was lost money. He didn't intend to marry until he'd finished sowing his oats. When he was forty, perhaps. He'd choose a woman whose company he enjoyed, someone he could be good friends with, and settle down to a life of fidelity and fatherhood. But that woman wouldn't be Eloïse Fortrose and the time definitely wasn't now.

He turned down the offer of a second glass of brandy. "I must be off. I have a dinner engagement."

This statement set off a round of catcalls.

"Off to scale the Fortress, are you?" someone asked, with a wink.

The crudeness of the comment put Dex's back up. Eloïse Fortrose wasn't a building to scale or a peak to summit. She was a person, not a conquest, and he wasn't trysting with her in order to carve a notch into his bedpost—if he stooped to such boorishness, which he most certainly didn't. He was trysting with her because he enjoyed her company, enjoyed making love to her *and* making her laugh.

But Dex didn't say any of that. He merely gave an inscrutable smile and sauntered off, leaving his fellows to their bawdy jokes and their brandy.

Dex wielded the door knocker with a brisk *rat-tat-tat,* relinquished his hat and gloves to a footman, followed the butler along the now-familiar corridor to the drawing room—and discovered that he wasn't the only dinner guest. Another of the comtesse's many admirers was ensconced on the settee.

The stranger had a decidedly foreign air. He looked to be in his early sixties, but despite his age he possessed a thick head of black hair with a dramatic widow's peak. His luxuriant mustache made him look rather like a Spanish grandee, an impression that was confirmed when he was introduced as Vizconde Pavoneo, who was newly arrived in London.

Dex made his bow to the man.

The vizconde bowed back with a flourish that was more flamboyant than anything Dex had ever achieved.

Dex was rather disconcerted. He took a seat and said politely, "I hope you had a pleasant journey, sir?"

The vizconde resumed his occupation of the settee. "I have been telling the ladies, it was most . . . how do you say . . . hair-lifting."

"Oh?"

"¡Si! My postilion, he was struck by lightning."

Dex blinked. "He . . . was?"

"¡Si! The poor man, he burn to a crispy."

There was nothing amusing about someone being struck by lightning, but Dex had to bite the tip of his tongue to stop himself laughing aloud at that "crispy." He swallowed the inappropriate mirth and managed to say, "How dreadful."

"It was the most terrible thing I ever have witness." The vizconde made a gesture in front of his nose. "Such a smell as you would not believe."

The gesture was so melodramatic, the man's expression of disgust so exaggerated, that Dex almost caught a whiff of charred postilion.

"The poor man," Comtesse de Villiers said gravely. "Such a tragedy."

"What of the horse?" Eloïse Fortrose inquired.

The vizconde gave a theatrical shudder. "The horse, he was crispy, too."

There was that word again. Crispy. The urge to laugh ambushed Dex. He glanced desperately at Eloïse. She was biting her lower lip, neat white teeth digging temptingly into pillowy pink flesh.

He dragged his gaze away from her. How could he want to kiss her when they were discussing a postilion being struck by lightning?

Could a postilion burn to a crisp?

Could a horse, for that matter?

"What an ordeal for you," the comtesse said, with solemn sympathy.

"*Such* an ordeal," Vizconde Pavoneo agreed. He covered his eyes with one hand, his distress as extravagant and showy as an actor hamming it up on stage.

Dex glanced at the ladies again, uncertain how to react. Ought he sympathize with the man? Attempt to jolly him out of his affliction of emotion?

Eloïse was biting her lip quite ferociously. Her cheeks were extremely rosy. She looked as if she was on the verge of hysterical laughter.

The comtesse wasn't biting her lip, but her mouth was quite rigid, as if she, too, was trying not to laugh.

Dex looked at Vizconde Pavoneo. The man peeked back at him from between his fingers. His eyes twinkled with mischief.

Hazel eyes.

Eyes that were surprisingly familiar.

Where had Dex seen those eyes before?

Realization slowly dawned. Baron Zhivot had had hazel eyes. And so had Colonel Withers. And Mr. Entwhistle. And Count von Klöppel.

Dex opened his mouth, and found himself speechless with outraged delight.

The vizconde lowered his hand. His eyes were bright with glee, his grin wide beneath the luxuriant black mustaches.

"You . . ." Dex uttered. "You . . ."

Eloïse dissolved into hysterical laughter. So did Comtesse de Villiers. So did the fake vizconde.

Dex followed suit, whooping in shocked disbelief. He'd never been so hoodwinked before, nor had he ever laughed quite this hard. He was breathless with laughter, aching with laughter, crying with laughter.

It took several minutes to recover his equilibrium. Dex wiped his eyes and struggled to catch his breath. He knew that his face was red, but so was everyone else's. "Who *are* you?" he managed to ask.

The spurious Spanish grandee stood and swept a theatrical bow. "Arthur Blake, at your service."

"An actor?" Dex guessed.

Blake puffed out his chest. "A star of the stage for more than thirty years." His accent was utterly unremarkable, the King's English without any trace of region or class.

"You were Zhivot and von Klöppel and Entwhistle *and* Colonel Withers."

"You're missing one," Blake said with a smirk.

Dex cast his mind back. Surely he hadn't met anyone else in this house?

Blake exhaled with a faint whistling noise.

"You were the butler, too!" Dex cried, leaping to his feet and pointing at Blake. "You fell asleep standing up!"

Blake puffed out his chest again and preened. "Liked that, did you?"

"It was magnificent," Dex admitted. "Those snores!" Lord, how he'd struggled not to laugh over his dinner. He stared at Blake, trying to see the bald, stoop-shouldered stork of a butler beneath the façade of Spanish grandee. "When you called the comtesse 'sir' and me 'ma'am' . . . that was deliberate?"

"Of course."

Dex shook his head and laughed out loud in admiration and disbelief. "You used to act in comedies, didn't you?"

"Acted in everything, but comedies were my favorite."

Dex could well believe that. "Zhivot and von Klöppel were . . ." He mimed a huge belly. "How did you do it?"

"Corset," Blake said, patting his trim waist. "Stuffed with feather pillows."

Dex laughed again, shook his head again, and turned to the ladies. "You *knew*," he accused them. "Both of you! You knew all along!" He wanted to feel outraged, but it was impossible. The imposture was too extraordinary, too magnificent. He wished he could go back and live through each of those encounters with Blake again, but with the knowledge he had now. Oh, how he'd laugh at himself!

"Are you cross?" Eloïse asked. Her cheeks were rosy from the exertion of laughing and her eyes sparkled brightly. She didn't look afraid of his wrath, not that Dex had any wrath. He only had admiration. *Such* a magnificent deception!

"Of course not." He crossed to her, swept her up from her seat, and danced her exuberantly around the drawing room, too elated and energized to care that dancing viscountesses around their drawing rooms was an outlandish thing to do. Eloïse didn't appear to mind. She was warm and vibrant in his arms, and when he levitated them several inches off the floor so that they were dancing on air, she clutched him close and laughed delightedly.

Dex spun them on two giddy circuits of the room, then carefully set her on her feet again. They were both panting, both laughing, both a little dizzy.

He was still too energized by the hoaxes they'd perpetrated on him, too elated and too awed, to sit down, so he turned to Comtesse de Villiers and swept her up and danced her around the room, too. He didn't sweep Blake up, but he hugged him, a rib-cracking, back-clapping embrace. "I swear I've never seen your equal on stage. Not even Kemble himself could outperform you!"

Blake's cheeks flushed and his chest inflated with pride. There was more than a suggestion of swagger in his stance, more than a hint of smirk in his smile.

Dex had a strange sense of déjà vu. It took him a moment to realize why. Looking at Blake was rather like looking at himself in the mirror—if he were a sixty-ish Spanish grandee with a widow's peak and lush black mustache. The set of Blake's shoulders, the set of his chin, that swagger and smirk—Dex had seen those in his own mirror often enough.

As realizations went, it was a rather disconcerting one. Dex pushed it to the back of his head to examine later, or most likely, to ignore. "I wish I could see your costumes."

"You can, if you wish. They're right here."

"In this house?"

"Of course. I live here."

Dex blinked in surprise. Were Blake and Comtesse de Villiers a couple? Living in sin beneath the unsuspecting noses of the aristocracy?

If they were, it was another extraordinary act of subterfuge. He was in awe of their daring.

"We each own a third of this house," Eloïse said.

Dex felt his eyebrows rise in astonishment. "You do?"

"Yes. We were all of us widowed, so we combined households."

That tidbit of information wasn't common knowledge among the *ton*. Dex's elation at the trick they'd played on him reshaped itself into another emotion: intense curiosity.

He eyed the trio standing before him. The viscountess who filled her house and wardrobe with bright colors. The regal little comtesse who had once been an opera dancer. The flamboyant chameleon of an actor.

He'd met them more than a dozen times now, but he'd barely scratched the surface of who they were. He'd only been shown their outermost layers. In Blake's case, not even the true layers.

Who was Blake when he wasn't putting on an act?

Who was the woman beneath the opera dancer and the comtesse?

Did he even know the real Eloïse Fortrose? They'd been

naked together, but people didn't show all of themselves to a temporary lover. One revealed one's body, not one's innermost self. He'd shown her Decimus, but not Dex. She'd shown him Eloïse.

Who was under Eloïse?

"Want to see my costumes?" Blake said. "We have time before dinner."

The four of them relocated to Blake's treasure trove of a costume room. It was considerably larger than Dex had imagined. In fact, he suspected it had been a drawing room in its former life. Instead of sofas and armchairs, the chamber now held an array of armoires, clothes presses, cabinets, and shelves, as well as two tall mirrors and a dressing table upon which little pots of cosmetics and adhesives were clustered. Garments such as tailcoats and waistcoats, pantaloons and breeches, shirts, collars, and cuffs were doubtless tucked away in the armoires and drawers, but a cornucopia of other items was on display. One glass-fronted cabinet held dozens of beards, another held mustaches, sideburns, and eyebrows. The eyebrows looked like a collection of disturbingly hirsute caterpillars.

A wall of shelves was devoted to wigs of all shades and styles. Other shelves held footwear, everything from court shoes with glittering buckles to a postilion's leather-and-iron boots to a macaroni's high-heeled shoes. Wherever Dex looked, he spotted another delight: a watchman's lantern, rattle, and staff; a rainbow array of masquerade masks; a collection of spectacles and quizzing glasses; a coachman's livery.

"Where are the corsets?" he asked, bouncing excitedly on his toes.

"In here," Blake said, crossing to one of the armoires. Inside it were corsets and the padding to stuff them with. Dex could give himself a little pot belly or something as large as von Klöppel's substantial paunch. Not only that, the armoire's drawers held pads to augment other parts of his anatomy: his calves, his shoulders, his rump.

Dex *had* to try on the largest corset and stuff it with padding, and he *had* to try on Entwistle's fluffy white wig. He longed to affix mutton-chop whiskers to his face, but dinner was mere moments away and he rather thought it would take more than a few minutes to apply the gum Arabic and position the whiskers correctly. Instead, he selected a pair of spectacles with thin silver frames and round lenses.

"What do you think?" he asked, parading in front of his audience. The comtesse had a tricorne on her head, with an ostrich feather curling down to touch her shoulder, Eloïse wore a turquoise loo mask with glittering spangles, and Blake had added a swirling red cape to his Spanish vizconde's ensemble.

The butler chose that moment to enter the room. "Begging your pardon, but dinner is served." He looked unsurprised to find them attired so strangely, but if he lived in this house he must be familiar with Blake and his changes of persona.

What an *odd* household to work in.

Eloïse helped him unlace the corset, but Dex didn't relinquish the wig or the silver spectacles. He was rather fond of the fluffy white hair. Together with the spectacles, it altered his appearance quite remarkably.

They trooped into the dining room and took their places. The table was set with great formality, but the mood felt very informal. Eloïse was still wearing her loo mask, Comtesse de Villiers her tricorne, and Blake was resplendent as a Spanish grandee.

The viscountess must have felt the informality, too, for she dismissed the footmen and butler once they'd been served.

"The servants all know, I take it?" Dex asked, once the door had closed behind the men.

"They know the truth about my background, but not Minette's," Blake said. "Only Eloïse and I know that. And you." There was no twinkle of mischief in the bright, hazel eyes. Blake's gaze was sharp and his tone held a note of warning.

"I shan't tell anyone. You have my word." Dex picked up

his soup spoon, then set it down again. "Aren't you worried about the servants, though? One of them might tell someone about your impersonations."

Blake laughed, his seriousness evaporating. "The servants? No. They're all theater folk, like me."

Dex felt his brow crinkle. "You mean . . . they're pretending to be servants?"

The ladies joined in the laughter that time.

"No," Blake said, through his chuckles. "They're not pretending—they are servants—but not everyone born into the theater wishes to stay there. It's a precarious existence. Here, they don't need to worry where their next meal is coming from or be afraid they'll have to sleep under a bridge next month."

"I see." Dex picked up his soup spoon again, and put it down a second time. He glanced from the elderly actor to the regal opera-dancer-turned-comtesse to the young dowager viscountess in her shimmering aquamarine gown and bright turquoise loo mask. "If you don't mind me asking . . . how is it that you all came to be living together?"

*C*HAPTER 14

*E*lla looked at Arthur. Arthur looked at Minette. Minette gave one of her elegant French shrugs. "The story, it is rather a long one."

Pryor glanced at the dishes arrayed on the table, as if to say, *We have plenty of time.*

Minette must have agreed, for she said, "When I came to England, I was but seventeen and I did not speak *l' anglaise.* My *protecteur,* he left me behind when he returned to France. I was pregnant, you see, and he did not like that."

Ella hadn't expected Minette to tell Pryor the whole story. She tried to exchange a shocked glance with Arthur, except that Arthur didn't appear at all shocked and he wasn't looking in her direction. He dipped a spoon into his bowl of green pea soup and nodded along to Minette's narrative.

Pryor hadn't started his soup yet. He was frowning, a serious expression quite at odds with the wig perched on his head.

"I tried to find work as a dancer, but no one would hire me. I would have ended up in the gutter, but *mon cher* Arthur and his wife took me in." Minette reached over to pat Arthur's hand.

Arthur twinkled a smile at her and continued to eat his soup.

"They were *mes anges*. My angels. They gave me a bed and they taught me English, and when the baby was stillborn, they looked after me."

"I'm sorry," Pryor said. His lips pressed together briefly, and then he said, as if offering understanding as well as sympathy, "My brother was stillborn."

Minette accepted this with a nod. "It was a difficult time, *oui,* but I had Arthur and Jenny. They looked after me, and when I was well enough, Arthur took me to the theater and I became a dancer again." Minette picked up her spoon, but didn't dip it in her soup. "I found many temporary patrons, but one day, I found *un grand protecteur.* Lord Cameron." She gestured at Ella with the spoon. Silver gilt gleamed in the candlelight. "Eloïse's uncle."

Pryor glanced at Ella, then back at Minette. He nodded.

"Lord Cameron, he was very tedious, but his wife, Clara . . ." Minette's expression softened. "She was perfection."

Once again, Ella was disconcerted by Minette's candor. It was one thing to imply that Clara and Minette had been bosom friends; it was something else entirely to disclose that they'd been lovers. But when she sneaked a glance at Pryor, Ella discovered that he didn't look scandalized.

"Fortunately, Lord Cameron, he did not live long."

Pryor uttered a short, startled laugh. Now he did look a little shocked.

"If you had met him you would agree, *monsieur.* He was, how do you say? A bully. Not a nice man."

Pryor accepted this evaluation of Lord Cameron's character with a nod. Belatedly, he picked up his spoon and dipped it in his soup. After a moment, Ella did, too. Arthur was ahead of them, soup finished, tucking into the partridges *à la Perigord* and the veal with sorrel sauce.

"Clara and I, we looked through her *généalogie* to find the most obscure person possible, and the Comtesse de Villiers was born." Minette gestured to herself with a flourish of her spoon.

"A magnificent portrayal, ma'am," Pryor said.

"*Oui, le plus magnifique,*" Minette agreed, with no modesty whatsoever. "Clara and I, we lived together thirty years, but then the influenza took her away from me."

Pryor opened his mouth, no doubt to offer sympathy again, but Minette was already continuing: "She left half her fortune to me and half to Eloïse, and me, I give half of mine to *mon cher* Arthur."

Pryor's eyebrows ticked up in surprise.

"Arthur was my savior," Minette said in reply to that silent astonishment. "I would not have survived my first year in England without him and his wife. Of course, I share my fortune with him!"

Pryor looked rather abashed. "Of course."

Minette began to eat her soup. Arthur took up the tale: "My Jenny died a few months before Clara, God rest their souls. Minette and I were both lonely, so we decided to live together, but it's not seemly for an old actor to share a house with a comtesse. I came and went through the servants' door—a butler if anyone asked, but no one ever did. When we went out on the town together, I dressed up as a foreign nobleman or a nabob or whoever struck my fancy, but at home, we were just ourselves." He exchanged a fond glance with Minette.

"Your servants knew," Pryor said, a statement, not a question.

"*Naturellement,* but Arthur, he chose them all, every last one. They would not betray us."

"The secret to loyal servants is to pay them well and to treat them even better," Arthur said gravely, and then he winked. "And to give them a day off every week."

Pryor looked startled, as well he might. Most servants received half a day off per month, not one day per week.

"And to let them sing while they work," Ella put in, because that was one of her favorite things about living in this house: that the kitchen maids sang while they stirred their pots, the housemaids hummed as they wielded dusters and made beds, and the footmen whistled while they fetched and carried and attended to their chores.

"And to stage *une grande production* every year," Minette said.

Pryor's brow creased slightly beneath the feathery tufts of white wig. "A production?"

"A play or a pantomime," Arthur explained. "Something we can all take part in."

Pryor's forehead creased further as he pondered the novelty of servants and employers performing in a play together.

"We usually do it in winter," Ella told him. "Our next one's to be a farce. *The Medley of Lovers*."

"I shall play Miss Biddy," Arthur declared, with a feminine toss of his head.

"And I will be Captain Flash." Minette tossed her head, too, almost dislodging the tricorne.

"And I'm to be Mr. Fribble," Ella said. "And Minette and I will duel!"

Pryor's eyes widened behind his spectacles, not in shock, but in glee. "By Jove, what a grand idea! My cousins and I should do something like that." His eyes grew even wider. "*I* could play Miss Biddy!"

He looked ready to charge off in pursuit of this enterprise, perhaps to Arthur's costume room, perhaps further afield, to wherever his cousins currently were—then he looked down at his green pea soup and deflated slightly, as if realizing that he couldn't pursue his grand scheme quite at that moment.

He dipped his spoon in the soup, stirred it, ate a mouthful . . . and then his posture changed, like a gun dog coming to point. His gaze lifted. He looked at Arthur, at Minette, at Ella, his eyes bright with curiosity through the spectacle lenses. "We're only halfway through the story. How did two become three?"

"We're nine-tenths of the way through," Ella said. "There's very little left to tell. Francis died less than a year after Aunt

Clara. My father and the new viscount both wished to have oversight of me, but Minette and Arthur invited me to live with them—and here we all are."

If Arthur and Jenny had been Minette's saviors, then Minette and Arthur had been Ella's. They'd shown her how to be herself, taught her how to truly live. She had shed the tight, constricting confines of her old life and become someone new through their kindness, their encouragement, their *joie de vivre*.

"You bought this house together?"

"Yes." Ella smiled across the table at Arthur and Minette. She might have chosen the colors that surrounded them, but Minette and Arthur were what made this house a home. It was safety and sanctuary and freedom because of them. It was the place where she'd spread her wings, where she'd learned to stand up for herself and to ignore her father's disapproval—not that he could disapprove now, from his grave. No man had power over her anymore. Not her father, not the current Viscount Fortrose, no one.

The tale now told to its end, talk turned to the stage. Arthur entertained them with stories of triumphs and *tours de force,* mishaps and outright disasters. At mention of *The Merry Wives of Windsor,* Pryor jolted in his seat. "*That's* the play I should stage with my cousins. I could make the Faeries fly! Imagine it . . ." He spread his fingers, wiggled them—and the salt cellar and pepper caster rose into the air. They twirled and pirouetted like dancers showing off in a ballroom, then set about harassing the epergne, darting and diving, as if the epergne was poor Falstaff and the pepper caster and salt cellar were two of the Faeries.

They were all in fits of laughter when the door to the dining room opened.

The salt cellar and pepper caster hastily descended to the tabletop, taking their proper places a mere half-second before the butler entered the room.

The first course was removed and the second one laid

before them. "No more magic in rooms without locks," Pryor said, once the servants had retreated again.

Arthur's eyes lit up. "I have an idea."

*C*HAPTER 15

*A*rthur's idea required them to take their tea in the library, because the drawing room had no lock and the library, for no reason that Ella had ever been able to discern, did. But first, they ransacked the costume room for Faerie wings left over from their production of *A Midsummer Night's Dream* two years ago.

"I'll be the Faerie queen!" Pryor declared. "Do you have any costumes for females?"

Fifteen minutes later, they were in the library, with the door locked and Faerie wings attached to their backs. All four of them wore loo masks—Ella's turquoise, Minette's scarlet, Arthur's bright purple, and Pryor's silver and gold. As the queen, Pryor had a wig of flowing blonde ringlets. He'd donned a voluminous round gown over his shirt and breeches. His Faerie queen was plump; beneath the gown, he had a belly, a rump, and a pillowy bosom. Ella had never seen anyone look so ridiculous, or so excited. He was brimming with glee, his eyes brighter than the spangles decorating his mask.

"Ladies, fasten your ribbons!"

Ella bent and gathered her hem close to her ankles. She tied a ribbon over the layers of petticoat and evening gown, to prevent her skirts from gathering around her ears if Pryor tipped her upside down.

"Are you ready?" he cried, bouncing on his toes.

"Yes," they chorused, and Ella only just stopped herself from bouncing up and down, too—then she thought, why shouldn't she bounce if she was excited?

So she bounced on her toes, too, and as she bounced, she rose up in the air, weightless in the grip of Pryor's magic.

A gasp caught in her throat and she felt the familiar exhilaration, the familiar delicious thrill skate across her skin. Alongside her, Arthur let out a whoop. Minette was laughing, and Ella discovered that she was laughing, too, breathless and giddy and disbelieving. She was *floating* three feet above the floor. They were all floating.

"Are you ready, Faeries?" the queen cried.

"Yes," they chorused again.

The queen began to sing in a falsetto: "Pinch him, Faeries, mutually; Pinch him for his villainy; Pinch him, pinch him, turn him all about, till the candles and starlight and moonshine be out."

The words weren't quite correct, but then neither was their Falstaff. A pile of cushions on an armchair stood in for the foolish, bumbling *roué*. They'd each chosen one item to adorn Falstaff. Arthur had gone first, deciding on a macaroni's high wig. Pryor had selected two shaggy eyebrows and carefully positioned them where Falstaff's forehead would be, if he had a forehead. Minette had perched a silly little Nivernois hat atop the wig, and Ella had chosen a gaudy pair of men's shoes with high heels and glittering buckles and set them on the floor at Falstaff's feet.

Voilà. They had a rake.

Arthur and Pryor had chortled when they'd stepped back to examine their creation. Ella had chortled, too, caught up in the sheer silliness of what they were doing.

"Pinch him, Faeries, mutually; Pinch him for his villainy," Pryor warbled again, his magic spinning them in midair. Ella found herself swooping at Falstaff, just as the salt cellar and the pepper caster had swooped at the epergne.

"Pinch him!" she cried. "Pinch him! Pinch him!" She didn't actually pinch their Falstaff as she flew past; the hat would have toppled off, and the wig and the eyebrows, too, and all the cushions would have tumbled to the floor, but it was fun to pretend. Arthur was on her heels. He let out a whoop as he dived low. So, too, did Minette.

Ella had never whooped in her life. She didn't think she *could* whoop, but she gave it a tentative try. The sound that emerged from her mouth was more squawk than whoop, but her second attempt was better, and her third was indisputably a whoop. The servants must think them playing a mad sort of game—and they'd be right: it was mad. Utterly mad. The maddest thing Ella had ever done, madder than anything she'd ever imagined, swooping around the room like gargantuan swallows, darting and diving at a make-believe Falstaff, whooping loudly, laughing exuberantly, crying, "Pinch him, pinch him!"

They flew fast, all three of them, but Ella wasn't afraid that they'd collide. She trusted Pryor, trusted his judgment, trusted his magic. He hovered in midair by the fireplace, warbling Shakespeare's silly song, waving his arms as if he was a conductor directing musicians. "Pinch him, Faeries, mutually; Pinch him for his villainy!"

When they were all pink-cheeked and breathless, Pryor lowered them to the floor. Ella was laughing as hard as she had when he'd made Arthur fly around the second-best parlor. She untied the ribbon around her ankles, pulled off her mask, and wiped her streaming eyes while her laughter subsided to panted giggles.

Pryor grinned at her from where he stood by the fireplace, blonde ringlets falling over his shoulders, fake bosom almost bursting from his bodice.

Minette had been correct all those weeks ago: Decimus Pryor's swagger had absolutely nothing to do with vanity or arrogance. No man with an ounce of either would dress as he was currently dressed. He looked utterly ludicrous, absolutely ridiculous—and she wanted to march across the room and kiss him soundly.

Doing so would be shocking and scandalous—one didn't kiss one's husband in public, let alone one's lover—but Minette and Arthur weren't easily shocked, so Ella seized her courage and crossed to where Pryor stood by the hearth. She stood on tiptoe, took hold of his face, and kissed him on his ludicrous, ridiculous mouth.

"Oh, I say," he said, startled, when she broke for air, and then his arms came around her and he kissed her back. While they kissed, her toes left the floor and they spun in midair, two feet above the Aubusson carpet.

Ella was blushing and breathless when they came back down. She wished they could go upstairs right at that minute, but there were costumes to put away and cushions to restore to their proper places, and they were all four of them in such high spirits and so thirsty that they rang for a fresh pot of tea and talked until late.

The clocks were striking midnight when they bade one another goodnight. Arthur retired to his suite of rooms on the ground floor. Minette elegantly ascended one flight of stairs and disappeared into her own apartments. Ella took Pryor's hand and tugged him up the second flight of stairs. She'd be sorry when their liaison was over. Decimus Pryor made everyone in his orbit laugh, and while lightheartedness wasn't valued as much as being wise or courageous was, it *ought* to be.

Pryor's eagerness matched her own. Their feet skipped and danced up the steps. They tumbled into the bedroom, breathless and laughing, and set to work divesting each other of their clothes.

Ella had intended to discuss riding St. George tonight, to make Pryor realize that there was no shame in allowing a woman to be uppermost, no emasculation, but the mood between them was too golden with laughter. Tonight was a night for joy, not for navigating the intricacies of male pride and challenging long-held misbeliefs. She set that conversation aside for next time and bent all her attention to the here and now, to enjoying the rake in her bedchamber, the man who made her laugh more than she'd ever thought possible.

*C*HAPTER 16

*T*he golden mood was still with her the next morning. Ella snuggled among the sheets in the bed that no lover had ever seen, in the room no lover had ever entered. She felt languorous and content, happy. Her heart was the same color as the walls: rich sunrise pink, warm sunrise orange.

When she went down to the breakfast parlor, Minette was there, lingering over her repast. Arthur had clearly been and gone, an abandoned teacup and scattering of crumbs all that remained of his presence at the table.

Ella hummed while she browsed the dishes on the sideboard.

"Someone is happy this morning," Minette observed, when Ella took her place at the table.

"Yes." Ella spread a napkin on her lap. Her heart felt rosy. For twenty-seven years, it had been colorless. Through childhood, through marriage, through widowhood and four lovers. But now, because of Decimus Pryor and his silliness, her heart had finally learned how to *feel*.

Ella picked up her fork. "Minette . . . last night, when you told Mr. Pryor about you and Aunt Clara, weren't you afraid that he'd be . . ." She sorted through adjectives, discarding "disgusted," "outraged," and "scandalized," settling on something milder. "Shocked?"

"But of course not. His uncle is like me and Clara, he has *un amoureux* he has lived with for a great many years."

Ella dropped her fork with a clatter. She gaped at Minette. "Which uncle?" Not the marquis, surely? But that only left Lord Tertius, and he was married, too. All three of the elder Numbers—as the Pryor men were known among the *ton*— were married, and seemingly in love with their wives. Was one of those marriages a lie?

"Mercury."

Ella's shock snuffed out. She'd forgotten about the Duke of Linwood's illegitimate son. The illegitimate son who'd been accepted into the bosom of the family decades ago but was rarely seen in Society. "That must be why he's so reclusive."

"*Non.*" Minette shook her head. "It is his nature to be reclusive. He does not like most people."

Ella eyed her with interest. "Have you met him?"

"Clara and I, yes. Several times. We moved in the same circle." Minette tapped the side of her nose and gave an exaggerated wink.

A circle of men who loved men and women who loved women. Yes, that circle would be very select, very clandestine.

Ella picked up her fork again. There was a great deal more to the world than met the eye, secrets concealed behind ordinary, everyday façades. Hidden lovers, comtesses who weren't really comtesses, barons who were in fact actors from Bristol, noblemen who wielded magic.

Did Mercury Pryor have a Faerie godmother? Could he do magic?

It was a question she doubted that Decimus would answer, even if she were prying enough to ask it—which she wasn't— so Ella set it aside and turned her attention to her breakfast. Her thoughts strayed to the previous evening's silliness, the exhilaration and the gaiety, the absurdity of Pryor dressed as a plump Faerie princess.

She wanted to do it all again, not necessarily Falstaff and the Faeries, but the lighthearted merriment, the rollicking exuberance, the sheer joy of being alive.

She would never remarry, never exchange the freedom of widowhood for the prison of matrimony, but she would like a long-term lover. Someone not unlike Pryor, who enjoyed laughing and making others laugh, and who didn't mind making himself look ridiculous while doing so.

Or . . . rather than a man like Pryor, why not take him as her long-term lover?

Ella's heart felt as if it grew a little rosier—and then common sense reasserted itself. Decimus Pryor was a rake, and rakes enjoyed raking. It was what defined them: the urge for conquest after conquest. Pryor wouldn't want to be confined to one bed and one lover. He might be happy to extend their liaison for another month, possibly even two, but then he'd grow bored and long for newer pastures.

Ella poured herself another cup of tea and took the last brioche bun. It was filled with preserved apricots this morning. Each bite tasted of the long golden days of late summer.

Arthur entered the parlor, a letter in his hand. "From Sarah," he said cheerfully, resuming his seat at the table.

"More drawings from *le jeune* Phillipe?"

"With any luck." Arthur broke the wax seal eagerly. Sarah was his youngest niece. His eldest niece had died in an accident four years ago, along with her husband, leaving Phillip an orphan. Sarah had stepped in to raise the boy. Arthur doted on them both, sending money every month and visiting Bristol several times a year.

He unfolded the letter but didn't immediately display its contents, from which Ella deduced that it contained news, not artwork. She sipped her tea and waited to be regaled with details of Phillip's latest exploits.

"Sarah's getting married," Arthur said. "To a man named John Stratton."

"Oh? That's . . . good." Ella knew that her views on matrimony were a little odd. Most women wished to marry. It was one of the pinnacles of female achievement.

Arthur read further, a frown gathering on his face.

Ella exchanged a glance with Minette.

Arthur put down the letter. His mouth was a thin line, his eyebrows knotted together. It looked like anger, but Arthur was rarely angry.

Trepidation clutched in Ella's chest. "What's wrong? Is Phillip unwell?"

"Stratton doesn't want to have the raising of another man's son. Sarah says I may take Phillip if I wish. If not, they'll send him to a boarding school."

"Not a boarding school!" Ella cried, at the same time that Minette said, "He comes here, of course."

Arthur looked from one of them to the other, his eyebrows still knotted. "I can set up my own household . . ."

"*Non.* Why would you do that?"

His eyebrows didn't unknot. "But a child, here . . ."

"Would be *merveilleux*! Do you not agree, *ma chère*?"

"We would love to have a child in the house," Ella said firmly.

"We shall raise him together," Minette declared, clapping her hands. "All three of us. It will be *très agréable*!"

Ella hadn't realized how tense Arthur was until his shoulders lowered and his jaw unclenched. "Thank you."

"Not at all. A child is just what this house needs. Is it not, *ma chère*?"

Ella nodded her agreement.

"Which room shall we give Phillipe? The nursery—"

"*Not* the nursery." Ella had sad, gray memories of nurseries and the lonely isolation of a child tucked away at the top of a house. "How old is he now?"

"Seven," Arthur said.

Old enough for his own bedroom. He'd be happier among the adults, knowing there were people nearby who'd keep him safe, people close enough to hear him if he had nightmares. "One of the guest rooms. The blue one or the—"

"The green one!" Minette said. "Next to me. And if you like, *mon cher*, you can move up to the blue one, so Phillipe

121

will have Oncle Arthur on one side and Tante Minette on the other."

Even more of Arthur's tension eased, the knot finally disappearing from his brow. "Yes, I'd like that." He glanced at Ella. "Is that all right with you?"

"Whatever makes you and Phillip happy makes me happy," Ella said.

There was a sheen of what might have been tears in Arthur's eyes. He pushed back his chair and came around the table to where Ella sat, bending to hug her and press a kiss on her cheek. It was something her father had never done, something her husband had never done—affection and gratitude in a simple hug, a simple kiss. It made Ella's heart feel as if it expanded a little in her chest, as if it grew warmer and rosier.

Arthur embraced Minette, too, kissed her cheek, too.

"*Bon,*" Minette said. "Now, off you go! You must hurry to Bristol. Ella and I will arrange everything."

"Thank you. I'll be back next week." Arthur strode from the room.

The breakfast parlor felt very empty without him. Ella looked down at her plate. One morsel of brioche remained, one bite of apricot and sweet summer sunshine.

"We must go shopping," Minette announced.

"Yes." The green bedchamber was a lovely room decorated in a dozen shades of green and gold, like a sunlit woodland dell, but it wasn't furnished for a child. They'd need a little washstand and a child-sized dressing table and steps so that Phillip could climb up into his bed.

Minette sprang to her feet. "At last, a child in the house! Clara could not have them and neither could you, I had only the one *tragédie,* and Arthur's Jenny, she had nothing but miscarriages, which was *beaucoup de tragédie,* but now at last it happens!" She clapped her hands briskly. "Come! We must decide what we need for Phillipe's room and then we shall go shopping. I will make a list!" She bustled from the parlor, intent upon her task.

Minette's excitement was contagious. Ella swallowed the last bite of brioche hastily and pushed back her chair. She caught up her skirts and hurried after Minette, vowing to give Phillip everything her own childhood had lacked. He'd be encouraged to laugh as loudly and as often as he could, allowed to run if he wished, shout if he wished. He'd be hugged every day, told that he was loved every day. He would grow up knowing that he was valued, and more than that, that he was treasured.

Ahead, Minette flung open the door to the green bedroom. "What shall we keep and what shall we replace?"

*C*HAPTER 17

*P*ryor dined with them the following evening. When he asked where Arthur was, Ella merely said that he had gone to Bristol—Arthur's family business was his own—but Minette excitedly informed him that Arthur was bringing his great-nephew back with him, and that they'd have a child in the house at long last, and they were refurbishing one of the bedrooms, and—

"I doubt Mr. Pryor wishes to talk about children," Ella said, trying to redirect an enumeration of the changes she and Minette had wrought in the green bedchamber.

But it appeared that she was wrong. Pryor eagerly plunged into a discussion about what they needed to buy. "You said he likes to draw? You'll need crayons and pencils and paints and lots of paper. He probably loves building things, too—I know I did!—towers out of dominoes and castles out of wooden bricks—and dressing up and playing pretend—Blake's costume room will be an absolute treasure trove for the boy!"

The discussion continued in the drawing room, over a pot of tea. "Little soldiers made out of lead," Pryor said. "You know the ones? Or the flat pewter ones. It's fun to paint them different colors, turn them into pirates and bandits."

Minette's shopping list was quite long by the time she

bade them goodnight and retired to her bedchamber. Ella and Pryor retired, too. Pryor talked all the way up the stairs. He seemed almost as excited by Phillip's arrival as they were. "Do you think he's too old for a rocking horse?" he asked as they entered her crimson-and-gold bedchamber. The room was cozy with candlelight, warm from the fire. The sheets were turned back, inviting them into the wide, soft bed.

Ella closed the door and turned to him. Tonight was the night to challenge his misconceptions about riding St. George. She'd show him that it wasn't emasculating at all, that he could enjoy it.

"Oh! I just had a thought!" His eyes opened wide. "A toy theater, with puppets!"

Ella placed her fingers over his mouth. "No talk of children in this room. It's for adults only."

Pryor inhaled, as if to protest, and then paused. His expression changed. The wide-eyed animation ebbed. She saw intention flow into his face. Intention—and desire. His eyes darkened. When she removed her fingers and stood on tiptoe to kiss him, he kissed her back hungrily. His hands settled at her waist, large and strong, holding her close.

Desire shivered through her from her scalp to the very tips of her toes. Her amatory muscles fluttered and clenched eagerly.

They undressed one another swiftly, murmuring and laughing, caressing and kissing. Ella's skin was taut with expectation. Anticipation thrummed in her blood and a full, tingling heat gathered in her loins. Tonight she'd ride him.

They tumbled onto the bed and Pryor showed her yet again how skilled he was with his fingers and his mouth. "I want to talk to you about something," Ella said breathlessly as she floated down from the second of the night's climaxes.

"What about?" Pryor's hair was wildly tousled where she'd gripped it while he worked miracles with his mouth. His eyes glittered darkly, his cheeks were flushed, and his wicked, sinful lips were plump and rosy. His virile member was plump and rosy, too. Its thick length strained towards her, its head eagerly bedewed, looking as ready to breach her as she was to be breached.

Ella reached out and touched his organ, wrapping her hand around it in bold familiarity.

Pryor jolted. His breath caught in a short gasp.

His virile member was a heavy weight in Ella's hand, a scorching heat. She wanted it to fill her, over and over again.

She ran her thumb lightly over that hot, blunt, dewy head, making his whole body twitch and shiver, before releasing it.

Pryor reached for her.

"I'd like to ride St. George tonight."

He froze in mid-reach.

His hair was still wild, his cheeks flushed and lips still rosy, but the tension in his body seemed to change from urgent outward need to a drawing into himself, a retreat.

Ella laid her hand on his arm, feeling firm muscle beneath hot skin. "When I was married, I didn't enjoy sexual congress at all. I thought it was tedious and disagreeable, and when Francis died I was *so* pleased that I wouldn't have to do it anymore."

Pryor frowned.

"It took me a long time to learn that I was wrong, and that everything I thought I knew about sex was a misconception." Ella held his gaze and said softly, coaxingly, "I think that if you try St. George, you'll find that your notions about it are misconceptions, too."

Pryor ignored this statement and instead said, "Did your husband not like sex?"

"Oh, he liked it well enough; he certainly took every opportunity to do his duty. But he never bothered to see to it that I liked it."

Pryor's frown became truly alarming. His arm tensed beneath her fingers, the muscles becoming as taut as steel. His hand knotted, clenching the wrinkled sheets. "That damned—"

"He's dead," Ella reminded him. "There's no point in getting angry now."

Pryor's fist didn't unclench.

Ella plowed on: "Francis controlled every aspect of my life, and after his death, when I believed that I was free, he continued to control what I thought about sex. Until I tested my misconceptions and discovered they were wrong."

"What do you mean, he controlled every aspect of your life?"

Ella sighed. This conversation wasn't going in the direction she wanted it to. "I mean that I was his marionette and he pulled the strings. He told me what to eat and what to say and even what to think. He chose my clothes every day, right down to my garters. He decided how my hair should be styled and which reticule I would carry when I went out. He told me what my activities would be and when I would do them. He read every letter I wrote or received. He controlled *everything*, even my name."

"What do you mean, even your name?"

"He called me Louise." Ella was frowning now, too, and the hand not resting on his arm had formed a fist. She deliberately flexed her fingers, releasing the tension. "But that is all by the by. Francis has been dead for six years and we're not talking about him; we're talking about you. And St. George."

It was a lost cause, though. "He called you Louise?" Pryor said, outraged. He sat up in the bed, a movement that caused her hand to slide from his arm. "He told you what to wear and what to eat?"

Ella sighed again and sat up, too. She could tell that there would be no riding St. George tonight. "Yes, he did. He had an autocratic disposition and a need to oversee every detail, and he is *dead*. I don't wish to talk about him, especially not here." She gestured at the tumbled pillows and the rumpled sheets and the crimson-and-gold hangings that Francis would have hated.

Pryor's rage folded in on itself and snuffed out. "No, of

course not. Forgive me." He looked contrite. His hair was still disheveled, his cheeks still flushed, but his virile member was only at half-mast, which was no good at all. Riding St. George was off the table tonight, but Ella still wanted him inside her—*needed* him inside her.

She leaned close and nipped his shoulder lightly, tasting salt, then kissed where she'd bitten, kissed the edge of his jaw, kissed that splendid, sinful mouth.

Pryor's hand came up to cup the back of her head. He returned her kiss, quite thoroughly. They eased down onto the bed again. Ella skimmed her hands up his arms, reveling in the sleek skin, the hard muscle. "Did you receive an invitation to the Chalmers' Michaelmas ball?"

She already knew the answer to that question. Of course he'd received an invitation; he was a Pryor. He was invited everywhere.

"Mm-hmm." Pryor devoted his attention to reacquainting himself with her collar bone, alternating kisses with tickling little flicks of his tongue.

Ella shivered and sighed with pleasure. "Shall we go together?"

"If you wish." His wicked, wonderful mouth abandoned her collarbone and moved to her breasts.

Ella gasped and arched and managed to say, "I do wish."

"I'll protect you from highwaymen," Pryor murmured against the swell of her breast.

"In Brook Street?"

He laughed, warm breath feathering over her skin. "It could happen." His mouth moved lower, tracing a tickling path over her ribs, making her squirm with anticipation. Was he going to? Yes. His teeth touched her skin in that perfect spot that only he had discovered. He bit her there, gently but firmly, a primitive, sensual act that sent pleasure jolting through her.

Ella relinquished her grip on the conversation and surrendered to Pryor's skill, surrendered to the delicious pleasure of being made love to by a consummate rake.

CHAPTER 18

The Chalmers' ball was something of a triumph for Dex. When he entered the ballroom with Eloïse Fortrose on one arm and Comtesse de Villiers on the other, heads turned and a murmur sprang up.

Eloïse was resplendent in violet satin. Amethysts gleamed at her throat and sparkled in her elegant coiffure. Her skin was as smooth and perfect as marble, her hair the color of moonlight, pale and lustrous, her gown striking and bold. She was the personification of temptation, and at the same time she was cool and untouchable.

Untouchable, except by him.

Dex couldn't resist strutting a little. He didn't need to look in any mirrors to know that they looked damned good together. Armed with knowledge of what she was wearing, Hicks had worked his magic again. Dex's tailcoat and breeches were a color that lay somewhere between indigo and periwinkle, a rich, deep hue that set the violet gown off to perfection.

He and Eloïse stood up for a *contredanse* and then a quadrille. Their steps fitted together as smoothly as if they'd danced many times before—which they had, if one counted activities between the sheets as dancing.

After the quadrille, Dex procured her a glass of champagne

and they went their separate ways. To do otherwise would have given the wrong message. He and Eloïse weren't besotted with one another; they were merely paramours—and not for much longer.

Tonight was the 29th of September. Tomorrow marked the end of their liaison.

Dex felt a sharp pang of regret. He would very much like another month. Eloïse had been resolute in setting an end date, but there was no harm in negotiating for an extension, was there?

He sipped his champagne and decided that he'd pose the question later that night, when she was sated with laughter and pleasure.

He made a circuit of the ballroom, idly scanning for fortune hunters as he strolled. Phoebe wasn't there, but it was an unbreakable habit—watching out for gold-diggers, chasing them away. One was in pursuit of an heiress right now, using his wiles on a bashful, apple-cheeked débutante and her equally apple-cheeked mother. Dex didn't recognize the man's quarry, provincials most likely, but he recognized the man, smooth and charming and insincere. The girl and her mother were wealthy—it looked as if an ocean's worth of oysters had vomited pearls over their gowns—and easy targets judging by their expressions, the mother flattered, the débutante shyly admiring.

It was none of his business, but the habit was too deeply ingrained. Dex ambled in their direction, paused alongside the trio, and said, "Marris, look for your prey elsewhere."

Marris flushed and his smile became momentarily ugly. He mastered his expression, turned on his heel, and stalked off, almost colliding with a footman.

The footman stumbled. Glasses wobbled on his tray.

Dex reached out with his magic, a fleeting touch of levitation, helping the footman catch his balance, steadying the glasses. He turned back to the pearl-bedecked heiress and her mother. "Fortune hunter," he told them. "I'd avoid him, if I were you."

The débutante uttered a squeak of dismay. Her mother frowned.

Dex inclined his head to them politely and strolled onward, completing another leisurely circuit of the ballroom, nodding to acquaintances, pausing to speak with friends. A stir of whispers followed him, his name and Lady Fortrose's bandied together *sotto voce*—or not so *sotto voce* in some instances. Rakes eyed him with envy, young widows with speculation, and that hateful sobriquet, Vigor, seemed to finally be on the wane.

The gossip circulating about him wasn't limited to his affair with Eloïse Fortrose. Dex was asked several times about the events on Wimbledon Heath. Flurries of excited conversation followed in his wake. The rakes and young widows weren't the only people eyeing him; dowagers and débutantes did, too, elderly gentlemen and young sprigs of fashion. It was impossible not to puff out his chest a little under the weight of all that admiration, impossible not to swagger a little. Why yes, he *had* singlehandedly routed three highwaymen.

Lady Swansea, who'd brushed him off at the Wimbledons' ball, claiming that dancing with him was too vigorous, flirted determinedly with him tonight, fluttering her eyelashes and sending him provocative glances over the top of her fan.

Dex smiled politely, ignored all her lures, and extricated himself from the conversation. Lady Swansea might be a diamond of the first water, but alongside Eloïse Fortrose she was insipid in her looks, her character vapid and shallow.

He exchanged his empty glass for one full of champagne and made another sauntering circuit of the ballroom. More than one young widow sent come-hither glances as he passed. His stride gained a little more swagger, a little more strut. Venetia Twyckham's comment was all but forgotten and he was once again *le jouet des jeunes veuves*.

Dex's feet took him in Eloïse Fortrose's direction. He was her plaything tonight, no one else's.

"Someone's ransacked the fortress," a young buck sniggered as he passed.

Dex wasn't one to brawl, but he wanted to turn and smash his fist into that particular buck's particularly stupid mouth. Eloïse Fortrose wasn't a fortress and he made love to her, not ransacked her like a bloody barbarian.

He fixed a smile on his face and continued on his way, and as he neared her side, the rage faded and his smile became genuine. "My lady," he said, with an extravagant bow. "You are the brightest of jewels and the most exquisite of flowers, the most luminous of stars on the darkest of nights." He kissed his fingertips to her.

Eloïse pressed her lips primly together, but dimples sprang to life in her cheeks. "And you are a grandiose flatterer," she said dryly.

Dex preened, as if she'd offered him a great compliment. "One does one's poor best."

She shook her head at him, lips pursed, dimples dancing, eyes laughing. Her hair gleamed like spun silver in the blaze of the chandeliers, amethysts winking and twinkling amid the pale, shining tresses.

She thought his compliments hyperbole, but they weren't. She *was* luminous, she *was* exquisite, she *was* jewel-bright, and he loved making her laugh, loved making her shiver and tremble, loved making her melt.

But their liaison was due to end. There would be no more nights of laughter, no more nights of passion.

Regret panged again, like a harp string being plucked. Dex didn't want their affair to end just yet. He wanted to be Eloïse Fortrose's plaything a while longer. If she would allow it.

They danced two more dances together, which would have been scandalous had she been a débutante, but was merely risqué for a widowed viscountess, and then sat down to supper, dining on white soup and lobster and veal fricandeau and, because it *was* a Michaelmas ball, goose—roasted goose and green goose pie, pickled goose and *petit pâtés* of goose— along with a profusion of tarts, jellies, flummeries, and other desserts.

Comtesse de Villiers joined them briefly, then departed again for the card room. Dex and Eloïse Fortrose lingered at their table. He was conscious of eyes on them, conscious of curiosity and envy.

Another lady would have simpered and preened beneath that regard, would have touched her hair and her neckline to draw more attention to those things. Eloïse was definitely aware of the scrutiny, but she didn't play up to it; she merely said, "Your star is on the rise again."

Dex liked that candor, that frankness. It was refreshing. There was nothing coy about Eloïse Fortrose, nothing arch or coquettish. She never angled for compliments, but he gave her another one anyway: "My star is but a flickering candle flame compared to yours. You are more radiant than the sun. Your beauty transforms darkness into daylight."

Eloïse didn't blush at that fulsome compliment. In fact, Dex had the impression that she barely resisted rolling her eyes. "Must you empty the butter boat over me?"

He laughed out loud, delighted by her dryness.

His laughter drew more attention to them, but Dex ignored it. "Very well, no butter boat, then." He raised his glass to her. "You're very beautiful, my lady."

He liked her frank candor, but his frank candor appeared to make her uncomfortable. She wrinkled her nose, a tiny contraction of muscles, and glanced away.

Dex lowered his glass. "Do you not like your looks?"

Her gaze returned to him. She shook her head.

"Whyever not?"

"Too cold. Too colorless."

She wasn't entirely wrong. Her beauty was pale and cool and icy—the white-blond hair, the alabaster skin, the wintry eyes.

Frosty Fortrose, he'd heard her called more than once in the clubs. He'd probably even called her it himself.

"Is that why you wear bright colors?"

She hesitated, and then said, "In part."

Dex wondered what other reasons she might have to wear such vivid colors.

"Shall we dance again?" she said, before he could ask.

Dex did want to dance with her again, but he felt obliged to say, "We'll shock the high sticklers."

"I don't care a button for them. Do you?"

Dex didn't care any number of buttons for the disapproval of sticklers and prigs. Music wafted in from the ballroom, joyful and gay, inviting them to kick up their heels and be merry. He pushed back his chair. "Two more dances?"

Eloïse smiled at him, bright, vivid, beautiful, and—for tonight—his. "Two more dances."

*C*HAPTER 19

*T*he night was half over by the time Ella's carriage set them down them in Old Burlington Street. Once inside, Minette bade them goodnight with a wink and an "*Amusez-vous, mes chéris.*"

Pryor laughed and said, "We will." He took Ella's hand, tugging her towards the staircase. They hastened up the steps and tumbled into the crimson-and-gold bedchamber out of breath and laughing.

They kissed eagerly, hungrily, and set about the task of disrobing one another—his tailcoat and waistcoat, her jewelry, his neckcloth, her hairpins—and with the disrobing, formality fell away. They were no longer Mr. Pryor and Lady Fortrose, but Decimus and Eloïse.

They set aside their shoes, peeled off their stockings. Decimus unfastened Ella's gown, carefully laying it to one side. Her petticoat was next, his breeches, her stays. He stood behind her, fingers moving deftly, undoing the laces, teasing her while he worked, placing tickling kisses where her neck met her shoulder, biting softly, making her shiver and gasp.

At last the stays were undone. Decimus tossed them aside, then stepped round to face her, taking her mouth in a kiss that was slow and sensual and full of promise.

Ella kissed him back, wrapped in a delicious haze of heat and desire. She loved this moment, when they were almost naked, he in his drawers and open-necked shirt, she in her chemise, thin linen whispering over bare skin. Her body seemed made of anticipation rather than flesh and blood, every part of her tingling in expectation of what was to come, the effervescent levity, the exquisitely delicious exertion, the sheer giddy delight that was making love with Decimus Pryor, the way he made her convulse with both pleasure and laughter.

But she wanted something different tonight. Something more.

Ella broke the kiss. They stood leaning into one another, lips barely touching, breathing raggedly. "Decimus?"

"Mmm?" He drew back enough to see her face. His smile was sultry, his eyes heavy-lidded, his hands large and strong at her waist, warm through the thin chemise.

"I know you're not enthusiastic about riding St. George and I understand why, but tonight . . . I would like to try it with you. Please?"

His sultry smile dimmed.

"Those pictures of the toothless old men—I know they're abhorrent, but if you could only understand." She bit her lip, then blurted, "In my marriage, that was me! I was toothless and passive and I hated it! I don't want sex to be like that. I don't want to feel that I have no control."

Decimus's smile vanished. "I make you feel like that?" His hands lifted from her waist. He took a step back.

Ella moved with him, capturing his hands, placing them at her waist again, holding them there, her hands over his, warm skin to warm skin. "No. You don't make me feel toothless, but . . . you take responsibility for everything, Decimus—for my pleasure as well as yours—and sometimes that's not what I want."

Firelight and candlelight illuminated his face. His expression held the dismay of someone confronted with an unpalatable truth.

"Sometimes I like to be the one who leads. Sometimes I like to ride St. George."

He didn't step back this time, just stood and gazed down at her, uncharacteristically serious.

Ella placed her hands on his chest, feeling his body heat through the linen shirt, then skimmed her palms lightly down his ribcage until her hands rested at his waist, mirroring him. "I'd like to try St. George with you tonight. Not if it makes you feel terrible, of course, but . . . I don't think it will. You have a talent for bedsports, Decimus. You make everything pleasurable and I think that if we rode St. George together, we would both enjoy it. So . . . can we please try that tonight?"

"Of course," he said, without hesitation.

CHAPTER 20

*D*ex had always prided himself on being a generous lover. It was mortifying to realize that he hadn't given Eloïse Fortrose what she wanted, that instead of giving her more orgasms, he ought to have given her more control over what they did together, more control over *him*.

He wasn't enthused by the idea of being ridden, but he hoped he'd hidden it from her. If riding St. George was important to her, then he'd make it as good for her as he could, as good for them both—which meant entering into it with zeal.

In Dex's opinion, enthusiasm was as essential to great sex as laughter was. Sex was pleasure and bliss and ecstasy, but it was also sweat and mess and body parts bumping awkwardly and unexpected, comical noises. There was no shame in the awkwardness or the noises or the mess, so why not laugh? Why not enjoy it all with unrestrained gusto?

There was no shame in being ridden either, Dex told himself, but his mind was less inclined to accept that statement as the truth. Apprehensiveness fluttered like moths at the back of his brain. He ignored it, concentrating on the here and now, devoting himself wholeheartedly to the caresses and kisses that were prelude to the main event, no hesitation, no reluctance, not allowing the apprehensiveness to take hold.

They played with one another amid the tumbled sheets, an escalation of passion and arousal. He brought Eloïse to climax with his fingers, but when he was about to repeat the deed with his mouth, she laughed breathlessly and said, "No," and pressed her hand against his chest.

Dex let her push him onto his back, submitting to her desire to be in charge of their pleasure tonight.

Eloïse straddled him on hands and knees. Candlelight burnished her pale skin, turning it a soft, warm gold. The view was rather splendid. Her breasts tantalized him—soft curves and rosy nipples.

She dipped low for a kiss, her hair falling in a silky veil around their faces. "Is this all right?"

"Yes."

"Good." She kissed him a second time, then sat back, reaching for his cock.

A kernel of discomfort took up residence in Dex's chest, a walnut-sized lump beneath his breastbone. He strove to ignore it, focusing on her face—the flushed cheeks, the sparkling eyes, the way she caught her lip between her teeth as she lowered herself onto him, the way her eyelids fluttered when he breached her.

It always felt amazing to sink into a woman—the hot, sleek, welcoming tightness. Dex repressed a grunt of pleasure, repressed an upward thrust of his hips, repressed the urge to take her by the waist, gather her close, and roll them both over. Tonight, Eloïse led. Tonight she chose what they did.

Her expression was blissful as she took him in fully and settled into place. She closed her eyes briefly, breathed a soft sound of pleasure, then opened her eyes and said, "It feels wonderful, doesn't it?"

"Yes," Dex said. It was a truth, if not the whole truth.

Eloïse leaned forward, a movement that changed the clasp of her body around his cock in rather interesting ways. Her pale silky hair cascaded like moonlight around them. She pressed a kiss to the very tip of his nose. "Is it so terrible?"

"No," Dex answered honestly. It wasn't terrible. There was pleasure in being inside her, frustration in not being able to take control. "May I touch you, or would you rather I—"

She took his mouth in a fierce, hungry kiss. Their lips clung together and then parted. She sat up halfway, her veil of hair tickling his skin, and braced her forearms on his chest. "Touch me," she said, her voice low and husky.

Dex stroked up her thighs to her waist, hands gliding over warm, smooth skin, and as he did so, she began to ride him, a rocking motion, rising up slightly, unsheathing his cock a few inches, then sheathing it again in slick, tight, welcoming heat.

The kernel of discomfort dissolved. He hummed in his throat, an involuntary noise of pleasure.

Eloïse heard it. She laughed and rose up again . . . and again . . . and again. Dex caressed her midriff, her waist, her thighs. The urge to roll them both over pricked at him, the urge to take control, but he concentrated on the joys of the moment, on the beautiful woman poised above him, the delight on her face, the delicious sensation of his cock sinking repeatedly into her warmth.

She sat up a little more, arms extending, head tipping back, a movement that thrust her breasts into prominence. Dex skimmed his hands upwards to capture those delicious, tantalizing globes.

Eloïse uttered a low, breathy groan. "That feels good." Her pace picked up.

Dex's cock liked that change of tempo. He still wanted to roll them both over, but being ridden was a great deal more enjoyable than he'd thought it would be. There was nothing ignominious about it, nothing emasculating. He caressed her breasts, then dipped back to her waist, feeling muscles flex beneath smooth skin.

Eloïse leaned forward before he could recapture her breasts. She placed her hands on his shoulders, pressing down, pinning him to the bed.

Pleasure went through Dex like lightning, intense and

unexpected, setting him ablaze from his balls to the very top of his head.

What the devil? He *liked* being pinned down?

Eloïse laughed joyfully, her hair cascading around them. "Good?"

It was a hell of a lot better than good, but when Dex tried to tell her so, all that emerged from his throat was a hoarse, inarticulate sound.

Eloïse laughed again, breathless and exhilarated. She was stunning. Her beauty was the opposite of pale and icy; it was rosy and impassioned, skin flushed with arousal and dewy with exertion, eyes dark and hot, irises engulfed by her pupils. Feverish color burned in her cheeks.

Her pace became fierce, urgent. She was panting now, panting and laughing, wild delight on her face. She pressed down on his shoulders more strongly.

Incandescent pleasure jolted through him again, making him gasp, making his muscles clench. Dex was suddenly close to climax, ready to go off like the fireworks at Vauxhall, lighting up the sky in a fountain of sparks, his legendary stamina obliterated.

Eloïse laughed down at him and gripped his shoulders harder, pressed more forcefully. Lightning licked through him. Dex laughed back breathlessly, took firm hold of her waist, and flexed his hips, plunging up to meet her. It was rough and wild and uncontrolled, a mad race to the finish line. Eloïse reached that goal first by a mere half-second; then Dex went up in a blaze of ecstasy.

He always pulled out and spilled his release into a handkerchief, but there was no chance of that tonight. It all happened too quickly, too urgently. One moment his hips were arching up to meet her downward plunge, the next he was wracked by paroxysms of pleasure.

Eloïse slumped bonelessly on top of him, breathing raggedly. Dex wrapped his arms around her and lay in the tangle of sheets, spent and panting, dazed.

His wits slowly picked themselves up, shook themselves off, and started working again, presenting him with belated reactions.

The first was astonishment. How could he have enjoyed being held down so much? How could it have been so deeply, intensely, and shockingly arousing?

The second was relief that Eloïse was barren. He'd never spilled his seed into a woman, not once in all his years of raking. It was bad *ton* for a rake to impregnate an aristocratic lover, but more than that, he was a Pryor. He dared not be reckless with his seed. Not when his sons would inherit a baleful Faerie godmother.

On their very first night, when Eloïse had informed him she couldn't conceive, he'd been relieved, but he still hadn't taken the risk. Not then, and not since—until tonight. It hadn't been a conscious choice; his body had taken control of that decision. Holding back long enough to withdraw had been physically impossible.

It ought to horrify him, but he felt oddly unconcerned. If Eloïse were to become pregnant, they would cope with that. Together.

She stirred in his embrace, hummed contentedly, then propped her forearms on his chest and looked at him. They were almost nose to nose. His eyes struggled to focus on her face without crossing.

She looked disheveled and debauched and thoroughly sated, lips ripely red, skin glowing, pupils still dilated. Dex was thoroughly sated, too. His cock nestled inside her, warm and happy and replete.

He stroked her hip, a light caress. "Go on, say it."

"Say what?"

"I told you so."

Eloïse laughed and sat up. The candlelight painted her hair and skin a soft, pale gold. "Do I need to?"

Dex shook his head.

Eloïse laughed again, still a little breathless. Dex thought he'd never seen anyone more beautiful. She glowed with exertion, glowed with happiness.

This was the real Eloïse, the woman beneath the cool, reserved veneer of Lady Fortrose.

"We've reached the end of September," he observed, stroking her hip again. It was well past midnight. September 30th was already several hours old.

"Yes." She bit her lip and dipped her chin, looking at him through her lashes. It wasn't a provocative come-hither glance, but something shyer.

"How about . . . ?" he said, at the same time that she said, "Shall we . . . ?"

They both paused. There was a beat of silence; then Dex said, "How about an extension?"

"Yes."

"Another month?"

"Another month."

She smiled at him, still with that faint air of shyness, and as she smiled, Dex's heart did something it had never done before, seeming to simultaneously clench and to melt. That strange sensation was accompanied by an upwelling of emotion: affection and fondness and tenderness, an inexplicable need to protect and to safeguard, to cherish.

It was as unprecedented as it was alarming. He was a rake. He had liaisons with women; he didn't fall in love with them. He didn't *want* to fall in love.

But Dex had a horrible feeling that that catastrophe might have befallen him and that—quite against his will—he had tumbled in love with Eloïse Fortrose.

In the morning, it no longer seemed like a catastrophe. In fact, none of the events of the previous night seemed as momentous as they had at the time. Dex surfaced from sleep slowly, listening to his manservant move around the bedchamber. Hicks wasn't a soft-footed valet any more than he was an ingratiating valet. He crossed to the window—*clomp, clomp, clomp*—and noisily drew open the curtains, letting in watery gray light. He left, returned with a ewer that he deposited loudly on the washstand, then departed again—*clomp, clomp, clomp.*

Dex yawned and climbed out of bed, padded over to the window, and peered out. As he'd suspected, it was raining again. How tedious. But then, London in autumn generally was tedious.

Last night hadn't been tedious.

Last night had been . . . deliciously unexpected.

It wasn't in Dex's nature to worry; he left that to his cousins Quintus and Sextus. What was the point in stewing over things that had already happened and therefore couldn't be changed, or in fretting over events that might happen but also might not?

The fact that he'd enjoyed being ridden and being held down was surprising, astonishing, baffling, mystifying, and however many other adjectives one wished to attach to it— but he wasn't going to waste time trying to unravel the puzzle of why he'd liked something that he ought to have hated and he certainly wasn't going to brood over it.

It had happened, and nothing that had been that good could be bad.

What *was* a little worrying were the emotions he'd felt for Eloïse Fortrose afterwards, the affection and the tenderness, the protectiveness, emotions that were as unexpected as the bone-melting pleasure that had preceded them, but far less welcome.

Love was for romantics and idealists and serious men who thought profound thoughts—or sentimental fools who believed in Faerie tales. It wasn't for devil-may-care fellows like himself and it definitely wasn't for rakes. He was too frippery for love. He wasn't capable of it. His *heart* wasn't capable of it—which it would realize soon enough.

Dex yawned again, rubbed his face, and headed for the washstand. The water in the ewer steamed gently. His shaving accoutrements lay on a folded towel.

He had another month with Eloïse. A month for that tender, unsettling feeling to dissipate. A month for his heart to realize that it hadn't fallen in love. A month during which to enjoy bedding—and being bedded by—the delectable Viscountess Fortrose.

Dex smirked at himself in the mirror. The next month was going to be capital. Quite superlative, in fact.

He took a moment to admire himself. What a handsome devil he was, even with his hair standing on end and stubble roughening his jaw. Decimus Pryor, rake extraordinaire, *jouet des jeunes veuves*.

He crossed his eyes at his reflection, then laughed and set about the business of shaving.

CHAPTER 21

T here were occasions that changed the course of one's life. Ella's marriage at fifteen to Francis Fortrose had been one such occasion. His death six years later had been another. When she hurried down to the entrance hall just after midday on a Wednesday, another life-changing moment occurred. A trunk, three portmanteaux, and several valises were littered about. Footmen converged on the luggage, the butler was issuing directions, and in the middle of all the noise and bustle stood Arthur.

A child held Arthur's hand. He had unruly brown hair and freckles across his nose and huge eyes. Or perhaps his eyes only looked huge because he was gazing around the vestibule in awe.

Arthur spotted her. "Eloïse! Come and meet my great-nephew."

Ella made her way through the portmanteaux and the footmen.

"This is young Phillip," Arthur said.

Phillip looked up at her shyly. His eyes *were* huge. And hazel, just like Arthur's.

"Phillip, this is Lady Fortrose. She lives here, too."

Phillip darted a glance up at his great-uncle. "Do I bow now?" he whispered.

"No," Ella said. "Let's just shake hands." She bent low and held her hand out.

Phillip hesitated, and shyly slipped his little paw into hers.

Ella had a moment of recognition: This boy was going to be a very important part of her life.

"You may call me Aunt Ella," she told him with a smile, and then: "Welcome to your new home."

He smiled shyly back, removing his hand from her clasp and using it to cling to Arthur's leg instead. Arthur laid a hand comfortingly on Phillip's head, stroking that messy brown hair.

"Would you like to see your room?" Ella asked. "You're next to your great-uncle."

Phillip nodded shyly, still clinging to Arthur's pantaloons.

"We bought toys and story books for you, and if there's anything else you'd like, just let us know."

Phillip glanced from her to Arthur and back again. Ella could almost see the cogs turning in his head. "May I have a puppy?" he whispered.

"Sarah wouldn't let him have one," Arthur told her, stroking the boy's hair again. "I said we'd think about it."

Ella had never been allowed pets as a child. "I think a puppy would be an excellent idea. And kittens, too, don't you think?"

A grin broke over Phillip's face like sunrise. Two of his front teeth were missing. "Yes!"

"Are you hungry? Come, let's see your room, and then we can all have luncheon."

Phillip released his grip on his great-uncle's pantaloons and took her hand.

They made their way up the staircase. Phillip's hand was small and warm in hers. Small and warm and trusting. Ella vowed to never betray that trust. She would be Phillip's champion, his place of safety.

Minette met them on the half-landing. "He's here!" she exclaimed excitedly, swooping down to hug Phillip in a flurry

147

of silk and lace and expensive scent. "*Mon chou,* welcome to your new home!"

Ella had been an inconvenience in her father's house, tucked away in the nursery and later in the schoolroom, feeling like an interloper on the rare occasions she'd been allowed down to the drawing room or parlor. She had lived in that house for fifteen years, but it had been a place of residence, not a home. She wanted the house in Old Burlington Street to be Phillip's *home.* He'd be at the center of everything, not spoiled and overindulged, but seen, listened to, encouraged. He'd know that he was safe and loved and that he belonged.

Ella hadn't dined with her father until after the occasion of her marriage, and she'd never breakfasted with him in her life—so those were two things that she was determined they'd do with Phillip. Breakfasting together entailed nothing more than the addition of an extra place setting, but dining *en famille* required a less elaborate menu, not to mention less elaborate tableware. The ornate centerpiece was removed, as was the tall epergne that Phillip couldn't see over, and the dinner hour was brought forward to suit his earlier bedtime.

When Ella had informed Arthur and Minette that she was extending her liaison with Decimus Pryor for another month, they'd been delighted, but when she'd suggested that perhaps it would be best if Pryor no longer joined them for dinner, they hadn't agreed.

"Nonsense!" Arthur said. "Why shouldn't he dine with us?"

"Because he'll meet Phillip."

"But why should he not meet Philippe?"

"Because it's inappropriate."

"Devil a bit!"

"If you introduce him as your *amoureux* it would be inappropriate, but you will not do that, will you?"

"Of course I won't!"

"Then what's to worry about? He'll dine with us as our friend."

"*Oui.* As our friend."

"I'd like him to meet young Flip," Arthur said. "Got a feeling they'll get along like a house on fire."

"I do not understood that expression. A house on fire is a bad thing, no? Get along like thieves at a fair—that is what we say in France. It makes much more sense, do you not agree?"

Ella refused to be diverted by semantics. "The meal won't be at all what he's used to—and so early!"

Arthur waved those quibbles aside. "Pryor won't care about that. His grandfather might be a duke, but he's no snob. You're worrying needlessly, my dear."

Ella couldn't help worrying, though. She liked Decimus Pryor more than she'd thought possible, but Phillip had to come first. This was his home now, and if Pryor didn't like that a child's needs were more important than his were, she'd have to end their liaison.

She hoped it wouldn't come to that. It would be difficult to replace him. London abounded with rakes and dandies, but there were none quite like Decimus Pryor. He was inimitable.

Ella sent round a note inviting him to an early dinner, *en famille.*

Pryor sent back a note accepting.

She found herself unaccountably anxious as the appointed hour drew near. Pryor had seemed interested in the preparations for Phillip's arrival, but he was a rake, and rakes had no time for children.

"You will chew your lip off," Minette told her. They were in the second-best parlor, awaiting their dinner guest. Phillip was on the floor building a tower out of dominoes, Arthur on his knees alongside him, everything comfortable and unceremonious.

Pryor arrived punctually. His face lit up when he spotted Phillip and the teetering construction of dominoes. "Oh ho! Who's this?"

Phillip looked up. He apparently recognized Pryor as a kindred spirit, for his face lit up, too.

Ella made the introductions and within half a minute Pryor was on the floor alongside Phillip, heedless of creases to his coat-tails or breeches. Perhaps she ought to be miffed that her lover preferred constructing towers from dominoes to conversation with her, but all she felt was relief.

By the time dinner was announced, Phillip and Pryor were on first name terms.

"Tante Minette calls me Philippe and Aunt Ella calls me Phillip," Phillip confided. "But you can call me Flip, sir. It's what Uncle Arthur calls me."

"Flip it is!" Pryor declared. "I have a nickname, too. Do you want to know what it is?"

Phillip nodded eagerly.

"Dex. You can call me Mister Dex, if you like."

Dinner was relaxed and informal, less than a dozen dishes to choose from, none of them fussy or elaborate. Afterwards, they retired to the second-best parlor again, until it was time for a yawning Phillip to go to bed. Arthur and Minette accompanied him, debating whose turn it was to read the first story. At the door, Phillip paused and looked back. "Will you come to dinner again, Mister Dex? Please?"

"I will."

"Tomorrow?"

Pryor hesitated, and glanced at Ella, but it was Arthur who replied, "If you don't already have engagements, you're more than welcome, Pryor. No need to stand on formality! Come whenever you like."

"Thank you," Pryor said. He waited until the door had closed behind the trio, then said, "Phillip seems to be settling in well."

"Yes."

"No homesickness?"

"A little, yes. But everything's new here, and exciting, and moreover, he can be as loud as he likes."

"His aunt didn't like noise?"

"From what he's said, no."

"Children should be noisy."

Ella agreed. "We've decided to get a puppy. And some kittens."

Pryor's face lit up, eyes sparkling eagerly. He opened his mouth.

"Yes, you may come and play with them," Ella said, before he could ask the inevitable question.

He grinned at her. "You know me well."

She did, rather. In fact she knew him better than she knew anyone, with the exception of Arthur and Minette.

It was an unsettling realization. How had this man become such an important part of her life?

Pryor's grin faded into something speculative. "Shall we wait for Blake and the comtesse to return, or . . . ?"

"It will be a good hour before they've finished reading the stories."

They eyed one another, and then simultaneously rose to their feet. Pryor held out his hand to her. Ella took it.

They held hands all the way up the stairs.

CHAPTER 22

The next day was a miserable one, rain sluicing down relentlessly. Dex generally spent such afternoons at his club, amid the cozy warmth and camaraderie of his fellows; today, though, he visited a nicknackatory and then caught a hackney to Old Burlington Street.

He ran up the steps under a deluge of rain and rapped imperatively on the door. Two footmen helped unload his purchases from the hackney and carry them into the entrance hall. Dex surreptitiously levitated most of the raindrops away from men and boxes.

"Is Blake in? And young Phillip?" he asked, once everything was indoors and the door had been closed against the cold and the wet.

Blake and Phillip appeared almost before he'd finished uttering the words.

"Mister Dex!"

"Hello, young Flip." Dex flourished dramatically at the mountain of pasteboard boxes. "I come bearing gifts."

"What are they?" Phillip asked, wide-eyed.

"Wooden building blocks. I thought we could build a fort big enough for you to get inside."

"Oh, yes!" Phillip cried, dancing excitedly on his toes. "Can we, Uncle? Can we please?"

Eloïse Fortrose came down the stairs. She was wearing marigold yellow today, perhaps in defiance of the weather.

Dex's heart lifted at the sight of her. "My lady," he said, sweeping her a florid bow. "You dazzle mine eyes. You are as glorious as the sun."

Eloïse laughed as if he were joking, but he wasn't. She *did* dazzle his eyes. She *was* as glorious as the sun.

Belatedly, Dex realized that Comtesse de Villiers had arrived on the scene. He bowed and presented her with an extravagant compliment, too.

The pasteboard boxes were carried into one of the parlors and the building of the fort commenced. Everyone helped, even the comtesse. They constructed three walls of wooden blocks between a settee, a *chaise longue,* and a red wingback armchair, creating a compound large enough to shelter two people. Blake fetched a bundle of paper. "Darts or spitballs?"

"Both!" Eloïse declared, to Dex's surprise.

He was even more surprised when she confessed that she'd never made a dart and that she had no idea what a spitball was. Her childhood had clearly been severely lacking. He showed her how to rip paper into tiny pieces, roll those pieces into balls and wet them, then he showed her how to fold sheets of paper to make the best darts. She copied him earnestly. It shouldn't have made his heart pang, but it did.

He had no time to worry about panging hearts, though, because a great battle commenced, Phillip and his great-uncle defending the fortress from assault.

Dex attacked everyone indiscriminately. "Take that, you bow-legged barnacle!" he cried, pelting Eloïse with spitballs from his perch on the *chaise longue.*

"I'm on your side!" she protested, batting the projectiles away.

"I know!" Dex cackled loudly and lobbed darts at Blake and Phillip and, for good measure, Comtesse de Villiers.

"You smell like a goat!" Blake bellowed, slinging several darts in Dex's direction.

"Hedge-pig!" the comtesse crowed, throwing a handful of spitballs at Dex.

Phillip picked up that insult. "Hedge-pig!" he cried gleefully, also throwing spitballs at Dex.

"Cross-eyed hobgoblin!" Eloïse joined in, aiming her darts at Dex, too.

Dex flung up his hands to protect himself from the barrage of missiles, uttered a shriek, and toppled melodramatically off the *chaise longue*.

It was childish and ridiculous and a thousand times better than spending the afternoon at his club, drinking brandy and catching up with the latest news and *on-dits*.

When the fortress had been reduced to a rubble of wooden blocks and they were all weak with laughter, the butler poked his head into the room. "Cook is icing some gingerbread shapes. She wishes to know if Master Phillip would like to assist."

"Yes, please!" Phillip cried, scrambling to his feet.

Dex saw longing on Eloïse's face, there for a split second and then gone. "Why don't you join them?" he suggested.

She hesitated, bit her lip, and said, "I've never iced gingerbread shapes."

"Then go."

She rose to her feet in a flurry of marigold skirts and hurried after Phillip.

Dex set to work picking up the scattered spitballs. It didn't do to aggravate one's servants, and it particularly didn't do to aggravate other people's servants.

The comtesse subsided on the settee, fanning herself with a crumpled sheet of paper. Several of her hairpins had come loose and a dart was lodged in the lacy hem of her gown.

Blake began gathering the wooden blocks. "Splendid idea. Thank you, Pryor."

Dex smirked. "I'm full of splendid ideas."

He had wonderful memories of rainy days spent constructing long tunnels out of furniture draped with sheets, then chasing his cousins—or being chased by them—everyone crawling rapidly and shrieking with glee, but today wasn't the day to suggest that particular activity. It wasn't a quiet game and it would disrupt the household on a much larger scale than a fort built between a settee, a *chaise longue,* and an armchair. They'd need to move all the furniture in this room, bring furniture in from other rooms, wheedle the housekeeper into relinquishing dozens of sheets . . . It was wisest to clean up this mess first and wait a week or two before suggesting such an activity.

"How's Phillip settling in?" he asked. "Eloïse said that he's not too homesick."

"We give him no time to be homesick," the comtesse said, from the settee. "All day he is busy, busy, busy." She was silent for a moment, and then added: "I haven't heard him crying at night. Have you, Arthur?"

Blake shook his head. "I think he's happier here than he was with his aunt, not that she was unkind to him, but . . ."

"We are better!" the comtesse declared.

Dex nodded. This struck him as a fabulous household for a child to grow up in. "It's to be a long-term arrangement, I understand?"

Blake's lips thinned. "Yes. Sarah wanted a husband, and he didn't want someone else's child. So yes, permanently."

"Their loss," Dex said.

The displeasure faded from Blake's face. "Their loss," he agreed.

Dex dug several spitballs out from underneath a *bergère.* "I know it's none of my business . . . but have you given any thought to his education?"

Blake and the comtesse exchanged a glance. Blake heaved himself off the floor and went to sit alongside her on the settee. "We've given a lot of thought to a lot of things," he said, holding out his hand to the comtesse. She placed her hand in his. "We're getting married. Special license."

Dex sat back on his heels, startled. "Congratulations."

"It is *un mariage de convenance*," the comtesse said, smiling fondly at Blake. "An arrangement between friends."

"Ceremony's on Monday. The notice will go out in all the newspapers."

"And after that, it will be *convenable* for us all to live together."

Blake nodded. "I can reside here openly, with no risk to anyone's reputation."

"Who will you be?" Dex asked. "Entwhistle? Withers?"

"Myself. Arthur Blake."

Dex gathered up more discarded spitballs. "Arthur Blake, the actor?" he said, trying not to sound dubious. It would ruffle more than a few feathers among the *ton* if an actor married a comtesse.

Blake shook his head. "Arthur Blake, obscure gentleman from the north, possessed of a fortune, an unblemished past, and a young great-nephew."

Dex nodded. "That should work."

"It will work," Blake said, still holding the comtesse's hand.

Dex tossed the spitballs he'd gathered into the fireplace. It had been prodigious fun flinging paper missiles all about, but now he regretted making quite so many of them. Paper darts and spitballs littered the parlor. They were underneath furniture, behind cushions, floating in vases, caught in his hair, his pockets, his boots, simply everywhere. "What about his schooling? If you need me to put in a word for you somewhere, I can. The Pryor name carries some weight."

"No boarding schools," the comtesse said firmly.

Blake nodded. "Ella's adamant about that. He'll stay with us."

Ella. Dex liked that nickname. It suited her, soft and sylphlike. "A day school, then? Or perhaps a tutor." He thought about the advantages of each while he ferreted several spitballs out from the folds of a curtain. "The Michaelmas term has already started, no point in him going to school until next year. You want him to move in the best circles, I take it?"

"Yes."

Dex hesitated, afraid of giving offense, but if anyone understood the importance of first impressions, it was Blake. "His accent . . ."

"Needs a little work. Yes, I'm aware."

"Philippe takes after *mon cher* Arthur," the comtesse said. "He has the ear."

"Natural mimic," Blake agreed. "It shouldn't take long."

"Good." The boy's Bristol accent wasn't strong, but it would influence the way some people judged him, and Phillip didn't need that. "His manners are excellent. No work required there."

"Sarah's a stickler for manners."

Dex liberated a paper dart from between two cushions. "It would be good for him to meet other boys his age. I wonder . . . My cousins Quintus and Sextus are older than I am. One or other of their friends may have sons the same age as Phillip. I can ask, if you like?"

"Thank you," Blake said. "We'd appreciate that."

"What about yourself?" Dex rooted among the ornaments on the mantelpiece, fishing out spitballs and paper darts. "If Arthur Blake is going to be a permanent resident here, shall I sponsor you to my club?"

"I . . . yes, thank you. That would be most kind."

Dex grinned at him. "You may regret it. I'm a sad rattle, and so are most of my friends!"

"You are both rattles." The comtesse rose from the settee. "If you will excuse me, I need to recoup my strength. Me, I am a very old lady."

"Nonsense!" Dex said. "You're as fresh-faced and nimble as a débutante in her first season."

The comtesse rolled her eyes. "*Quelle absurdité.*"

Dex leaned down and plucked the paper dart from her hem as she passed. "*Merci,*" she said, and tottered theatrically from the room.

It took another fifteen minutes to track down the last of

the spitballs and paper darts. Dex wasn't certain that it *was* all of them. They'd probably lurk in nooks and crannies for the next decade. Possibly longer. Perhaps someone would find one in a hundred years' time, lodged in a crack between the floorboards.

It had been worth it, though.

He glanced around the room. The *chaise longue* and settee were back in place, the blocks returned to the pasteboard boxes.

"You'll stay to dine?" Blake said.

Dex hesitated. He'd never dined at Old Burlington Street two nights in a row. "Eloïse may prefer that I don't."

"You're my guest tonight—and Phillip's. He'll be delighted if you stay."

"Thank you." Dex was conscious of an unfamiliar feeling in his chest, a warmth, a flush of pleasure. In this house, he was now more than merely Eloïse Fortrose's lover. He was Blake's friend, Phillip's friend. Quite possibly the comtesse's, too.

It was always nice to gain friends.

"Let's see how those gingerbread shapes are getting along." Blake led him out of the parlor, along a corridor, and through a green baize door.

Dex uttered a faint sound of protest. "Your cook won't like it if we—"

"She won't mind," Blake said cheerfully.

In Dex's experience, servants didn't like it when one invaded their domain, but this household was run more casually than he was used to—although no less well. The servants were always smartly turned out, the meals first-rate, everything sparkling clean, not a speck of dust anywhere. Casual clearly didn't equate to careless.

He followed Blake down a staircase and along another corridor. The scents of sugar and spices and roasting meat wafted to his nose, tantalizing his tastebuds and making his mouth water. Somewhere ahead, several people were singing.

The kitchen was an oasis of warmth and delicious smells. It was also the origin of the singing. Eloïse and Phillip were at a long, scrubbed wooden table in the middle of the room, both swaddled in aprons, both intent on their task, both adding their voices to the song. Kitchen maids stirred and chopped and whipped and sang. The cook sang, too, while tending to whatever was in the cast iron roasting oven, and from the scullery came the sound of scrubbing and slopping water and two more voices singing.

Standing on the threshold, looking in at all the warmth and busyness, Dex had a strange sense of homecoming, as if this large, noisy, fragrant room that he'd never seen before in his life was a place he'd been missing, a place where he was meant to be. As if this kitchen was his *home*. And it wasn't merely the kitchen that was his home; the people in it were, too: Phillip, standing on a footstool, Eloïse alongside him.

Except that she wasn't Eloïse at this moment. She was definitely Ella, bundled up in an apron, a smear of flour on one cheek, flushed and glowing and inordinately beautiful. Rows of gingerbread biscuits lay before her, circles and stars and half a dozen other shapes, decorated with swirls of white icing, delicious treats waiting to be eaten, thin, crisp, crunchy mouthfuls of sweetness and spice.

Blake advanced into the room with a bouncing stride and a merry greeting. Kitchen maids smiled and greeted him back, the cook nodded a welcome and kept singing, and it appeared that Blake had been correct: no one minded their invasion of the kitchen.

Phillip beamed at them. "Uncle Arthur! Mister Dex! Come and see!"

Eloïse pointed a stern finger at them from across the rows of gingerbread biscuits. "Wash your hands before you touch anything!"

*C*HAPTER 23

*D*ex had taken his dinner at Old Burlington Street many times as Eloïse Fortrose's guest, but dining as Blake's guest felt different in a way that he couldn't quite pinpoint. He was the same person he always was, his hosts were the same people they always were, the house was the same house, so why did it feel different?

He finally decided that it was because he wasn't there as a rake; he was there as a friend. A friend who was dressed casually in buckskins and top boots. A friend who'd spent the afternoon playing with building blocks, spitballs, and paper darts. A friend who'd been invited down to the kitchen and had spoiled his appetite for dinner by scoffing some freshly iced gingerbread biscuits.

Later that evening, it turned out that he was there as a rake as well. Dex accompanied Eloïse up the stairs to her boudoir and spent a very pleasurable few hours in her bed.

When she expressed the wish to ride St. George, Dex said, "Yes, as long as you hold my shoulders down."

She did, and it was just as remarkable as it had been the first time. Being held down was highly arousing. Bafflingly arousing.

Not that Dex wasted any time wondering why he liked

it. He had something far more important to think about. Namely, his feelings for Eloïse Fortrose.

Dex had never attached emotion to sex before. Now, sex and emotion were inextricably entwined. Every time he kissed Eloïse, his feelings for her grew more tender. When she straddled his hips and held his shoulders down, his foolish, frippery heart felt like singing, and when his climax finally burst from him, that same heart felt as if it, too, might burst, not with effort, but with emotion.

Despite the fact that Dex wasn't a worrier, it was rather worrying.

When he went back to Clarges Street in the early hours of the morning, he had the disconcerting realization that the house on Old Burlington Street felt more like his home than the rooms he'd lived in for several years. Damn it, what was happening to him? Was he becoming a romantic?

He'd better bloody not be. He was only twenty-seven. Far too young to hang up his raking hat. The *ton* abounded with young widows he hadn't yet played with.

Mindful of his promise to Blake, Dex wrote to his cousins Quintus and Sextus, asking whether they knew anyone in London with sons Phillip's age. He followed these letters with one to his sister.

Dearest Fleabee, yesterday I fought a pitched battle with hedge-pigs and hobgoblins. I would like to tell you that I emerged victorious from this engagement, but alas, I was overwhelmed by superior forces.

Below that, Dex drew two pigs covered in hedgehog-like spines. He gave them maniacal grins and, after some consideration, sharp teeth. The hobgoblins also had sharp-toothed, maniacal grins, along with hooked noses and catlike ears.

Lastly, he drew himself. No heroic figure this time, but a spindly creature with knobbly knees, cowering before an onslaught of paper darts.

It ought to make his sister laugh.

He drew the same picture for Phillip, too.

He could have sent Hicks round to deliver it, but Dex decided to hand the picture over in person. He told himself it was because he wanted to see Phillip's face when he saw it, but that wasn't the only reason.

His feet traced the familiar route from Clarges Street to Old Burlington Street. The door knocker rapped out its familiar *rat-tat-tat*. Dex wiped his feet on the mat, greeted the butler by name, and stepped into the entrance hall with its warm yellow walls and bold red carpet and blue *trompe l'oeil* sky. The sense of homecoming wasn't as strong as it had been in the kitchen, but it was still undeniable.

Damn.

"Is Master Phillip in? I have something for him."

"If you'll follow me, sir."

Phillip was in the library with his great-uncle and soon-to-be great-aunt. To Dex's disappointment, Eloïse Fortrose wasn't present.

The comtesse was spinning a globe. "The dragons, they live here, in this énorme desert. And the sea monsters, they are here." She placed her finger on the globe with authority.

"Mr. Pryor, to see Master Phillip," the butler announced.

"Mister Dex!" Phillip cried joyfully, scrambling down from the chair on which he was perched.

At the other side of the library, someone straightened to standing. Eloïse Fortrose, holding a book so large it could only be an atlas.

Dex's foolish, frippery heart gave a leap of pure joy when he saw her.

Damn, damn, and triple damn.

He advanced into the library with a swagger and a smirk, telling himself that he was barely a week into the second month of his liaison with her. The foolish, unwelcome feelings would die away soon.

The feelings didn't abate.

Five days passed. Ten days. Fifteen days, and the only thing that changed was that Dex's silly, frivolous heart fell more in love with Eloïse Fortrose with every minute he spent in her company. That, and they discovered that if he liked having his shoulders held down while she rode him, he *loved* it when his wrists were tied to the bedposts.

How could ceding control be so extraordinarily arousing? It was an unfathomable mystery, but Dex was glad they'd discovered it.

He wasn't glad about the feelings, though. In fact, he was beginning to feel rather desperate. Why weren't time and familiarity quashing them? Wasn't that how it was supposed to work? One's heart grew accustomed to things—to people—to having one's wrists tied to bedposts—and those things and people and moments spent tied to bedposts stopped being exceptional and became merely ordinary, and one's heart realized that it wasn't in love after all.

Except that that wasn't happening.

When the kittens became involved, it grew even worse.

Dex found the kittens by the simple expedient of asking his grandfather's servants. Servants knew pretty much everything, in his experience. He needed kittens? Yes, sir, there was a litter in the stables behind Hanover Square. Five kittens, born last month.

He'd long since ceased to be surprised by such instances of servantly magic.

Arthur accompanied him when he took Phillip to view the kittens for the first time. So did Eloïse Fortrose. She'd never seen a litter of kittens, she confided, and Dex knew her well enough to see that she was almost as excited as Phillip. She didn't bounce up and down on the carriage seat and ask a thousand eager questions, but her cheeks were flushed and her eyes shone and she practically vibrated with anticipation.

She didn't balk at the ladder to the hayloft, simply removed her bonnet and gloves, set them aside, and climbed. Nor did she balk at crawling through the dusty, prickly hay. The expression on her face when she saw the kittens, the wide-eyed wonder, the awe, made Dex want to give her all the kittens in the world.

They stayed in the loft for almost an hour, lying on their bellies, watching the mother cat tend to her offspring. The cat's tail twitched to and fro and her ears were aimed at them, but as the minutes passed she grew less and less wary. The kittens were four weeks old, ears pricked and eyes open, but still clumsy on their feet. They clambered over one another in search of sustenance from their mother's nipples, cheeping like birds.

After half an hour, Dex dared to wriggle closer and to slowly, carefully, reach out and stroke a replete, sleeping kitten. He kept his gaze on the mother cat and she kept her gaze on him.

Dex wriggled back to where the others waited. "You try," he told Phillip. "Slowly and carefully, just like I did. Watch the mother. If she takes alarm, back off. We want her to grow accustomed to our visits and recognize us as friends."

Phillip wormed forward and carefully touched a kitten, a familiarity that the mother cat permitted.

When he wormed his way back to them, his face was ablaze with excitement.

"You wish to touch one?" Dex asked Eloïse.

"Oh, yes," she breathed.

She did exactly as Dex had done, as Phillip had done, inching forward carefully, reaching out slowly. She touched a kitten with a gentle fingertip, let her hand rest on its tiny flank for a moment. Her expression was intent and awed, wide-eyed, and Dex thought she was holding her breath.

She glanced back at them. Her smile was even wider than Phillip's had been, lighting her whole face with wonder and joy.

In the hayloft in the stables behind his grandfather's townhouse on Hanover Square, Dex's heart rolled over and presented its belly to Eloïse Fortrose in submission. *Take me,* it said. *I'm yours. Forever.* Which was more than a little alarming. Forever wasn't a word that had been in his heart's vocabulary before.

Dex tried not to panic.

They remained in a hayloft for another twenty minutes. Twenty minutes during which he waited for his heart to roll back over and pick itself up, carefree and unattached.

It didn't happen.

Nor did it happen when they clambered back down the ladder and returned to Old Burlington Street by way of Gunter's Tea Shop.

Nor later that evening, when he left Eloïse Fortrose's bed and went back to his rooms on Clarges Street.

Nor the next day, when he visited Old Burlington Street and they all played at dress-up.

Nor the next day. Or the next.

The kittens were scampering all over the loft, the end of October was upon them, and still his heart stayed flat on its back, presenting its belly to Eloïse Fortrose and declaring itself to be hers.

Dex's panic solidified to a heavy sense of doom. When Eloïse suggested extending their liaison for another month, he gave the only answer possible: "Yes."

He was beginning to feel rather desperate, though. Thinking about his predicament wasn't helping; he needed to talk it over with someone. The person he wanted to talk with was at Linwood Castle, though, so he informed the inhabitants of the house on Old Burlington Street that he was going to be out of town for a few days, hired a post-chaise, and went to Gloucestershire.

CHAPTER 24

*D*ex was so familiar with Linwood Castle that he no longer noticed its grandeur. It was a ducal castle, but everything about it felt comfortable and welcoming. He'd run wild here as a child, larked about with his sister and cousins, raced up and down staircases and along miles of corridors, played thousands of hours of hide-and-seek, climbed trees and splashed through ponds, slid down bannisters and constructed furniture forts. Linwood Castle might overawe the casual observer, but to Dex, it was family and laughter and belonging. Clarges Street was where he resided, but this castle was home, just as much as his parents' estate in Surrey was home.

He found himself viewing everything with new eyes as the post-chaise made its way through the acres of parkland. What would Eloïse think of the wooded hills and meadows? Of that first glimpse of Linwood Castle, with its ramparts and honey-colored walls and glittering banks of windows? What would Phillip say when he spotted the crenelations and the turrets?

Would they ever see it? Was it wishful thinking to hope that they would, or arrant foolishness?

Arrant foolishness, most likely. When Eloïse Fortrose remarried—if she remarried—she'd choose someone more responsible and serious-minded than he was. Someone who'd make a worthy husband.

On that gloomy note, the post-chaise entered the carriage sweep and rolled to a halt in front of Linwood Castle's towering central façade. Dex flung open the door and jumped down rather than wait for a footman. Gloucestershire was only a day and a half's journey from London, but it was still a long time to be cooped up in a carriage. His feet were grateful to be on solid ground again, his body grateful to be standing instead of sitting, his lungs grateful for fresh air.

His arrival was unexpected, but the butler greeted him with unruffled calm, instructing two footmen to assist his valet, Hicks, with the luggage and another to show the postilions to the stables.

"Do you know where I might find my mother?" Dex asked.

"I believe she's in the art room, sir."

"Is the marquis still here?"

"Yes, sir."

"I need to speak with him and my grandfather. Before dinner, if possible. Shouldn't take more than half an hour." He had to confess that he'd revealed the family secret to Eloïse Fortrose and her companions, and he preferred to get that ordeal over with as soon as possible. "M' father, too, if he's around." Might as well kill three birds with one stone.

"I'll see what I can arrange, sir."

"Thank you, Brockmole."

Dex waylaid a footman bearing one of his valises, gave the man his hat and gloves to take up to his room, and strode off in search of his mother.

When he peeped into Linwood Castle's airy, light-filled art room three staircases and seven corridors later, he was relieved to find his mother sitting in front of an easel, and even more relieved that she was alone. In formal circles, his mother answered to the name Lady Secundus Pryor. In more informal circles, she was known as Lady Deuce. Here at Linwood, among family, she was Imogen. To her husband, she was Midge. Dex thought his mother always looked like a Midge when she was painting. Today's outfit was a round gown that was more than a few years out of fashion, shabby at the cuffs and liberally flecked with paint.

"Darling!" his mother said, looking up from her easel. "Were we expecting you?"

"No." He crossed the room and bent to kiss her cheek. "Surprise visit. I wanted to talk with you."

"With me?" His mother didn't lay down her delicate brush.

"Yes. That's beautiful." The watercolor was almost finished, a *fritillaria imperialis* from the greenhouse rendered in glorious, painstaking detail, the petals richly yellow, the leaves lush and verdurous. It was the sort of work he hadn't the patience or skill for—or the desire—but that didn't mean he couldn't appreciate its beauty.

"Thank you, darling. How long are you here for?"

"Only one night."

"Only one?" Now, his mother did put down her paintbrush.

"I have to get back to London." This journey was costing him the first four days of his third month with Eloïse Fortrose. "But I was hoping to speak with you."

"That sounds serious, darling," his mother said, beginning to clean her brushes.

"It is rather." Had he ever said that to anyone? That he wished to speak to them about something serious? He didn't think he had.

"Should I send for your father?"

"No." Not that he didn't love his father, but Secundus Pryor didn't have a serious bone in his body. He turned everything into a joke, and falling in love wasn't something Dex could joke about. Not yet, at any rate.

There was a settee beneath one of the art room windows, a comfortable thing with a serpentine back and sun-faded damask. Dex crossed to it, weaving his way between easels and stools. He wasn't prone to fidgeting, but he found himself fiddling with his cuffs and toying with his buttons while he waited for his mother to see to her brushes.

169

At last, she rose from her stool and came to join him on the settee. She sat close enough that their legs almost touched and placed one comforting hand on his knee. Green paint had found its way under her fingernails. "What's so serious, darling?"

Dex had had ninety miles to think about how to pose his question and he still didn't know how to say what he wanted to say. He looked down at his hands, twisted his fingers together, stopped himself twisting his fingers together, took a breath, and said, "You and Father . . . you have a bond. A deep bond. You love each other as much as Grandfather loves Grandmother, and as much as Uncle Ace and Uncle Terce love my aunts and Uncle Mercury loves Jack. Don't you?"

He glanced at his mother in time to see her brow crease slightly. The angle of her head was ever so slightly perplexed.

"Yes, we do," she answered. "Why?"

Dex hesitated, trying—and failing—to find the right words. He didn't know how to talk about this sort of thing, feelings and emotions and weighty matters like love.

His mother waited patiently for him to speak.

"Father didn't always love you that much, though, did he?" Dex blurted out. "Because my uncles and Grandfather, they're serious, but Father's not."

The angle of his mother's head became more perplexed, the creases in her brow more pronounced.

Dex plowed on. "Father and I, we're not serious. We're frippery and lighthearted and . . . and real love—*lasting* love—is deep and profound. But Father *does* love you and . . . it was my brother's death that did it, wasn't it? That's what made Father's love for you so strong and enduring. Because he's too frippery for real love, isn't he? Just like I'm too frippery for it?"

His mother was silent for a long moment, her gaze steady on his face. When she finally replied, she didn't answer his question, but instead posed one of her own: "Have you fallen in love, darling?"

Dex looked away, partly because he was embarrassed to

170

be talking about love with his mother, but mostly because it was such an enormous question, such a *weighty* question, and he couldn't answer it while looking at her. "I think so," he confessed to the nearest easel. "But I'm like Father, and it took a tragedy for him to be able to love deeply, and I haven't had a tragedy and . . . it's doomed to fail, isn't it?"

His mother didn't answer immediately. Dex darted a glance at her.

Again, she answered his question with one of her own: "Why do you think your father didn't love deeply before Septimus?"

"Because he never takes anything seriously." But a stillborn child was serious. Not even the most flighty of flibbertigibbets could laugh a tragedy like that off.

The creases pleating his mother's brow grew deeper. "What is it you want me to tell you?"

What did he want her to tell him? Dex returned his gaze to the nearest easel and puzzled his way through the answer to that question. "I want you to tell me whether Father was a good husband before Septimus. If he loved you enough to make you happy. Because I'm as like him as if I was spat from his mouth, and if *he* failed at being a good husband, then I likely will, too." He sighed. "I know I shouldn't offer for her. I guess . . . I want you to confirm it."

The easel received this confession stoically and silently. His mother was silent, too. After a moment, Dex glanced at her again.

As if she'd been waiting for him to look at her, she said, "You are as like your father as if you were spat from his mouth—a terribly vulgar expression, darling, but quite true in this case—but that doesn't mean you aren't capable of love. Quite the opposite, in fact."

"What do you mean?"

"Our love was deep from the very beginning. It was your brother's death that nearly broke us."

Dex frowned. "I don't understand."

It was his mother's turn to sigh. "We grieved differently, your father and I. I closed myself off from him and he tried to reach me, but I wouldn't let him."

Dex shook his head. He couldn't imagine his mother closing herself off from his father. She was so warm, so loving.

"I felt that my loss was greater than your father's, that he couldn't understand how I felt." She laid one hand on her belly, a gesture Dex thought she wasn't aware of making. "I'd felt your brother grow within me, felt him move. I'd talked to him and sung to him. He was a real person to me, even though he wasn't yet born. I was inconsolable when he died. Your father tried so hard to comfort me, but I wouldn't let him."

Dex touched his mother's hand lightly, where it rested on her abdomen. "I'm sorry. I shouldn't have brought it up."

"No. Sometimes we need to talk about these things." She turned her hand over and took hold of his fingers. "We all grieve differently. Your poor father . . . he turned to me, but I turned away. I thought his grief trifling and insignificant compared to mine. All he'd done was rub my feet and fetch me pickled onions in the middle of the night, whereas I'd carried Septimus for nine months." Her fingers tightened on Dex's. Her grief might be nearly thirty years old, but it still ran deep. "Your grandfather helped us find a way through it. He sat us down and made us speak the truth to each other. He wouldn't let me turn away or be silent. And I was partly right, our grief over Septimus *was* different—he was a real person to me, but only a dream to your father—but your poor father, he wasn't only grieving a son who hadn't lived to be born, he was grieving the loss of his wife. He was grieving *me*. So that is the truth: when your brother died, it almost destroyed our marriage."

Dex held his mother's hand and absorbed that flood of information. The silence in the art room was so profound that he thought he could hear his watch ticking in his pocket, hear his heartbeat, possibly even his mother's heartbeat.

"I had no idea," he said finally. "I always assumed . . ." The story he'd concocted years ago as the reason for his father's deep love for his mother was complete and utter fiction. "Thank you for telling me."

"Does it answer your question?"

"I think so." But just to be absolutely certain, he said: "So men like me—like Father—who are frippery and lighthearted instead of serious . . . we *can* still love deeply?"

"Of course you can. You may not be serious, but you both have a gift for being happy, and for making others happy, too. The world needs people like you, just as it needs men like your uncle, Ace."

Dex didn't completely agree with that statement—surely wisdom and profundity were more valuable to the world than levity?—but he felt considerably more optimistic than he had when he'd sat down on the sun-faded art room settee.

"May I ask who she is? Do I know her?"

"Eloïse Fortrose."

His mother blinked in surprise. Her expression became a little dubious. "Lady Fortrose?"

"Do you not like her?"

His mother hesitated, and said, "I've scarcely spoken to her, but from what I've seen, her nature is very different to yours."

"Very different," Dex agreed. "She's not like me at all. She's . . ." How to describe Eloïse Fortrose in a way that did her justice? "She doesn't put on airs or simper and she's never missish. She's quick-witted and unconventional and she likes to laugh. She's very forthright, very matter-of-fact, and she stands up for herself, stands up to *me*." She'd persuaded him to try riding St. George, had challenged him to test his assumptions, and he'd discovered a facet of himself that he'd had no suspicion existed—not that *that* was a topic he was going to discuss with his mother. "She is rather reserved and private, but once you get to know her, she's not at all. She's open and warm and kind and *fun*." And, now that he thought of it, Eloïse Fortrose's reserve was probably due to the secrets

Blake and the comtesse—now Madame Blake—were hiding, as much as anything.

And on the subject of secrets . . .

"She knows about my magic." He spilled the story out: Wimbledon Heath and the highwaymen, the invitation to take tea, the cross-examination, his divulgence of the great family secret.

His mother's expression grew grave. "Does your grandfather know about this?"

Dex grimaced. "I'm seeing him after I've spoken to you."

His mother patted his hand sympathetically. "He won't lose his temper. He never does."

"No, but he'll be disappointed, and he'll be right to be—I *was* foolish and I *did* show off and now three people know our secret!" Dex huffed out a breath, annoyed with himself for being so cocky that night on Wimbledon Heath. "But Eloïse won't tell anyone. I trust her completely. And the Blakes, too. They're good people. Unusual, but good."

"Unusual how?"

Dex shook his head. "If I marry her, then you'll see for yourself. And if not . . . then it doesn't matter, does it?"

"You've decided, then?" his mother asked, her expression still grave. "You'll ask her?"

Had he decided? "I think so, yes. But she's given no indication that she'll welcome my suit. I'm not exactly the best of catches."

"Nonsense. You're an excellent catch."

Dex shook his head again. Not everyone wanted to marry a fribble, however good-looking and well-connected he was. Eloïse Fortrose might be of the opinion that he made a good lover, but not a good husband. "I think she's the one for me, but I might not be the one for her."

"Then it will be her loss."

Dex grinned at her wryly. "Cold comfort, Mother."

She laughed, and embraced him. "I wish you luck, darling."

"Thank you." He hugged her back.

"Was that all you wished to speak with me about?"

"Yes." Dex climbed to his feet. "Now I have to confess to Grandfather." But that encounter on Wimbledon Heath had led to his liaison with Eloïse Fortrose, so while he might regret his mistakes, he didn't wish them undone.

His mother returned to her easel and the *fritallaria imperialis*. Dex headed for the door, his stride buoyant. Fribbles *could* love deeply and enduringly. His mother had told him so, therefore it must be true.

A footman stood in the corridor.

"Are you waiting for me?"

"Yes, sir. Mr. Brockmole said not to disturb you."

Dex was grateful for that courtesy.

"The duke will see you in his sitting room, sir."

"Now?"

"Any time between four and five, sir."

Dex pulled out his pocket watch. The time was seven minutes past four. "Is the marquis with him, do you know?"

"He is, sir, and your father."

Dex stuffed the watch back in its pocket. "Thank you, Basil."

He turned left and went down one flight of winding stone stairs. He wasn't looking forward to confessing to the sins of cockiness, showing off, and revealing family secrets, but his stride was still buoyant as he navigated the warren of corridors that led to the duke's private sitting room.

CHAPTER 25

The Duke of Linwood's private sitting room was a comfortable space that managed to be both masculine and cozy, all dark polished wood, soft brown leather, and plum red damask. The room was the duke's den, his sanctum, his retreat, a place of gentle conversations and quiet contentment. Whenever Dex set foot in it, he had a sense of shedding his burdens, a feeling that the world slowed its hectic pace, that troubles and worries and disappointments couldn't intrude. Which was silly. Of course troubles, worries, and disappointments could intrude. He was bringing all three into the sitting room right now.

Maximus Pryor, Duke of Linwood, was ensconced in his favorite armchair. His heir, Primus—Ace to family and friends; the Marquis of Stanaway if one was being formal—had chosen an armchair, too. Dex's father Secundus—Deuce—lounged on a sofa. The men Dex needed to confess his mistakes to. His grandfather because he was head of the family, his uncle because he was the duke's representative in all matters, and his father because . . . well, because he was his father.

All three men held glasses, sherry, by the looks of it.

"Dex!" his father cried, putting down his glass and leaping to his feet. "Good to see you, my boy."

He embraced Dex enthusiastically, clapped him heartily on the back, and bounded across to the sideboard and the array of decanters lined up there. His hair was salt-and-pepper, but his figure hadn't thickened and he still had the energy of men half his age.

Dex greeted his grandfather, shaking his hand and bending to kiss the old man's cheek. He always kissed the duke's cheek. His grandfather was in his eighties, still as sharp as a tack, but increasingly frail. Who knew how long he had left to live? This might be the last time Dex ever saw him, so . . . always a kiss on the cheek.

He didn't kiss his uncle's cheek; he shook his hand. "I hope you're well, Uncle Ace?"

Dex's father returned and presented him with a glass. Dex took a grateful sip. It was the very best of sherries, pale strawgold, light and dry and with a lingering taste of almonds.

"You wish to speak with us about something?" his grandfather said.

"Yes, sir. I know I could have written, but . . . I wanted to tell you face to face."

"It's serious, I take it?" his uncle said.

"I've dealt with it, but yes, it could have been." Dex took another fortifying sip of sherry and put the glass down. He didn't sit. "I don't know whether you heard, but I had an encounter with highwaymen back in September."

He launched into a description of the events on Wimbledon Heath. He found himself almost acting it out, striding to and fro, gesticulating wildly. When the last highwayman had run off into the dark, his father broke into enthusiastic clapping. "Bravo, my boy. Bravo!"

"Thank you, Father, but you're premature in your applause." Dex took a deep breath, exhaled gustily, and continued with his confession: "Lady Fortrose and her companions were less distracted by the highwaymen than I'd thought. Even though it was dark they saw enough to make them suspect my magic."

His audience's expressions grew grave as he recounted

what had come next. Even his father acquired a furrowed brow and pursed lips when Dex described the exchange of secrets in Eloïse Fortrose's parlor. "They won't tell anyone. I trust them implicitly."

"What is the comtesse's secret?" his grandfather asked.

"I can't tell you, sir, any more than I could tell them what your magic is, or Uncle Ace's or Father's."

Since his grandfather's magic was the ability to hear lies, Dex knew the old man could hear he was telling the truth.

"I swear that her secret's not terrible—she's done nothing to harm anyone. She's a grand old lady. I think you'd love her, if you met her. And Blake, too. They're delightfully odd and the very best of people."

Three pairs of dark brown eyes appraised him gravely.

"I know I made a mull of things and I know it was my own fault—showing off!—but they won't tell anyone. I *swear* it."

The duke and the marquis exchanged a glance. "I'd feel safer if I could meet them," Dex's uncle said, which Dex had anticipated.

"I'd prefer to meet them, too," Dex's grandfather said, with a frown. Dex had also anticipated that answer, and the frown. Now that he was in his eighties, the duke no longer traveled to London. If he wished to speak with Eloïse Fortrose and the Blakes, they would have to come to him.

"Of course you should meet them, Grandfather—and once you *hear* them say they won't tell anyone, you'll know our secret's safe!—and perhaps they will come to Linwood Castle soon, because . . . I intend to ask Lady Fortrose to marry me."

A stunned silence met this declaration.

"She might say no!" Dex said hastily. "She might not wish to marry me, but . . . she might, and then you'll meet her and the Blakes—the comtesse and Blake married last month, by the way—and if Eloïse comes to Linwood, they will, too, because they're as close to her as family—and I'll tell them you can hear lies, Grandfather, and that they have to be truthful here, and you'll learn their secrets just as soon as you meet them, because their secrets are—well, I can't tell you what they are, but they're not *bad* secrets, just the sort of secrets that one doesn't want anyone else to know. Like our secret."

He stumbled to a halt. His audience looked rather bemused by the avalanche of words. Dex gulped down the last of his sherry and gave them time to unpack what he'd said. He was trying to unpack it all, too. Had he really blurted out that he wanted to marry Eloïse Fortrose?

Before embarrassment could set in, Dex's uncle said, "I hadn't planned on going to town just yet. Perhaps it can wait. What do you think, Father? Deuce?"

Dex's father replied first: "It's already been, what, a couple of months?"

Dex nodded confirmation.

"What's another couple of months?" his father said with a shrug of his eyebrows, a shrug of his shoulders.

"I suppose I can wait another month or two before speaking to Lady Fortrose and her companions," the marquis said slowly.

"I can't speak to them unless they come here," the old duke said. "Which they may soon do if someone's suit prospers." He tipped his head slightly and sent Dex a glance that was sidelong and almost impish. For a fleeting moment, his resemblance to Dex's father was strong.

Dex felt a blush rise in his cheeks. "She may refuse me, sir."

"If she does, she's a fool!" his father declared.

"She's not a fool, but she may wish for a steadier husband."

His father gestured at the marquis. "Like old sobersides, here? How boring!" There was no animosity in the jibe; it was said with a grin and a wink.

The marquis rolled his eyes, but didn't rise to the bait; he merely sipped his sherry and said, "So we'll leave it a couple of months? If Lady Fortrose and her companions don't pay us a visit by the end of the year, I'll speak with them in London. Agreed?"

"Agreed," the duke said.

"I'll come with you," Dex's father announced. "I want to meet this woman. Especially if she refuses my son. I'll have a good word with her! Make her change her mind."

"Father, don't you dare!" Belatedly, Dex spotted the glint in his father's eye. The old rascal was teasing him. "You're a dashed loose fish," he grumbled.

"From the moment I was born," his father agreed.

"That's the truth," the duke said, rather dryly.

"It most certainly is," the marquis said, in a tone of great long-suffering. He downed the last of his sherry, fetched the decanter, and refilled everyone's glasses.

At last, Dex felt able to sit. The atmosphere in the sitting room seemed to change, to ease and to soften. It became a place of cozy contentment again, a place where worries retreated and the world slowed down.

*C*HAPTER 26

*D*inner was informal and relaxed, a family meal, people talking across the table and serving themselves, no footmen or butler hovering in attendance. Phoebe wasn't there. Dex's cousin, Octavius, and his new wife had taken her down to Dorset with them, which Dex was pleased about—it was splendid that Fleabee was no longer the only young female in the family, splendid that she and Pip had become bosom friends—but he was sorry, too; he hadn't seen his sister since August and he missed her.

As family dinners went, this was a relatively quiet one. Of the Numbers—as the *ton* called the Pryor males—only one, two, five, nine, and ten were present. Dex's uncle, Tertius, and his wife were in Derbyshire, his cousin Sextus was in Westmorland, and Octavius was in Dorset. His uncle, Mercury, who'd escaped the numerical nomenclature, wasn't there, and neither was Mercury's companion, Jack, but despite all those absences, it was a cheerful, almost rowdy, table.

Dex was reminded of dining at the house on Old Burlington Street; Blake weaving tall stories and cracking jokes, the comtesse—Madame Blake now—interposing droll utterances, Phillip chiming in eagerly, Eloïse watching it all with a smile in her eyes and dimples peeking in her cheeks, offering the occasional dry comment and turning pink with pleasure when she made the others laugh.

A pang of homesickness stabbed him just below his breast-bone, even though Linwood Castle was a thousand times more his home than the house on Old Burlington Street. He missed that house, though, missed its bright walls and bright carpets and bright curtains, its flamboyant furniture, the vivid reds and oranges and yellows, the vibrant greens and blues—but most of all he missed the people.

They'd fit in well at this table, Eloïse and the Blakes and young Phillip. He could imagine Blake entertaining everyone with stories of the stage and tales of pretending to be this baron or that count. He could imagine Madame Blake lowering her façade of aristocratic dignity and allowing her real self to peek through, mischievous and a little earthy. He could imagine Phillip, the only child at the table, but far from alone, blossoming under the attention of so many new aunts and uncles like a plant given water and sunshine.

And he could imagine Eloïse seated beside him. She'd be one of the quieter people present, more of an observer like Sextus than a loud gabster like Nonus—who was about to knock over a decanter of particularly fine claret.

"Careful, you muttonhead," Dex said, righting the decanter with his magic before it could spill its precious contents over the beef tremblant and the grenadine of duck.

Nonus—Ned, as he insisted on being called—grinned, unrepentant, and helped himself to another serving of partridge.

Dex moved the decanter out of Ned's reach. Did he really want to introduce Eloïse to his gigantic idiot of a cousin?

Yes. Yes, he did. He wanted to introduce her to everyone, wanted her to see them for who they were beneath the ducal mantle that most people never bothered to look past—and he wanted them to see her, to realize that she wasn't frosty at all and that her inner colors were as vibrant as the gowns she wore.

After dinner, rather than the ladies withdrawing to drink tea and the men staying at the table to toss back glasses of port and brandy, they all trooped into one of the smaller drawing rooms and continued their many conversations—until Dex's cousin, Quintus, said, "What's this I hear about a ruckus with highwaymen?"

Ned came to alert like a hunting dog. "Highwaymen? Do tell!"

Dex was more than willing to obey this behest. But first, he levitated one of the Windsor chairs to in front of the door, tilting it so that its high wooden back tucked neatly under the handle, preventing any servants from entering and discovering the family secret.

The door secured, he reprised his rôle as raconteur, acting out the tale to his relatives, only this time, when he tiptoed up to the beleaguered coach (which was the sofa upon which his mother and his aunt sat) and snatched the first highwayman from his horse, he plucked Ned from the armchair in which he was sprawled and whisked him up to dangle beneath the high, intricately molded ceiling.

"And hung him in a tree!" Dex proclaimed, over Ned's surprised yelp.

His uncle uttered a very un-marquis-like yap of laughter—then flicked a glance at the door. When he saw the chair holding it shut, he relaxed.

"Put me down!" Ned squawked indignantly, so Dex did, setting him carefully on the floor before continuing with his tale: "Then I crept around the carriage and punched one of the highwaymen and knocked him clear across the road, into the ditch."

He tiptoed around the sofa and mimed a great punch—and used his magic to lift Ned off his feet again, swooping his cousin backwards across the room, over sofas and armchairs, settees and tables.

This time, Ned didn't yelp; he shouted, "Huzza!"

Dex's uncle didn't glance at the door, but his grandfather did, and Quintus. They, too, relaxed when they saw the chair.

Dex set Ned down in front of the fireplace.

"Oi!" Ned protested loudly, but he was grinning, so Dex decided that his cousin didn't mind being part of the story.

"The toby tried to jump on his horse, so I gave him a bit of a hand . . ."

He sent Ned up and over a high-backed armchair in a gigantic standing leap.

Ned shouted another loud, "Huzza!"

The duke began to chortle. Alongside him on the sofa, Dex's silver-haired grandmother, the Duchess of Linwood, giggled and set her teacup aside.

"That poor highwayman," Dex said sadly, shaking his head. "He just could *not* get on his horse."

A twitch of his magic and Ned leaped over the armchair again. "Huzza!"

And again. "Huzza!"

Dex's audience was laughing uncontrollably by now, even Ned, who was hooting like a maniac.

Dex grinned at them all and recounted what happened next, using Ned to pantomime the last, reeling punch. Then he sent his cousin on a careening circuit of the parlor, plunging over chairs and tables, mimicking the hapless highwaymen fleeing into the night, although the highwaymen had been silent and Ned was whooping loudly enough to wake the dead.

His tale concluded, Dex bounced on his toes and surveyed his wheezing, red-faced, wet-eyed audience, feeling prodigiously pleased with himself. There were few things better in life than making people laugh.

He regretted that his sister hadn't witnessed the performance, or his cousins Octavius and Sextus, but he could always repeat it at Christmas, when they all gathered at Linwood Castle to see in the new year.

And perhaps the Pryor family would have grown by then. Perhaps he'd have a wife.

Dex dared to hope for a few seconds, dared to dream.

People caught their breaths. Handkerchiefs emerged to wipe faces. Reviving cups of tea were drunk. Calm returned to the drawing room.

Dex's aunt tenderly felt her ribs. "I haven't laughed that much in a long time."

Dex smirked, feeling very smug. He couldn't help strutting a little, couldn't help preening a little. "It's a hardship being so heroic and so talented," he told Quintus and Ned loftily.

Quintus ignored this utterance, but Ned gave a start, held up one finger as if he'd just had a thought, and rushed from the room with a great *thud-thud-thud* of his huge clodhoppery feet.

Dex and Quintus exchanged a glance and a shrug.

Ned returned half an hour later. "Dex, Quin, come with me," he said, seizing them both by a wrist and hauling them up to standing.

"Why?" asked Quintus, and "Where?" asked Dex, but Ned just said, "Come and see."

So they went and saw.

The object of their perusal was in one of the smaller parlors. Dex studied it in the scant and flickering light of the single lit candelabrum in the room, and turned to Ned, perplexed. "A sofa table?"

"A *rosewood* sofa table!"

The wood was cinnamon brown with darker veins, so yes, probably rosewood, but Dex wasn't certain why that was worth noting. He felt his brow pucker. "And that's significant because . . . ?"

"Because we're the Knights of the Rosewood Sofa Table! Don't you remember? It was Otto's idea. We use our magic to right wrongs!"

Vague memory stirred. Octavius asking earnestly whether any of them had ever considered using their magic to help others; Ned turning it into a joke.

"You used your magic to give three highwaymen the right-about; therefore, you deserve an honor!"

"You mean . . . a knighthood of the, er, the rosewood sofa table?"

Ned batted this suggestion aside with one hand. "Of course not. We're already knights of the rosewood sofa table."

They were? As far as Dex remembered, all it had ever been was a joke.

"Now you need to be decorated!"

"Decorated? As what?"

"As a *hero* of the rosewood sofa table!" Ned declared triumphantly.

Dex had learned years ago that it was easier to go along with Ned in whatever nonsense he was set on than to try to talk him out of it. "Very well. But if I'm to be decorated, then Otto should be, too, for what he did to Rumpole."

Ned batted that suggestion aside, too. "Later," he said, turning away and then swinging back, a long rapier in his hand.

Dex took a prudent step backwards. Ned and swords weren't a good combination.

Ned clambered up onto the rosewood sofa table. Octavius wasn't there to say, "No shoes on the table," so Quintus did it for him: "No shoes on the table."

Ned ignored him. "Come along!" he said, with an imperative gesture.

"What? You mean . . . up on that table?"

"Of course!"

"It'll collapse." Dex eyed the straining table. As sofa tables went, it was moderately large, with frieze drawers along each side and flaps at either end that hadn't been extended. It was perfectly designed to write letters upon or to store half-read magazines in, not for lumbering louts to use as a stage. "I'm astonished it hasn't already."

"Nonsense. It's a sturdy thing. See?" Ned gave a little jump.

The table swayed and creaked.

186

Dex winced, waiting for it to disintegrate. It didn't, but he had no doubt it would if he joined Ned atop that precarious perch. Those four slender legs could only hold so much weight. "I'll stay on the floor," he said firmly. "You can knight me from up there."

"Decorate you," Ned corrected.

Dex rolled his eyes. "Decorate me." He stepped closer.

Ned flourished the rapier aloft. Dex braced himself, trying—and failing—not to wince as the weapon slapped against first one shoulder and then the other. The wince wasn't because he thought Ned would deliberately skewer him, but because Ned was an abysmal swordsman. "Vigor and no finesse" perfectly described his fencing style.

"I, Nonus Pryor, Knight of the Rosewood Sofa Table, pronounce you, Decimus Pryor, to be a Hero of the Rosewood Sofa Table!"

It was the ideal opportunity to strut and preen and puff out his chest, to play up to the spectacle of the moment, but Dex found himself ducking his head and blushing instead.

Ned held the rapier out to Quintus, pommel-first. "Peon, take this sword!"

Quintus, who was an earl, rolled his eyes and stepped forward to take the rapier. Not for the first time, Dex wondered whether Ned noticed that he went through life surrounded by people rolling their eyes.

"Step closer, hero," Ned intoned. They were all of them tall, but Ned was the tallest, fully six foot six, and burly to match. Atop the table, he towered like a giant.

Dex exchanged a glance and a shrug with Quintus and stepped closer.

"Your hero's medal!" Ned pulled something from his pocket with a flourish. It looked like a loop of twine with a round silver pendant threaded onto it. "Bow your head, hero."

Dex did as requested. The twine slipped over his head.

Ned jumped down from the table with a thud that made the nearest vase wobble. The ceremony was clearly over.

Dex examined his hero's medal in the feeble candlelight. "Is this . . . a button?"

"Yes. It has a rose on it. See? For rosewood! Clever, ain't it?" Ned smirked smugly.

The smirk was rather familiar. Dex had seen it in his own mirror often enough.

"Wherever did you get it?" Quintus asked.

"Came off one of my court ensembles," Ned said, taking the rapier from Quintus.

One of his hideously expensive court ensembles. Ned's valet would doubtless utter several profanities when he discovered that desecration.

They left the small parlor and headed for the room where the weapons were stored, Ned carrying the rapier, Quintus the candelabrum, and Dex his silver hero's button.

"I've been thinking," Ned said, as they ambled along the candlelit corridors.

"Always dangerous," Quintus muttered.

"That costume you found in the attic in town—"

"No," Quintus said firmly.

"But—"

"No. We are absolutely *not* resurrecting the Ghostly Cavalier."

Ned pouted. "But it would be so much fun!"

"And very wrong of us," Quintus said.

"You're such an old sobersides," Ned told him.

The comment reminded Dex so strongly of his father and uncle that afternoon that it felt as if time doubled up on itself, past and present overlaying one another for a few seconds.

"I'm not a sobersides; I'm just sensible!" Quintus protested, although, in fact, he was quite as much of a sobersides as his father. Dex didn't hold it against him, though. He'd always thought that it would be impossible not to be a sobersides if one were born an earl and would one day become a marquis and eventually a duke. It was a monstrous weight of responsibility to have looming over one.

Ned swung to face Dex. "Tell him, Dex! We *have* to resurrect the ghost! We could roam all over London—a glimpse here, a glimpse there. It'd be devilish good fun!"

Ned was correct: it would be devilish good fun to tease the *ton* with sightings of the Ghostly Cavalier. Unfortunately, Dex felt obliged to side with Quintus. Being a voice of reason wasn't a rôle he was used to playing, but . . . "You know that Grandfather wouldn't like it."

Ned reeled back dramatically and pressed the hand not holding the rapier to his breast. "*Et tu, Brute?*"

Honestly, how many times a day did he roll his eyes when he was in Ned's company?

"He forbade our fathers," Quintus said, somewhat pompously. "You know he'd forbid us, too."

Ned dropped the rapier with a clatter and clapped his hands over his ears. "I can't hear you!" he sang. "La-la-la-la-la!"

Dex and Quintus exchanged another glance, another eye-roll.

"A drink?" Dex suggested.

"A drink," Quintus agreed.

They turned and headed for the drawing room, leaving the gigantic idiot that was their cousin singing *la-la-la* in the corridor. "I asked around," Quintus said, as they walked. "Rhodes Garland's oldest boy, Melrose, is seven."

"Is he?" Rhodes Garland was currently the Marquis of Thane, but one day he'd succeed to a dukedom, just like Quintus—and like Quintus, he was sober, serious, and conscientious.

"They're in Staffordshire right now, won't be back in town until the new year, but he's looking to hire a tutor then. He'd be open to someone sharing lessons with Melrose—if the boys hit it off."

Phillip sharing lessons with Rhodes Garland's son? That would establish him in the very best of circles.

"Tell me about this Blake. Who is he?"

"No one you'll find in *Debrett's Peerage*. He's a capital fellow, though. One of the best."

Quintus sent him a sidelong glance. "You vouch for him? And for the boy?"

"Unreservedly."

Quintus accepted this with a nod.

They arrived at the drawing room. The door stood ajar. Lamplight and the murmur of familiar voices spilled into the corridor.

"Brandy?" Dex said.

"Brandy," Quintus agreed.

*C*HAPTER 27

*E*lla's heart had been golden and rosy and sunshiny for long enough that it felt familiar, but not so long that she didn't still pause every day to rejoice in it.

What color is my heart today? she asked her reflection in the mirror that morning, and the answer was that her heart held all the colors of dawn, blushing pinks, soft golds, and glowing oranges.

Her heart didn't feel like something made of muscle and blood. It felt like a rose. A rose that had come into full bloom, basking in warm sunshine with its petals spread joyously wide.

Hedgepeth sang under her breath while she tidied the dressing table, a tune that Ella hummed on her way down the stairs. The breakfast parlor was warm and cozy, brimming with scent and sound. She paused in the doorway and took it all in: the dark, rich fragrances of coffee and chocolate, the sweet smell of pastry and the spiciness of kedgeree, the deeper aromas of eggs and meat, the clatter of cutlery and burble of a cup being filled, rain pattering against the windowpanes, Phillip's chatter as he attacked the sausages on his plate, the rumble of Arthur's reply from the sideboard, where he stood pondering the eggs and the sirloin.

How fortunate she was, how blessed, that this was her life.

Phillip looked up from his sausages. A smile lit his face. "Good morning, Aunt Ella!"

Ella felt an answering smile brighten her own face, felt the rose in her chest bloom a little more fully. "Good morning."

After breakfast, they decamped to the library, which had become their favorite place to spend a rainy day, not merely because of the wide fireplace and the mellow burgundy-colored walls, the hundreds of books and the pianoforte, but because the library was where the maps and the globes were, the dissected geography puzzles, the wooden building blocks, the huge foolscap sheets of paper, the pencils and pens and paints, the toy theater and the puppets, until it was as much playroom as library, a place where they all loved to be, adults and child alike.

Phillip headed for the picture he was coloring in, Arthur for the fireplace and the morning's newspapers, and Minette for the pianoforte, an instrument she had learned to play when she'd set aside her dancing shoes and assumed the persona of Comtesse de Villiers.

Ella enjoyed playing the pianoforte as much as she enjoyed embroidery, which was to say not at all. As a daughter and a wife, she'd devoted hours of her day to both pursuits. Dutiful, painstaking hours. As a widow, she listened to Minette play and did no needlework at all. She'd replaced both of those activities with reading. Her father and Francis had restricted her access to books, deeming novels dangerous to the female mind and too much knowledge unnecessary. It gave her great pleasure to spend the money they'd left her—Francis's sizable jointure, her father's more modest legacy—on the silliest and most shocking of novels and on publications that stretched her understanding of the world.

She didn't feel like reading right at this moment, though. She wandered around the library to the sound of Bach's suites, running her fingers along gilded spines, pausing to gaze out the rain-speckled window, idly setting the globe spinning, enjoying the happiness and contentment in the library, the joy of knowing that this room, these people, this *life*, were hers.

As Ella wandered, she found traces of Decimus Pryor. Arthur had purchased the wooden skittle soldiers and the flat pewter ones, but it was Pryor who'd suggested embellishing the uniforms with polka dots and stripes and who'd sat for all of one rainy afternoon helping Phillip do just that. The pair of them had decorated the counters used to play backgammon and lottery tickets, too. Not the mother-of-pearl counters—they were too beautiful to need any enhancement—but the round wooden ones and the ones made of bone and shaped like fish.

She picked a fish counter up and turned it over in her fingers. Someone had daubed it with indigo and teal paint and then added a scattering of tiny pink scales. The work was too delicately done to be Phillip's, which meant that Pryor had painted this particular counter—a realization that prompted another of the annoying little pangs of longing that had plagued her yesterday and the day before, and that clearly intended to plague her today, too.

Ella put the counter down with a brisk little *click*. Decimus Pryor was her lover and her friend, but he didn't live in this house, he wasn't a member of her family, and she refused to pine for him while he was in Gloucestershire.

She continued her circumnavigation of the library, but everywhere she looked she saw traces of Pryor. The wooden blocks were courtesy of him, as was the delightful pocket globe that so fascinated Phillip and the dissected geographical puzzles. Pryor was responsible for the stack of foolscap paper, too—a stack so thick that Ella had been certain it would take a full year to get through, but which was already more than half gone, because Decimus Pryor loved drawing quite as much as Phillip did—a thought that provoked yet another of those little pangs and the feeling that something—someone—integral was missing from the library.

Ella shook her head in annoyance and continued her perambulations.

Examples of Pryor's work were everywhere. Maps of make-believe lands populated with dragons and oceans teeming with sea monsters. Outlines of sailing ships and castles and winged horses for Phillip to color in. And caricatures. Dozens of caricatures.

Caricatures of Arthur, of Minette, of Phillip, of Ella, even some of Pryor himself, each person laughably ludicrous and instantly recognizable.

Minette had been wrong all those weeks ago. If Pryor hadn't come into the world shod and hosed and with a golden spoon in his mouth, he wouldn't have been an actor, he'd have been an artist. Not a Hogarth or a Gainsborough, but a Rowlandson or Gillray, someone who lampooned public figures and whose drawings were pinned up in shop windows for a delighted populace to view.

In addition to the make-believe maps, the winged horses and the castles, the caricatures, Pryor had drawn more serious things. Alphabet cards to help Phillip learn his letters. Copies of illustrations from encyclopedias. Phillip was coloring in one such illustration now, the tip of his tongue caught between his teeth as he concentrated on staying within the lines.

Ella pulled out a chair and sat opposite him. Phillip looked up and grinned at her.

Ella grinned back. "What are you coloring in?"

Phillip explained eagerly, telling her all about eggs and caterpillars and chrysalises, and how a butterfly's wings were small and wrinkled at first and it had to wait until its wings were strong enough to fly.

Ella hadn't known that last fact. She fetched Swiffen's *Cyclopaedia* and they read the entry on butterflies together. *I was that caterpillar,* Ella thought. *I was in that chrysalis. I am that butterfly now.*

Phillip had colored his caterpillar yellow and red and blue; the caterpillar that Ella had been in her father's house, and later in her husband's, had been the dullest, drabbest, most fading-away shade of pale gray.

Phillip's chrysalis was bright green with orange spots; Ella's chrysalis had been the black of widowhood.

Phillip had colored one wing of his butterfly. It was violet and turquoise and yellow.

That is me now, Ella thought. *I am color and freedom.*

She closed the *Cyclopaedia* and put it aside. Phillip set to work coloring the second wing of his butterfly. Ella shuffled through the caricatures, looking for one to color in. Arthur as a stork with extremely knobbly knees and a tailcoat? Empress Minette atop a throne, her hair in a towering coiffure reminiscent of fashions fifty years ago? Phillip as a bumble bee? Or—

She stopped, arrested by a sketch she'd not seen before. Herself in a ballgown, wearing a masquerade mask and with large, outspread butterfly wings.

When had Pryor drawn it?

How had he known she was a butterfly?

"May I color this one?" she asked Phillip.

"Of course!" He gave her a beaming smile and went back to his work, a study in concentration: brow furrowed, tip of his tongue once again caught between his teeth.

Ella's heart seemed to clench a little and then to expand again, an emotion she recognized as maternal love, even though Phillip wasn't her son and she would never be a mother. But it didn't matter whether she'd given birth to Phillip or not. She could love him just as fiercely as any mother, and protect him just as fiercely, too.

Ella watched him in silence, loving his focus, his concentration, loving *him,* and then she looked down at the drawing she'd chosen. Herself, as a butterfly.

How had Pryor *known*?

He hadn't, was the answer. He couldn't possibly know. No one did. It was a good guess, that was all. A perfect guess.

Ella set to work coloring herself as brightly as possible. When the door to the library opened, she didn't look up, too immersed in pinks and yellows and oranges.

Phillip uttered a wordless shout.

Ella leaped in her seat, heart beating wildly. Across the table from her, Phillip scrambled from his chair. "Mister Dex!"

Ella turned hastily.

There, in the library doorway, was Decimus Pryor, back from whatever errand had taken him to Gloucestershire.

She watched Phillip run to him, watched Phillip hug him exuberantly, watched Pryor swing the boy up and then set him on his feet again, both of them laughing.

No one rebuked Phillip for the shout; everyone in this house was united on that front. Exuberance should never be squashed, delight never crushed, and children should never be scolded for expressing joy.

Ella wanted to express her joy, too, wanted to run to Pryor and hug him. It was an urge, an ache, almost a need. Now that her heart no longer beat madly with fright, it felt as if it was blooming more fully, petals turning a deeper shade of happiness.

She might be a butterfly, but her heart was a rose.

Ella tutted under her breath. What idiotic flights of fancy she had.

"I'm *so* glad you're back, sir!" Phillip declared.

"I'm glad to be back." Pryor's grin encompassed the library: Arthur by the fire, Minette at the pianoforte, Ella at the table.

His gaze came to rest on her in a brief moment of shared connection. Ella felt her cheeks grow warm, felt the foolish rose that was her heart bloom even more fully.

Phillip captured Pryor's hand and tugged him towards the table. "Come see what I've done, Mister Dex!"

Pryor spent several minutes looking through the pictures Phillip had worked on during the last four days, the ones he'd drawn, the ones he'd colored in, offering praise and encouragement; then he came around the table and took the chair alongside Ella. Her heart seemed to give a sigh as he sat. Not a sigh of melancholy, but one of contentment.

Pryor smiled at her. Not his rake's smile, but something warmer and friendlier. Ella knew that her own smile was the same. Her pleasure in seeing him wasn't sexual. She didn't want to grasp his hand and drag him up the stairs to her bedroom;

196

she wanted to sit alongside him in the library, basking in his nearness like a cat basking in the warmth of a cozy fire.

Pryor leaned close to see what she was working on and uttered a low laugh. "You're coloring a butterfly, too."

Ella didn't tell him that she *was* a butterfly. "I like butter-flies," she said. Her cheeks still felt flushed with color and her heart was flushed with color, too, the petals turning a rosier shade of pink.

"I'll draw some more then, shall I?"

They set to work, all three of them, Phillip and she coloring, Pryor drawing, while Minette meandered through more of Bach's compositions, Arthur read by the fire, and rain tapped against the windowpanes. It was peaceful and cozy and companionable, domestic and ordinary and unexciting—and somehow, because of those things, it was also perfectly idyllic.

After luncheon, Ella, Phillip, and Pryor visited the mews behind the Duke of Linwood's townhouse on Hanover Square. Or rather, they visited the six-week-old kittens who lived in the stables. It was Ella's fifth visit to the mews, and perhaps it wasn't quite proper for dowager viscountesses to climb up into haylofts, but she didn't care about such things. Not when there were kittens to be played with. She discarded her bonnet and gloves, scrambled up the ladder with as much alacrity as Phillip, and crawled through hay that smelled of long ago summers. Down below in the stables, lanterns cast warm pools of light, but up here it was twilight. Rain drummed on the slate roof overhead, almost drowning out the rustle of hay and the *peep-peep-peep* of kittens.

"I see them!" Phillip said in an excited whisper.

They approached at a snail's pace, then lay on their stomachs while still several yards from the kittens.

The mother cat eyed them for a second, flicked an ear, and resumed grooming her offspring.

Ella watched, entranced. Everything about the kittens was fascinating—the way they submitted to that rough grooming, the way they clambered over one another in single-minded pursuit of their mother's nipples, the way they fell asleep while still suckling. How, when they weren't suckling or sleeping, they were endlessly active, endlessly curious, exploring their domain on legs that became stronger and sturdier with each passing day.

She loved that sometimes the kittens tiptoed with wary caution and at other times they hurtled madly about the hayloft, performing acrobatic leaps and ambushing one another, backs arched and tails sticking up like little furry exclamation marks.

She loved that the kittens had come to recognize them as friends and playmates. She loved that their fur was as soft as down and their teeth and claws as sharp as needles. She loved their round, plump little bellies. She loved the wild bursts of activity and equally sudden collapses into angelic sleepiness. She loved the rapid pitter-patter of their heartbeats and the purring thrum of their contentment.

"Puss, puss, puss," Phillip called softly.

The mother cat's ears twitched and two of the kittens noticed that they had playmates.

Ella stretched out an arm and turned her hand palm-up. She wiggled her fingers enticingly.

Alongside her, Phillip did the same.

Naturally the kittens came to investigate, sniffing their hands and batting at their fingers with clumsy, needle-edged paws. Ella saw delight on Phillip's face, the same delight that she felt.

Not for the first time since Pryor had introduced them to this ducal hayloft, she asked herself why it had taken her so long to realize that she needed kittens in her life. Her father hadn't liked animals and neither had Francis, but why hadn't she acquired a kitten just as soon as she'd moved into the house on Old Burlington Street? Why had she waited for Phillip to arrive and for Decimus Pryor to ask among his grandfather's servants, before embarking on pet ownership? Why hadn't she done it herself, years ago?

A kitten clambered onto Ella's forearm, claws digging into her pelisse and quite likely ruining it. Not that Ella cared. The pelisse was an old one, as was her gown, and anyway, haylofts and kittens were more important than clothes. "Come and explore, little puss," she whispered.

As if it understood that invitation, the kitten set off determinedly for her shoulder.

It would be another fortnight before the kittens were old enough to leave their mother. Two were to stay in the ducal stables, destined for a career hunting rats and mice; their three siblings would relocate to Old Burlington Street. Ella was waiting for that moment as eagerly as Phillip. She imagined kittens climbing curtains, scampering over sofas, and launching ambushes from behind half-closed doors. She imagined them lying warmly in her lap, purring.

Kittens were adorable and fascinating and she needed them in her life just as much as she needed color.

Hay rustled behind her, not a kitten-rustle, but something much larger. She glanced back to see Decimus Pryor crawling to join them. He stretched out on his stomach alongside her. A kitten immediately set about investigating the enticing folds of his coat-tails. The coat was a much newer and more expensive garment than Ella's old pelisse, but Pryor made no move to redirect the kitten's attention. He looked back over his shoulder, watching the little creature, a small, indulgent smile on his mouth, then lifted his gaze to Ella. His eyes were black in the dim light, but it wasn't a predatory black; it was a black that matched his smile, warm and affectionate and surprisingly sweet.

Ella smiled back at him.

"Peep-peep-peep," said one of the kittens, but it wasn't

until it nipped her fingers with sharp teeth that Ella tore her gaze away from that smile.

This side of him was almost as unexpected as his magic. Who'd have thought that Decimus Pryor could smile like that, with such openness and sweetness and warmth? Who'd have thought he was the type of rake who spent hours drawing pictures for a child? The sort of dandy who crawled up into haylofts and let kittens play in the expensive folds of his tailcoat?

Ella certainly hadn't. If she'd thought about Pryor at all—which she rarely had before that night on Wimbledon Heath—she'd have assumed that the only reason he'd have for venturing into a hayloft would be to tup someone. A literal tumble in the hay.

She'd have been wrong.

She had been wrong about a lot of things with regard to Decimus Pryor. He had depths one didn't expect in rakes and dandies. He was surprisingly thoughtful, surprisingly good at giving gifts, and not merely gifts such as pocket globes and dissecting puzzles, but gifts of time.

The time it had taken to draw each and every one of those pictures.

The time it had taken to decorate the game counters.

The time it had taken to talk with his grandfather's servants, to discover this litter of kittens, to bring them here, not once, but five times.

Pryor could be drinking wine with his cronies right now, in whichever club he patronized; instead, he was lying in a dusty hayloft and letting a kitten explore the topography of his tailcoat.

Her offspring fed and groomed, the mother cat stalked off to attend to her own needs. Phillip set about making a cave in the hay. Two of the kittens thought this was a fine game. A third lay in Ella's cupped hand, belly-up, almost asleep. She stroked that round little belly, feeling the vibration of a purr through her fingertips. The purr wasn't merely the kitten's; it was her own purr as well, a hum in her blood, a resonance in her bones: happiness.

A fourth kitten was navigating Pryor's shoulder, claws determinedly digging into the superfine of his coat. Ella looked for the fifth kitten, but couldn't spot it. It was either exploring the loft or fast asleep somewhere.

Rain beat on the slates overheard, too loud for conversation, but Ella liked that, liked not talking, liked simply existing in the present. These were the sorts of moments that brought pure contentment. Not balls and soirées and visits to the theater, but this: kittens and hay and rain.

If she had Pryor's skill with a pen, she'd attempt to draw this scene, to preserve it forever. He would undoubtedly draw it for her if she asked—and she might just ask—but for now she set about capturing it in her memory. The sound of rain. The dusty late-summer scent of hay. The horse and leather smell of the stables. A faint hint of wet wool that probably came from Pryor's coat. The prickle of straw and the softness of the kitten's fur, the vibration of its purr in her hand. The play of shadow and light, the cozy, peaceful gloom. Phillip laughing. Pryor stretched out alongside her while a kitten navigated its way along the slope of his back.

Ella shuffled sideways, a few inches only, until her shoulder touched his. He gave her a quick, surprised glance before his face relaxed into another of those startlingly sweet smiles. He leaned closer, pressing their shoulders more firmly together. There was nothing flirtatious about the movement, just a sweet smile and a friendly press of shoulders that made a surprisingly perfect moment even more surprisingly perfect.

This man, whom she'd once dismissed as a peacock and a popinjay, had become one of her favorite people. He was more than her lover; he was her friend.

Ella didn't have many friends. She'd certainly never had one her own age before. Not as a child. Not as a wife. Not as a widow. But Pryor was her friend, and the press of his shoulder against hers warmed her in a way that wasn't sexual at all. It made her feel known. It made her feel *liked*.

Minette and Arthur knew and liked her. Her Aunt Clara had known and liked her. And now Pryor did.

Being liked was a thousand times more important than being desired. Ten thousand times more important. Desire was something one felt for a person's outside, their form and their shape: hands and nape of neck and the silly smirk you wanted to kiss off their lips. Desire was shallow and ephemeral, inconstant, volatile, here today and gone tomorrow. Friendship and liking however . . . those were what you felt for a person once you knew who they were on the *inside*. They took time and intimacy to build—not sexual intimacy, but the emotional intimacy of conversation and laughter and the sharing of confidences—and once the foundations had been set, they lasted. Not merely for days or for weeks, but for years. Forever.

Decimus Pryor fitted into her life as if he belonged there as much as Phillip and Arthur and Minette did.

Ella opened her mouth to say, *Let's make our liaison a long-term arrangement*—and closed it again. This wasn't the time or place, and not merely because Phillip was within earshot. Long-term was the sort of word that was too easily misunderstood. Pryor might think she meant marriage, he might take fright, take *flight*, and she wanted that as little as she wanted a husband.

An extension of their liaison until the end of winter . . . that was a proposal that surely wouldn't scare him off. And as spring approached, she'd suggest continuing until summer. Season by season they could keep each other company.

She would like that.

Pryor leaned even closer, the press of his shoulder against hers becoming firmer. "Would you still like a puppy?" he asked, his voice barely audible above the drum of rain on the slates overhead.

"Yes." Because puppies were undoubtedly something else that she hadn't known her life had been missing. "You've found one?"

"Possibly."

Ella tilted her head towards him. Their cheeks almost touched, an intimacy that wasn't at all erotic, a companionable closeness of the sort she'd never thought could exist between a man and a woman, let alone was something she could have. "Where?"

"Linwood Castle. The head gardener's dog is with pup. No saying how many there'll be or what they'll look like, but he says you're welcome to have one." Pryor drew back slightly. Something about the angle of his head, the way he studied her from beneath his lashes, made him look almost shy—which was a ridiculous notion. Decimus Pryor didn't have a shy bone in his body. It was the dim light making him look bashful and uncertain. "You and Phillip could come up to Gloucestershire and see them for yourselves . . . if you like?"

Ella suddenly felt shy herself. Visit Linwood Castle? She looked down at the kitten cupped in her hand. "We could do that, yes. Thank you."

The fifth kitten came pouncing out of nowhere, leaped onto Pryor's wrist and promptly got its claws tangled in his cuff. It thrashed and floundered, squeaking indignantly.

Pryor chuckled and detached the kitten, setting it free to scamper off again; then he leaned close and bumped his shoulder companionably against hers. "I'll write to the gardener, tell him we want one of the pups. It won't be until January, though. You may not wish to wait that long?"

"Oh, no," Ella said hastily. "January is perfectly fine."

A foolish blush heated her cheeks and a silly little smile crept to her lips.

Pryor was thinking long-term, too.

*C*HAPTER 28

*T*he three kittens made the move to their new home a fortnight later. They were confined to the smallest of the parlors until they learned what the box filled with sawdust was for. Once that leap of understanding had been made, their domain expanded.

The occasional accident occurred, but Arthur taught Ella and Phillip how to clean up the little puddles, saying that they didn't want the servants to find the kittens a bother, did they?

Ella most certainly did not want the servants to find the kittens a bother, because she didn't think she could go back to living in a house without rapscallion feline companions. She cleaned up puddles before the servants noticed they were even there, and watched the kittens explore their new home, curious and bold, clumsy and exuberant. She played with them and stroked them and coaxed them into her lap, feeling blessed whenever a kitten chose to purr for her, chose to sleep on her. November drew towards its close, damp and gray, but Ella's heart was filled with sunshine, because her life had Phillip in it, and Minette and Arthur. And kittens. And Decimus Pryor.

The kittens stopped having accidents and started sharpening their claws on the furniture. Pryor and Arthur put their heads together and came up with a solution for that: doormats of plaited rushes. Soon every room had a scratching mat and a box of sawdust. Every room also had pencils lost behind cushions and down the backs of sofas, pictures in the process of being drawn or colored in lying on tables, story books piled on chairs, toys discarded under furniture and behind curtains and on windowsills—wooden blocks and soldiers and spinning tops for Phillip, tassels and feathers and long pieces of string for the kittens.

The house on Old Burlington Street had never been hushed and silent. Footmen had whistled and maids had hummed, there had been snatches of song—Hedgepeth tidying the dressing room, choruses drifting up from the kitchen. There'd been the rumble of Arthur's voice, the rumble of his laugh, Minette's vivacious conversation and her melodies on the pianoforte. Added to those sounds was now the mewing of kittens and giggles of a child, the scamper of paws and boyish feet. The house had always been colorful, but it had never been so noisy, so busy, so messy, so alive, so happy, so much a *home*. And Decimus Pryor was part of it all. He was there every day, adding to the noise and the busyness, bringing more warmth and more laughter, more happiness.

Ella wanted everything to stay exactly as it was. Forever. It couldn't, though. Kittens grew and children grew and nothing remained the same, not even for a month, let alone forever.

The final days of November sped past, autumn hastening towards its end. The anniversary of her latest agreement with Pryor approached. Several times, in the privacy of her crimson-and-gold bedchamber, in that lull after lovemaking and before he dressed to leave, Pryor inhaled as if to say something of importance, something significant, then released his breath without speaking.

Ella knew what those unsaid words were. They were ones she'd almost uttered several times herself.

Shall we extend our liaison?

Pryor was leaving it up to her to make that suggestion. He was being a gentleman. Not pushing.

On the twenty-eighth of November, after an afternoon spent dressing up in Arthur's costume room while rain battered at the windows, and after they'd dined *en famille,* and after they'd played jackstraws in the parlor, and after Phillip had departed for bed, kittens gallivanting at his heels and Minette and Arthur arguing over which of them would read the first of that evening's stories, Ella tidied away the scattered jackstraws and said, "Shall we go upstairs?"

Tonight was the night. Tonight she'd broach the subject they'd both been avoiding for the past week: a renegotiation of their agreement.

This time she'd ask for longer than a month. She'd be bolder and more assertive, more ambitious. She'd suggest extending their liaison until the end of winter. Another three whole months.

CHAPTER 29

*F*or the entirety of Ella's marriage, sex had been a chore, a duty, something that she'd submitted to because that was what wives did, a nightly obligation to her husband where she was a passive receptacle of his seed. Discovering that sex could be not only pleasant but varied had come as rather a shock, but after four lovers Ella had thought that she'd understood sex in all its permutations.

She'd been wrong.

Sex with Decimus Pryor was unlike anything she'd ever experienced. Even during the first month of their tryst, when he'd been unwilling to relinquish control, it had been more carefree and lighthearted than she'd thought possible, more enjoyable, but once he'd given her equal charge of what they did together, it had become something else again, an exploration of boundaries and desires, an intimate adventure.

On the night when she'd playfully, teasingly, looped silk stockings around his wrists and tied him to the bedposts, Decimus's reaction had surprised them both. His virile member had strained desperately against his stomach, leaking with urgent excitement.

That revelation had resulted in a great deal of pleasure in the four-poster bed.

It was exhilarating to take charge, exhilarating to make him writhe and beg, to wring paroxysms of bliss from him. When he lay trembling, waiting, letting her do whatever she wished, all that strength and muscle restrained by thin silk bindings . . . it was heady and intoxicating in a way that Ella had never imagined was possible. She exulted in it. *They* exulted in it.

But there was more to it than mere sexual pleasure. When Decimus ceded control, allowed her to bind his wrists, made himself vulnerable to her . . . it was a surrender, and that wasn't merely arousing; it was humbling. It made her want to protect him even while she tied him up, to be tender *and* dominating, to master him *and* cherish him.

Tonight's mood was quiet but still playful, a little intense. Ella rode him, but didn't bind his wrists, held his shoulders down and watched him come apart with pleasure.

Afterwards, they lay among the rumpled sheets, entwined in a loose embrace. The bedchamber was a haven of stillness, candlelight, and shadows, the midnight hush broken only by the sound of their panted breaths slowly steadying. Ella stroked Decimus's sweat-damp skin with an idle fingertip, basking in the warm, drowsy contentment of the moment, the mellow afterglow of exertion and orgasm.

Mixed in with her drowsy contentment were other emotions: tenderness and liking and a sense of connection that went beyond the physical act of two bodies joining together in sexual congress, a connection that was affection and rapport and . . . not love, of course—definitely not that—but friendship. The liking and affection and rapport of friendship.

Ella traced a path down his arm with her fingertip. How astonishing that this man should have become one of her closest friends. One of her most necessary friends. Someone whose arrival she looked forward to every day. Someone she missed when he was gone. Someone who made her life brighter, better, happier.

It was time.

Ella sat up. "Decimus?"

"Yes?" His smile was soft and fond and as far from a smirk as night was from day.

"I've been thinking . . . why don't we continue this until spring?"

His smile faded.

"Not if it doesn't suit you," Ella said hastily. "If you'd rather not make such a commitment, I perfectly understand."

Decimus sat up and reached for one of her hands. "It does suit me. I'm very happy to continue until spring."

An absurd surge of relief welled up in Ella's throat. "Oh," she managed. "Good."

"Good," Decimus echoed. He was still holding her hand. His fingers entwined with hers, linking them together. "Eloïse . . . I've been thinking, too."

"Oh?" she said hopefully. Did he wish to make their relationship long-term, too? They were remarkably in tune with one another, more in tune than she'd thought a man and a woman could ever be. It was entirely possible that they both wanted the same thing.

Decimus bit his lip and glanced at her from beneath his lashes. Such glances were usually followed by a playful pounce and a kiss, but there was nothing flirtatious about this particular glance, nothing mischievous. If anything, he looked uncertain, diffident, even a little shy. "We can continue longer than spring, if you wish?"

The relief wasn't a surge this time, more a melting of tension. They *were* on the same page, she and Decimus Pryor.

"I do wish," Ella said. It might be the middle of the night, but it felt as if there was sunshine in her chest, sunshine in her smile.

Decimus's smile was still diffident, though, the upward glance through the dark fan of his lashes still uncharacteristically shy. He took a breath and said, "Eloïse . . . will you marry me?"

CHAPTER 30

Ella recoiled, pulling her hand free from his clasp, scrambling off the bed. "No! I'm sorry, Decimus, but no. Absolutely not!" She snatched her chemise from where it lay on the floor and held it to her bosom, a ridiculous attempt at modesty given the intimacies they'd shared in this room. Her heart beat wildly, frantically.

Decimus scrambled off the bed, too. "Eloïse . . ."

"Why on earth would you wish to marry me?" she snapped, taking refuge in anger.

"Because I love you," he said simply.

"Well, I don't want you to! I don't want any man to!" Ella dragged the chemise on hastily, taking refuge in the thin, wrinkled linen. "I don't want to marry you! I don't want another husband!"

"I can see that," Decimus said quietly. "I beg your pardon. Please accept my apologies." He made no move to cover his nudity. His nakedness wasn't erotic. He looked defenseless cloaked in nothing but shadows and candlelight, vulnerable, as if she could make him bleed merely by stabbing him with words.

His defenselessness, that sense of defeat and forlorn-ness—Ella recognized those as the dangers they were. Men were never defenseless, never helpless. They always held more power than women. They took, they claimed, they caged, and if she was foolish enough to fall for that forlornness she'd end up in the same prison she'd been freed from six years ago.

Her heart longed to comfort him, to give him the words he hoped to hear. Her brain knew better. The last thing she wanted was to shackle herself to another husband.

"I think it's best if we conclude this affair," Ella said stiffly.

Decimus didn't argue. He pressed his lips together and nodded.

Ella walked a wide path around him, her steps quickening until she was almost running. She wrenched open the door to her dressing room, hurried through it, slammed it. Her heart hammered in hard, panicked beats, as if she'd barely escaped from a trap.

The door had no lock. Ella leaned against it and pressed with her full weight, every muscle tensed. This dressing room and the sunrise-colored bedchamber beyond it were her refuge, her place of safety. She wouldn't let Decimus Pryor in, any more than she would let him into her heart.

Her ears strained for the sound of pursuit. It didn't come. After a long moment, she heard the faint rustle of clothing being donned, and finally, footsteps.

The footsteps didn't come towards her, but away. They headed for the door to the corridor, the staircase, the street.

Ella's tension melted into relief. She closed her eyes and rested her forehead against cold, hard wood and listened to Decimus Pryor leave.

If footsteps could be sad and subdued and woebegone, those footsteps were.

If ears could listen with guilt, then her ears were listening with guilt.

She hadn't thought him capable of falling in love, had never even considered it a possibility. He was a *rake,* capable of liking and friendship and desire, but love?

It was unthinkable. Impossible.

But the unthinkable and the impossible had happened and his heart was presumably now breaking.

Her heart felt as if it was breaking, too. Not because she loved Decimus Pryor, but because she'd hurt him. That pain in her chest, that sting behind her closed eyelids, that was regret. Regret, because she hadn't meant to hurt him. Regret, because she'd lost more than a lover tonight; she'd lost one of her closest friends.

CHAPTER 31

$\mathcal{E}$lla didn't fall asleep until nearly dawn. She woke late, feeling lethargic and hollow and angry at Pryor for ruining everything. She knew the anger was unfair. It wasn't his fault he'd fallen in love, but she wished with all of herself that he hadn't.

Listlessly, she climbed out of bed and washed her face. Listlessly, she allowed Hedgepeth to dress her. Listlessly, she stared at herself in the mirror. The gown she wore was the warm, rich color of saffron, but inside she was brown and gray. The brown of sodden leaves in a gutter, the gray of low, heavy rainclouds.

Ella gave herself an angry shake. She was the blue of spring skies, the green of new grass, the yellow of buttercups, because she was independent and *free*. She was living the life she had chosen, the life she'd been *lucky* enough to be able to choose. Few women were as fortunate as she was. She'd inherited money from Aunt Clara, from Francis, from her father. She had freedom and independence, the privilege of wealth, the protection of her dead husband's title—*and* she had Minette and Arthur and Phillip.

Ella glared at herself in the mirror. *My life. My choice.*

She made her way down to the breakfast parlor. At this hour, it was empty.

One of the footmen brought her a basket of brioche and a fresh pot of tea. Ella poured herself a cup. She stared at the steaming liquid. After several minutes, she selected a brioche and put it on her plate.

She sighed, and remembered to pick up her teacup and drink.

She hadn't handled last night well.

Decimus Pryor had offered her his heart, and instead of returning it to him gently but firmly, she'd hurled it back at him and run away.

It was quite possibly the worst thing she'd ever done to a person. If she'd ever done anything crueler, she couldn't remember it.

She needed to apologize to him. But not face to face. She didn't think she could bear that. It would be awkward and painful to set the apology down on paper, but a thousand times less awkward and painful than actually being in the same room as him.

Ella sighed into her tea, sipped it, put the cup down, broke the brioche open, and decided she wasn't hungry. She pushed the plate away, but couldn't find the energy to stand and go in search of Arthur and Minette and Phillip.

She sighed again and rubbed her forehead, where a headache was making its presence known. Decimus Pryor was one of the people closest to Phillip's heart. The boy would be devastated to lose his friendship.

This house wasn't solely hers; it belonged to Arthur and Minette, too. It was their home, and Phillip's, and if they wanted Pryor to visit—if he still wished to visit—then he was welcome. As their friend. And as her friend, too, if friendship was possible after what she'd done to him. But he was not welcome as a lover. She would make that quite clear in her letter.

Ella sighed, and sipped her tea, and sighed again, and realized that the brioche was filled with bramble preserves. Juice leaked onto the plate, a red so rich it was almost black.

The torn open brioche looked like a bleeding heart.

Ella averted her gaze. She pushed her chair back and went in search of a quiet parlor and some writing paper.

Minette found her in the parlor that looked out over the back garden, where she was struggling to write what was the most difficult letter of her life. "Is everything all right, *ma chère?*"

Ella sighed and laid down the quill. She didn't want to have this conversation any more than she wanted to write to Decimus Pryor, but she had to, and then she'd have to have the same conversation with Arthur. She sighed again. It was all she'd been doing this morning: sighing.

"I've terminated my liaison with Pryor."

"What? Why?" Minette crossed to her in a flurry of expensive silk, worry sharp on her face. "Did something happen? Did you argue?"

"We didn't argue. He . . ." It seemed wrong to tell Minette what had happened. Surely Pryor wouldn't want anyone else to know? Not merely for the sake of his pride, but because his offer of marriage, his declaration of love, had been a baring of his soul, intensely private, not something to be divulged to others.

Minette mistook her hesitation. Wrath kindled on her face. "Did he hurt you? Did he hit you? *Mon Dieu!* I had not thought it of him!"

"Of course he didn't hit me."

"Then what? I thought you were *très compatibles.* I do not understand."

They had been *très compatibles.* More compatible than Ella had thought a man and woman could be.

She felt a flare of anger towards Decimus Pryor. Why had he proposed? Why had he destroyed one of the best friendships of her life? Why had he had to change things, to ruin things?

Her anger was unfair. She knew that. Falling in love wasn't something one had control over.

She sighed for the hundredth time that morning and pressed her fingertips to her forehead, where a headache throbbed. "He wanted one thing and I wanted another."

"Ah." Minette's expression softened into sympathy. She sat down beside Ella. "He wanted to end it? *Ma pauvre chèrie.* I had not thought it. He seemed so . . . what is the word? Enamored."

"He was. He is. He . . ." How to explain to Minette without divulging something that Pryor wouldn't wish to be shared? "I wanted our liaison to be long-term, but he wanted it to be permanent."

Minette's brow creased in confusion, as if she didn't understand the difference between long-term and permanent.

"I wanted what you had with my aunt," Ella clarified. "A long-term liaison. He wanted . . . something more."

Minette's whole face lit up. She leaned forward. "Marriage? Did he offer marriage? *Mon Dieu!*" Confusion gathered on her brow again. She sat back in her chair. "But that *is* what Clara and I had."

"No, it wasn't. It wasn't legal. My aunt didn't have power over every decision in your life. You weren't a piece of chattel. You could have walked away whenever you chose."

Minette gave a single, resolute shake of her head. "What I chose was marriage. We gave our vows to each other *en privé.* It was not in a church, there was no license, but for me and for Clara, it was marriage."

Ella give a single headshake of her own. "You could have walked away. You were *free.*"

"Me, I could not have walked away. Clara was my best friend. Why would I leave her?"

"If she treated you like a possession, a pet, a child who had to be told what to do, you would have left! If she controlled your money and made all your decisions and tried to lock you in a cage, you would have left!"

Minette's eyes widened. "A cage? Did Francis—"

"A metaphorical cage."

"Ah, *la métaphore.*" Minette nodded sagely, and said, "But of course Clara did not do any of those things, and neither did I. We loved each other." Her brow creased again. She cocked her head to one side. "You did not object when Arthur and I married."

"Because you're friends. You might belong to him in the eyes of the law, but he'd never abuse that."

"And you think Monsieur Pryor would?"

No, she didn't think that he would, but she'd certainly not give him the opportunity to do so. "That's beside the point. I have no intention of marrying again."

"A love match is very different from a *mariage arrangé*—"

"I am not in love with Decimus Pryor," Ella said stiffly.

"No? You turn to him like a flower turns its face to the sun."

"No, I don't!"

Minette pursed her lips dubiously.

"He's a friend, nothing more. My heart isn't capable of love." Ella picked up the quill again and stabbed it into the inkwell.

"No? You love Phillip, I think."

"Romantic love," Ella clarified. "I'm not capable of *romantic* love."

Damnation. She'd split the tip of the quill.

Ella wanted to throw the wretched thing across the room; instead, she laid it down carefully. "Were you looking for me for a reason? I have a letter to write."

Minette's gaze flicked to the sheet of hot-pressed paper. At its top, clearly legible, were her attempts at crafting an adequate salutation. *Dear Mr. Pryor* had been crossed out. So had *Mr. Pryor* and *Dear Decimus*. She'd finally decided on *Decimus*, a greeting that acknowledged the intimacy of their relationship, but omitted an affectionate adjective.

"I was a little uncivil last night," Ella admitted. "I need to make it clear that he's still welcome to visit Phillip."

Minette's eyes widened in alarm, as if she'd not considered the possibility of Pryor avoiding Old Burlington Street altogether. "But of course he must continue to visit! Me, I shall write to him *immédiatement* and tell him so. Phillip will be most upset to lose so good a friend!" She hastened to her feet and headed for the door—then turned back, her gaze narrow and shrewd. "And I think you will be upset to lose so good a friend as well, *ma chère*."

Ella was upset. Upset to lose Pryor as a friend. Upset to lose him as a lover. Decimus Pryor was one of a kind. He was irreplaceable. She'd never find another man like him.

A surge of unreasonable anger rose in her breast. Why had Pryor fallen in love with her? Why had he destroyed what they had?

"I don't need a man to make me happy. *I* can make myself happy." Ella opened a drawer in the escritoire, hunting for another quill.

Minette sniffed. "A dildo can give you pleasure, but not love."

Ella slammed the drawer shut. "That's not what I—"

But Minette had already gone, sweeping from the parlor, intent on writing her own letter to Decimus Pryor.

Ella blew out a harsh breath. Her headache was worsening. She dug her fingertips into her temples. "Botheration."

CHAPTER 32

"Gentleman to see you, sir."

Dex looked up from Eloïse Fortrose's letter. "I'm not at home to visitors."

Hicks grunted and withdrew from the bedchamber.

Dex read the letter again, tilting it to catch the light seeping in through the windowpanes. He wanted the letter to say something different, but with each re-reading, the words remained the same.

Hicks returned and presented a visiting card with all the finesse of a butcher offering a scrap of flyblown meat for perusal. "Most insistent he is, sir."

Dex's temper flared. "I told you, I'm not at home to visitors!" He snatched the card from Hicks's hand, preparatory to flinging it across the room.

A name caught his eyes.

Arthur Blake, Esq.

Dex crumpled the card in his hand, its edges biting into his palm. He wanted to tell Hicks to tell Blake to go to blazes, but what if he brought word from Eloïse? A change of heart?

He dropped the card on the floor, folded the letter into a tight wedge of paper that hid all those apologetic, unpalatable words, and climbed from the shelter of his bed.

He shaved hastily, dressed hastily, and emerged into his sitting room to discover that Blake had brought another letter with him.

It wasn't from Eloïse, though; it was from Madame Blake, expressing regret at the unfortunate turn of events—as she phrased it—and inviting him to visit Phillip that afternoon.

Dex refolded the letter, disappointment stinging painfully in his breast. "Please thank madame, but—"

"I extend the invitation, too," Blake said. "Phillip has been talking about that rocking horse all morning."

Dex hesitated. He'd promised to paint zebra stripes on the rocking horse with Phillip that afternoon. He didn't want to disappoint the boy, but his heart was currently hemorrhaging blood. Setting foot in the house on Old Burlington Street wasn't something he could face today. Or tomorrow, or any other day in the future.

"I realize that things are awkward with Eloïse right now," Blake continued earnestly. "But I want you to know that you're always welcome in our house. I count you as a friend, as does Minette. It would pain us if you refrained from visiting, and as for my great-nephew . . ."

Blake went down on one knee.

There was a beat of silence—horrified silence on Dex's part—and then Blake clasped his hands at his breast and said, entreaty throbbing in his voice, "Pryor, I beg you not to cease your visits to Phillip."

The throb told him that Blake was acting and tipped the moment from the horrifying to the ludicrous. Belatedly, Dex spotted the gleam in Blake's eyes, a gleam that was hopeful and earnest and impassioned, but also a little impish.

Thespians. Always so dramatic.

Dex raised his gaze to the ceiling for a moment.

When he looked back down at Blake, the man was still on bended knee, still clasping his hands at his breast, still shamelessly projecting hopefulness.

"For heaven's sake, get up, man."

"You'll visit us?"

Dex blew out a breath. "I'll visit," he said grudgingly.

"Now?"

It was almost two o'clock, the hour of the day when he usually found himself on the doorstep of Eloïse Fortrose's house. And he had promised to paint that rocking horse with Phillip.

"Now," Dex agreed, even more grudgingly.

If dealing with overly dramatic thespians was awkward, meeting Eloïse Fortrose face to face was infinitely worse. She entered the library while Dex, Blake, and Phillip were still setting out the paints. "Mr. Pryor? If I might have a quick word?" Her manner was gracious, her smile as wooden as the rocking horse's.

Dex patted Phillip's shoulder. "I'll be back in a few minutes."

He followed Eloïse out into the corridor, past two doors, and into a parlor. Dread gathered in his gut with each step. He was so tense that it felt as if his belly was going to reject everything in it, casting its contents up for their horrified inspection.

Dex crossed to the fireplace, where at least he could vomit on the tiled hearth if he needed to.

Eloïse closed the parlor door and turned to face him. Her hands were clutched together at her waist, a small white-knuckled shield that she held in front of herself. The patently false smile was gone. Her skin was paler than it usually was, washed out and waxen, and her lips were almost bloodless. Her gaze met his for a fraction of a second, then skipped sideways, coming to rest on his shoulder instead. She inhaled a short breath and visibly braced herself. "I apologize for my behavior last night. It was unpardonably rude of me."

"There's nothing to forgive," Dex said, his voice as wooden as hers. "The apology is mine to make. I hadn't realized my offer would be so unwelcome. Please forgive me. I didn't mean any offense."

Her gaze flicked to his eyes and away again. "You didn't offend me, Mr. Pryor. I apologize if that is what you thought."

If not offense, then horror. His proposal had—quite literally—sent her fleeing.

"I am conscious that you did me a very great honor," she continued stiffly to his shoulder. "But I have no intention of remarrying."

Yes, she'd made that quite clear last night. Dex wished he'd known that fact before he'd opened his stupid mouth.

Her gaze flitted past his nose and landed on the mantelpiece behind him. "It shames me that I responded to your offer so ungraciously. My behavior was unconscionable."

"You were surprised."

"Surprise is no excuse for egregious incivility." Her gaze met his squarely for a half-second, then veered away again. "Please believe that it was never my wish to cause you pain."

"Nor was it my wish to cause you distress."

"I esteem you greatly as a friend," she told the mantelpiece, or perhaps it was the clock that ticked with such meticulous precision upon that mantelpiece. "But I regret that I cannot return your feelings."

Dex regretted it, too.

"Thank you for coming to visit Phillip today. I hope that you will continue to do so."

"Do you?" he asked bluntly.

Her gaze jumped to his face. For a long, intense second, their eyes met; then Eloïse looked away. "Yes, I do. Very much. He's lost enough people in his life. I would hate it if my actions caused him to lose you, too."

"He shan't lose me," Dex told her.

"Thank you."

An awkward silence fell. The clock increased the loudness of its ticking.

"I should get back to the library."

"Of course." She turned towards the door and opened it. "I'm very sorry for my behavior last night," she said as he stepped past her, out into the corridor. "It was not my intention to be cruel. Please believe me."

Dex turned back to face her. "It's forgotten," he told her, not because it was true—last night's events were seared into his soul—but because it was the polite thing to say.

Her gaze grazed his chin and settled on his neckcloth. Her grip on the door handle was white-knuckled. "I hope that we can remain friends," she said, stilted and formal, words that were uttered because they, too, were the polite thing to say.

"I hope that we can, too." He sketched her a courteous bow, twitched his lips into a grimace of a smile that she didn't see because she was still staring at his neckcloth, and turned towards the library.

Behind him, the door closed with a decisive little *snick,* Eloïse retreating back into the parlor and shutting herself away from him.

CHAPTER 33

Dex halted in the corridor and let out a long, shaky breath. That had, without any shadow of doubt, been the most painful conversation of his life.

He stood in silence, simply breathing. The dread had subsided to a feeling of heaviness. Heaviness in his heart, heaviness in his chest, his limbs, his lungs. His stomach felt heavy, too, and still undecided on the subject of casting up its contents. It might possibly do so. Not out of dread, but out of mortification. He had never been so mortified on so many fronts before. Mortified that his love was so unwelcome. Mortified that his proposal had sent Eloïse fleeing. Mortified that she could barely meet his eyes now. Mortified that he was going to have to tell his mother that he'd been resoundingly rejected. And his father. And his uncle. And his grandfather.

Dex groaned under his breath.

Why the devil had he told them all? His mother, yes, but he'd had no reason to tell anyone else.

No reason except that he'd been too confident—overconfident—so certain that he—a Pryor!—grandson of a duke!— could never be rejected, and as a result of that overconfidence he had four people to inform of his dashed hopes and four people who would pity him instead of merely one.

This was undoubtedly a salutary lesson.

It didn't feel salutary. It felt like heartbreak and grief and despair—and that, right there, *was* the salutary lesson: Falling in love was a fool's game. He should have known better than to do such a thing, just as he should have known better than to counter Eloïse Fortrose's offer of a sexual liaison with a marriage proposal. Affairs—fun, frivolous, throwaway—were as different from the lifelong commitment of marriage as black was from white.

There was no retrieving the situation now, no going back to what he and Eloïse had had. He'd burned his bridges too thoroughly for that. There was only forward.

Going forward meant continuing to visit this house. It meant pretending that he hadn't given his heart to someone who didn't want it, pretending he wasn't devastated, pretending to be Eloïse Fortrose's friend and not her spurned lover.

It meant being friends with the Blakes, which wasn't pretense at all, and it meant visiting young Phillip. Given a choice between spending afternoons at his club or spending them with Phillip, he'd choose Phillip, so that was no hardship.

Dex heaved a belly-deep sigh and coaxed his heavy legs into movement, *clomp, clomp, clomp,* as graceless as Hicks. He gave vent to another gusty sigh at the door to the library.

Phillip looked up at his entrance. The boy's face was bright with excitement. "We're ready, Mister Dex!"

Dex's legs didn't feel quite so heavy as he crossed to the table where Phillip and Blake stood. He took in the preparations: the old sheets covering the table and carpet, the bright array of paints from Ackermann's, the brushes and the cleaning cloths. "It looks good." He reached out to ruffle the boy's hair.

Phillip beamed up at him—and then swooped on a kitten that was attempting to ascend a fold of fabric from floor to tabletop.

Blake removed the kitten to the safety of the armchairs by the fire, and Dex and Phillip set to work transforming the

225

rocking horse into a rocking zebra—and not just any rocking zebra, but a rocking zebra with yellow and red stripes and bright blue hooves.

The transformation took all afternoon. When the curtains were drawn and the lamps and candles lit, Phillip said, "You'll stay for dinner, won't you, sir?"

Dabbling with paints in the comfortable coziness of the library had been surprisingly enjoyable. Dinner, sitting at the same table as Eloïse Fortrose, making polite conversation, forcing himself to eat, to chew, to swallow . . . "Not tonight."

Phillip's face fell. "But you'll come tomorrow, won't you, sir?"

Blake looked up from Wordsworth and Coleridge's *Lyrical Ballads*, which he was reading in a wingback armchair by the hearth. "Yes, please do, Pryor."

"*Oui*," said Madame Blake, from the pianoforte, where she was perusing new musical scores. "You are always welcome in this house, Monsieur Pryor."

Eloïse wasn't there to voice an objection; she'd avoided the library all afternoon.

She *had* asked him to continue visiting Phillip.

Dex glanced at the boy, and found himself the object of a beseeching stare. It was impossible not to capitulate. "I'll stop by tomorrow afternoon."

"Hoorah!" Phillip cried, and danced a capering little jig.

To his astonishment, Dex found himself laughing. It was a ragged sound, only a breath long, as abrupt as it was unexpected, quickly quenched, but genuine.

He kept his word, stopping by the next afternoon, staying for several hours, declining another dinner invitation, but agreeing to visit the following day. It wasn't merely that he didn't want to disappoint Phillip; he didn't want to disappoint himself. The boy's delight in his company was balm for his eviscerated heart. The hours spent with Phillip were the best of his day, one of the few brightnesses in the gray, damp, chilly descent into winter.

The kittens also helped. Kittens made even the worst of days better, with their purrs and their squeaks and their acrobatics.

He rarely saw Eloïse—a few minutes here, a few there. If she was in the library when he arrived, she greeted him with polite civility and friendly reserve, and then, within a very few minutes, excused herself. There were no afternoons sitting side by side drawing, no throwing of paper darts and spitballs at one another, no shared glances, no laughter, no conversation beyond a courteous, "How do you do, Mr. Pryor?" and then an equally courteous, "Pray excuse me, I have a letter to write . . . I need to have a word with my maid . . . I have an appointment at the modiste."

Each time she retreated from his presence, it felt like rejection anew. But still Dex visited, because Phillip's joy in his company—and his own joy in Phillip's company—made it impossible not to.

Four days after Eloïse Fortrose's rejection of his suit was the Oliphants' ball.

Dex had assiduously been putting off his commitments. He hadn't written to his parents or his uncle or his grandfather to inform them that his suit had been declined. He'd canceled an appointment with his tailor and another with his bootmaker. He hadn't replied to his sister's latest letter. After one visit to his club, which had been unbearably tedious, he'd taken to spending his evenings in his rooms, desultorily thumbing through Walpole's *Castle of Otranto*.

He would have ignored the ball, except that when he'd encountered Lord Oliphant two weeks ago, he'd given his word to attend the wretched event.

He dressed in the ensemble he'd requested Hicks to lay

out, donning each garment like a knight putting on armor, and unenthusiastically made his way to Grosvenor Square.

He was late enough that there was no receiving line. Music wafted into the entrance hall, a faint melody that grew louder with each reluctant step Dex took, until he was standing on the threshold of what some people might call a ballroom, but which was in fact a genteel battlefield where mamas pursued eligible gentlemen for their daughters, not-so-eligible gentlemen chased less virginal prey, and fortune hunters stalked heiresses.

Heat rolled out the door at him, along with the smells of perfume, pomade, and perspiration. The sound of voices was a low roar, like surf on a beach. Lady Oliphant would be pleased; the ball was a crush. Or as much of a crush as was possible in early December.

Dex paused in the doorway. This was his hunting ground. His *milieu*. So why did it seem too loud, too bright, too busy? Why did he want to walk back to the entrance hall, reclaim his hat, and retreat into the night?

When the devil had he turned into a shrinking violet?

Dex twitched his cuffs, annoyed with himself, and plunged into the fray. He would have swaggered, but his legs appeared to have forgotten how to swagger. He settled for a saunter.

"Vigor!" Someone clapped him on the shoulder. "What rock have you been hiding under?"

The rock of crushing rejection, Dex was tempted to answer. "No rock," he said lightly, and accepted a glass of punch from a passing footman.

Outside, it was winter; in this room it was a hot summer's day. Chandeliers blazed overhead and the members of the orchestra weren't the only people sweating. The punch glass was warm. Dex ventured a sip and discovered that the punch was warm, too.

"Did you hear about Bayton?" his interlocutor said cheerfully. "Lost his entire stables to Henderson in a game of picquet."

Dex couldn't care less about Bayton's horses, but he said, with a decent simulation of interest, "Oh? I bet he's not pleased."

"Mad as fire!" his companion jovially agreed. "Picquet's never been his game. Fool to keep playing it."

Dex nodded, and tried not to search the crowd for a shining white-blonde head.

Two dandies sidled up. "We thought you'd left town, Pryor," one of them said, a comment to which the other added, "Is it true that you've cut Lady Fortrose loose?"

No, it wasn't true at all. She'd cut *him* loose. But his pride didn't want that truth out in the world.

"Mutual cutting loose," Dex said, with forced joviality, and gulped a mouthful of unpalatably warm punch.

A rather notorious rake joined their little group. "I hear you're on the prowl again, Vigor."

"Perhaps we should call him Finesse now?" the first dandy said, with a titter.

Dex shifted his weight to the balls of his feet. Where was his swagger when he needed it, damn it? "You both have it wrong," he said loftily. "It's vigor *and* finesse."

This rejoinder provoked a gust of merriment.

"I wonder who'll be next to scale the Fortress's walls?" the second dandy mused, with a sly sideways glance at the rather notorious rake.

The rather notorious rake smirked.

Dex experienced an almost overpowering urge to punch both men. "If you'll excuse me, I see someone I need to speak with."

It wasn't a lie; he'd spotted two familiar faces across the room. The Blakes. Which meant that Eloïse Fortrose was probably somewhere in the crush, too.

She was, as Dex discovered less than a minute later, when he'd found a footman to hand off his too-warm punch to. He turned away from the man and came face to face with her: Dowager Viscountess Fortrose, aloof and eye-catchingly beautiful in a ballgown of poppy red.

Her gown was the exact shade of his waistcoat, which was unfortunate.

Dex rather thought that she was wearing her brightest, boldest red for the same reason that he was wearing his: as armor to deflect the *ton*'s curiosity.

He was aware of a pause in the conversations nearest them, aware of heads turning and glances darting their way, aware of his ribcage clenching around his heart, aware of the tiny flinch of muscles around her eyes, aware that the warm smile she bestowed on him was as false as the one he bestowed on her.

"Mr. Pryor. How delightful to see you."

Dex bowed with a flourish. "The pleasure is mine, Lady Fortrose."

Under the weight of so many gazes, they uttered several commonplaces and then strolled the length of the ballroom together, her gloved hand barely resting on his arm, before parting ways with more warm, insincere smiles.

Eloïse hadn't needed to do that—walk with him, talk with him—but Dex knew why she'd done it: it was public confirmation that their parting of ways was amicable, proof that she'd not kicked him from her bed. It was an act of charity on her part, done so that he could hold his head up amid the *ton*, a kindness that stung as if it were a wagoner's lash, another mortification to add to all the other mortifications.

A similar piece of playacting occurred three days later, at the Winstanleys' rout, and five days after that, at the Endicotts' soirée: a smiling conversation, the pretense of an amicable end to their liaison, another painful welt laid upon Dex's flayed pride.

Eloïse wasn't merely talking to him, she was talking *about* him, dropping hints of his prowess, just as she'd promised she would when they'd embarked upon their affair. Dex had never been so popular among the young widows. He'd had to fend off more than a few wives, too, and several of the bolder débutantes.

No doubt her panegyrizing was meant as another kindness, but it was a kindness Dex could have done without. He didn't want to flirt with anyone. He didn't want to exchange laughing come-hither glances. He didn't want to steal kisses in shadowy alcoves.

He left the Endicotts' soirée early, having extricated himself from the clutches of his third eager young widow of the evening, and stood on the damp cobblestones, purposeless and adrift.

He could go carousing. He could gamble. He could drink claret at his club and invent stupid wagers for the betting book. He could even visit one of the more exclusive brothels and attempt to find his missing libido.

Instead of doing any of those things, Dex went home, where he huddled in an armchair by the fire like a tortoise in its shell and apathetically turned the pages of Walpole's *Castle of Otranto*.

He was the plaything of young widows and he was vigor *and* finesse—and he didn't want to flirt and he didn't want to have sex. He didn't even want to toss off into his own hand, which would have been alarming if he could have mustered the energy to be alarmed.

Instead of being alarmed, he was restless and dissatisfied and reading books he didn't want to read. The French had a word for it: *Ennui.* It was an emotion Dex had never experienced before.

He set the book aside and went to bed.

In the morning, his ennui was still firmly in place. *Clomp, clomp, clomp* went Hicks's footsteps as he opened the curtains, as he filled the ewer with hot water, as he set out the razor and a fresh towel. *Clomp, clomp, clomp* as he laid out clothes for Dex to wear.

Dex didn't want to get out of bed. He didn't want to shave. He didn't want to get dressed.

With a groan, he flung back the bedclothes.

Hicks's "Good morning, sir," was more grunt than words, but even that gruff greeting was far too cheerful.

Dex halfheartedly climbed out of bed.

What was the point in washing one's face and brushing one's teeth? What was the point in fiddling with one's neck-cloth until it looked just right? There was no point, but he did those things because he'd always done those things. He also ate breakfast although he wasn't particularly hungry and read the newspaper even though he didn't particularly care what was happening in the world. Those activities completed, Dex was at a loss. He didn't want to go riding in the persistent December rain. He didn't want to go to his club. He didn't want to venture out to Tattersalls or to his tailor, or anywhere else for that matter.

He didn't want to write to his sister and fill a sheet of paper with anecdotes and jokes and silly little caricatures.

He didn't want to write to his parents and inform them of Eloïse Fortrose's rejection, and he definitely didn't want to tell his uncle and grandfather about it yet.

Drawing had always been his default activity, but he didn't even want to draw.

Dex had never felt the lack of an occupation before, but he'd felt it in the thirteen days since Eloïse Fortrose had rejected his suit. What he wouldn't give for a purpose, a reason to leave his bedchamber, something worthwhile to do with his time.

But when the clock hands reached a quarter to two, he *did* have a reason, he *did* have a purpose.

He walked around to Old Burlington Street, deflecting raindrops and hopping over puddles, and knocked on the door, *rat-tat-tat*. A footman escorted him to the library. "Mr. Pryor," he announced.

Dex's gaze darted around the room, finding Phillip and the Blakes, but not Eloïse. The tension in his shoulders eased; the pain in his breast increased.

"Mister Dex!" Phillip cried, leaping from his seat.

Dex bent and returned the boy's hug, his heart swelling almost to bursting. It was a toss-up for a moment: laugh or cry. He managed to choose laughter and stood and swung Phillip around, whooping as he did so.

He set the boy on his feet. "What are we doing today, Master Flip?"

"Pirates!" Phillip said, taking Dex's hand and tugging him towards a table scattered with encyclopedias, story books, maps, and paper.

"Are we drawing them or dressing up as them?"

"Both!"

Eloïse didn't join them for their piratical high jinks, but that was all right. There was happiness in spending an afternoon with Phillip and the Blakes, enough happiness to give Dex's life purpose and reason: reason to draw, reason to joke and be silly and play games, reason to make other people laugh.

CHAPTER 34

Ella hovered outside Arthur's bedroom. On the other side of that closed door a battle was taking place. She heard bellows of "Ahoy!" and "Avast!" and shrieks of laughter. Bedchambers weren't usually the place for pirate battles, but Arthur's bedroom was decorated in blue—cobalt and duck-egg blue, smalt and gentian and indigo and dozens of shades in between. It was a sea grotto of a bedroom, which was presumably why it had been chosen as the site of the skirmish currently taking place.

The four-poster bed was probably the pirates' sailing ship.

Ella wanted to peep into the room. She wanted to see what the pirates were up to.

One of the kittens wanted to participate in the mayhem, too. It scratched at the door, the tiny *scritch-scritch* of its claws lost beneath the tumult within.

Ella scooped it up. "Pirate battles are no place for kittens," she scolded quietly. "You'll be squashed if you go in there."

Someone within the bedroom uttered a warbling shriek. The ghastly sound went on—and on—and on—and on—until it was drowned out by gales of laughter.

Ella yearned to join the pirates, to be silly with them, laugh with them; instead, she retreated to the garden parlor. She took the kitten with her.

The kitten didn't want to be in the parlor. It scratched at that door, too, and once released, scampered down the corridor in search of adventure.

Ella sighed and closed the door. She wandered across to the rain-specked window. How dreary the garden looked, all bare branches and dead leaves.

If she focused on the windowpanes, she could see a faint reflection of herself.

She looked as transparent as she felt, as colorless.

Ella turned away from the window and crossed to the fireplace, her cozy nook, where books and soft cushions and a steaming teapot awaited.

"My life. My choice." She *chose* to be in this parlor while everyone else enacted pirate battles in Arthur's bedroom. It was her choice. Her decision. Her life.

She was free and she was independent and she was *happy*.

The next day, when Decimus Pryor was due to visit, Ella went to Hatchard's. She spent a full hour browsing the books, one of the footmen dutifully attending her. It was a footman's job to accompany his mistress on errands and carry her purchases; he was being *paid* to wait, but Ella still felt guilty. It was all very well for her to hide among the bookshelves, but it was a dreadful waste of the footman's time.

Ella turned the five minute walk home into a half hour promenade that included a circuit of Berkeley Square, but that, too, was a waste of the footman's time. Rain spat at them from above the rooftops, a squall sweeping in to harry them home.

As they entered the house, she caught an echo of distant laughter. What were Phillip and Decimus Pryor up to this afternoon?

Resolutely, she didn't pause in the entrance hall to listen. Resolutely, she didn't go in search of that laughter. Instead, Ella climbed the stairs to her dressing room and exchanged her damp cape and walking dress for a kerseymere round gown and a cashmere shawl.

The kerseymere was raspberry red and the shawl the color of sunrise, pink blending into orange.

Ella glanced at her reflection in the mirror. The dress was warm, rich, cheerful, the shawl a bright splash of color, but she herself looked like one of the waxwork effigies at Westminster, dull and pale.

What color is my heart today?

Not raspberry red. Not daybreak orange or sunrise pink.

If her heart had been a rose in full bloom last month, now it was a shriveled wad of brown petals.

Ella snorted under her breath. Her heart was a shriveled wad of brown rose petals? "Ridiculous fustian," she muttered, turning away from the mirror.

"I beg your pardon, ma'am?"

"Nothing, Hedgepeth." And it *was* nothing. She was free and she was independent and she was living the life that she had chosen.

Ella marched downstairs with her purchase under her arm, a copy of Mary Wollstonecraft's *Letters Written During a Short Residence in Sweden, Norway, and Denmark*. As she passed the library, heading for the garden parlor, childish laughter caught her attention.

Ella didn't mean to halt; her feet did it without her telling them to.

The door to the library was closed, but she heard someone speaking inside. The words were indistinct, impossible to make out, but her ears instantly recognized that baritone. It belonged to Decimus Pryor.

Phillip replied, light and eager.

Ella leaned closer.

Pryor said something. Phillip answered. A third voice

joined in: Arthur's. There was a pause, and then all three of them laughed.

Ella wanted to be in the library, laughing with them. The wad of brown petals in her chest *yearned* for it.

"*Ma chère,* why are you standing in the corridor?"

Ella almost leaped out of her skin. The book slipped from her grasp and thudded to the floor. She whirled around, hands pressed to her chest.

Minette stood there, eyebrows arched, eyes bright with curiosity. "Is the door locked?"

"Oh, no! I was just passing." Ella bent and snatched up the book.

"You should join us," Minette said, reaching for the door handle.

"Perhaps another time." Ella clutched the book to her bosom and scurried for the garden parlor.

Unfortunately, Minette followed her. "Very snug," she said approvingly.

It was snug. The servants had been in before her. Lamps glowed warmly, a fire burned in the grate, and a tea tray sat on the table. Steam curled from the spout of the teapot. It was an oasis, cozy and peaceful, secluded. A place to be alone. A place to be lonely.

Minette crossed to the settee by the fire and sat. "Now, tell me, why do you not wish to join us in the library?"

"Because I want to read my book," Ella said, displaying *Letters Written During a Short Residence in Sweden, Norway, and Denmark.*

Minette barely accorded the volume a glance. "You do not need to banish yourself. We would all be happy if you joined us."

"I'm not banishing myself," Ella said indignantly. "This is where I wish to be! It's my *choice.*" She sat decisively in the armchair opposite Minette.

"You are avoiding Monsieur Pryor."

"For his sake, not mine. I don't care whether I see him or not."

"No?"

"He's the one with feelings, not me!"

"You have no feelings for him? It seems to me that you do, *ma chère;* otherwise you would not be hiding in this parlor."

"I'm not hiding," Ella snapped, even though that was precisely what she was doing. She crossed her hands firmly over the book on her lap. "I cannot return Mr. Pryor's romantic feelings; therefore, it's kinder that I remove myself from his presence."

"Cannot return?" Minette said, furrowing her brow. "Me, I do not always understand English perfectly. Do you mean that you are unable to return his feelings or that you refuse to return them?"

Ella glared at her.

Minette smiled serenely, picked up the teapot, and poured for them both. "Monsieur Pryor is not a martinet," she said, placing one blue-and-gold *chinoiserie* teacup in front of Ella. "He is not Francis or your father. And he is not a bully, like my poor Clara's Norman." She picked up her own cup, sipped, set it back in its gilt-edged saucer. "Me, I think that he will make some lucky woman a very fine husband."

He would, but that woman wouldn't be her.

"I don't want another husband. I don't need one. I'm free and I'm *happy.*"

"Are you happy, *ma chère*? It seems to me that you are not." Minette's gaze was as sharp as one of the knives that Cook used in the kitchen. Ella felt skewered by it, cut open, her shriveled brown heart exposed to Minette's merciless gaze.

She tossed her head. "Of course I'm happy!"

Minette didn't look convinced. She picked up her cup and sipped her tea once, twice, a third time. After the third sip, she said, "It does not happen often that one finds a person who lights up one's life."

"He doesn't light up my life! And I don't wish to discuss this any further!"

Minette put down her cup and gave a very elegant and

very Gallic shrug. "As you wish." She rose to her feet and patted Ella's cheek, before heading for the door. "Do not saw off the branch you are sitting on, *ma chère*. It is not a wise thing to do."

*C*HAPTER 35

T here was a limit to how long Dex could procrastinate. Fifteen days after the end of his affair with Eloïse Fortrose, he reached that limit. With great reluctance, he wrote to his parents, informing them that his suit had not prospered.

Next, he wrote to his uncle. At the bottom of that brief note, he wrote: *Can you please tell Grandfather?*

And just like that, the ordeal he'd been avoiding was over.

It wasn't a relief to have the letters written. If anything, it lowered his mood further. Informing his family only served to underscore the reality of what had happened: He'd offered his heart to Eloïse Fortrose, and she had handed it back. Thrown it back and fled, if one were truthful, but he and she were the only people who knew just how emphatically she'd rejected him.

Dex pushed the letters aside and capped the ink pot. That task done, he gazed at the window. Rain pattered down. After ten minutes of watching raindrops run down the window-panes, he dragged himself across to the fireplace. He halfheart-edly stirred the coals. He flung himself into the armchair and slouched there. He picked up *The Castle of Otranto,* glanced perfunctorily at the page he was up to, and put it down again. His gaze strayed to the clock on the mantelpiece. Still nearly two hours before he was due at Old Burlington Street.

He could go to his club.

He could write to his sister.

He could nap in the armchair, like an old man.

Dex decided on that last activity as the one most suited to his lethargy and general dissatisfaction with life, but before he'd done more than sink deeper into his slouch, a forceful *rat-a-tat-tat rat-a-tat-tat* sounded on the door to his rooms.

Dex only knew one person who knocked that long and that loudly.

He groaned and pushed to his feet.

The forceful banging started up again, even louder this time, shaking the door in its frame. *Rat-a-tat-TAT. Rat-a-tat-TAT.*

Dex yanked the door open. His cousin Ned loomed in the corridor, his many-caped greatcoat making him look like one of the giants in *Gulliver's Travels*.

"Excellent! You're home! I need your help."

"What nitwittery are you up to now?" Dex said wearily.

"The Ghostly Cavalier. The costume fits, but it doesn't look right."

"I told you before, I'm not helping you pretend to be a ghost. Grandfather wouldn't like—"

"I just want to get the cavalier looking right, that's all." Ned gave him a grin that showed all his teeth—a grin that Dex didn't trust in the slightest. "What's the point in having the costume, if we don't at least dust it off?"

"We could put it back in the trunk where we found it," Dex pointed out.

Ned wrinkled his nose. "When did you become such a killjoy?"

The accusation stung, because it was true. He might be in the doldrums, but that didn't mean he had to spoil other people's fun. "Sorry, I'm a bit out of curl today. The rain, you know." He stepped back and gestured for Ned to enter.

"Never-ending, ain't it?" Ned said cheerfully, shedding water off the many capes of his coat as he strode inside.

Dex closed the door. "When did you get to town?"

"Last night. Took two and a half days, can you believe? Would have been faster in a boat." Ned took off his beaver hat and shook it, spraying the sitting room with water. "So, will you help me?"

Dex hesitated. As long as he didn't levitate the Ghostly Cavalier, there was no harm in helping his cousin perfect the costume, was there?

"Just help me get it looking right. I promise not to ask you to . . ." Ned darted a glance around the room, as if expecting to find Hicks lurking in a corner. "You know." He wafted one hand in the air, mimicking levitation.

"All right. Let me put on my coat."

Ned followed him into the bedroom, dripping water. *Clomp-clomp-clomp* went his boots, even louder than Hicks.

The *clomp-clomp-clomp* made Dex feel better about his decision. Ned was such a thundering gollumpus that he would never learn to walk quietly enough to play a ghost.

Ned flung open an armoire, found only waistcoats, slammed it shut, flung open the next one and pawed through the tailcoats hanging there. "Hicks!" he hollered. "Where are the greatcoats?"

"He's out," Dex said. He shoved his cousin aside and located his second best greatcoat.

Five minutes later, they splashed down Piccadilly to the Albany, where Ned had a set of rooms.

The Albany had been York House until recently, abode of Prince Frederick until that gentleman had found himself at ebb-water and sold it. The property had been converted into lodgings for bachelors. It was a warren of entrances, staircases, and passageways, but the rooms themselves were high-ceil-inged and spacious. No women were permitted to set foot in the place, which was why Dex hadn't snapped up one of the leases. He'd never live somewhere his sister couldn't visit.

They left their outerwear in Ned's vestibule, trod through the sitting room, and into the bedchamber. The cavalier costume was laid out on the bed.

"Where's your man?"

"Given him the day off."

Dex picked up the wide-brimmed cavalier's hat with its curling ostrich feather. He ought to encourage Ned to pack the costume back in its trunk, but . . .

It *was* a very fine costume. It might have lain forgotten in an attic for the past thirty years, but it wasn't at all moldy. The gold braid on the doublet still gleamed brightly.

There was no harm in helping Ned dress as a cavalier, was there? It was just a bit of bobbery, something to fill in a few hours. Ned would never parade the Ghostly Cavalier around town. Not today. Not any day. He might be able to make himself invisible, but he was as loud as a herd of stampeding cattle. Without someone to levitate him, he'd never be able to pass himself off as a ghost.

Twenty minutes later, Ned was arrayed in the blue velvet doublet and breeches, the broad lacy collar, the knee-high boots with their turned-over tops and elevated heels, the leather gauntlets, the hat with its jaunty ostrich plume, the flowing cape. He'd even put on the leather baldric and sword and the wig. Black ringlets cascaded over his shoulders and down his back. The only things he hadn't donned were the pointed vandyke beard and the curling mustache.

"You see my problem?" Ned said, gazing disconsolately at himself in the mirror.

Dex did see the problem. The costume was authentic in its detail, but Ned didn't look remotely Jacobean or Carolinian or whatever era it had been when men wore such clothes. He looked like a modern-day gentleman playing at dressing up. An imitation cavalier.

Ned held the beard and mustache up to his face. It didn't help. He gusted out a sigh, his burly shoulders sagging. "No one will believe I'm a real ghost."

"Not that you're going to pretend to be one, are you?" Dex said, and then winced internally. That was exactly the sort of comment their cousin Quintus would make.

"Well, of course I'm not going to! Not if I look like this." Ned turned away from the mirror and flung the mustache and beard on the bed. "Help?" he said plaintively.

Dex surveyed him from top to toe. He walked around Ned several times. Everything looked right—and yet it looked all wrong.

Arthur Blake was a master of disguise, able to turn himself into stork-like butlers and stout Russian barons. He'd be able to wear this costume with aplomb. He'd *be* a cavalier so thoroughly that no one could doubt it.

How did Blake do it? And more to the point, how could Ned accomplish such a feat?

"I have a friend who's very knowledgeable about the theater and costumes and such. He lives just around the corner, in Old Burlington Street."

"Fetch him!" Ned said, with an imperative gesture at the door.

"What? Now?"

"Of course now. It's raining. What else is there to do?"

Dex shrugged. Ned was right; there wasn't a lot to do in London on days this wet and cold. "Can't guarantee he'll come, but I'll ask." He took a step towards the door, then turned back. "If you've given Kettley the day off, you might want to clean up this mess."

Ned looked down at the clothes strewn across the floor as if he couldn't imagine how they'd come to be there.

In the vestibule, Dex shook out his greatcoat and donned it. As he was arranging its folds, his ears caught the sound of a stealthy footstep. *Ker-lomp.* And then another one. *Ker-lomp.* A glance over his shoulder told him that the sitting room was empty.

Ker-lomp.

Ker-lomp.

"I can hear you."

"No, you can't," Ned said sulkily, from the seemingly empty sitting room.

Dex pulled on one glove.

Ker . . . looomp.

Ker . . . looomp.

"I can still hear you."

"Curse it!" In the blink of an eye, Ned came into view, a disgruntled scowl on his face.

"Please tell me you haven't been practicing that within Kettley's hearing." Ned's valet might be in his fifties, but there was nothing wrong with his ears.

"Of course, I haven't!" Ned said indignantly. "I only ever do it with family. And you always hear me. But one day I'll creep up on you, mark my words!"

"It'll never happen," Dex said, pulling on his other glove.

"It will! Because I'm going to take lessons! That's why I've come to town."

Dex laughed. "Lessons in walking quietly? Pray, where do they teach that?"

"Lessons in dancing, fencing, and deportment," Ned said loftily.

Dex put up his eyebrows. "Dancing, fencing, and deportment? You loathe all those things."

Ned wrinkled his nose in agreement. "It was Pip's idea. She says I need to learn the art of moving."

Pip was their cousin Octavius's new bride. She'd been a governess and she was a great deal cleverer than Ned was. "She's not wrong. You do need to learn. You're a thundering clodhopper."

Ned sniffed, but didn't deny this truth. "Just you wait. In a year's time, none of you will be able to hear me coming."

"In *ten* years' time, we'll still be able to hear you," Dex said, putting on his beaver hat. "Honestly, Ned, I don't know why you chose invisibility. It was a stupid thing to wish for."

"Levitation is just as stupid!" Ned retorted.

"No, it's not." Although the truth was, they'd both chosen frivolous gifts. Their wishes couldn't be large—ridding the world of famine or plague was beyond the scope of Faerie magic—but they both could have wished for something useful, as Quintus and Sextus had done.

But Quintus and Sextus were serious sorts of fellows, and he and Ned were not.

Dex let himself out the door, leaving his scowling cousin in the vestibule.

When he returned fifteen minutes later, an intrigued Blake at his heels, Ned was no longer scowling. He welcomed them enthusiastically, wrung Blake's hand, and capered in a pirouette, showing off his costume. "Well?" he said eagerly. "What do you think?"

Blake put his hands on his hips and pondered Ned thoughtfully. "What's this for? A masquerade?"

"A performance, and I'm not just a cavalier, I'm the *ghost* of a cavalier—I'll need to paint my face white for that, but that's by the by—first I need to look like a cavalier, and I don't. I look like . . . like . . ."

"Like a side of beef trying to dress as a turkey," Dex supplied helpfully.

"A side of beef trying to dress as a turkey," Ned agreed, his shoulders drooping as he surveyed himself in the mirror over the fireplace. "I look fake."

"You're still you," Blake said. "You're not inhabiting the cavalier's skin."

Ned turned to him hopefully. "How do I do that? Can you teach me?"

Blake shrugged. "I can give it a try."

"Now?" Ned said, even more hopefully.

Blake glanced at the clock on the mantelpiece, then at Dex. "Shall we take this to my house? It's nearly two o'clock."

"You don't mind?" Dex asked.

"Not at all. I think Flip will enjoy it."

"Who's Flip?" Ned wanted to know.

"You'll see." Dex shooed his cousin into the bedroom. "Let's get you out of that rig."

Ned hastily stripped off the costume and donned the clothes he'd worn earlier, everything wrinkled from lying on the floor. The doublet and wig and other items were bundled into a portmanteau and the three of them set off, walking briskly, dodging puddles, the collars of their greatcoats turned up against the cold and the rain—not that Dex let many raindrops land on them.

Less than five minutes later, they hurried up the steps to the house on Old Burlington Street. Ned gaped when he saw the entrance hall. He turned on his heel, taking it all in—the yellow walls, the red carpet, the *trompe l'oeil* sky. "I say, this is rather nice."

It was more than rather nice; it was cheerful and vibrant and welcoming and it felt like Dex's home. Which it wasn't.

A kitten mewed at them from the half-landing and then scampered away. Phillip's laugh echoed from somewhere close by.

The sense of homecoming became stronger. Dex felt it in his guts, in his bones—the knowledge that this house was where he belonged and that the people in it were his family.

Which was wrong, of course. This wasn't his house and these people weren't his family. But they were his friends and they were important to him . . . and he was introducing his jingle-brained oaf of a cousin to them.

He hoped it wasn't a grievous mistake.

CHAPTER 36

Yesterday, Ella had looked through every book at Hatchard's. Today, she went further afield, to Ackermann's Repository of Arts on the Strand. The carriage set her and a footman down on the flagway and departed, wheels splashing, with instructions to return two hours later.

In the middle of the season, Ackermann's was thronged with people; on a rainy afternoon in mid-December, only a few customers were present. The shop was aglow with lamplight, the better to see the framed pictures hanging on the walls, the prints displayed on stands and in racks, the busts and the miniatures, the decorative borders and the frames, the shelves of illustrated books. Two ladies perused the miniatures, their voices a low murmur, and a shop assistant attended to an elderly couple at the counter.

A shopman approached with soundless footsteps. "May I assist you, ma'am?"

"No, thank you. I wish to browse."

Ella handed her swansdown muff into the footman's keeping, crossed to the nearest rack of prints, and began to leaf through them, not swiftly and cursorily but with intention, pausing at each print, examining it in detail, giving it the attention it deserved, that the artist deserved—and that the poor wet coachman and poor wet horses deserved, and the footman, too, otherwise why had she rousted her servants out in this rain?

She tried to find at least one thing that she liked in each image: a lamp in a window, the curve of a hillside, a flower, a smile, a rosy red apple. She came to a set of prints depicting the four seasons, each beautifully tinted by hand.

Ella stared at winter—the bare branches, the barren fields, the snow in the hollows, the hoarfrost, everything brown and gray and icy. *This is me,* she thought. *This is my heart.* She flicked through the seasons and found spring, with its delicate green leaves and gauzy pink and white blossoms. That was who she'd been three months ago, when Decimus Pryor had taught her how to laugh in bed and her heart had begun to gain color.

The next print, summer, brought a stinging rush of tears to her eyes and made her heart clench with something that felt like grief. Ella blinked rapidly, and when that wasn't enough, fished in her reticule for a handkerchief. She dabbed her eyes, dabbed again, and told herself not to be foolish. A hand-tinted print of a garden she'd never seen shouldn't make her cry. That feeling in her chest wasn't grief! It was . . . it was tiredness. Tiredness and a longing for summer sunshine. She hadn't been sleeping well, and the rain was dreary, and the print had caught her by surprise, that was all.

She shoved the handkerchief back in her reticule and resolutely looked at summer again, determined to prove herself right. See? There was nothing in the image to make her sad. Nothing at all. The scene was exuberantly joyful, bursting with color, the flowers in full bloom, bold and bright, everything bathed in golden sunshine, a butterfly dancing on the breeze.

The butterfly with its gaudy wings had her fishing for her handkerchief again.

She'd been that butterfly. Her heart had been that exuberant, joyful, colorful garden.

Ella gave a loud, resolute, unladylike sniff, turned her

back on the print racks, and marched across to the display of illustrated books. Knowledge and beauty spilled from the pages. Here was a book on classical architecture and another containing prints from grand tours of Europe. This volume was filled with botanical sketches and that one with drawings of exotic animals. Look at that! A crocodile.

She resolved to bring Phillip here. He'd love these books. He could select some to add to their library. That one of drawings from voyages in the Pacific, perhaps. Or the one alongside it about insects found in England.

Ella turned the pages of that latter tome, enthralled. Grasshoppers. Dragonflies. Bees.

Inevitably, in a book of insects, there were butterflies. Ella examined them in ruthless detail. See? There was no stinging rush of tears while she admired the yellow brimstone and the red admiral, the purple emperor and the six-spot burnet, no foolish clenching of her heart.

She turned the page and was confronted by the life cycle of the peacock butterfly, from pale green egg to black caterpillar to gray-green chrysalis to fragile, newly emerged butterfly clinging to a twig, and finally to colorful beauty with striking azure eyes on its widespread orange-brown wings.

Ella touched a light, careful fingertip to the illustration.

She had been that black caterpillar. She had been in that gray-green chrysalis. She had spread her wings and flown, bright and colorful and free. *That is me, that flying butterfly.*

No, her heart said. *That's you, clinging to the twig.*

Ella shut the book with a snap and crossed to the cabinets where the watercolor cakes were displayed in their multitudinous colors. Blue Verditer and Chinese Vermilion. Red Orpiment and Prussian Green. Royal Smalt and Dragon's Blood.

She studied the various hues, trying to pick her favorites. That watercolor cake over there was the rusty color of the peacock butterfly's wings, and that light blue was the exact shade of those disconcerting and decorative eyes. There were the colors of spring—delicate greens, pale pinks and yellows—and those cakes were summer, flourishing colors, bright and bold, the colors she surrounded herself with, the colors she wore.

Ella's gaze tracked to the browns. Bistre and Brown Lake. Brown Ochre and Cologne Earth. Van Dyke Brown. Egyptian Brown. The colors of dead leaves and dead grass and wads of dead rose petals.

Ella stared at the array of watercolor cakes, the myriad of different colors. More colors than one saw in a rainbow, more colors than one found in a garden. Colors for every season and every mood. Colors that matched who she was on the outside—and who she was on the inside.

She wanted the colors in her wardrobe and the colors in her heart to be the same, but they weren't. They were the opposite. Summer and winter.

Ella stared at the display of watercolor cakes, but what she saw was a bleak winter landscape: bare branches, icy hollows, barren fields.

Those winter colors—dreary grays and dank browns, unyielding blacks and icy, aloof whites—weren't the colors she wanted to be on the inside.

She returned to the display of books, opened the one on England's insects, and found the plate illustrating the peacock butterfly's life cycle.

Ella blew out a breath, smoothed the page flat with her palm, and studied the illustration, not merely with her eyes, but with her *heart*.

That plain black caterpillar was who she'd been in her girlhood and in her marriage, a creeping, timid little thing.

The first year of widowhood had been her chrysalis.

She'd emerged from that time of metamorphosis a butterfly, wings colorful but fragile, clinging to a twig, not yet strong enough to fly.

And then she'd flown. For the past five years, she'd flown, bright and free.

Hadn't she?

Or had she spent those years clinging to a twig, fluttering her wings but not actually flying? Had she only let go and truly flown, truly *soared*, when she'd let Decimus Pryor into her life?

Her heart said that's what she'd done.

It said that she was no longer flying, that she was clutching the twig again.

My life, my choice, Ella thought, staring at that clinging butterfly.

What did she choose?

To hold on to the twig? Or to fly?

Fly, of course. But flying meant inviting Decimus Pryor back into her life, into her bed, into her heart.

It meant accepting his offer of marriage, because she didn't want to fly halfheartedly. If she flew, she *flew*. No reservations, no retreat to the safety of that twig. Nothing but wholehearted commitment.

It was terrifying to think of marrying again, of letting a man control her happiness . . . but didn't Decimus already have that power? Not a husband's power, but a loved one's power. His absence made the world dull, made *her* dull, leached all the color from her heart.

And while the thought of marriage was terrifying, it was also uplifting. Because with Decimus, she wouldn't be a butterfly clinging to a twig. Her heart would be colorful and her wings would be strong and she'd be free. Free to fly, free to laugh, free to love.

But also shackled.

She'd be chained to Decimus as a wife was chained to a husband, as Minette was chained to Arthur—except that Minette didn't think she was chained, because Arthur was her friend and would never abuse his marital power.

Decimus wouldn't abuse that power, either. He was her friend, just as much as Arthur was Minette's friend. He was the sunshine in which she flourished. He wouldn't try to control her. He'd let her bloom, let her be herself, let her fly free. He'd *help* her to fly free.

Ella closed the book decisively. The clock above the counter told her that the carriage wouldn't return for another hour.

She couldn't wait that long.

The hackney disgorged them in Old Burlington Street. Ella and the footman ran up the steps. "Send round to the stables, please, Chisnall," she told the butler. "Let them know I don't need the carriage again."

"Yes, ma'am."

Ella handed the footman her muff, untied her bonnet and gave him that, too, then took off her cardinal red cape and piled it into his arms. "Take those up to Hedgepeth, please." Then she set off for the library.

It was empty, but sounds of hilarity led her to Arthur's costume room. Ella tapped lightly on the door. Her heart was beating faster than running up the steps from the street warranted and she felt a little breathless.

The inhabitants of the costume room didn't hear her knock. The sounds of hilarity continued unabated.

Ella opened the door and looked inside.

She saw a tall cavalier with a pointed black beard, curling mustache, and ghostly pallor.

The cavalier was engaged in a sword fight with a very small pirate who also had a beard and mustache and a ghostly pallor. *Clack!* went the wooden sword blades, and *clack!* again, the pair of them uttering whoops as they attacked and then danced out of range.

Ella felt that she ought to recognize the cavalier. There was something quite familiar about him. He wasn't Decimus Pryor, though, because Decimus was standing with Minette and Arthur, all three of them laughing and clapping and whooping almost as loudly as the combatants.

The room was a chaos of costumes and color and noise, of frivolity and merriment. Her late husband would have taken one look at such a scene and recoiled in horror. Ella wanted to be part of it.

A kitten darted past her and into the room, keen to join in, too.

Ella stepped resolutely over the threshold, closed the door behind her, and stood with her back pressed to it. Her heart was still beating too swiftly. She felt as if she stood on the parapet of Westminster Bridge, preparing to jump off.

No, not preparing to jump; preparing to fly.

Clack! went the wooden swords. Phillip laughed, and the cavalier laughed, and Arthur and Minette and Decimus laughed.

Ella wanted to laugh, too. Not over by the door, but with them, shoulder to shoulder with Minette and Arthur and Decimus Pryor.

My life. My choice.

She pushed away from the door and crossed to where the others stood.

Decimus was the first to notice her. He glanced over his shoulder. The laughter on his face snuffed out instantly. He seemed almost to flinch. He looked briefly away and then back again. A courteous smile stretched his lips but didn't reach his eyes. He inclined his head politely. "Lady Fortrose," he said beneath the noise.

Ella's heart beat even faster. She felt a little breathless, a little lightheaded. "Mr. Pryor."

"*Ma chère!* I thought you were spending the afternoon at Ackermann's."

"I changed my mind," Ella said, her gaze still holding Decimus's. Had he heard the meaning in her words? That she'd changed her mind about more than merely Ackermann's? "I realized that I was wrong about something."

She stepped closer. Close enough to touch Decimus's arm if she chose to. Close enough to take his hand if she wished.

Clack! went the wooden swords. Phillip whooped and the unknown cavalier uttered a booming laugh.

"Bravo!" exclaimed Arthur, clapping heartily.

Decimus didn't look at the combatants. He held himself very still, his gaze on her face. He looked uncertain, wary, braced for rejection.

Marriage didn't mean subjugation. Arthur and Minette were friends, equals, partners. She and Decimus Pryor could be those things—and lovers, too, which Minette and Arthur weren't. Friends, equals, partners, lovers.

Ella stepped even closer, until her sleeve brushed his. "I changed my mind," she said again, and reached for his hand.

Startlement crossed Decimus's face, followed by dawning hope. His fingers flexed around hers, returning her clasp tentatively. His gaze searched her face.

Ella smiled at him and tightened her grip on his hand.

His touch soaked into her like rain soaking into dry soil. It warmed her like sunshine and brought color flowing back into her heart.

"Aunt Ella!" Phillip cried. "Look at me! I'm a pirate ghost!"

Ella forced herself to look away from Decimus's dark, intent, hopeful eyes. "I can see that. Who is your foe?"

The cavalier swept off his plumed hat and made her a magnificent leg. "Nonus Pryor, ma'am. At your service."

That was Nonus Pryor beneath the pallor and the pointed beard and the long black ringlets? "Good gracious. I didn't recognize you at all."

The cavalier put on his hat, puffed out his chest, and strutted a few steps. The resemblance between the two cousins leaped to the eye—then the cavalier spun around, uttered a yodeling cry, and rushed at Phillip. The battle recommenced.

Ella turned to Decimus. "We need to talk," she murmured beneath the sounds of combat and merriment.

"Now?" he murmured back.

"Later. This evening." Right now, she wanted to hold his hand and bask in his nearness and feel the color return to her heart.

It was her life, her choice, and this was what she chose: color and laughter and friendship and love. She chose Decimus Pryor.

CHAPTER 37

After Ned died—very loudly and theatrically—Blake tried to teach him to walk like a ghostly cavalier. The lesson was not successful.

Ned might look like a ghost now, his skin a luminous white thanks to something Blake had called bismuth, but he was incapable of moving like either a cavalier or a ghost. Blake minced in high-heeled court shoes; Ned clomped in the cavalier's high-heeled boots. Blake strolled elegantly; Ned clomped. Blake wafted; Ned clomped.

Dex held Eloïse's hand and watched. Part of him wanted Ned gone, so that he and Eloïse could slip away and talk. The rest of him wanted the lesson to last forever, because he was afraid that an enchantment lay over the costume room and that when they stepped out into the corridor the spell would break and she would stop holding his hand, stop glancing at him with shy warmth in her eyes, stop smiling at him so softly and so joyfully.

I changed my mind.

I was wrong about something.

What did that mean? Did she want them to be lovers again . . . or did she mean what he hoped she meant: that she wanted to marry him?

Dex clung to her hand and hoped.

Wigs, beards, mustaches, and cosmetics were removed. The ladies withdrew from the room, so that costumes could be removed, too. Dex reluctantly released Eloïse's hand, reluctantly watched her go, then set to work assisting Ned out of his cavalier's attire. Ned talked the whole while with Blake, who was helping Phillip revert from pirate to seven-year-old boy. By the time Ned was back in his usual garb, it had been decided that after a year of deportment, dancing, and fencing lessons, Ned would come to Blake for acting lessons.

Dex probably ought to be worried—Ned wouldn't be rash enough or foolish enough to truly resurrect the Ghostly Cavalier, would he?—but he had more important concerns, namely Eloïse Fortrose and her change of heart. He paid scant attention to the conversation between Ned and Blake or to the possible consequences of a collaboration between a master actor and his prankster of a cousin.

Blake invited them both to stay for dinner. Dex and Ned accepted.

The dining room was just a dining room—more colorful, certainly, than most dining rooms in England, but still merely a room where one ate one's dinner. Why, then, did his heart lift when he entered? Why was it such a tremendous relief to sit at that familiar table? And why did it make him happy to see Ned taking a place at that table, too, and getting along so well with everyone?

They dined *en famille*—and that phrase was why it felt so good to be at the table again. Family. He wanted to belong to the family in this house in Old Burlington Street in the same way that he belonged to his family at Linwood Castle. Having Ned here was a glimpse of a future he desperately craved.

I've changed my mind, Eloïse had said, and then she'd held his hand for a full half hour.

Did that mean what he wanted it to mean?

Hope grew, taking up the space in Dex's belly where hunger should be. He picked at his chicken fricassée, picked at his broccoli à la *Flamand,* picked at his Rhenish cream. Would he and Ned and Eloïse and the Blakes and young Phillip soon be at another table? A table at Linwood Castle?

He hoped so. Lord, how he hoped.

He wanted to look up from his plate and see his family and Eloïse's family dining together, talking and laughing with one another.

Dex toyed with a Savoy cake and decided that if Eloïse wanted a long-term affair rather than marriage, he would agree. Between them, they had sufficient cachet to pull off such a feat, she a viscountess, he the grandson of a duke. They could become one of society's open secrets, known by all, ignored by all. She could visit Linwood as his friend, and the housekeeper would give them rooms side by side, and there'd be no scandal.

It wasn't what he wanted, but it was doable. It would be bearable.

After dinner, they played several merry games of fish, until it was time for Phillip to go to bed. "You'll come tomorrow, Mister Dex?"

"I'll come tomorrow," he promised.

Phillip withdrew, hand in hand with Madame Blake, discussing bedtime stories with his great-uncle, kittens frisking at their heels.

Dex caught Ned's eye and tipped his head at the door, a message that his cousin failed to understand.

Dex frowned at the dolt and jerked his thumb at the door, forcefully.

That message, Ned caught. He smirked, climbed to his feet, and took his leave, heading into the night with the portmanteau containing the cavalier tucked under one arm.

At last, Dex and Eloïse were alone.

Dex's throat was suddenly dry. "You wished to talk?"

"Yes. But not here. Somewhere we won't be disturbed."

Somewhere they wouldn't be disturbed turned out to be the crimson-and-gold bedchamber, which Dex took as a hopeful sign. Eloïse didn't cross to the bed, though; she went to stand by the fireplace, gesturing for him to take one of the armchairs there.

Dex would rather stand, but he was taller than she was and she didn't give the impression of someone who wished to be loomed over right now. She looked a little nervous, a little anxious—two emotions that he was currently in the grip of, too.

He sat.

Eloïse knitted her fingers together, took a deep breath, and said, "If your offer still stands, I accept it."

She didn't look overjoyed; she looked like someone bracing for an ordeal—which was not how Dex wanted her to look while accepting his suit. Unease rose in his chest. "Have your feelings for me changed?" he asked.

"No."

The unease intensified into foreboding.

"My feelings for you are what they have been for some time," Eloïse continued, clearly uncomfortable. Her gaze flitted from Dex's face to his neckcloth to his shoulder, where it settled. Her grip on her hands tightened.

"I didn't think I was capable of romantic love," she told his shoulder. "I still don't think I am. What I feel for you doesn't feel *romantic*. It feels . . ." She pressed her lips together, met his gaze fully, and burst out: "You give my heart color."

The words robbed Dex of breath.

He gave her heart *color*.

He exhaled slowly, shakily. Eloïse's gaze skipped away again, to land on the brocade arm of the chair he sat in. Her pale cheeks were flushed, her hands knotted together at her breast.

"You give my heart color, too," Dex said, meaning it.

Her gaze rose to meet his.

Long seconds passed, while the fire murmured encouragingly in the grate; then Eloïse said gravely. "I think it means I love you."

Dex smiled at her. "I know it means I love you."

Her flush deepened. She returned his smile shyly, hesitantly.

Dex stood and stepped close and took her clenched hands in both of his, holding them lightly. "We don't have to marry. We can stay as lovers—"

"I want to marry you, because then you'll live with us, and that's what I'd like. It's what I *want*."

Dex clasped her hands more firmly. "I want that, too."

Her gaze dropped. She stared at his lapel. "I'm scared of marriage," she whispered.

Dex released her hands and gathered her in his arms, not crushingly close, not caging, not smothering, but gently and comfortingly, an embrace she could easily break free of. "I'm not Francis Fortrose," he said, dipping his head to speak quietly in her ear. "I won't crib and confine you. You have my word."

She breathed out a sigh. Her shoulders relaxed and she leaned into his embrace, resting her forehead against his breastbone. "I know."

"I won't tell you what to read or eat or wear or do—and I will *never* call you Louise. I promise."

"You can call me Ella if you like," she whispered shyly.

"You can call me Dex."

They stood like that for several minutes. Quiet minutes. Long minutes. Minutes when Dex didn't think about the future at all, didn't think about marrying Eloïse or about taking her to Linwood Castle as his bride and introducing her to his family. Minutes when he simply existed in the here and now: the softness of her hair beneath his lips, her warmth in his arms, the way that she leaned into him so trustingly.

"I'm sorry about last month," she said finally, into the superfine cloth of his lapel. "I panicked."

"I should have led up to it more circumspectly."

Eloïse shook her head against his chest. "I think I would have panicked regardless." She pushed away far enough to look up at him. "I thought I would regret marrying you, but what I regretted was *not* marrying you. Minette was right: it's not often you find someone who lights up your life."

Dex felt a blush invade his cheeks, felt a foolish, besotted smile take possession of his lips. "I light up your life?"

She blushed, too, and nodded.

"Good, because you light up mine. You're like no one I've ever known." She delighted him, challenged him, made his life richer, better, brighter. He'd learned things about himself that he would never have learned but for her.

Dex's foolish, besotted smile became a laugh. He caught Eloïse close and swung her around, lifted them both off the carpet with his magic and twirled in an exuberant pirouette. He laughed again, loudly and joyfully, and she laughed, too, clutching him as they spun. Then he set her carefully on her feet and kissed her. Not a breathless, giddy kiss, but something gentle and reverent.

They disrobed without haste, helping one another with buttons and hooks, speaking in low murmurs, gifting light kisses and soft touches. They made love just as quietly, just as simply. There was no frolicking, no wrists tied to bedposts, just connection, tender and meaningful.

Afterwards, as they lay entwined, Eloïse said, "I surrounded myself with color, but there was never any in my heart until you. I was colorless inside, and now I'm not."

Dex felt his nose sting, as if he was about to cry. His instinct was to retreat into flippancy. He bit the tip of his tongue to stop a joke spilling out. Now wasn't the time for jokes.

Before he could come up with a suitable response, she said, "When I'm with you, I fly—and I don't mean because of your magic. You make me fly by being you."

Dex released her and groped for the sheet, but he was laughing as he mopped his eyes. Laughing and crying.

When he was no longer a watering pot, he said, "Everything you just said is how I feel about you." He smoothed the damp, wrinkled sheet and glanced at her, suddenly shy. "I never thought I'd fall in love."

"Neither did I."

They shared a smile, while the candles cast soft light and the fire mumbled contentedly in the grate. Eloïse's hair was a messy silver halo, her skin a pale candlelit gold. She looked like an angel, a goddess, a nymph.

His nymph.

"My raking days are over," Dex told her. "You have my word. The only bed I'll be in from now on is yours." He patted the mattress emphatically.

"This isn't my bed. My real bedchamber is through there." Eloïse pointed to the door she'd fled through after his disastrous marriage proposal. "Would you like to see it?"

Dex did wish to see it. He climbed off the four-poster and took the hand she held out to him.

Through the door was a dressing room decorated in blues and sea greens. Stepping into it was like stepping into a magical undersea world illuminated by soft lamplight.

A bathtub stood beside a fireplace in which embers glowed. "Do you wish to bathe?" Eloïse asked. "The water should still be warm."

"No. Do you?"

She shook her head and drew him across the room and through another door. Her real bedroom. It was no crimson-and-gold den of sybaritic delight, no blue-and-green undersea world. It was like sunrise, like summer, like the heart of a rose. The colors were lush and rich and warm. It felt like a sanctuary. Eloïse's sanctuary, rosy and restful.

"Would you like to stay the night?" she asked.

"Would you like me to?"

"Yes."

Dex's heart felt as if it grew two sizes with happiness. "Then I'll stay."

The bedclothes were turned back invitingly, a warming pan tucked cozily between the sheets. Dex pulled it out and laid it on the hearth. "Which side do you prefer?"

"I don't know. Francis and I had separate rooms. I've never slept the night with anyone."

She looked so adorably perplexed that Dex laughed and laid a light kiss on the tip of her nose. "Let's find out then, shall we?"

Her smile was bright and shy. "Yes, let's."

Climbing into bed was something Dex did every night, but this time it felt momentous. Life-changing. They slipped between the sheets and made themselves comfortable in each other's arms. Dex's heart swelled several more sizes until it felt as if it might burst out of his chest with joy. He felt giddy, dizzy. This was going to be his future: sharing a bed with the woman he loved, sharing a *life* with the woman he loved.

He pressed a kiss to her pale, silky hair, pressed a kiss to the smooth skin of her shoulder. His giddiness, his joyfulness, was too great to contain. He wanted to levitate the bed two feet in the air and set it dancing. He didn't think Eloïse would enjoy that right at that moment, so he kissed her shoulder a second time and blew some of his giddiness against her skin in a silly toot of sound.

She huffed a laugh. "You are ridiculous," she told him, her breath a warm caress against his chest, then she pressed her lips where her breath had been, a soft kiss. "I love your ridiculousness," she whispered. "Don't ever stop."

Dex's nose stung with tears again. It took him several minutes to master his emotions, by which time she was asleep in his arms, warm and relaxed. That felt momentous, too. Life-changing. Eloïse Fortrose was asleep in his arms. Eloïse Fortrose was going to become Eloïse *Pryor*.

He liked that: Eloïse Pryor.

Dex sighed happily and followed his soon-to-be wife into sleep.

CHAPTER 38

Waking with a man in her bed—waking in a man's arms—ought to have been claustrophobic and caging. It wasn't. Instead of panic, Ella felt contentment, joy, relief. Her heart was filled with rainbows today, filled with happiness and freedom.

They'd changed position while they slept. They now lay like spoons nestled in a drawer, her back to his chest. One of Decimus's arms was around her waist, his fingers entwined with hers.

Hedgepeth had been into the room; the curtains were open. Gentle morning light illuminated the bedchamber.

Ella spent several minutes admiring Decimus's hand, admiring his fingers, his knuckles, his nails. It was a very masculine hand, strong and capable, and yet beautiful, too. Her favorite hand in all the world.

His mouth was her favorite mouth in all the world, too. His ridiculous, smirking, laughing mouth. And his heart was her favorite heart.

Ella slipped her fingers free from his clasp, carefully eased herself out from under his arm, and crept out of bed. She didn't want to leave that cozy nest, but she wanted to see . . . *needed* to see . . .

Hedgepeth had laid out a dressing gown for her at the end of the bed, and one for Decimus, too.

Ella donned her dressing gown, belted it at her waist, and tiptoed around the four-poster. Bedclothes were drawn up around Decimus's shoulders in a warm, snug cocoon. Against the creamy whiteness of the pillows, his hair was as black as ravens' feathers. There, glimpsed between tousled locks of hair and that cozy cocoon of bedding, was the nape of his neck—smooth skin and firm muscle and the vulnerable knobs of his vertebrae.

The sight plucked at Ella's heartstrings. She wanted to cover his nape with her palm, to keep it safe forever, to keep *him* safe.

She leaned down and pressed a soft kiss to that bare, vulnerable skin.

Decimus stirred, snuffled into the pillow, then rolled towards her. His eyelids fluttered open. He gave her a sleepy smile. "Morning."

Ella gazed down at him besottedly. "Good morning."

Decimus rubbed his face and raked a hand through his hair, making it stand on end. Stubble was dark on his cheeks and jaw. He didn't look like a suave, smooth-tongued rake or perfectly turned-out dandy. He looked rumpled and half-awake and heartbreakingly beautiful.

Ella leaned down and kissed him again, this time on the lips. A good morning kiss. The first good morning kiss she had ever given anyone.

She would have lingered in that kiss, but now that she was out of bed, her body was informing her that it had a rather pressing need. A pressing need that Decimus probably had, too.

"Would you like to join us for breakfast?"

The sleepiness fell from his face. He sat up amid the rumpled sheets and indented pillows, naked, unshaven, disheveled, and utterly gorgeous. "For breakfast?"

"Yes."

Decimus blinked several times, and then said, "Yes, thank you. I would."

Ella beamed at him. "Good." She tapped the bedside cabinet with a fingertip. "There's a chamber pot in here and a dressing gown on the end of the bed. Come through to the dressing room when you're ready." She turned towards the door. If Hedgepeth had had the presence of mind to fetch a dressing gown for Decimus, she probably also had clothing and a razor laid out for him.

"Eloïse?"

She turned back.

Awake and with the strong musculature of his chest and arms on display, his nape hidden from view, Decimus no longer looked defenseless or vulnerable. He managed to look shy, though, diffident and hopeful. "You're still certain? About us? You still wish to marry?"

Ella gave an emphatic nod. "I'm very certain. I'd marry you this morning if it were possible."

A joyful smile lit his face. "We can marry tomorrow, if you like? I'll purchase a special license today."

"Don't you wish to get married in Gloucestershire? Your family . . ."

From Decimus's expression, it was clear that he would like his family to be present when he married, but what he said was, "They already know of my intentions. If you want to marry this week, in town, we can."

Ella had everyone she loved in this house, but Decimus didn't. "Purchase a special license, but we'll get married in Gloucestershire."

"But we'll live here, yes?" He patted the bed, clearly meaning Old Burlington Street, not merely London.

"You like it here?"

"It feels like home."

Ella desperately needed a chamber pot, but she ran back to him, placed a hasty kiss on his lips, and said, "Yes, we'll live here." Then she hurried for the door.

Ella dressed in her raspberry-red kerseymere gown and sunrise-pink-and-orange cashmere shawl—colors that matched how she felt inside—and left Decimus in the capable hands of one of the footmen. The breakfast parlor was occupied, Minette sipping hot chocolate, Arthur making inroads into eggs and sirloin, Phillip cutting up his sausages. Every servant in the house was probably aware of Pryor's presence in her bedchamber that morning, but Minette didn't look at her knowingly over the rim of her cup and Arthur didn't surreptitiously wink at her. Whatever gossip was circulating among the servants hadn't reached here yet.

Ella exchanged greetings, crossed to the sideboard, and chose from the array of dishes. There was more food than usual. A fifth place had been set at the table. How had Arthur and Minette not noticed the extra food? That extra setting? Or perhaps they had. Perhaps they were waiting for her to say something?

Ella took her seat at the table.

Minette continued to drink her hot chocolate. Arthur continued to eat his sirloin.

Phillip grinned at her across the table.

Ella grinned back. She spread a napkin on her lap, poured herself a cup of tea, sipped it.

The first few times she'd invited Decimus Pryor into her bed, Minette had asked her if she'd learned anything. Minette hadn't asked that question for a long time, but Ella wanted her to ask it today. If she did, Ella would say that she'd learned that she could be filled not just with sunshine, but with rainbows. She'd learned that happiness could make her feel as if she walked on air, that love truly could give you wings.

She'd learned that giving her heart to another person didn't mean putting it in a cage; it meant setting herself free to fly.

Minette selected a brioche from the basket and broke it

open. The scents of vanilla and cinnamon wafted enticingly across the table. *Ask me,* Ella wanted to say. *Ask me what I've learned.*

Minette glanced at her. Her eyes narrowed slightly. She cocked her head. "You look different this morning, *ma chère.* Is that a new way of doing your hair?"

Ella laughed. "No. I don't know. Perhaps?" She hadn't paid any attention to what Hedgepeth had done with her hair. "That's not what's different, though."

Minette's thin, elegant eyebrows arched. "Oh?" She picked up her cup again and pursed her lips to sip.

Behind Ella, the door to the breakfast parlor opened.

Minette halted in mid-sip, her eyes wide.

Ella glanced over her shoulder. Decimus Pryor stood on the threshold. They exchanged a brief smile; then he stepped into the room and closed the door. There was no dandy's flourish, no rake's smirk or swagger, just the simple, ordinary everydayness of a man entering his own breakfast parlor, unexceptional and unremarkable—but definitely not unmemorable. This was an occasion to remember: the first time Decimus breakfasted in this house. The first morning of their life together.

Ella's heart grew lighter, freer, more joyful.

Minette put her cup down with a clatter.

Arthur glanced up from his plate and did an impressive double take. Arthur's valet might have supplied Decimus with dressing gown, drawers, stockings, shirt, neckcloth, and razor, but he'd clearly been discreet about doing so. So discreet that his master hadn't been aware of it.

"Mister Dex!" Phillip cried. "You're here for breakfast!"

"He'll be here for breakfast every day soon," Ella told him. "He's going to live with us."

Phillip gave a delighted whoop. He jumped from his chair, ran to Decimus, and flung his arms around his waist. For a moment Decimus looked as if he might cry; then he laughed and swept Phillip off his feet, swinging him up and around.

There may have been a little magic in that swing, but Phillip didn't notice.

Ella looked away and found both Minette and Arthur staring at her. "We're getting married," she told them.

"*Oh là là!*" Minette exclaimed, clapping her hands in delight. She sprang up from her chair and came around the table to embrace Ella in a cloud of silk and expensive perfume.

Arthur hugged her, too, and so did Phillip, and after everyone had hugged everyone they possibly could, sometimes twice, sometimes three times, they sat down to their breakfast again.

The first breakfast of their life together as a family.

$\mathcal{A}$FTERWARDS

$\mathcal{T}$wo days after Christmas, Ella went down to the Linwood Castle stableyard with her husband. *Her* husband. Decimus Pryor. Dex. The man who'd not only filled her heart with color, but had given it wings.

The afternoon was chilly and gray, bleak, but Ella's heart skipped as joyfully as if it were midsummer. The stableyard smelled of horses and hay and manure, scents that were earthy and unrefined, but not at all unpleasant, not even the manure. Dex called one of the grooms over. "Bryce, can you fetch Mr. Conran for us, please?"

The groom departed in the direction of the kitchen gardens, a vast expanse of beds and trellises and succession houses that Ella hoped to explore soon.

Dex took her hand and drew her into the dim, fragrant warmth of the stables. It was a cavernous place, far larger than the stables behind Hanover Square where the kittens had been born. There were scores of stalls, scores of horses—carriage horses, riding horses, work horses—and dozens of grooms and stableboys to tend to them.

Dex knew most of the men by name and he had a cheerful word for everyone. They strolled the length of the stables, looking the horses over, rubbing inquisitive noses, slowly making their way towards the far end.

The head groom joined them when they were halfway down the long row of stalls. Woodrow was a wiry man with a weatherbeaten face and a shock of gray hair. "Come to see the pups, have you?"

"Yes," Ella replied eagerly. "We have!"

This wasn't the first time she'd visited the puppies. She'd snatched a glimpse of them the afternoon they'd arrived at Linwood Castle, another glimpse the day before her marriage, a third glimpse the day after, but this was the first time she would be able to linger, to pet them and play with them and properly make their acquaintance. The last fortnight had been a whirlwind, but finally the hurly-burly of preparing to travel—and actually traveling—and arriving—and meeting everyone—and preparing for a wedding—and actually *getting married*—and then celebrating Christmas immediately afterwards had subsided and at last she had time to catch her breath, time to relax, time to explore, time to play with puppies.

The exploring would take weeks. Linwood Castle was a great deal larger and more splendid than Ella had anticipated, but also a great deal more welcoming. The castle and its inhabitants had opened their arms and gathered them close, herself and Minette, Arthur and Phillip.

Her first interview with Maximus Pryor, Duke of Linwood, had been daunting because he was a duke, daunting because Dex had urged Arthur and Minette to be honest about their pasts, daunting because he'd told them that the duke could actually *hear lies*. Ella had walked into that interview with her stomach clenched as tightly as a fist—but it had turned out that there'd been nothing to fear. Arthur and Minette had seemed to sense a kindred spirit in the old duke immediately, and while Linwood had been surprised by their revelations, even shocked at times, he'd responded with chuckles rather than condemnation. By the end of that interview, the French opera dancer, the actor from Bristol, and the Duke of Linwood had been friends—and Ella had gained a grandfather.

The old man was certainly remarkable, and not at all what Ella had expected in a duke. Instead of being stern, stand-offish, and supercilious, he was warm-hearted and wise. It was clear that he loved his family deeply, and equally clear that he was loved deeply in return—and now that love encompassed her and Phillip, Arthur and Minette. The duke's seal of approval had been all that was needed for the Pryors to welcome them with open arms. Her family had expanded beyond Decimus Pryor to his parents and his sister, his uncles and aunts, his cousins, his grandparents, all of them opening their hearts unreservedly. Ella had everything she'd longed for as a lonely child in an attic nursery. She had a father-in-law who teased her and a mother-in-law she could confide in, a sister to giggle with. And for the first time in her life, she had a female friend her own age, because if Arthur and Minette had found a kindred spirit in the old duke, she'd found one in her cousin-in-law Lord Octavius's wife, Pip.

It was beyond anything Ella had ever imagined, a cornucopia of unhoped for joys.

They strolled further, Woodrow and Dex conversing with the easy familiarity of men who'd known each other for years. As they neared the last stall, the head gardener joined them. "You wished to see me, sir?"

"Yes." Dex tipped his head at Ella, handing her the reins of the conversation.

"We've come to see the puppies, Mr. Conran. Will you tell us which ones you wish to keep and which ones we may choose from?"

The gardener smiled at her. "Of course, ma'am."

They entered a stall that smelled of horse and hay, but that was currently inhabited by a dog called Bess and her six-week-old pups.

Ella knelt on the straw, heedless of harm to her dress. Dex knelt alongside her. Together they observed the exuberant, noisy nest of puppies.

"Oh . . ." Ella breathed. She beamed at her husband, her

excitement too big for a mere smile, too big even for a grin. Her whole face seemed to be radiating excitement and delight.

Dex laughed and put an arm around her, hugging her close, before releasing her again. "You look as if you want to take them all home with us."

"I do," Ella admitted. Six puppies and three kittens. Was that too much for one household?

It possibly was. Best to start with one puppy. But which one?

Bess was a mid-sized dog, brown and long-legged. Her pups were a range of browns, too—chocolate brown, toffee brown, honey brown—but they all currently had short legs. Short, clumsy, adorable legs and fluffy, adorable coats and pink, adorable tongues and floppy, adorable ears. Even their needle-sharp teeth were adorable.

Bess was an affectionate creature, dispersing her licks as lavishly to humans as she did to her offspring. She didn't mind Conran picking up the puppies, lifting their tails to check which were male and which female. "Dogs come in all types, like people. There's timid ones, like this 'un here, and bold ones, like this wee lass, and ones that are curiouser than a cat."

"You can tell their characters already?" Ella asked, surprised.

"Oh, aye," the gardener said.

Woodrow, the head groom, nodded and said, "Starts showing when they're about five weeks old." He hunkered down on the straw alongside them. The puppy Conran had called bold scrambled over to nip at Woodrow's breeches. He chuckled and rubbed its ears.

"Will you keep only the bold ones?" Ella asked.

"Bold's best for poachers," Conran said. "But timid's useful, too. A timid dog can keep rabbits from the cabbage patch just as well as any dog."

Ella nodded, absorbing this information. "Which would be best for a child? Timid or bold?"

"Soft," Woodrow said, still rubbing the puppy's ears. "That's what you should be thinkin' of. Soft or hard."

Conran nodded his agreement. "There's dogs as are soft and dogs as are hard. The soft ones will want nothing more than to please you, like Bess here, and the hard ones will push against every limit you give 'em. You can train 'em, and they're sharp, but you need to keep on top of 'em every day."

"Oh." Ella observed the squirming pile of puppies thoughtfully. "May we have one that's soft, but not too timid? Is there one in this litter? Can you tell that yet?"

Conran's sun-browned face creased in a smile. "This one," he said, handing her a puppy. "She's the softest of the lot. She won't need much correcting."

"Is she timid or bold?" Ella asked, accepting the warm, fluffy bundle.

"Neither. Friendly is what she is. She'll lick the young master to death given half the chance."

Since the puppy was currently attempting to lick as much of her face as it could, Ella believed him. She laughed and avoided that eager tongue, cuddling the little creature close. Her puppy. Their puppy. She looked at Dex, her heart full to bursting.

"Someone's stealing our puppies!" a voice declared from the entrance to the stall. Nonus Pryor loomed there, Phillip riding on his broad shoulders. "Dastardly fiends!"

"They're Conran's puppies," Dex informed his cousin. "And we're not stealing; we're choosing." He glanced at Ella, his eyes bright and smiling. "Shall we show Flip our new puppy?"

Nonus swung the boy down. Phillip came to crouch alongside Ella, his face bright with excitement. She carefully passed him the puppy. The little creature set to work licking whatever parts of Phillip it could reach, tail wagging joyfully.

Phillip giggled and squirmed, and the puppy licked and squirmed, and Ella's heart had more color than it could contain; it brimmed to overflowing, rainbows spilling everywhere.

Dex put an arm around her. She leaned into his warmth, his strength. *My life*, she thought. *My choice*.

But it was more than that now, bigger than that, better than that.

Our life. Our choices.

Hers and Decimus Pryor's.

The new year was just around the corner, the first year of their lives together. There was magic in that togetherness, freedom in it, color. More magic and freedom and color than Ella had ever hoped for, more than she'd ever imagined was possible.

"Happy?" Dex murmured, beneath the sound of Phillip's laughter and Nonus's conversation with Woodrow and Conran and the puppies' shrill little yips.

"Yes." Ella pulled away slightly, enough to see his face. "You?"

He smiled back at her. Decimus Pryor, plaything of widows and trouncer of highwaymen, friend and lover and husband, keeper of her heart. "Yes."

$\mathcal{A}$UTHOR'S $\mathcal{N}$OTE

The sentence "My postilion has been struck by lightning," allegedly appeared in a Hungarian phrasebook in the 1800s. Apparently it was also used in Dutch, Norwegian, Portuguese, Russian, and French phrasebooks, but no one has ever found a copy of a phrasebook containing this sentence, so these claims are likely apocryphal. Apocryphal or not, it's still a great phrase and has appeared in *Punch* and the *New Yorker* and even spawned a comic poem.

If your eye delighted in the word "nicknackatory," that gem is from Francis Grose's 1811 *Dictionary of Vulgar Slang.* "Riding St. George," also comes from Grose, but "diligence de Lyon," is from *Dictionnaire* Érotique *Moderne,* by Alfred Delvau, which was published in the 1800s.

The history of the Albany, where Ned has his rooms, is rather interesting. It was built for Viscount Melbourne in 1771 and went by the name Melbourne House. In 1791, the viscount swapped houses with Prince Frederick, Duke of York and Albany. (Yes, they swapped houses!) Melbourne House became known as York House. Alas, Prince Frederick was rather too extravagant with his spending and was forced to retrench, selling York House in 1802. Henry Holland converted it into 69 bachelor "sets" (sets of rooms), and it became known as the Albany. It was a very fashionable residence in Regency times—and still is, because yes, the Albany still exists!

In its early days, women weren't allowed on the premises. It's going to be interesting to see if I can sneak one into Ned's rooms when I write his book. (Ned's book will be the last in the series, because he has a *lot* of growing up to do.)

Real-life residents of the Albany included Lord Byron and Georgette Heyer, the doyenne of Regency romance.

The Medley of Lovers (or, Miss in Her Teens) was a farce in two acts written in 1747 by the actor and playwright, David Garrick. The play finally made its way onto the silver screen in 2014, with a cast including the great Sir Ian McKellen. It's a gorgeously filmed and very silly romp titled *Miss in Her Teens.*

The names of the watercolor cakes that Ella saw at Ackermann's are all genuine. Yes, Dragon's Blood really was a paint color!

Do you like listening to books?
The Baleful Godmother series is available in audio!

Praise for the narrators:

**"An intelligent, well-paced performance
that shows once again why Ms. Landor is such a
beloved narrator of historical romance."**
~ AudioGals, on *Ruining Miss Wrotham*

**"Landor really gets under the skins of the leads, unerringly
pinpointing the emotional heart of their relationship."**
~ Caz's Reading Room, on *Trusting Miss Trentham*

**"Landor delivers another flawless performance.
Accomplished, nuanced, emotionally resonant."**
~ AudioGals, on *Unmasking Miss Appleby*

**"As usual Hamish Long is amazing! All the characters
come alive. A pure delight to listen to."**
~ Audible reviewer, on *Claiming Mister Kemp*

Available wherever audiobooks are sold.

Listen to samples at
www.emilylarkin.com/audio-books

$\mathcal{T}$HANK $\mathcal{Y}$OU

Thanks for reading *Decimus and the Wary Widow*. I hope you enjoyed it!

If you'd like to be notified whenever I release a new book, please join my readers' group, which you can find at www.emilylarkin.com/newsletter.

If you enjoyed this book, please consider leaving a review on Goodreads or elsewhere. Reviews and word of mouth help other readers to find books and are the best gift you can give an author.

Decimus and the Wary Widow is part of the Baleful Godmother series. I'm currently giving free digital copies of the series prequel, *The Fey Quartet*, and the first novel in the original series, *Unmasking Miss Appleby*, to anyone who joins my readers' group. You'll also receive exclusive bonus scenes and other goodies. Here's the link: www.emilylarkin.com/starter-library.

Decimus and the Wary Widow is the second book in the Pryor Cousins series. The first Pryor novel, *Octavius and the Perfect Governess*, stars Dex's cousin, Octavius, who goes undercover to protect a governess in jeopardy. For the first chapter of *Octavius and the Perfect Governess*, please keep reading.

OCTAVIUS
and the
Perfect Governess

*O*ctavius Pryor should have won the race. It wasn't difficult. The empty ballroom at his grandfather-the-duke's house was eighty yards long, he'd lined one hundred and twenty chairs up in a row across the polished wooden floorboards, and making his way from one side of the room to the other without touching the floor was easy. His cousin Nonus Pryor—Ned—also had one hundred and twenty chairs to scramble over, but Ned was as clumsy as an ox and Octavius knew he could make it across the ballroom first, which was exactly what he was doing—until his foot went right through the seat of one of the delicate giltwood chairs. He was going too fast to catch his balance. Both he and the chair crashed to the floor. And that was him out of the race.

Octavius ignored the hooting and sat up. The good news was that he didn't appear to have broken anything except the chair. The bad news was that Ned, who'd been at least twenty chairs behind him, was now almost guaranteed to win.

Ned slowed to a swagger—as best as a man could swagger while clambering along a row of giltwood chairs.

Octavius gritted his teeth and watched his cousin navigate the last few dozen chairs. Ned glanced back at Octavius, smirked, and then slowly reached out and touched the wall with one fingertip.

Dex hooted again.

Octavius bent his attention to extracting his leg from the chair. Fortunately, he hadn't ruined his stockings. He climbed to his feet and watched warily as Ned stepped down from the final chair and sauntered towards him.

"Well?" Dex said. "What's Otto's forfeit to be?"

Ned's smirk widened. "His forfeit is that he goes to Vauxhall Gardens tomorrow night . . . as a woman."

There was a moment's silence. The game they had of creating embarrassing forfeits for each other was long-established, but this forfeit was unprecedented.

Dex gave a loud whoop. "Excellent!" he said, his face alight with glee. "I can't *wait* to see this."

When Ned said that Octavius was going to Vauxhall Gardens as a woman, he meant it quite literally. Not as a man dressed in woman's clothing, but as a woman dressed in woman's clothing. Because Octavius could change his shape. That was the gift he'd chosen when his Faerie godmother had visited him on his twenty-fifth birthday.

Ned had chosen invisibility when it was his turn, which was the stupidest use of a wish that Octavius could think of. Ned was the loudest, clumsiest brute in all England. He walked with the stealth of a rampaging elephant. He was terrible at being invisible. So terrible, in fact, that their grandfather-the-duke had placed strict conditions on Ned's use of his gift.

Ned had grumbled, but he'd obeyed. He might be a blockhead, but he wasn't such a blockhead as to risk revealing the family secret. No one wanted to find out what would happen if it became common knowledge that one of England's most aristocratic families actually had a Faerie godmother.

Octavius, who could walk stealthily when he wanted to,

hadn't chosen invisibility; he'd chosen metamorphosis, which meant that he could become any creature he wished. In the two years he'd had this ability, he'd been pretty much every animal he could think of. He'd even taken the shape of another person a few times. Once, he'd pretended to be his cousin, Dex. There he'd sat, drinking brandy and discussing horseflesh with his brother and his cousins, all of them thinking he was Dex—and then Dex had walked into the room. The expressions on everyone's faces had been priceless. Lord, the expression on *Dex*'s face . . .

Octavius had laughed so hard that he'd cried.

But one shape he'd never been tempted to try was that of a woman.

Why would he want to?

He was a man. And not just any man, but a good-looking, wealthy, and extremely well-born man. Why, when he had all those advantages, would he want to see what it was like to be a woman?

But that was the forfeit Ned had chosen and so here Octavius was, in his bedchamber, eyeing a pile of women's clothing, while far too many people clustered around him—not just Ned and Dex, but his own brother, Quintus, and Ned's brother, Sextus.

Quintus and Sextus usually held themselves distant from high jinks and tomfoolery, Quintus because he was an earl and he took his responsibilities extremely seriously and Sextus because he was an aloof sort of fellow—and yet here they both were in Octavius's bedchamber.

Octavius didn't mind making a fool of himself in front of a muttonhead like Ned and a rattle like Dex, but in front of his oh-so-sober brother and his stand-offish older cousin? He felt more self-conscious than he had in years, even a little embarrassed.

"Whose clothes are they?" he asked.

"Lydia's," Ned said.

Octavius tried to look as if it didn't bother him that he was going to be wearing Ned's mistress's clothes, but it did. Lydia was extremely buxom, which meant that *he* was going to have to be extremely buxom or the gown would fall right off him.

He almost balked, but he'd never backed down from a forfeit before, so he gritted his teeth and unwound his neckcloth.

Octavius stripped to his drawers, made them all turn their backs, then removed the drawers, too. He pictured what he wanted to look like: Lydia's figure, but not Lydia's face—brown ringlets instead of blonde, and brown eyes, too—and with a silent *God damn it,* he changed shape. Magic tickled across his skin and itched inside his bones. He gave an involuntary shiver—and then it was done. He was a woman.

Octavius didn't examine his new body. He hastily dragged on the chemise, keeping his gaze averted from the mirror. "All right," he said, in a voice that was light and feminine and sounded utterly wrong coming from his mouth. "You can turn around."

His brother and cousins turned around and stared at him. It was oddly unsettling to be standing in front of them in the shape of a woman, wearing only a thin chemise. In fact, it was almost intimidating. Octavius crossed his arms defensively over his ample bosom, then uncrossed them and put his hands on his hips, another defensive stance, made himself stop doing that, too, and gestured at the pile of women's clothing on the bed. "Well, who's going to help me with the stays?"

No one volunteered. No one cracked any jokes, either. It appeared that he wasn't the only one who was unsettled. His brother, Quintus, had a particularly stuffed expression on his face, Sextus looked faintly pained, and Ned and Dex, both of whom he expected to be smirking, weren't.

"The stays," Octavius said again. "Come on, you clods. Help me to dress." And then, because he was damned if he was going to let them see how uncomfortable he felt, he fluttered his eyelashes coquettishly.

Quintus winced, and turned his back. "Curse it, Otto, don't do that."

Octavius laughed. The feeling of being almost intimidated disappeared. In its place was the realization that if he played this right, he could make them all so uncomfortable that none of them would ever repeat this forfeit. He picked up the stays and dangled the garment in front of Ned. "You chose this forfeit; *you* help me dress."

It took quite a while to dress, because Ned was the world's worst lady's maid. He wrestled with the stays for almost a quarter of an hour, then put the petticoat on back to front. The gown consisted of a long sarcenet slip with a shorter lace robe on top of that. Ned flatly refused to arrange the decorative ribbons at Octavius's bosom or to help him fasten the silk stockings above his knees. Octavius hid his amusement. Oh, yes, Ned was *never* going to repeat this forfeit.

Lydia had provided several pretty ribbons, but after Ned had failed three times to thread them through Octavius's ringlets, Dex stepped forward. His attempt at styling hair wasn't sophisticated, but it was passable.

Finally, Octavius was fully dressed—and the oddest thing was that he actually felt *un*dressed. His throat was bare. He had no high shirt-points, no snug, starched neckcloth. His upper chest was bare, too, as were his upper arms. But worst of all, he was wearing no drawers, and that made him feel uncomfortably naked. True, most women didn't wear drawers and he was a woman tonight, but if his own drawers had fitted him he would have insisted on wearing them.

Octavius smoothed the gloves over his wrists and stared at himself in the mirror. He didn't like what he saw. It didn't just feel a little bit wrong, it felt a *lot* wrong. He wasn't a woman. This wasn't him. He didn't have those soft, pouting lips or those rounded hips and that slender waist, and he most definitely did *not* have those full, ripe breasts.

Octavius smoothed the gloves again, trying not to let the others see how uncomfortable he was.

Ned nudged his older brother, Sextus. "He's even prettier than you, Narcissus."

Everybody laughed, and Sextus gave that reserved, coolly amused smile that he always gave when his brother called him Narcissus.

Octavius looked at them in the mirror, himself and Sextus, and it *was* true: he was prettier than Sextus.

Funny, Sextus's smile no longer looked coolly amused. In fact, his expression, seen in the mirror, was the exact opposite of amused.

"Here." Dex draped a silk shawl around Octavius's shoulders. "And a fan. Ready?"

Octavius looked at himself in the mirror and felt the wrongness of the shape he was inhabiting. He took a deep breath and said, "Yes."

They went to Vauxhall by carriage rather than crossing the Thames in a scull, to Octavius's relief. He wasn't sure he would have been able to get into and out of a boat wearing a gown. As it was, even climbing into the carriage was a challenge. He nearly tripped on his hem.

The drive across town, over Westminster Bridge and down Kennington Lane, gave him ample time to torment his brother and cousins. If there was one lesson he wanted them to learn tonight—even Quintus and Sextus, who rarely played the forfeit game—it was to never choose this forfeit for him again.

Although, to tell the truth, he was rather enjoying himself now. It was wonderful to watch Ned squirm whenever

Octavius fluttered his eyelashes and flirted at him with the pretty brisé fan. Even more wonderful was that when he uttered a coquettish laugh and said, "Oh, Nonny, you are so *droll*," Ned didn't thump him, as he ordinarily would have done, but instead went red and glowered at him.

It had been years since Octavius had dared to call Nonus anything other than Ned, so he basked in the triumph of the moment and resolved to call his cousin "Nonny" as many times as he possibly could that evening.

Next, he turned his attention to his brother, simpering and saying, "Quinnie, darling, you look so *handsome* tonight."

It wasn't often one saw an earl cringe.

Dex, prick that he was, didn't squirm or cringe or go red when Octavius tried the same trick on him; he just cackled with laughter.

Octavius gave up on Dex for the time being and turned his attention to Sextus. He wasn't squirming or cringing, but neither was he cackling. He lounged in the far corner of the carriage, an expression of mild amusement on his face. When Octavius fluttered the fan at him and cooed, "You look so *delicious,* darling. I could swoon from just looking at you," Sextus merely raised his eyebrows fractionally and gave Octavius a look that told him he knew exactly what Octavius was trying to do. But Sextus had always been the smartest of them all.

They reached Vauxhall, and Octavius managed to descend from the carriage without tripping over his dress. "Who's going to pay my three shillings and sixpence?" he asked, with a flutter of both the fan and his eyelashes. His heart was beating rather fast now that they'd arrived and his hands were sweating inside the evening gloves. It was one thing to play this game with his brother and cousins, another thing entirely to act the lady in public. Especially when he wasn't wearing drawers.

But he wouldn't let them see his nervousness. He turned to his brother and simpered up at him. "Quinnie, darling, you'll pay for li'l old me, won't you?"

Quintus cringed with his whole body again. "God damn it, Otto, *stop* that," he hissed under his breath.

"No?" Octavius pouted, and turned his gaze to Ned. "Say you'll be my beau tonight, Nonny."

Ned looked daggers at him for that "Nonny" so Octavius blew him a kiss—then nearly laughed aloud at Ned's expression of appalled revulsion.

Dex did laugh out loud. "Your idea, Ned; you pay," he said, grinning.

Ned paid for them all, and they entered the famous pleasure gardens. Octavius took Dex's arm once they were through the gate, because Dex was enjoying this far too much and if Octavius couldn't find a way to make his cousin squirm then he might find himself repeating this forfeit in the future—and heaven forbid that *that* should ever happen.

Octavius had been to Vauxhall Gardens more times than he could remember. Nothing had changed—the pavilion, the musicians, the supper boxes, the groves of trees and the walkways—and yet it *had* changed, because visiting Vauxhall Gardens as a woman was a vastly different experience from visiting Vauxhall Gardens as a man. The gown undoubtedly had something to do with it. It was no demure débutante's gown; Lydia was a courtesan—a very expensive courtesan—and the gown was cut to display her charms to best advantage. Octavius was uncomfortably aware of men ogling him—looking at his mouth, his breasts, his hips, and imagining him naked in their beds. That was bad enough, but what made it worse was that he knew some of those men. They were his friends—and now they were undressing him with their eyes.

Octavius simpered and fluttered his fan and tried to hide his discomfit, while Ned went to see about procuring a box and supper. Quintus paused to speak with a friend, and two minutes later so did Sextus. Dex and Octavius were alone—or rather, as alone as one could be in such a public setting as Vauxhall.

Octavius nudged Dex away from the busy walkway, towards

a quieter path. Vauxhall Gardens sprawled over several acres, and for every wide and well-lit path there was a shadowy one with windings and turnings and secluded nooks.

A trio of drunken young bucks swaggered past, clearly on the prowl for amatory adventures. One of them gave a low whistle of appreciation and pinched Octavius on his derrière.

Octavius swiped at him with the fan.

The man laughed. So did his companions. So did Dex.

"He *pinched* me," Octavius said, indignantly.

Dex, son of a bitch that he was, laughed again and made no move to reprimand the buck; he merely kept strolling.

Octavius, perforce, kept strolling, too. Outrage seethed in his bosom. "You wouldn't laugh if someone pinched Phoebe," he said tartly. "You'd knock him down."

"You're not my sister," Dex said. "And besides, if you're going to wear a gown like that one, you should expect to be pinched."

Octavius almost hit Dex with the fan. He gritted his teeth and resolved to make his cousin *regret* making that comment before the night was over. He racked his brain as they turned down an even more shadowy path, the lamps casting golden pools of light in the gloom. When was the last time he'd seen Dex embarrassed? Not faintly embarrassed, but truly, deeply embarrassed.

A memory stirred in the recesses of his brain and he remembered, with a little jolt of recollection, that Dex had a middle name—Stallyon—and he also remembered what had happened when the other boys at school had found out.

Dex Stallyon had become . . . Sex Stallion.

It had taken Dex a week to shut that nickname down—Pryors were built large and they never lost a schoolyard battle—but what Octavius most remembered about that week wasn't the fighting, it was Dex's red-faced mortification and fuming rage.

Of course, Dex *was* a sex stallion now, so maybe the nickname wouldn't bother him?

They turned onto a slightly more populated path. Octavius waited for a suitable audience to approach, which it soon did: Misters Feltham and Wardell, both of whom had been to school with Dex.

"You're my favorite of all my beaus," Octavius confided loudly as they passed. "Dex Stallyon, my *sex stallion.* You let me ride you all night long." He uttered a beatific sigh, and watched with satisfaction as Dex flushed bright red.

Feltham and Wardell laughed. Dex laughed, too, uncomfortably, and hustled Octavius away, and then pinched him hard on his plump, dimpled arm.

"Ouch," Octavius said, rubbing his arm. "That hurt."

"Serves you bloody right," Dex hissed. "I can't believe you said I let you ride me!"

Now that was interesting: it was the reference to being ridden that Dex objected to, not the nickname.

Octavius resolved to make good use of that little fact.

He talked loudly about riding Dex when they passed Lord Belchamber and his cronies, and again when they encountered the Hogarth brothers.

Both times, Dex dished out more of those sharp, admonitory pinches, but Octavius was undeterred; he was enjoying himself again. It was fun ribbing Dex within earshot of men they both knew and watching his cousin go red at the gills.

He held his silence as two courting couples strolled past, and then swallowed a grin when he spied a trio of fellows sauntering towards them. All three of them were members of the same gentleman's club that Dex frequented.

Dex spied them, too, and changed direction abruptly, hauling Octavius into a dimly lit walkway to avoid them.

Octavius tried to turn his laugh into a cough, and failed.

"You're a damned swine," Dex said. It sounded as if he was gritting his teeth.

"I think you mean bitch," Octavius said.

Dex made a noise remarkably like a growl. He set off at a fast pace, his hand clamped around Octavius's wrist.

Ordinarily, Octavius would have had no difficulty keeping up with Dex—he *was* an inch taller than his cousin—but right now he was a whole foot shorter, plus he was hampered by his dress. He couldn't stride unless he hiked the wretched thing up to his knees, which he wasn't going to do; he was already showing far too much of his person. "Slow down," he said. "I've got short legs."

Dex made the growling sound again, but he did slow down and ease his grip on Octavius's wrist.

Along came a gentleman whom Octavius didn't recognize, one of the nouveau riche judging from his brashly expensive garb. The man ogled Octavius overtly and even went so far as to blow him a kiss. Instead of ignoring that overture, Octavius fluttered his eyelashes and gave a little giggle. "Another time, dear sir. I have my favorite beau with me tonight." He patted Dex's arm. "I call him my sex stallion because he lets me ride him all night long."

Dex pinched him again, hard, and dragged him away from the admiring gentleman so fast that Octavius almost tripped over his hem.

"*Stop* telling everyone that you ride me!" Dex said, once they were out of earshot.

"Don't you like it?" Octavius asked ingenuously. "Why not? Does it not sound virile enough?"

Dex ignored those questions. He made the growling sound again. "I swear to God, Otto, if you say that one more time, I'm abandoning you."

Which meant that Octavius had won. He opened the brisé fan and hid a triumphant smile behind it.

Dex released his wrist. Octavius refrained from rubbing it; he didn't want to give Dex the satisfaction of knowing that it hurt. Instead, he walked in demure silence alongside his cousin, savoring his victory . . . and then lo, who should he see coming towards them but that old lecher, Baron Rumpole.

"I warn you, Otto," Dex said, as Rumpole approached. "Don't you *dare*."

293

Rumpole all but stripped Octavius with his gaze, and then he had the vulgarity to say aloud to Dex, "I see someone's getting lucky tonight."

The opening was too perfect to resist. Warning or not, Octavius didn't hesitate. "That would be *me* getting lucky," he said, with a coy giggle. "He's my favorite beau because he lets me ride—"

"You want her? She's yours." Dex shoved Octavius at the baron and strode off.

Octavius almost laughed out loud—it wasn't often that he managed to get the better of Dex—but then Rumpole stepped towards him and the urge to laugh snuffed out.

He took a step back, away from the baron, but Rumpole crowded closer. He might be in his late fifties, but he was a bull-like man, thickset and bulky—and considerably larger and stronger than Octavius currently was.

Octavius tried to go around him to the left, but Rumpole blocked him.

He tried to go around him to the right. Rumpole blocked him again.

Dex was long gone, swallowed up by the shadows.

"Let me past," Octavius demanded.

"I will, for a kiss."

Octavius didn't deign to reply to this. He picked up his skirts and tried to push past Rumpole, but the man's hand shot out, catching his upper arm, and if he'd thought Dex's grip was punishingly tight, then the baron's was twice as bad. Octavius uttered a grunt of pain and tried to jerk free.

Rumpole's fingers dug in, almost to the bone. "No, you don't. I want my kiss first." He hauled Octavius towards him and bent his head.

Octavius punched him.

If he'd been in his own shape, the punch would have laid Rumpole out on the ground. As it was, the baron rocked slightly on his feet and released Octavius's arm.

Octavius shoved the man aside. He marched down the

path, his steps fast and angry. How *dare* Rumpole try to force a kiss on him!

Behind him, Rumpole uttered an oath. Footsteps crunched in the gravel. The baron was giving chase.

Octavius was tempted to stand his ground and fight, but common sense asserted itself. If he were a man right now he'd *crush* Rumpole, but he wasn't a man and Rumpole outweighed him by at least a hundred pounds. Retreat was called for.

Octavius picked up his skirts and ran, even though what he really wanted to do was pummel the baron to the ground. Fury gave his feet wings. He rounded a bend in the path. The shadows drew back and he saw a glowing lamp and two people.

The baron stopped running. Octavius didn't, not until he reached the lamp casting its safe, golden luminescence.

He'd lost his fan somewhere. He was panting. And while rage was his predominant emotion, underneath the rage was a prickle of uneasiness—and that made him even angrier. Was he, Octavius Pryor, *afraid* of Baron Rumpole?

"The devil I am," he muttered under his breath.

He glanced over his shoulder. Rumpole had halted a dozen yards back, glowering. He looked even more bull-like, head lowered and nostrils flaring.

The prickle of unease became a little stronger. *Discretion is the better part of valor,* Octavius reminded himself. He picked up his skirts again and strode towards the people he'd spied, whose dark shapes resolved into two young sprigs with the nipped-in waists, padded shoulders, and high shirt-points of dandies. "Could you escort me to the pavilion, kind sirs? I'm afraid I've lost my way."

The sprigs looked him up and down, their gazes lingering on the lush expanse of his breasts.

Octavius gritted his teeth and smiled at them. "Please? I'm all alone and this darkness makes me a little nervous."

"Of course, darling," one of the sprigs said, and then he had the audacity to put his arm around Octavius's waist and give him a squeeze.

Octavius managed not to utter an indignant squawk. He ground his teeth together and submitted to that squeeze, because a squeeze from a sprig was a thousand times better than a kiss from Baron Rumpole. "The pavilion," he said again. "Please?"

The man released his waist. "Impatient little thing, aren't you?" he said with a laugh. He offered Octavius his arm and began walking in the direction of the pavilion. The second sprig stepped close on Octavius's other side, too close, but Octavius set his jaw and endured it. The pavilion was only five minutes' walk. He could suffer these men for five minutes. They were, after all, rescuing him.

Except that the first sprig was now turning left, drawing Octavius down one of the darker paths . . .

Octavius balked, but the second sprig had an arm around his waist and was urging him along that shadowy path. "I don't like the dark," Octavius protested.

Both men laughed. "We'll be with you, my dear," one of them said, and now, in addition to an arm around Octavius's waist, there was a sly hand sidling towards his breasts.

Octavius wrenched himself free. Outrage heated his face. His hands were clenched into fists. He wanted nothing more than to mill both men down, but he was outweighed and outnumbered and the chances of him winning this fight were slim. "I shall walk by myself," he declared haughtily, turning his back on the sprigs and heading for the lamplight.

Behind him, he heard the sprigs laughing.

Octavius gritted his teeth. A plague on all men!

He reached the slightly wider walkway, with its lamp, and glanced around. Fortunately, he didn't see Baron Rumpole. Unfortunately, he couldn't see *any*one. He wished he'd not steered Dex towards these out-of-the-way paths, wished they'd kept to the busier promenades, wished there were people around. He picked up his skirts and headed briskly for the pavilion, but the path didn't feel as safe as it once had.

The lamplight didn't extend far and soon he was in shadows again. He heard the distant sound of music, and closer, the soft crunch of footsteps.

They weren't his footsteps.

He glanced around. Baron Rumpole was following him.

Octavius began to walk more rapidly.

The footsteps crunched faster behind him.

Octavius abandoned any pretense of walking and began to run, but his skirts restricted his strides and the baron caught him within half a dozen paces, grabbing his arm and hauling him into the dark mouth of yet another pathway.

"Let go of me!" Octavius punched and kicked, but he was only five foot two and the blows had little effect.

"Think too highly of yourself, don't you?" Rumpole said, dragging Octavius deeper into the dark shrubbery. Rough fingers groped his breasts. There was a ripping sound as his bodice gave way. Octavius opened his mouth to shout, but the baron clapped a hand over it.

Octavius bit that hand, punched Rumpole on the nose as hard as he could, and tried to knee the man in the groin. He was only partly successful, but Rumpole gave a grunt and released him.

Octavius ran back the way he'd come. There were wings on his feet again, but this time he wasn't fueled solely by rage, there was a sting of fear in the mix, and damn it, he *refused* to be afraid of Rumpole.

The path was still too dark—but it wasn't empty anymore. There, in the distance, was Sextus.

Sextus was frowning and looking about, as if searching for someone, then his head turned and he saw Octavius and came striding towards him.

Octavius headed for him, clutching the ripped bodice with one hand, holding up his skirts with the other. He heard fast, angry footsteps behind him and knew it was Rumpole.

The baron reached him first. He grabbed Octavius's arm and tried to pull him towards a dark and shadowy nook.

Octavius dug his heels in. "No."

"Stupid bitch," Rumpole snarled, but Octavius was no longer paying him any attention. He was watching Sextus approach.

His cousin's stride slowed to an arrogant, aristocratic stroll. His expression, as he covered the last few yards, was one that Sextus had perfected years ago: haughty, aloof, looking down his nose at the world. "Rumpole," he drawled.

The baron swung to face him, his grip tight on Octavius's arm. "Pryor."

Sextus glanced at Octavius. He saw the torn bodice, but his expression didn't alter by so much as a flicker of a muscle. "I must ask you to unhand the lady."

Rumpole snorted. "She's no lady. She's a piece of mutton."

"Always so crass, Rumpole. You never disappoint." There was no heat in Sextus's voice, just boredom. His tone, his words, were so perfectly insulting that Octavius almost crowed with laughter.

Beneath that instinctive laughter was an equally instinctive sense of shock. Had Sextus actually said *that* to a baron?

Rumpole flushed brick red. "She's mine."

"No," Sextus corrected him coolly. "The lady is a guest of my brother tonight."

"Lady?" The baron gave an ugly laugh. "This thing? She has no breeding at all."

"Neither, it appears, do you." Again, Sextus's tone was perfect: the boredom, the hint of dismissive disdain.

Octavius's admiration for his cousin rose. Damn, but Sextus had balls.

Rumpole's flush deepened. He released Octavius. His hands clenched into fists.

"I believe that's Miss Smith's shawl you're holding," Sextus said, and indeed, Octavius's shawl was dangling from one meaty fist, trailing in the dirt.

Rumpole cast the shawl aside, a violent movement, and took a step towards Sextus.

Sextus was the shortest of the Pryors, but that didn't mean he was short. He stood six feet tall, eye to eye with Rumpole, but whereas the baron was beefy, Sextus was lean. He looked slender compared to Rumpole.

Octavius found himself holding his breath, but Sextus gave no hint of fear. He returned the baron's stare with all the slightly bored arrogance of a duke's grandson.

For a moment the threat of violence hung in the air, then the baron muttered something under his breath that sounded like "Fucking Pryor," turned on his heel, and stalked off.

Sextus picked up the shawl, shook it out, and put it around Octavius's shoulders. "You all right, Otto?"

Octavius wrapped the shawl more tightly around himself, hiding the ripped bodice. "You were just like grandfather, then. All you needed was a quizzing glass to wither him through."

Sextus ignored this comment. "Did he hurt you?"

Octavius shook his head, even though his arm ached as if a horse had kicked it. Damn Rumpole and his giant-like hands. "It's a shame you're not the heir. You'd make a damned good duke."

"Heaven forbid," Sextus said, which was exactly how Octavius felt about his own ducal prospects: heaven forbid that *he* should ever become a duke. It was little wonder Quintus was so stuffy, with that multitude of responsibilities hanging over him.

"Come on," Sextus said. "Let's get you home." He took Octavius by the elbow, matching his stride to Octavius's shorter legs.

They were almost at the Kennington gate when someone called out: "Sextus!" It was Dex. He reached them, out of breath. "You found him! He all right?"

"Rumpole practically ripped his dress off," Sextus told him. "What the devil were you doing, leaving him like that?"

Dex looked shamefaced. "Sorry, I didn't think."

"That is patently clear," Sextus said, a bite in his voice. "Tell the others I'm taking him home."

Dex obeyed without argument, heading back towards the pavilion.

"It was my fault," Octavius confessed, once they were through the gate and out in Kennington Lane. "I pushed Dex too far."

Sextus glanced at him, but said nothing. He still looked angry, or rather, as angry as Sextus ever looked. He was damned good at hiding his emotions.

Several hackneys waited in the lane. Sextus handed Octavius up into one and gave the jarvey instructions.

"It *was* my fault," Octavius said again, settling onto the squab seat.

"What? It's your fault that Rumpole almost raped you?" A shaft of lamplight entered the carriage, illuminating Sextus's face for an instant. Octavius was surprised by the anger he saw there.

"He didn't almost rape me," he said, as the carriage turned out of Kennington Lane and headed towards Westminster Bridge. "And honestly, it *was* as much my fault as Dex's. Neither of us thought Rumpole was dangerous. I didn't realize until too late just how puny I am." He remembered the baron forcing him into the dark shrubbery and gave an involuntary shiver. And then he remembered Sextus facing Rumpole down. "I can't believe you spoke to him like that. He'd have been within his rights to call you out."

Sextus just shrugged.

The carriage rattled over Westminster Bridge. When they reached the other side, Octavius said, "When I was fourteen, Father and Grandfather had a talk with me about sex. Did your father . . . ?"

"We all had that lecture," Sextus said.

Octavius was silent for several minutes, remembering that long-ago conversation. He'd given his word of honor to never force any woman into bestowing sexual favors, regardless of her station in life. "I'd wager Rumpole didn't have a talk like that with his father."

"No wager there," Sextus said dryly.

They sat in silence while the carriage trundled through the streets. Octavius had given his word all those years ago—and kept it. He'd never forced women into his bed, but he had ogled the ladybirds, snatched kisses, playfully pinched a time or two. It had seemed harmless, flirtatious fun.

Harmless to *him*. But perhaps those women had disliked it as much as he'd disliked it tonight?

Octavius chewed on that thought while the carriage rattled its way towards Mayfair.

Like to read the rest?
Octavius and the Perfect Governess is available now.

$\mathscr{A}$CKNOWLEDGMENTS

A number of people helped to make this book what it is. Foremost among them is my developmental editor, Laura Cifelli Stibich, but I also owe many thanks to my copyeditor, Maria Fairchild, and my proofreader, Martin O'Hearn.

The series logo was designed by Kim Killion, of the Killion Group, and the cover and the print formatting are the work of Jane D. Smith. Thank you, Jane!

Emily Larkin grew up in a house full of books. Her mother was a librarian and her father a novelist, so perhaps it's not surprising that she became a writer.

Emily has studied a number of subjects, including geology and geophysics, canine behavior, and ancient Greek. Her varied career includes stints as a field assistant in Antarctica and a waitress on the Isle of Skye, as well as five vintages in New Zealand's wine industry.

She loves to travel and has lived in Sweden, backpacked in Europe and North America, and traveled overland in the Middle East, China, and North Africa.

She enjoys climbing hills, reading, and watching reruns of *Buffy the Vampire Slayer* and *Firefly*.

Emily writes historical romances as Emily Larkin and fantasy novels as Emily Gee. Her websites are www.emilylarkin.com and www.emilygee.com.

Never miss a new Emily Larkin book. Join her readers' group at www.emilylarkin.com/newsletter and receive free digital copies of *The Fey Quartet* and *Unmasking Miss Appleby*, as well as exclusive bonus scenes and other goodies.

OTHER WORKS

THE BALEFUL GODMOTHER SERIES

Prequel
The Fey Quartet novella collection:
Maythorn's Wish
Hazel's Promise
Ivy's Choice
Larkspur's Quest

Original Series
Unmasking Miss Appleby
Resisting Miss Merryweather
Trusting Miss Trentham
Claiming Mister Kemp
Ruining Miss Wrotham
Discovering Miss Dalrymple

Garland Cousins
Primrose and the Dreadful Duke
Violet and the Bow Street Runner

Pryor Cousins
Octavius and the Perfect Governess
Decimus and the Wary Widow